BEYOND THE HUMAN REALM

TO RENA:
THANK YOU FOR
BRINGING YOUR
VISION TO LOPEZ!

Cen

BEYOND the HUMAN REALM

A NOVEL

GENE HELFMAN

LUMINARE PRESS

WWW.LUMINAREPRESS.COM

Beyond the Human Realm

Printed in the United States of America

Luminare Press
442 Charnelton St.
Eugene, OR 97401
www.luminarepress.com

LCCN: 2021909739
ISBN: 978-1-64388-659-6

For Judy: it's only gotten better.

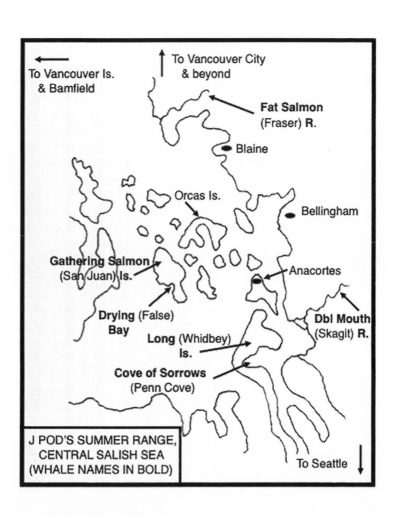

To Vancouver Is.
& Bamfield

To Vancouver City
& beyond

Fat Salmon
(Fraser) **R.**

Blaine

Orcas Is.

Bellingham

Gathering Salmon
(San Juan) **Is.**

Anacortes

Drying (False)
Bay

Dbl Mouth
(Skagit) **R.**

Long (Whidbey)
Is.

Cove of Sorrows
(Penn Cove)

J POD'S SUMMER RANGE,
CENTRAL SALISH SEA
(WHALE NAMES IN BOLD)

To Seattle

"But who would ever try to write a story about a whale!"

M. WYLIE BLANCHET, *The Curve of Time*

PART ONE

CHAPTER 1

We're living at a time when claims are being made for
a moral authority that lies beyond the human.

RICHARD POWERS, *The Overstory*

E ach day was a replica of the one before. And the one
before that, as far back as he could remember. His routine only changed when they wanted him to perform
silly tricks, before they gave him food.

A split-tail got into his pool (he hated that). She blew a
whistle twice, pushed a ball with her nose, and threw the
ball to another on the hard land. It was obvious what they
wanted him to do.

He immediately swam over, came up under the ball,
carried it across the pool and tossed it to a split-tail by the
edge. They clearly approved.

Someone blew the whistle twice.

He ignored it. He had shown them that he understood
but would not perform for them. It was clear this made them
unhappy. When they were unhappy, they would skip a feeding.
Although he was hungry, he took pleasure in their frustration.

Afterward, one of the split-tails, usually a female, would
wait until others weren't around and then pour a bucket of
food into his pool.

He'd lost his freedom so long ago he had no memory of
it. He was very young when he was brought here. He had a

vague image of swimming close to his mother, in the open ocean. But then the split-tails caught him and brought him to this place, a small oval, smooth, featureless, broken only by a window. A constant swim around the oval, over and over, day and night. Alone.

He did come to like one particular female split-tail. She always vocalized softly to him (did the others think he couldn't hear?). Everything about her actions indicated she cared. To reward her, he allowed her—and only her—to ride on his back as a trick. She did this with a four-finned, furry animal that he also liked. Maybe it, too, was a captive. He certainly had no reason to treat that animal badly.

His favorite female did something else special. Late at night, she would come alone, take off the outer skin they always wore, and slip into his pool. She waited for him to swim to her and then she would slide up onto his back and he would carry her around the pool until he sensed she was shaking from the cold. Then he would swim to the pool's edge and she would get off, after giving his back fin a hug. He enjoyed her company.

This went on for many moon cycles. Then she came one night with a male. They both removed their outer skins and swam with him. But something was wrong about that, and he never saw her again.

Each day was the same as the one before.

⸻

Then his life turned around. Another being was lowered into the pool. Her body shape triggered a memory of what his family members looked like. He approached the new being slowly, scanned it with his sonar, and knew it was a female. A very frightened female. She made sorrowful sounds, terrified sounds. Although he couldn't understand what she was saying, he sensed she wanted him to leave her alone.

He backed away, not wanting to cause her more distress. He concluded that she was another captive. He would do whatever was necessary to make her less frightened and miserable. Having a companion stirred something deep inside, a positive feeling he could barely remember.

At first, she wouldn't let him near and never approached him. But slowly, over many weeks, she grew less afraid. To make her comfortable, he always circled the pool ahead of her. Then one day she sped up until she was alongside him, and they swam together. Together!

It was clear that she hated the food they were given. To him, food was food, tasty or not. She felt otherwise and the split-tails would poke her with a sharp stick that made her sleepy and then force food down her throat. She often vomited it back. Eventually, she ate what they gave her, but without enthusiasm.

When they were alone, he showed her the tricks they expected him to perform, mimicking the whistle sound they used for each. She caught on immediately and surprised the split-tails when she performed a trick without being taught. He decided it might make things easier for her if he caused less trouble by also doing the tricks. Anything to win her confidence.

He didn't talk much, having had no one to talk to. He had gotten out of the habit. But he wanted to communicate with her. He decided to learn her language. To show his willingness, he repeated what she said, knowing his pronunciation was terrible. But she seemed to appreciate his effort and taught him constantly. And they had nothing but time. *If only she would talk slower.*

"I am Nan. What's your name?" she said.

"I am Nan. What's your name?" he repeated.

"No, silly. *I* am Nan. That's *my* name."

He hesitated, puzzled. He hated to disappoint her. But he caught the meaning from her emphasis. It occurred to him that he had no idea what he called himself.

"I do not have a name," he finally said, choosing his words carefully. "The split-tails call me Mahguy, when they want me to do tricks."

Nan also hesitated. Finally, she said, "Well, we don't want them to rule every part of our lives. So, I guess I'll have to give you a name. Let's see. I had an uncle named Sam when I was free. He was big and wise and always treated me well. You're big and treat me well. I'm not sure how wise you are, but you remind me of him. So, we'll call you Sam. Your name is Sam."

"Sam?" he said, pronouncing it slowly and carefully.

"Yes, Sam. You are Sam."

"Okay, my name is Sam," he said. *Anything to make her happy.*

"Good. Then another thing. In my family, we don't call them split-tails. We call them logriders, because we always see them riding on logs."

Sam wasn't sure what a log was. It didn't matter.

"Logriders, not split-tails," Sam repeated. "Logriders."

"Which brings up something else," she said. "What do you remember from before they captured you?"

"Not much, really," Sam answered. "I do remember them hurting my mother, her lying still while I cried out to her, before they caught me in a mesh. I've always assumed they killed her."

"Wow. I'm really sorry. I guess that makes you an orphan."

"I hadn't really thought about it that way, but you're right. It was the beginning of my hating the split...er, logriders."

Nan performed one trick that Sam never even attempted. In fact, it frightened him. She would jump out of the pool onto the smooth land, to excited shouts of the logriders. Then they would push her back into the pool. Just the thought of beaching himself made him shudder, imagining his weight pushing down, crushing him, without the water to hold him up. He asked her why she did this.

"I imagine I'm escaping," she said, matter-of-factly. "I know it's a fantasy, but, for a brief moment, I'm away from here."

Her response hurt his feelings, knowing that she would rather be somewhere else than with him. But she had known freedom, while he had been a captive essentially all his life.

Sam did everything he could to make Nan more content. He had never been so happy. But it was clear that she did not feel the same way. She constantly told him about her family members and what life was like in the open ocean.

Nan had a rudimentary ability to project a sound image, taking the sonar echo from an object and rebroadcasting it, an ability she said she had been learning from her Uncle Sam. At first, the objects were simple, the floats, their food, objects in their pool. Even when crudely copied, Sam was able to identify them. As her skill improved, she taught him how to project sound images. He caught on, again slowly. But, over time, they would challenge each other, improving their skills. She especially liked to show Sam her family members, introducing him to each one.

Their lives together continued. Then one day he felt her swimming closer to him, actually rubbing against him, running a side fin along his body. He was surprised at her intimacy and at how his body was reacting. Nan didn't seem at all surprised. In fact, she encouraged him. It didn't require much explanation. This became part of their daily routine and a new source of happiness for Sam.

Then, after a few moon cycles, she stopped encouraging him and, in fact, rebuffed his attempts. He was hurt, confused. He finally asked why.

"You don't know?" she scolded.

"I have no idea," he answered.

"Well then, look at me," she said, encouraging him to give her a deep scan.

He saw...a small body inside her.

"Is...is that what I think it is?" he said to her.

"Yes," she said, with obvious pride. "We did this."

And they waited. Sam gave Nan scanning updates on their child's development. Nan's appetite grew. The logriders must have sensed what was happening. They fed her more and demanded less.

Finally, their baby was born. It was a difficult birth. Nan cried out for her aunts, for their assistance. Sam felt helpless, ignorant, frightened. Their baby, a female, was weak at first. Both mother and baby had difficulty nursing. But things improved, and Sam felt a new pride in being a father. The three swam together, although Nan now paid little attention to him. It didn't matter. She was happy, consumed with joy. They named the baby Rosie, after Nan's younger sister.

And then the unimaginable happened. The logriders lifted their child from the pool. Rosie cried out for her mother; Nan called to her child.

Then Rosie was gone.

Nan stayed by the side of the pool for hours, days, calling for her baby. She refused to eat. Nothing Sam could do or say lessened her grief. She screamed at him to leave her alone. Her condition worsened. Early one morning, Sam found her lying motionless on the bottom of their pool. He was back to being alone.

Time passed. Sam returned to being uncooperative.

Then, one day, a new female appeared, younger than Nan had been. Sam swam over and spoke to her. The new female cried out, her words unintelligible.

It took Sam perhaps thirty seconds to understand. The logriders had brought him a new mate. They wanted him to produce babies. He became filled with hatred and anger.

The anger rose inside him. It boiled into a blinding, seething rage. He would be no part of this. Unthinking, he raced across the pool and smashed into…not the poolside, but the new female. Yes! He rammed her again, and again, and again. He bit and thrashed and didn't stop until he knew he had killed her.

Not long after, Sam felt the sting of the sleeping stick. When he awoke, he was in an entirely different place.

They had taken everything from him: his mate, their child. All that was left were his memories. And his hatred.

PART TWO

CHAPTER 2

Melville needed an editor.

RUDY LAGUNA

I t took only two weeks after being booted out of Hamilton College for Dr. Rudy Laguna to get his life in a semblance of order. The whiplash from being almost tenured to being unemployed still stung, but he had to admit the affair had been ill-advised. He had resisted Rachel's advances for two semesters, but then his willpower failed. Technically, she was no longer a student, having graduated a few hours earlier. Technically. And it had been unquestionably consensual, Rachel having made the initial advances. Didn't that count for something? How was he to know her parents were influential, her father head of the Board of Regents, her mother president of the Alumni Foundation? Hamilton's dean spelled it out in no uncertain terms: her parents were irate, wanted him gone, no recourse. His academic pink slip was attached to a tarnished golden parachute, a faculty position on the west coast at a tiny school called Northwest Washington State University. Rudy didn't have much choice.

He drove across country in early July, stopping infrequently. Other than sweltering heat in a Volvo that lacked air conditioning (but with a fully functional heater), the trip was largely uneventful. It took a week.

But Rudy had lots of time to think. He decided to avoid dwelling on the recent past. Water under the bridge, although it felt more like a raging torrent, and he had been forced to swim upstream. Unsuccessfully.

Best to look to the future. His new home in the Pacific Northwest was a couple hours north of Seattle, in Blaine, a small zit on the map. A web search didn't reveal much, other than Blaine was the last stop on the interstate before the Canadian border, if you decided to stop. "Where America Begins," the rather generic chamber of commerce website declared. Or ends, as seen through your rearview mirror. Please wave as you go past.

Importantly, what kind of research might he conduct, assuming his teaching duties permitted time for research? All his training was in animal behavior, watching little fish in small streams while partially submerged. A colleague at Hamilton had accused him of being an underwater bird-watcher. It wasn't meant as a compliment. At least summertime stream temperatures in upstate New York had been almost bearable. From what he could glean from the internet, streams in northern Washington State were fed by melting snowpack. Brrr. And the Pacific Ocean wasn't a lot warmer, even in summer. Brrr.

Somewhere in one of the Dakotas—was it near the Corn Palace?—he reflected on animals, other than minnows, that he found fascinating and that lived in the Pacific Northwest. High on the list were whales and dolphins, owing to his time spent as a commercial tuna fisherman, watching dolphins drown as part of the by-catch. He left that job because the dolphin deaths got to him. During his sleazy motel stops en route west, he started reading everything he could about dolphins, especially about killer whales, the biggest dolphins. Orcas were amazing: very intelligent, more so than humans in terms of relative brain size, especially the part of the brain involved in thought. More than one author had suggested they exceeded humans in brainpower. Not surprisingly, they were socially and behaviorally complex. And declining in numbers.

Rudy had seen orcas only once, but the vision was etched indelibly in his memory. He'd attended a fish behavior conference in Vancouver, British Columbia, his first year at Hamilton. An evening social was held at the Royal Vancouver Aquarium, otherwise closed to the public. Attendees had free range of the place. Rudy tired of shouting over the racket of the unwanted local band in a smoke-filled meeting room and drifted outdoors. The night was clear and cool, the air fresh, smelling of pine trees. He walked until he was overlooking a large circular pool, maybe three times the size of a backyard swimming pool. The lighting was dim, and nothing seemed to be happening.

Then he heard the whales.

There were three of them. One was huge, easily twenty-five or thirty feet long and had a tall dorsal fin bent over almost in a semi-circle. Another was slightly smaller with a shorter fin. The third was obviously an infant, swimming between them. He sat and watched and lost sense of time. He was mesmerized, almost hypnotized by the regularity of their movements. But his fascination darkened as he realized the regularity was the result of methodical behavior, the three animals circling the pool and breathing once each lap at the exact same place, the two larger animals exhaling simultaneously, the smaller a moment later.

Round and round the pool they went in a tight circle, almost mechanically, never changing their speed or direction, each circling of the pool taking exactly thirty-seven seconds. These animals weren't swimming. They were pacing. The pool was a tiny cage. Animals this size and this active shouldn't be held captive. It was obviously inhumane. He left the arena feeling angry and depressed.

So now he was moving to where orcas lived and were clearly worthy of study. Almost every website he looked at about the Pacific Northwest included photos of leaping orcas, either in the wild or in public display facilities, where they were forced to perform tricks. Like the ones in Vancouver. That memory still made him angry. But, clearly, these charismatic predators were in the public conscience. Blaine apparently even had an orca sculpture in its seaside park. Public awareness and concern were always good criteria when choosing a research topic. Minnows had never qualified.

Okay then, what would it take to become an orca researcher? A small boat and binoculars? Well then, how about one of those little rubber inflatable dinghies? At least that would be drier, and hopefully warmer, than diving research. It was fun to imagine. He'd start seriously researching orcas as soon as he got to Washington. It gave him something to look forward to, and maybe, just maybe, would help him forget the past.

Blaine turned out to be as far north in Washington State as you could get and still be in America. Only five minutes to a civilized country. Welcome to Blaine, Washington: "Gazing north with envy." The town was so insignificant that residents weren't sure how to spell it, some signs in town leaving off the final "e."

He rented a small two-bedroom house on Cedar Street, a quiet dead-end east of what passed for downtown Blaine, all one block of it. Other than the muted traffic noise and the faint smell of car exhaust from nearby Interstate 5, it was fine. The house looked like it had been built in the fifties and never remodeled. But it was only ten minutes to his new place of employment. After hearing horror stories about the rental market in Seattle, where bidding wars erupted over vacancies and people read the obituaries in their hunt for housing, he was prepared for the worst. Thankfully, rent was a whopping seven hundred a month. Blaine was not Seattle.

Next stop: higher education.

It was pretty much a straight shot to the campus, although Rudy drove right by, thinking it was an elementary school. He just caught a glimpse of the none-too-bold sign proclaiming Northwest Washington State University—Go Wolf Eels!

The entire university consisted of an aging compound of similar, one-story buildings linked by covered walkways. The impression of an elementary school was reinforced by a fading marine-motif mural painted on the exterior walls along the walkway. The artists couldn't have been older than ten, probably younger. Anatomical correctness had been sacrificed to creativity.

Rudy knocked on a door that read simply, "A. D. Christianson, Head."

"Come in," said a low, gravelly male voice.

The small room contained a single desk and some filing cabinets. Cracked, colorless linoleum on the floor, cheap Masonite paneling on the walls. Fluorescent lights buzzed overhead. Sitting at the desk was a late-middle-aged man in a white shirt, Hawai'ian print tie, and a blue sports coat that was a size or two too large. Thick horn-rimmed glasses framed a wide, bearded face, magnifying gray eyes that were underlined by bags. His hair was white and tousled, matching his beard. Bushy white eyebrows almost met above a bulbous nose. Santa Claus as department chair.

"Dr. Christianson?" Rudy asked.

"You must be Laguna," the man answered in a friendly tone. "Welcome to Northwest."

The joviality reinforced the St. Nick image.

"Yes, sir," replied Rudy. "Reporting for duty."

"Great. We're glad to have you, Dr. Laguna."

"Rudy's just fine, sir."

"Even better. I'm Alfred. Not many of the faculty here go by last names. And, in truth, I never finished my PhD. In fact, most of our faculty fell short of getting their doctorates. You're part of an elite."

"I guess. Uh, how many wound up here via the route I took?" Rudy asked. *Let's get this over with.*

"Oh, we all have histories of one sort or another. Yours is a little more colorful than most. But first things first. Your past is really of little consequence. I personally consider Northwest to be lucky to land someone with your background and credentials. We emphasize and reward teaching here and, from what Dean Jacobsen at Hamilton told me, you're a topnotch teacher. Do that, obey the most basic rules of conduct, and I think everything will be just fine."

Rudy didn't need to interpret the basic rules statement, but was grateful that Christianson didn't elaborate. It looked like he could leave his baggage behind and be judged on the merits of his teaching.

"Thank you then, sir, er, Alfred. Things have gone by quickly the last few weeks, and I apologize for not being more communicative. Can you tell me what classes I'll be teaching?"

"Of course. You'll be in our science department. That's the last building to your left outside, the one that looks like it might have housed a custodian and groundskeepers. Which, in fact, it did. You'll teach beginning, intermediate, and advanced biology, what we call Bio 101, 102, 103. Freshmen, sophomores, juniors. All are team-taught, so you'll have lots of support coming up to speed. In addition, you can teach a course of your choosing. All told, that's four courses a semester, a little more than what you did at Hamilton. But, on the upside, our classes tend to be rather small, like a dozen or so students."

"And my office?"

"Already set up," Christianson said. "Just head on down to the science department building, and you'll find a spot with your name on it."

"Um, I do have another question, if you don't mind."

"Certainly. What is it?"

"Well, my appointment here at Northwest was kind of sudden. I was never interviewed. I'm sort of accustomed to advertised position announcements and competitive job searches, but that appears to have been, er...well, bypassed."

"No, not at all. When my old friend Dr. Jacobsen at Hamilton called me, the timing couldn't have been better. We had a vacancy that had to be filled quickly. Jacobsen's description of you seemed a perfect fit, and we wanted to capitalize on your, um, special circumstances. We checked with our legal people, and they said there was a provision in our charter for emergency hires. We advertised, but only in the local weekly, the *Northern Beacon*. We ran it for a day, made the job description match your qualifications—there aren't too many folks who read that paper who have expertise in minnow behavior—and *voila*. The job was yours. Anything else?"

"What about tenure?" Rudy asked.

"Of course. It's seven years up or out. Based almost entirely on teaching, mostly student evaluations of your classes, which are carefully read and usually disregarded unless they seem other than self-serving."

"Do I get any credit for my years at Hamilton?" Rudy asked.

"No, sorry. That's set in stone by the state. No time off for good, or in some cases bad, behavior."

Realizing he was on weak ground, Rudy decided to put his questions about research support and salary aside for now.

"No, sir. That covers it, I guess."

"So, go check your space out," Christianson said. "Please feel free to drop in if you have any questions. I'm usually here because of my administrative duties. And my door is always open."

At the end of the covered concrete walkway sat another cookie cutter single-story rectangular building. Light brown stucco with darker brown trim around the door and windows, faded ocean creatures rampant across most surfaces. The sign on the door said, "Science Department." Someone had painted the menacing, tooth-studded, open jaws of a large shark, the door handle in the shark's mouth. He revised his age estimate of the artist upward. This was a topic more popular with twelve-year-olds.

The door opened directly into a fifteen- by twenty-foot room with a large, worn, oak veneer table, surrounded by a dozen metal folding chairs. The veneer was peeling along the edges. A small refrigerator sat next to a card table with a coffee pot and numerous stained mugs on a plastic cafeteria tray. The smell of old coffee was hard to ignore. Obviously, the faculty lounge and meeting area.

The faculty lounge opened into a hallway, office doors to both the left and right. Rudy found a door with a plaque that said, "Dr. R. Laguna, Biology." His nameplate was screwed into a space that obviously had once belonged to someone else.

Rudy's office was maybe ten by fifteen with an old gunmetal gray desk and a clunky black telephone. Behind it was a heavily padded rolling chair, a seeming luxury in an otherwise Spartan setting. Against one wall was an off-white, three-drawer filing cabinet. Overhead fluorescents buzzed. And that was it, nothing else. Except for the stale smell of pipe tobacco.

"Home sweet home, I guess."

Walking back down the hall, Rudy glanced at the names on the doors and their specialties: Botany, Geology, Zoology, Genetics, Chemistry & Physics, Microbiology, Anthropology, Political Science, Consumer Science. Wait a minute. Political and Consumer Science? Were those sciences? Wasn't Consumer Science what they used to call Home Economics?

CHAPTER 3

Housing and employment secured, Rudy started his orca research in earnest. But first he needed a boat. Anything bigger than an inflatable rubber dinghy would tax both his budget and the hauling capacity of his old Volvo.

He found one on Craig's List, a used ten-foot-long Zodiac inflatable boat. The Zodiac sat on a rusty trailer, both engulfed in luxuriant English ivy, as much planter as sea-going vessel. With minimal haggling, he and the seller reached a mutually acceptable price. The seller even threw in the outboard motor, an air pump, oars, and a small, green metal box.

"The ammo box is a safety feature," the seller declared. "It's got spare spark plugs, hammer, screwdrivers, pliers, a flashlight, and a flare gun. 'Ceptin' I'm pretty sure the light and the flares are kinda old."

The seller stopped and pointed out that Rudy's Volvo lacked a trailer hitch. The seller held the boat while Rudy went to get one installed. Rudy quickly learned that a professionally installed hitch would cost nearly a thousand dollars, so he decided to do it himself. He bought a trailer hitch kit, deciphered the mangled English instructions, drilled holes in his rear bumper that almost aligned with the ones in the hitch assembly, and bolted the parts together.

Returning to the seller, boat and trailer dropped into place remarkably easily. Maybe a little too easily. Lots of wiggle room.

Rudy drove off, trailing only a few strands of ivy. He was now ready to go study whales.

Rudy's initial whale watching was limited to short trips. He hauled the dinghy up and down I-5 to launching ramps that might get him close to the action. Blaine, Bellingham, Anacortes, San Juan Islands (despite the expensive ferry rides), Whidbey Island.

But one thing was certain. The trailer hitch he had bolted onto his bumper was getting looser and looser. The rattling became increasingly disconcerting, sort of like opening the fridge and seeing something move out of the corner of your eye. Rudy's prime suspect was the mismatching bolts and holes he had hastily installed. Wrenches in hand and wearing a headlamp, he crawled under the car.

His suspicions were confirmed. The bolts had worked back and forth, enlarging the holes he had drilled. The bolts had to be replaced, maybe with one size larger. Putting a wrench on a nut, he applied some torque. Nothing happened. More torque. Same result. Repeated dunkings in salt water, without many washdowns, had thoroughly corroded the nut, basically welding it to the bolt.

The corrosion might yield to solvent. Out from under the car and back again, Rudy sprayed stinky WD-40 lubricant liberally on the nut, wiped off the excess, and some from his eyes, put the wrench on and gave a mighty tug. The lubricant did what it was supposed to. It lubricated. The wrench slipped, and Rudy slammed his hand into the sharp edge of the bumper.

"Jesus-Christ-Holy-Mary-Fucking-Mother-Of-God!"

Deep rich crimson blood flowed freely from three knuckles on his right hand.

Which was when he heard the thumping, like someone hitting a wooden broomstick lightly against one of the tires. Thump, thump, thump.

He was confused, and his hand hurt like hell. He needed to clean the stinging lubricant off his bleeding knuckles. Sliding hastily out from under the car, he quickly sat up. Well, he was almost out from under the car. He hit his head against the underside of the bumper, shattering the headlamp.

"Jesus Christ!"

Thump, thump, thump.

Emerging more carefully now, slightly dazed, Rudy sat up and looked around. Standing next to the right rear tire, wagging its tail, was a large brownish-yellow dog. Thump, thump, thump.

"Uh. Hello, fella."

The dog sat down next to the wheel and looked Rudy in the eyes.

Forgetting his hand and head for a moment, Rudy said, "Where'd you come from?"

The dog just sat there, staring at him.

Rudy looked back down at his knuckles. They were bleeding worse than he had realized.

"Jeezus, what a dumb fucking move."

Thump, thump, thump.

Rudy looked at the dog. "Jesus?"

Thump, thump, thump.

"Your name is Jesus?"

Thump.

Rudy looked more closely at the dog. It was tall, or at least had long legs. Curly yellow-brown fur all over, including on its face and out to the end of its tail. A little gray under the chin. Obviously male. An older mutt with maybe

Airedale somewhere back in its heritage. Alert eyes. Erect ears. No collar.

"Okay, fella. Let me clean up this clusterfuck and find out where you belong."

The dog followed Rudy to the kitchen door, wagging its tail. Rudy washed his hands, bandaged his knuckles, and got a bowl of water. Half expecting the dog to have continued on to wherever it was supposed to be, Rudy found him sitting just outside the kitchen door. He put down the bowl, and the dog lapped up the water, then raised his head, water dripping from the curls around his mouth. He wagged his tail.

"If you're lost, you don't seem too concerned. But, clearly, you're a well-trained companion and someone should be missing you. Someone with a sense of humor and less sense of propriety."

The dog sat there, looking up and wagging his tail. Rudy had owned several dogs as a kid, but that had been years ago. He considered himself a dog person. But his career, what with all the fieldwork, made dog ownership, or at least what he considered responsible dog ownership, impractical.

This dog belonged to someone, but Rudy also knew that students would get dogs without much thinking and then abandon them at the end of the school year. Still, as much as it disrupted his life, he felt obligated to try to find the owner, assuming the dog stayed put. Things would be simpler if the dog just wandered off. Rudy decided to just wait and see.

Back inside, Rudy puttered around the house, trying to distract himself. Occasionally he'd look out the kitchen window, hoping the dog had left. It hadn't. It was sitting attentively just outside the kitchen door. When Rudy opened the door, the dog walked over to a small throw rug, stretched and yawned, and laid down.

Fine then. Get comfortable and we'll do the right thing.

Composing a "Dog Found" poster on his laptop, Rudy easily described the dog and the when and where. But he couldn't bring himself to include "Answers to the name Jesus." He could just hear the irate messages on his answering machine.

"Okay. This is a stretch. You look like you could be pretty fast, what with those long legs. How about Cheetah?"

No reaction.

"Well then. You're kind of more yellow than brown, so how about Cheetos?"

No reaction.

Looking around the kitchen, Rudy noticed a jar he'd left on the counter from last night's hastily prepared dinner.

"Cheez Whiz?"

The dog wagged his tail.

Rudy sat back down at the kitchen table and said, "Here, Cheez Whiz."

The dog got up, padded quickly over to him, sat down, and wagged his tail.

"Cheez Whiz it is then. Cheez for short. That shouldn't offend anybody, other than Kraft Foods."

The poster finished and a half dozen copies printed, Rudy grabbed his car keys. Cheez followed him outside. On a hunch, Rudy opened the back door of the Volvo, and Cheez jumped in, hopped into the front seat and looked out the passenger side window.

"I guess you're going to ride shotgun while we find your home."

Driving around Blaine, Rudy stapled posters to a variety of stop signs and light poles. On his way home, he stopped at a 7-Eleven and bought a five-pound bag of cheap dog food.

"Hope you're not too fussy," he said to the dog. "This will have to do while we wait for someone to claim you."

The dog looked at him as if he understood, or at least made eye contact. Rudy shrugged it off.

Back home, Rudy called "We Work, Like Dogs," the local animal shelter. He gave them the details and his phone number and said he was happy to hold the dog until the owner showed up, either from the posters or by contacting the shelter. The shelter said that was good. This was a busy time of year, and they didn't keep strays for more than a week before euthanizing them.

"Especially mutts without collars and tags."

Rudy shuddered. That had never occurred to him.

"Fine. I'll keep him in the meantime and get back to you. Or wait for your call. Thanks for your time."

And no one ever called.

One day, a month or so later, after Rudy had adjusted to owning a dog once again, he looked at Cheez Whiz and said, "Well, Cheez, I guess I've finally found Jesus."

Or was it the other way around?

CHAPTER 4

Cheez easily made himself at home. It was almost a seamless transition from life apart. When Rudy was home, Cheez stayed inside. The dog didn't necessarily follow him around, but somehow was always in the same room as Rudy. Rudy never raised his voice around the dog, and the dog seemed to understand what it was that Rudy wanted, without being told. When Rudy went off on his own, Cheez went outside, which is where he was when Rudy returned.

At first, Rudy drove back to the bungalow with a certain degree of trepidation, for fear the dog wouldn't be there. But there he was, sitting in the carport, wagging his tail. On whale-watching days, as soon as Rudy started hooking the trailer up to the Volvo's new, professionally-installed, welded trailer hitch, Cheez would walk over and sit outside the passenger door. At a boat ramp, the dog quickly assumed his self-assigned place in the front of the boat.

Once out on the water, Cheez stood in the bow, feet firmly planted, shifting effortlessly with the bouncing boat, nose in the wind and tail wagging slowly. His balance was extraordinary on the often-wet, slippery surface. For some reason, Rudy had a brief flashback to the movie about the Maori girl in New Zealand who rode whales.

The dog seemed to love boating as much as, or even more than, Rudy. How the dog caught on that it was orcas they were looking for was another mystery. It certainly hadn't been deliberate on Rudy's part. But, after their initial trip together, Cheez often spotted whales first. He would give one quick bark and turn in their direction. Rudy, not seeing anything, often thought it was a false alarm. But, invariably, Rudy would soon see a spout off in the distance where Cheez was facing. Pretty amazing. The dog greatly improved his whale watching.

So, who had adopted whom?

Rudy often reflected on why he hadn't gotten a dog long ago. The answer was simple, one word, "puppy." Too much was required to raise a well-behaved animal that would fit into his lifestyle. It was a time and energy commitment he hadn't been willing to take away from his research. For much the same reason, he had avoided long-term relationships. His one failed attempt at marriage had left him with a once-bitten-twice-shy mindset. It seemed unlikely he could find a compatible partner with shared interests, much less a tolerance for his 24/7/365 work ethic. Why waste his or some poor woman's time proving the point?

Cheez performed what he considered to be his sworn duties. Teamwork, protection of the den, and loyalty to the pack were utmost, as Rudy quickly learned.

Cheez took to sleeping on a throw rug in Rudy's bedroom. He never attempted to get up on the bed. That was clearly Rudy's sleeping territory. The rug was plenty comfortable and provided a view of the kitchen and back door. Cheez always slept facing the kitchen. Rudy didn't think much about it.

Until late one night. Rudy was out pretty cold from a rough day on the water and put the pieces together after the fact. A poorly informed burglar had apparently thought Rudy's bungalow was laden with riches, the aging Volvo in the driveway notwithstanding. But criminals seldom came from an intellectual elite. This guy barely tipped the scale. His tools included gloves, a glass cutter, a suction cup, and a knapsack.

The idea must have seemed brilliant at the time: remove the left-hand glass pane from the kitchen door by attaching the suction cup, then cut the glass just inside the wooden frame. Pull the cut piece out and lay it quietly on the ground outside. Reach in to unlock the door from the inside. Everything worked to perfection. Except that last part.

This was evident from what was left behind. A bloodied glove in Cheez's mouth, and the glass, suction cup still attached, plus a knapsack on the ground outside. Rudy didn't get into the act until he was awakened by a scream and a curse and the sound of rapidly retreating footsteps. Cheez apparently heard the guy scratching at the glass with the cutter. It probably was a fairly quiet operation, except to a dog who was acutely aware of ordinary and extraordinary sounds in a darkened house. Cheez must have walked to the door and watched as the glass pane was withdrawn and the would-be burglar reached inside for the knob. Cheez didn't bark or growl. He just bit down, very hard, and apparently thrashed back and forth. It wasn't a difficult scenario to reconstruct.

Cheez sat there, pulverized calf-skin glove in mouth, wagging his tail, looking like a birddog that had retrieved a large cock pheasant.

Rudy walked over, gave him a pat on the head for a job well done. Cheez dropped the glove at Rudy's feet and went over to the throw rug in the kitchen and lay down, facing the door. Rudy picked the glove up gingerly—you never know what pathogens it might harbor—and placed it in the trash. Then he went back to bed, knowing the pack and den were well protected. He'd replace the broken glass pane with a piece of wood in the morning.

CHAPTER 5

Rudy spent what remained of his first summer trying to bring what he hoped would be orca research up to speed. He was successful beyond his wildest expectations. The Southern Resident killer whales (SRKW in the local parlance), which consisted of seventy-plus animals in J, K, and L pods, spent the summer feeding on Chinook salmon as the fish migrated from the Pacific to their spawning grounds in British Columbia and Washington rivers. To find the whales, you looked for them while on the water, but this was largely hit or miss, Cheez aside. Instead, he looked for commercial and recreational whale-watching boats or fishing boats trolling for salmon. The whales followed the migratory paths of the fish, routes documented since the earliest First Nations and Native American tribes inhabited the region. This greatly reduced time wasted just cruising and looking. Once Rudy got the hang of it, he found whales at least half the time he went out.

Next, Rudy had to learn characteristics of the individual whales, a crucial component in any behavioral study. But the groundwork had been laid meticulously over several decades by the pioneering whale researchers in both BC and the US. Catalogs of photographs and genealogies of every animal were available in books and posters and on the web. What first appeared as subtle differences in fin shape and color patterns, especially the gray "saddle patch" behind the dorsal fin, turned out to be diagnostic and reliable. Before long, he was getting to know the whales intimately. It just took time on the water, and time was something he had in abundance.

Unfortunately, others used the same methods to find the whales. The whales were local celebrities and always drew a crowd. Hordes of over-exuberant tourists followed the animals throughout daylight hours. The whales seldom had privacy. The established whale researchers found that the presence of boats, any boats, affected the whales' feeding success. This was especially troubling because Chinook salmon runs were way down from historic levels, which meant the whales were having trouble finding food. Motors and depth sounders interfered with the sonar the animals used to find and capture prey, as well as their ability to communicate with one another. Engine exhaust from all the boats clung to the water, meaning the whales inhaled the fumes with every breath.

Whale-watching guidelines existed to reduce many of these impacts. They mandated keeping a distance from the animals, not pursuing them or cruising alongside them, nor placing yourself on a line ahead of the animals so as to intercept them. Most boaters followed the rules, but there was always the small minority of assholes who somehow didn't think such restrictions applied to them. Rudy didn't hesitate to confront such scofflaws. Most backed away, but a few of the more belligerent men (always men) told him to "fuck off" in no uncertain terms. He always made a point of conspicuously taking their picture and noting the boat registration numbers of these miscreants. He had the satisfaction of reporting a few to the authorities for expired registrations, which carried a hefty fine and a chance of boat impoundment. He fantasized about revenge on the others.

In addition to the SRKW, which ate salmon and nothing else, there were transient orcas, also called Bigg's killer whales, that fed on seals, sea lions, dolphins, porpoises, and whales. Other transient-type orcas around the world munched on seemingly anything that swam in the water, including whale sharks, white sharks, and an occasional moose. These animals behaved entirely differently from the salmon-eating SRKW. Local transients lived in smaller groups or family units, vocalized much less than the SRKW, and could occur almost anywhere, but especially near rocks where harbor seals hauled out.

———

The summer went by all too fast. Rudy avoided the Northwest campus and its promise of a heavy fall teaching load. But, finally, two weeks before classes started, it was time to face reality.

Christianson didn't appear to have changed his clothes since their initial meeting. The fluorescent lights were buzzing even louder than Rudy remembered.

"Ah, Dr. Laguna. Welcome back. Starting to get antsy about the start of school, no doubt. What can I do for you?"

"Well, Dr. Christianson, I—"

Christianson interrupted. "Alfred, please."

"Er, yes, of course. Sorry. Alfred, I have a couple of lingering questions. I know I'll be teaching one-third of the intro bio courses. I'm apparently replacing a prof who retired last year, and I'll be responsible for the lectures he gave."

"Yes," said Christianson. "Old Man Thompson stayed on several years past his effectiveness. Toward the end, he had a habit of falling asleep at the lectern. Sometimes in mid-sentence. It became common practice for the students to rotate the responsibility of waking him up at the end of the hour. He was a bit of an embarrassment, but all we could do was drop strong hints. I don't think he had looked at a course evaluation in decades, or not after the one that read something like, 'If I were told I only had an hour to live, I'd spend it at one of Dr. Thompson's lectures because they last forever.' You will be a welcome relief from that uncomfortable situation."

"Why did he finally retire?" Rudy asked.

"He never did really retire, at least not officially. He fell asleep at his desk one day and just kind of never woke up. Since folks were accustomed to him sleeping in his office, it took us three days to realize he had died. One of the custodians—we only clean offices every couple of days because of budget constraints—found him late at night and couldn't rouse him. She called campus security, who called the Blaine sheriff's office, who confirmed that he was indeed dead. We had a rather resounding wake in his honor."

Rudy was almost afraid to ask. "And his office space?"

"I think you'll find it comfortable. Thompson had the softest chair of any of our faculty. I'm pretty sure he got it at a garage sale, because it's far more commodious than our standard issue office furniture."

Rudy tried to show no reaction to this revelation. The mention of a chair reminded him he'd been standing all this time. He sat down on a metal folding chair.

"But, Rudy, you said you had other questions."

"Yes, I do. You mentioned that I could teach an additional course of my choosing. I've started a new research program. I've always had a deep interest in marine mammals, especially whales. And, with the wealth of knowledge and public attention given to the plight of orcas in these waters, I've begun making my own observations."

"No more minnows, I take it," Christianson said.

"Correct. I'm beginning to think my ex-wife, among her other complaints, was right to view my minnows as kind of insignificant. My little fish were perfectly healthy and abundant; orcas are clearly in trouble. While one can argue that healthy minnows indicate healthy streams, saving orcas seems a more immediate concern."

"Hmm," said Christianson. "Sounds like a midlife crisis, adult-onset stupidity, that period when insurance salesmen want to be Navy Seals and Seals want to...sell insurance."

"I guess that's a possibility," Rudy admitted.

"I'm sure the minnows will miss you. But where does your teaching fit in here?"

"I'd like to lead a senior seminar on orca biology and behavior. It would only be taught in the spring. One credit, one meeting a week. I'd do some lecturing, but students would read and report on the current literature. It would be highly interactive and participatory. My hope is to prepare students for grad school and to eventually work in the field. This class, if it goes as I anticipate, would look very good on their resumes."

"Well." Christianson hesitated a moment. "I can see where it fits into your research program, which is good. We like to have students participating in faculty research if at all possible, even though we give so little support—little meaning basically none—for faculty research."

Rudy stood back up. The metal chair felt like it was designed to be uncomfortable.

"Which answers my second question," Rudy said. "I guess I'll just have to chase after all those big bucks on my own."

"Unfortunately, that is the reality of our situation," Christianson said.

"Okay. But, on the off chance I manage to finagle research funding, can I buy my way out of teaching responsibilities?"

"Oh my, yes. We can hire part-time, underpaid and overworked adjunct faculty at a moment's notice. They're a dime a dozen here in the Northwest. Local universities are producing them faster than the market can absorb. I've got a list of at least twenty such poor souls in a folder somewhere on my desk. You buy your time at your salary rate, and we hire someone at half that. The other half goes into our general account and supplements many things our budget doesn't cover. Anything else?"

"Not that I can think of," Rudy said.

"Fine then. I look forward to your joining us at our first faculty meeting next Monday, nine a.m."

"Yes, sir. The weather's good so I guess I'll go hunt some whales and some funds. Thank you for your forthrightness."

"Happy hunting, Rudy."

CHAPTER 6

The science faculty met the next Monday, as scheduled. *Ah, faculty meetings: mutual assured destruction on a parochial scale. A bonfire of the inanities. The battles are so pitched because the stakes are so small.* Then again, Rudy's claim to the moral high ground was tempered by his all-too-often participation in the fray.

The faculty lounge was half full at nine. Several people came up to Rudy and introduced themselves. Rudy tried to match names with the titles on the doors in the hallway. Heavily male, heavily white and middle-age, heavily overweight. Two women, one also very white and large, the other short with a wide face and dark hair. Rudy guessed she was Native American.

Christianson walked in at fifteen past and sat at the oak veneer table's end.

"Welcome back, one and all," Christianson said. "I'll try to keep this meeting as short as possible as I know you all have lots of catching up to do. Since teaching assignments remain as last year, I don't have to go over those. But we do need to welcome a new faculty member, *Doctor* Rudolph Laguna, who is the newest member of our intro bio team. *Doctor* Laguna has offered to teach an additional class, a senior seminar in orca biology and behavior."

Rudy stood up and nodded. He had winced at Christianson's emphasis on the word "doctor" but decided the culture wars would be unavoidable. He smiled as broadly as he could while he looked around the table, attempting to make brief eye contact with as many as possible. Several people nodded approvingly. *The more I teach the less they have to.*

"Okay then," Christianson said. "Anything else?"

What followed were some questions about room assignments, the academic calendar, and, of course, parking spaces. *Ah yes. Parking. The international blood sport of academia.* Christianson adroitly dodged them all.

"Okay then," Christianson said. "Unless someone else has a pressing question, let's call this meeting a success while we still can."

Rudy was about to leave when he noticed people standing around, talking to one another. He figured it might be rude to exit hastily, so he decided to remain a little while.

"Ah, Laguna. Welcome aboard."

Rudy turned to face a thin, balding, middle-aged man wearing horn-rimmed spectacles and a corduroy sport coat with suede elbow patches, and a tie—the only formally dressed person he'd seen on campus. His face was remarkably white, even for the Pacific Northwest. The man stuck his hand out. Rudy obliged.

"I am Orrin Rockwell, the department's consumer scientist. I suspect you are wondering where I fit in with all these hard science types. It is really a quirk of history; won't bother you with the details. But, more importantly, I am delighted to have another scholar in our group, someone with such an extensive publication record and, I understand, plans for an ambitious research program too. We are a minority in this outpost of academic civilization."

Rudy never really considered his publication record to be that extensive. A dozen papers on minnow behavior and a manuscript on orca social structure in preparation, a meager output by any serious yardstick.

"Why, yes, of course, Dr. Rockwell. Happy to meet you. What's your specialty?"

"The history, science, and sociology of consumer paper products. Most recently, I published a volume on toilet tissue and its role—pardon the pun—in shaping modern society."

Why did academics always refer to their books as volumes?

"I've traced its history back to the sixth century AD in China, reviewed alternative products—did you know that Rabelais in *Gargantua and Pantagruel* suggested using the downy neck of a goose? I've also cataloged recent advances, including the Northern Tissue Company who, in the 1930s, championed their product as splinter free. We are all beholden to Joseph Gayetty, who created modern commercially available toilet paper in 1857. I titled the volume *The Essential Role of Toilet Tissue*, pardon the pun."

Rudy found he was holding his breath. Maybe this was some sort of joke? Was he being tested for a sense of humor, some form of get-the-new-guy? But Rockwell seemed genuinely serious and self-absorbed, as if Rudy couldn't be more interested.

"Really? I'd love to see a copy. Is it available on Amazon?"

"Of course," Rockwell said. "But the publisher has given me twenty-five complimentary copies for my book tour. I'd be happy to autograph one for you."

Rudy paused appropriately, then said, "I couldn't ask you to do that. You should save those for your book tour. I'll pick one up on Amazon and bring it over to you to be signed."

"If you insist," Rockwell said. "But use the code AU-5 and you can get my author's discount."

Rudy thanked the man and said, "Oh, I just remembered I have to ask Christianson about the audiovisual setup in the intro bio lecture room, see if my PowerPoints are compatible with the projection equipment. Nice to meet you, Dr. Rockwell."

"Call me Orrin, please."

"Sure thing, Orrin. Nice talking to you."

Rudy slid away to where Christianson was standing. Without looking up, he said, "Is Rockwell for real?"

"I see you got ensnared. Yes, he is for real. I bet he even offered you a signed copy of his book. Don't feel too special. My wife and I both have copies. Rockwell even calls himself the toilet paper king when he lectures to community groups. He's becoming quite a hit on the local public-speaking circuit."

"No shit," Rudy said. "Oh, pardon the pun."

Things progressed in that vein, people coming up to Rudy, asking how he was doing and hardly waiting for his reply before launching into a discourse on their personal interests. Somehow the concept of dialogue had difficulty making inroads in academia. Academics as a rule were great talkers but poor listeners. Rudy wondered if his colleagues would have noticed if he had slipped a life-sized cardboard cutout of himself in his place and walked away. Maybe the cutout would draw a crowd, being such an attentive audience.

It was close to eleven. Surely a safe time to leave. But then he noticed the Native American woman off by herself, a metal water bottle in hand.

"Hi. I'm Rudy Laguna."

"Yes, of course. I'm Doris Laq'mash' Whitesalmon," she said, softly. Rudy had to listen carefully. "My mother is Sherri La't'chl Whitesalmon and my father is Lester

Lam'tsha Whitesalmon. Her mother was Cathy Longisch Frank and her father was Cliff Stashn'um Frank. Our ancestors are Qwakwaw'a' orca clan."

"Wow. The Lagunas don't go back very far, I'm afraid," Rudy said, trying to be polite and stay on the topic. "No one knows for sure what our name was before some immigration officer changed it to Laguna when my grandparents came to America, from somewhere in eastern Europe."

"I didn't think you were Hispanic," Doris said.

"No, not a drop. Just a twist of fate, I guess. Grandpa probably got in the wrong line at Ellis Island. They were pretty clueless, because neither spoke any English. Sort of low men on the totem pole," Rudy said with a smile.

Doris looked at him sternly. "That's a totally inaccurate and demeaning figure of speech. There is no hierarchical positioning of the carved images, crests, and symbols on our traditional posts. It's a typical Anglo misinterpretation of our culture."

"Um. Sorry, I really meant no offense," Rudy said.

Doris just stood there.

Rudy finally said, "Well it was nice meeting you." And he slipped away.

On his way out, he stopped by Christianson to express his thanks.

"I'm glad you stayed a bit to meet folks," Christianson said. "I see you even had a pow-wow with Doris White-salmon, our anthropologist."

"That's a totally inaccurate and demeaning figure of speech," Rudy replied.

"Ah, Doris gave you a tongue lashing, eh? Doris is a member of one of the Native American groups in the area. She's proud of her heritage and more than a little resentful of past mistreatment. Understandably so, once you know more about it. Such as the uncomfortable fact that our esteemed university sits on unceded Coast Salish Territory, meaning we've stolen their traditional land to educate Europeans."

"I'm admittedly ignorant of the various indigenous groups around here," Rudy said. "I have trouble remembering their names, not to mention which is a nation, a tribe, or a band."

"All part of your education, Rudy. I think you'll find Doris and her relations worth your time. And I think you have one thing in common."

"What's that?" Rudy asked, more than a little perplexed.

"An extreme reverence for orcas, although coming at them from very different perspectives."

"She mentioned something about that, as part of her genealogical recounting."

"She's very serious, but she has a heart of gold and is trustworthy. Just don't expect light banter with her."

"I'm forewarned. Anyway, I think I'll go prep for my first lectures now that I've met everyone."

CHAPTER 7

Rudy remained bound and determined to make the Pacific Northwest home. He could have pouted and bemoaned the circumstances that banished him to NWSU. But here was a chance for a clean break and a new life. Time to make lemonade.

Rudy looked back on his former research efforts and couldn't help but think, *what did it matter?* Orcas were different. Everybody cared about them, for good reason. Justification required little mental gymnastics, minimal explanation. And although orcas were no longer killed for sport or economic gain, at least not quickly, they were the poster children for the damage to the environment caused by human greed. Why not become a champion for whales and a crusader against all the insults modern society heaped on them? The evidence was everywhere and the opportunities were endless, unfortunately.

The transition mentally to becoming a marine mammal biologist was pretty seamless. But the whales were only present in the summer, and so he threw himself into his fall semester teaching and daydreamed about his research. And looked for ways to fund it.

The uniformly green hills and rocky shorelines of the San Juan Islands slipped by as Rudy rode an aging ferry to Orcas

Island. The horizon was framed by the snowcapped peaks of the Olympic Peninsula to the southwest, with volcanic Mount Baker dominating the eastern skyline. His was the last car allowed on, which somewhat softened the sting of the fares the state charged its citizens to ride these overworked, and frequently late or disabled, green and white vessels.

This boat was called the *Elwha*. Rudy could see it was in desperate need of drydock time, its lower sides a patchwork of flaking bottom paint and rust. Many of the Washington State ferries, such as the *Elwha*, were named after the local Native tribes that the white man decimated a hundred years ago. One boat was even named the *Sealth*, which was close to Si'ahl, the actual name of the chief mispronounced as Seattle. That man had been a great philosopher, and his sayings were incorporated extensively into the lexicon of modern-day conservation organizations. Unfortunately, little of that wisdom seemed to have been heeded.

The twentieth century had brought rampant deforestation, decimating the old-growth forests that Lewis and Clark had to negotiate on their halting voyage to the Pacific. What the early white settlers had referred to as a "green hell" was cut down to provide wood for the steam engines of boats and to burn lime to produce concrete to build the burgeoning town of Seattle. Much of the landscape had been cleared and burned to create agricultural land; photos from the time showed farmers standing in mud amidst tree stumps. Then FDR blocked the Columbia River with dams and locks, creating irrigation and barge transport for apple and berry growers, while wiping out the salmon runs. Had anyone been paying attention, it would have been obvious that the salmon-eating orcas, at the top of the food chain, were destined to suffer. Compared to a time of abundant salmon and a large orca population, today's world was, from the whales' viewpoint, decidedly dystopian and post-apocalyptic.

The *Elwha* slowed and stopped to allow a behemoth oil tanker from one of the giant refineries in Anacortes to pass. A massive spill from one of these tankers was another threat that the remaining, starving orcas faced. But an oil spill might be a moot point because the orca's reproductive efforts had already failed to recover from pollutants continually liberated from the sediments of Puget Sound. These byproducts of a pollution-based economy passed up the food chain and culminated in the orcas eating the few remaining, contaminated salmon. Few baby orcas made it through their first year, given the toxins they ingested from their mother's milk. *Try to have faith*, thought Rudy. *Nature is resilient if not vengeful.*

Rudy's destination, hilly Orcas Island, was the third stop on the run. Orcas was not named for the whales, but by a Spanish explorer to honor some benefactor. Most of the islands in the Pacific Northwest were named for the people who bankrolled exploratory voyages, although many honored minor shipboard persons who were otherwise lost to history. Rudy wondered what an eighteenth century cabin boy had to do to get an island named in his honor.

Orcas Island came after Lopez Island and sparsely-populated Shaw Island. Lopez remained renowned for its nature-goddess-worshipping left-wing radicals. The typical Lopez car was old, rusty, Swedish, and tattooed with stickers. Liberals plastered their cars with bumper stickers; conservatives washed theirs.

Despite different personalities and topography, the one thing all the San Juan islands had in common was their ferry landings. At each stop, you drove off the ferry and passed under a signboard blazoned with leaping orcas. Killer whales, the remaining ones, were iconic to these parts. Rudy had scheduled a meeting with Jason Gaddis, head of SeaMedic, a non-profit with headquarters on Orcas. Sea-Medic channeled funds into marine conservation efforts, and Rudy wanted to explore the possibility of tapping into that money. Always a long shot, but still a necessity when you had few other sources of research dollars. He was early, the ferry schedule having been poorly coordinated with his late morning appointment with Gaddis.

Killing time, Rudy walked into a coffee shop near the ferry landing. A young woman sat on a stool behind the counter and barely glanced up as he entered. She half-heartedly slipped off her stool and stood opposite him, looking as much past his left ear as into his eyes. Silence. He ordered a large black coffee – no pretenses about size denominations. Add your own damn cream and sugar. No decorative flourish on the surface. Toto, we're not in Seattle any more.

The girl's name tag said Willow. *Did islanders consult herbalist's guides when naming their children?*. She was wearing a gray t-shirt with large black letters across the front that read ORCATRAZ. Slender, straight black hair, high cheekbones, incredibly black eyes, a slight olive tinge to her smooth skin, and a strikingly beautiful face *(probably mixed ethnicity, maybe some Native American)*. Nice body, Rudy couldn't help but notice, although she carried herself in the characteristic American teenage girl posture, her shoulders slumped forward.

Willow's face suggested mid-teens but her appearance otherwise was early to mid-twenties, a mature young woman. Local schools were in session. If she was a teenager, shouldn't she be in school? She certainly had the body of a young woman, but she carried it as something of a burden. Or maybe it was just the job.

Rudy watched as Willow poured his coffee and set it on the counter. He paid (no tip) and sat at a corner table, the only customer. Willow went back to her stool and looked out the window.

Willow Silvermoon Johnson hated her life, everything about it. She was only sixteen, but had been passing for much older for a couple of years now, like since when she turned thirteen and her breasts grew. Older men had been hitting on her ever since, and she hated it. And, although she was sixteen, she didn't have a driver's license because her stepfather, the creep, wouldn't teach her, and her mother always gave in to him.

That wasn't the half of it. When she said she wanted to learn how to drive, her stepfather had taken her aside, where her mother couldn't hear, and said he would teach her, but it would cost. And he gave her that leering smile he often used when she was around. She told him to fuck off. He just smiled.

"Hey, the offer still stands. Just let me know."

Since then, she had taken to hiding in her bedroom whenever her mother wasn't home, with a chair propped up against the door. She also kept her bedroom window held in place with a wooden stick because the latch mechanism had been mysteriously broken, just like the lock on her door.

Why her mother ever married the jerk was a mystery. Her mother was half Native American, a member of one of the tribes that were scattered around northern Washington and the coasts of British Columbia. She didn't know which one because her mother never talked about it. She remembered her grandmother, a full-blooded Native American, telling stories about tribal legends and myths, but Grandma had died when Willow was little. Her dad must have been a large part Native American, too, because Willow looked more Native American than her mother. And she guessed that's why she had a Native American middle name. But her dad disappeared even sooner than her Grandma. Willow had no memory of him.

Her stepfather was pure Anglo and pure ugly. Beer belly, red-faced most of the time. Among his other endearing traits was his job. He owned the local septic tank pumping service, driving around in a rusting, stained tanker truck with "Steve's Honey Jar. Hit me easy, I'm loaded" painted on the side. When he wasn't working, which seemed most of the time, he slumped in a lazy-boy recliner, still wearing his filthy work coveralls, drank beer, watched golf on TV (although he never played), and bossed her mother around. And her mother always gave in.

Willow had a younger brother. He was just a pain.

Although she didn't know how to drive, she at least had a fake driver's license. She'd bought it from a guy in Anacortes, someone she'd met on the ferry. She hitched a ride into town with him and complained about her stepfather refusing to teach her to drive. The guy had, like, a studio or lab in his parents' basement where he made licenses. He had her pose for the picture ("Don't smile. Only kids smile on their driver's licenses.") and printed up the license right there. He gave her a birthdate that said she was twenty-two. She asked how much she owed him, and he hit on her. She ran out of the house after kicking him in the balls.

School was a total waste. A joke. Her classes were of no interest, the subject matter less than irrelevant. Her social standing in school, not that she gave a damn, was not improved by her jerk of a stepfather pumping outhouses for a living. Her classmates were equally disinteresting, the boys full of themselves and immature. She'd been dumb enough to go out on a couple of dates. They were clumsy and anxious. The one boy who seemed a little more worth her attention, and whom she let get a little farther than unhooking her bra, suffered from what she later learned was called premature ejaculation. More embarrassing to him than her. She found it funny, actually. She wasn't a virgin by any means, thanks to a college kid she'd spent time with the previous summer, a guy who worked at one of the summer camps and whom she met, of course, on the ferry. She was also very, very careful. That much she'd learned, and not in school. When she attended.

Willow lived for the summers, when she could move around freely without drawing much attention. Just another teenager riding the ferries and blending with the hordes of tourists who descended on the San Juans each summer. She almost never had to buy a ferry ticket. Foot passengers didn't have to pay for moving between the islands, although there was little reason to go to Lopez or Shaw. Friday Harbor on San Juan Island was a stronger draw. It even had a movie theater and several bars within walking distance of the ferry landing.

Anacortes and beyond (America, to kids on the islands) was, of course, better, but that involved hitchhiking into town if she couldn't hop a ride with someone on the ferry. Her mom, who worked cleaning houses on Orcas, tried to keep track of where Willow was, but didn't seem too concerned as long as she came home at night. And it wasn't unusual for her to miss a night or two. For incidental expenses, she'd use money she'd saved from her minimum wage job at the coffee shop. She was just dying to get the hell off the rock.

Rudy's meeting with Gaddis at SeaMedic seemed to go well. No promises of funding were made, but it was clear that Gaddis felt more information on the lives of local orcas was needed, given how their population seemed to be in steady decline. Rudy should apply when the next funding cycle began in the next spring. At least he hadn't said no. Nothing ventured, nothing gained.

CHAPTER 8

A pril was indeed the cruelest month, pretty much indistinguishable from March or May, weather-wise. Yes, daffodils and tulips and crocus were in bloom, probably because they didn't need sun to grow. *We have way more than fifty shades of gray here.*

The spring school term ending Rudy's first year at Northwest still had two months left. The whales were unlikely to show up for another two months, so Rudy worked on his data. He had written a paper on his previous summer's observations, charting the movement of members of J Pod. The paper was accepted for publication in a regional journal, sandwiched between studies on intertidal isopods and photos of the sperm of marine worms. His research was classified as "descriptive natural history," something anybody could do. He watched and recorded, as faithfully as he could. Rudy suspected the paper was accepted because people were interested in orcas.

He also wrote up stories for the "science section" of the *Northern Beacon*, the weekly newspaper that covered non-events in the Blaine area. The *Beacon* was more than happy to print his stories, showing they were attuned to local environmental issues. Hey, the paper even had an environmental reporter. The guy's byline also appeared on high school sport stories, so clearly he was forced to multitask. Maybe he even wrote out parking tickets.

Regardless, Rudy's articles gained him some recognition, which led to speaking engagements to school and civic groups. They seldom paid for these talks, but he usually got a free dinner for his troubles. Which was just fine. He liked talking about orcas and would do it for free to anyone who would listen.

Early one April afternoon, as he sat preparing lecture notes for the next day's biology classes, someone knocked at his door. He remembered Northwest's open-door policy and tried to sound as welcoming as possible, despite how much he resented an intrusion.

"Come in," he said, barely loud enough to be heard.

Rudy looked up to see two tall men dressed in almost identical dark suits, dark ties, polished black shoes. Their hair was short and neatly combed. Both in their late twenties, early thirties. His strongest impression was of cleanliness and neatness. They could have been federal agents but lacked the necessary dark glasses, earbuds, and curly cables snaking down to their shirt collars. Plus, they were imposing but not menacing, despite the serious looks on their faces. Tweedledum and Tweedledee in Men's Wearhouse apparel.

"Dr. Laguna?" asked Dee.

"Yes. What can I do for you?"

"Dr. Laguna," began Dum, "we represent a person who would like to employ you in an exercise that requires your particular skills and, especially, your discretion. If you agree, you will be adequately compensated."

"Well, that's intriguing, I have to say. But I guess I'd like to know which of my many particular skills it is your person needs me for."

"We apologize, but we are not at liberty to discuss things any further until you meet with our employer. He is, by habit and necessity, somewhat secretive and prefers to conduct business face-to-face, one-on-one. All we can say is that this involves nothing illegal nor immoral."

Rudy was happy about the legality issue but would have found immorality a little more intriguing. He also suspected he was being subjected to a practical joke, although April first was long past. He decided to play along.

"Okay. Let's say yes for now and tell me what it is I have to do."

"Excuse us, but we have researched your teaching schedule, and it appears that you do not have lecturing responsibilities until tomorrow afternoon. So, if you will come with us, we can proceed with the interview and have you back here this evening."

"Sure, why not," Rudy said. "Let me just close down here. I'm guessing you're taking me somewhere."

"Yes, sir. Our car is waiting in the university's parking lot. From there, we will proceed to the Bellingham Airport, from which you will fly to our employer's location. The flight will take two hours and four minutes. The interview will take approximately one hour. We will then fly you back to Bellingham and drive you back here to your office or to your home at 498 Cedar Street, whichever you prefer."

Rudy suspected that his address was no secret. Still, it was a little disconcerting that these guys had committed it to memory. Plus, they spoke as if they'd learned English from a robot. If this was, in fact, a practical joke, it was well planned. What the hell. April was otherwise pretty boring.

Rudy put his laptop in his briefcase, grabbed his hoodie sweatshirt—the black one with the Northwest tribal orca motif—off the back of his chair, and followed the two outside. They walked ahead of him down the canopied walkway and into the small parking lot in front of the "administration" building.

Looking around, it didn't take much perceptiveness to guess which car was theirs. His fellow faculty members, and much of the student body, drove older, small, foreign cars. In one corner was a very dark, very new, Lincoln Town Car with tinted windows. Dum opened the rear door for Rudy, then got in the front passenger seat. Dee drove. The likelihood of a practical joker springing the bucks necessary to rent this car and the two automatons was decreasing by the moment. Neither man said anything during the drive.

All doubts vanished as the Lincoln was admitted through a guarded security gate at the Bellingham International Airport (*After all, we do fly to Canada.*) and drove up to a small private jet. Rudy knew little about airplanes and next to nothing about private jets. His experience was limited to reading about such excursions in the thriller novels he enjoyed.

The plane's cabin was tastefully furnished but, looking around, Rudy didn't see a bar nor provocatively dressed flight attendants. Just a small fridge next to a nice wooden table, an equally small stainless steel sink, and some comfortable stuffed chairs with seatbelts.

"We can offer you a soft drink or bottled water if you'd like before we take off, Dr. Laguna," Dee said. "Then we will be occupied with the flight. We apologize for any inconvenience."

"Looks great," said Rudy, glancing around. "I'll just sit here and enjoy the ride."

"That would be appreciated," Dee answered. "Please excuse us."

Rudy sat back as the plane taxied and then took off with little delay. He looked at his watch. It read 2:17. He felt the craft climb and bank and complete a circle and then head southwest, snowbound Mount Baker receding off to his left. They then entered dense overcast and emerged above the clouds, the view nice but monotonous. Despite the excitement of his first private jet ride and the ambiguity of this entire venture, he dozed off.

The hydraulic whine of the plane's landing gear being lowered woke him as the plane decelerated. His watch read 4:15. Looking out the window, he saw a vast plain of what were possibly salt flats and a huge lake, everything backed by a long line of snow-covered peaks and terraced benches marching up the mountains' flanks. He had been to Salt Lake City before and guessed that's where they were, the Wasatch Mountains in the background.

The plane taxied to a hangar, far from the commercial jets. A similar dark Town Car sat just outside the hangar. Dum and Dee led him to the Lincoln, Dum once again opening the rear door for him, Dee again driving.

Dum turned around in his seat and said, "The drive to our employer's will take about forty-five minutes."

The Lincoln headed opposite from where Rudy thought Salt Lake City lay. They drove along an interstate, then a two-lane blacktop road, and then a well-maintained gravel road. As they crested a hill, Rudy looked down on an oval lake, maybe a mile long and half as wide. It was quite lovely, sparkling beneath a blue sky and bright sun, weather Rudy hadn't experienced in weeks. Small, single-story buildings, painted in subdued earth tones, sat at one end of the lake. A dock connected the lake to the buildings, large, shiny metallic pipes running along the dock's length. Golf carts and small, all-terrain vehicles moved around the compound. Large sprinklers shot water into the air at a half dozen places in the lake. Rudy thought he saw something splash momentarily at the far end.

As they descended toward the cluster of buildings, Rudy looked up and saw a small drone hovering above, paralleling their course. A red light flashed on the Lincoln's dashboard. Dum punched numbers into a keypad, the light went off, and the drone vanished. The gravel road ended at the buildings, where Rudy noticed a parked refrigerator truck, "Charlie's Seafood" painted on its side.

Dum and Dee escorted Rudy to the center building and punched numbers on a keypad before the door opened. Glancing up, Rudy saw several video cameras pointing in different directions. The place was clearly secure. What could they possibly be protecting?

Walking down an undecorated but well-lit hallway, the three men approached a door at its end. There was no name plaque or other signage on the door. Dee knocked and Rudy heard a voice respond, "Yes?"

Dee opened the door slowly and said, "Mr. Alexander, Dr. Laguna is here to see you, sir."

"That's great, Randolph. Please show him in. I'll give you a call when we're finished. Thank you for your help."

The office was also well-lit, the lighting recessed and soft, the room perhaps thirty feet by thirty feet, with richly paneled walls and a dark hardwood floor. Rudy noticed a number of plaques on the wall and several photos of people shaking hands. Otherwise, it was undecorated. An elderly man sat behind a beautifully constructed wooden desk made from dark wood with wavy lines across its lustered surface. Behind him was a large, slightly tinted window that provided a view of the lake behind the buildings.

The man looked to be in his eighties. He wore a light blue, embroidered cowboy shirt with a bolo tie. He was totally bald, his head reflecting the glow of the overhead lighting. Clean shaven, thin but not gaunt, a sharp nose and alert dark eyes. He closed a small book he had been reading and laid it down on the desk next to a thick manila folder and a yellow legal pad. Smiling, he walked around the desk, and Rudy saw he was wearing jeans and cowboy boots.

"Dr. Laguna, what a pleasure to have you here. I'm J. B. Alexander, and I apologize profusely for all the cloak-and-dagger. I promise I'll answer all your questions, or at least any you may still have after I explain your seeming abduction from your busy life."

Rudy shook his hand, the handshake noticeably firm for a man of Alexander's apparent age.

"Hey, if this is a kidnapping, I'm afraid my department lacks the funds necessary to meet any ransom you have in mind, assuming they care. Meanwhile, I'm enjoying this tremendously."

"As I hoped and anticipated. Which is part of the reason I've chosen you, in particular, for this venture. Your reputation for unflappability precedes you."

Rudy didn't necessarily consider himself unflappable. He wasn't prone to panic, but neither was he impossible to fluster. Too much time in boats, with the many opportunities to get into trouble and get out of it, usually.

"Before we do any more talking, I'd appreciate if you'd accompany me to the lake and see what this is all about," Alexander said.

He punched a button on an intercom panel that appeared suddenly from the surface of the desk. "Joseph, could you arrange for a Gator to take Dr. Laguna and myself out to the dock?"

A voice that Rudy recognized as Dum's replied quickly, "Yes, sir, Mr. Alexander. Please meet us out front."

"This way, please, Dr. Laguna. Chuck! Let's go!"

On the way out, Alexander grabbed a cowboy hat off a sculpted wooden coat hook. Rudy heard a scrambling from behind the desk, and a short-haired dog, medium size, bluish gray fur—probably a blue healer hound—appeared and trotted alongside Alexander. Rudy followed. Exiting the building into bright sunlight, Rudy saw Joseph waiting in a green golf cart-like vehicle. Rudy and Alexander buckled themselves into the back seat. Chuck jumped into the luggage space behind them.

Joseph drove to the end of the well-built, sturdy dock, made from what Rudy knew was recycled plastic. The stout pilings supporting the dock were made from the same material. Rudy liked the idea that all the construction material was recycled plastic, a good sign. Of what, he was still uncertain.

Alexander got out remarkably spryly and invited Rudy to sit in an Adirondack chair, similarly constructed. Several small aluminum boats were tied to the dock, all fitted with oars and small electric motors. *Good, no outboard noises or pollution.*

Alexander said, "This might take a few minutes, but not much more." And he gazed out across the lake.

Rudy took in his surroundings. The snow-covered Wasatch Mountains were clearly visible off in the distance. When seen up close, the sprinklers he had noticed on the drive were actually fountains that shot lake water maybe fifty feet up in the air, apparently mixing and aerating the water. The six fountains were spaced around the lake's perimeter, each maybe a hundred feet from shore. The afternoon sun shone through those on the west side, creating a series of rainbows. Very pleasant. This old guy obviously enjoyed spending his money, although from what Rudy knew about the Great Salt Lake, he couldn't imagine much life in such highly saline water, rainbows or not.

Rudy's gaze had been directed at the snowcapped peaks and he wasn't really paying attention to the water. He almost jumped out of his chair—difficult to do, given how deeply he sat in it—when a large male orca with a dorsal fin in the shape of a question mark surfaced not twenty feet from the dock, exhaling loudly in the unmistakable whoosh of a killer whale's breathing. The whale disappeared, swimming from right to left.

Rudy ran to the dock's edge and stood there, gazing at the telltale flukeprint left in the water by the whale's tail as it dove. He stared off to the left where he thought it might next appear, wondering whether this was some sort of animatronic robot whale. Thoughts tumbled through his mind. He was in the middle of the country, or almost, far from the sea, staring at a salty lake in a desert landscape. Things didn't add up.

And then the whale surfaced and breathed again, and there was no doubt that it was a very large, very live, male orca. No one had come close to creating a robot with the suppleness and grace of a living orca.

He turned to Alexander.

"If you didn't have my interest before, you certainly do now."

Alexander smiled and said, "Let's just watch for a while. It's always the highlight of my day."

He motioned to Rudy to sit back down, but Rudy just stood there, rooted to the spot, gazing out at the water.

For five minutes, both men watched the whale work its way around the lake, just inside the fountains of water, surfacing every thirty or forty seconds before slipping back beneath the water. Rudy had been looking at his watch to time the breaths. It wasn't hurried, nor did it show the methodical, stereotyped swimming of a captive whale in a public-display aquarium, showplaces that Rudy despised going back to his formative three-orca experience at the Royal Vancouver Aquarium. This animal's breathing was periodic but somewhat unpredictable. The whale was swimming, not pacing like a caged animal.

When it got to the far end, it turned toward the middle of the lake and leapt entirely out of the water, landing back with a tremendous splash, followed by a delayed *whoomp* as the sound reached them. Rudy could see that the whale was huge, larger than any he could remember. It resurfaced and then dove straight down, its tail fin clearly visible in what Rudy knew was the beginning of a deep and probably long dive. But how deep could such a lake be? Rudy recalled reading that nearby Great Salt Lake was less than fifty feet deep, which would hamper any vertical dives of an animal more than thirty feet long.

Alexander said, "Ninety feet deep, in case you're wondering. We figured this animal should be given the luxury of a somewhat natural depth realm in which to exercise."

Among the questions swirling in Rudy's mind was the issue of the saltiness of the water. Great Salt Lake was something like ten times saltier than seawater, not a healthy environment for a marine animal such as an orca. He lay down on the dock and took a handful of water and tasted. It didn't seem especially salty. It also was quite cool.

"We keep it just around thirty-five parts per thousand, same as sea water. Any higher could lead to health issues. The water temperature is around sixty degrees, and we even let it cool down ten degrees in winter. We keep it cool in summer with refrigeration. The fountain system helps, and also mixes new water as it's pumped in. I'll be happy to show you the water control facility if you'd like."

Such technical details were indeed interesting, but Alexander was clearly skirting the major question.

Rudy turned and asked, "Who is this whale?"

"And therein lies the main reason I've brought you here. We'll have to go back to my office so I can give you the complete story."

CHAPTER 9

As they headed back up the dock, Rudy twisted around, trying to get another glimpse of the whale. They were passed by a green cart heading down the dock, a large plastic tub in the luggage area filled with fish, their tails protruding. Rudy recognized them as salmon.

Back in Alexander's office, Rudy had a thousand questions. He wasn't sure where to start.

"Excuse me, Mr. Alexander. And please don't take this as a lack of interest on my part. But your assistants, Joseph and Randolph, said I would be here about an hour. It's going on considerably more than that. Should I be concerned?

"By no means, Dr. Laguna. I have already ascertained that you are the correct person for this venture. We'll get you back in plenty of time for your classes tomorrow, no matter how long it takes us to finish. The final decision of how long you're here will be up to you."

Alexander opened the manila folder that sat on his desk.

"This whale has gone by a variety of names. You probably know him as Makai, although that is just one of several. His age and origin are obscure. Based on his DNA profile, he is from one of the North Atlantic orca lineages, perhaps near Iceland or Norway. The records are unclear. Our best guess is he is at least forty-five years old, based on his captivity record."

Alexander slid the manila folder across to Rudy. It contained several dozen sheets of paper.

"That's a summary of the whale's personal history. It's yours to study at your leisure, Dr. Laguna, if the arrangement we're considering interests you."

Rudy looked at the papers, then at Alexander. He decided to clear up two very critical issues.

"As important as the whale's name and curriculum vitae might be," Rudy said, "what's more important is how he came to be here and why and how you have acquired him. Keeping an orca in captivity involves running an incredibly complex gauntlet of federal regulations. I admit I'm unaware of any other person who owns one."

"You are correct," Alexander replied. "I am, in fact, the only person to own one, at least openly. There are a couple of sheiks in the Arabian Peninsula and a member of the Japanese mafia who also have one, but, in each case, the titular holder is a corporation.

"As to your first question," Alexander said as he leaned back in his chair, "how Makai came to be here is a long and involved story. The details are in that folder. But the salient facts are that he was housed for many years at the old Marineworld of the Pacific, in southern California, part of one of those hideous marine circuses, where captive animals are subjected to neglect, abuse, and sensory deprivation. Marineworld gave him a romantic Hawai'ian name, disregarding the fact that he was captured in the north Atlantic."

Alexander seemed to chuckle to himself, then continued. "Makai proved to be a lackluster performer. So, his captors decided to bring in a playmate, a young female named Tama, who was captured in the notorious August 8, 1970, orca roundup in Penn Cove in Washington State. Five of her family members drowned at that time, and she, along with six other members of J Pod, were captured and distributed to marine parks."

Alexander stood up and stared out the window.

"Makai and Tama got along well and mated," he said, not turning around. "She, unfortunately, died a few years later, shortly after giving birth, after her calf was taken away. Makai then refused to perform and became aggressive toward the staff. The Marineworld administration, assuming Makai was lonely, brought in another young female captured in the Bering Sea. Makai rammed her mercilessly, killing her. He was then considered a liability and was sold to some disreputable traders."

"Parts of this story are coming back to me," Rudy said.

"Since then, he has been on display at a series of marine parks, refusing to perform or mate. Each of these establishments went bankrupt, in no small part because orcas require a huge investment in food and veterinary care. He was eventually orphaned and became the responsibility of the U. S. Fish and Wildlife Service, who had scheduled him for euthanasia."

Alexander pointed at the folder Rudy was holding. "That is when I acquired him via a special permit, probably granted to avoid the bad publicity that would accompany killing a member of a charismatic species, one protected by a number of national and international laws. I managed to get a variance to bring him here from his former location of internment."

"Okay," said Rudy. "That explains a lot, and I'm anxious to read the details. But you have yet to tell me why you, in particular, are undergoing the substantial expense, one that has apparently bankrupted several other organizations, of keeping an orca in captivity. The last I read, just the purchase price of an orca is between seven and ten million dollars, plus hundreds of thousands in annual costs. I'd also like to know what you eventually plan to do with him."

"Of course." Alexander turned and faced Rudy, his head down slightly and shoulders slumped.

"Basically, I have amassed a considerable fortune as a result of owning many paper mills. Very large paper mills. They were scattered around the country, but several were in the Puget Sound, excuse me, the Salish Sea region. My factories decimated giant swaths of old-growth forest to produce a number of products, but Sempervirens-brand toilet tissue was our largest money maker. Toilet paper is the ultimate disposable commodity. Re-use is under-standably minimal. Americans consume more than seven billion rolls annually, an average of twenty-three rolls per person. At eighty-four cents per roll, that's five point nine billion dollars each year, just in the U. S. The profits add up after a while."

Alexander picked up a book on his desk and showed it to Rudy. "I'm fairly certain you are familiar with this book and its author."

Rudy recognized the book. It was the one that Dr. Rock-well, the self-anointed toilet paper king, had written and touted so proudly at Northwest faculty gatherings. Rudy nodded somewhat reluctantly.

"Dr. Orrin Rockwell and I are well acquainted," Alex-ander said. "He and I have had many conversations on the topic of toilet paper production. I provided a great amount of the detail that appears in this book. He is also quite a fan of your work and was the person who suggested I contact you about this matter."

That one threw Rudy for a loop. He had been rather dismissive of Rockwell's scholarship. He should at least say thank you to Rockwell.

"Over the years," Alexander continued, "I am probably personally responsible for decimating more forests and dumping more toxic chemicals, especially PCBs and their relatives, into U. S. waters. I know you are aware of the harm these pollutants have done and how orcas, in particular, suffer as a result of my activities. Simply put, I want to make amends for my ecocidal practices."

Alexander began to pace in front of the window, his hands behind his back.

"There is little I can do or undo regarding the long-lasting carcinogens, mutagenic compounds, and endocrine disruptors I've dumped into the Salish Sea. They are in the sediments and will continue to enter the food chain and poison these wonderful animals for decades to come. I am contributing millions anonymously to clean-up efforts, but I hold little hope for any immediate improvement. In the meantime, I intend to take at least one small step while I'm still alive to improve the lot of the orcas."

Alexander stopped pacing and looked at Rudy. "In a nutshell, I want to return Makai to the wild, and I am asking you to spearhead that effort."

Rudy caught his breath. He mentally went through a number of scenarios, many unpleasant.

After several seconds he said, "First, I'm assuming you are aware of the track record of attempts to reintroduce orcas into the wild. Keiko, the star of the *Free Willy* movies, died of pneumonia less than two years after release. Other attempts have been similarly unsuccessful, although less publicized. Springer is the sole exception, but that was an international rescue-rehabilitation-release effort involving an orphaned animal that never left the wild, was brought back to health in a short period, and was released back into her home family group. Her rehabilitation involved many scientists, multiple government and non-government groups, and hundreds of volunteers. Lolita and Morgan are the objects of similar efforts that are in legal limbo. Basically, it hasn't been, and probably can't be, done. Orcas live in complex, closed societies, creating language, dietary, and other cultural barriers."

"I have read that literature," Alexander said. "And I am aware of the mountain I am proposing we climb. I have encountered numerous challenges in my professional life and succeeded where others failed. And I think, as you read through Makai's dossier, you will see there are reasons to be optimistic. And I am also counting on your extremely deep knowledge of these animals, their behavior and social structure, and your creativity. And discretion. The ultimate decision as to whether or not to finally attempt a release will be yours."

Rudy couldn't help himself. "Why me?" he blurted out. "The world is full of large orca conservation organizations already working in this area. A dozen quickly come to mind, like The Orca Coalition, The Free Morgan Foundation, OrcaLab, Orca Network, Orca Research Trust, Center for Whale Research, *mmmmmm.*"

Rudy hesitated, going through the mental checklist of organizations whose acceptance he would love to earn. "And the Orca Behavior Institute, Wild Orca, Hakai Institute, Project SeaWolf Coastal Protection. Not to mention the larger Cetacean Society International, Whale and Dolphin Conservation Society, and the International Marine Mammal Project of Earth Island. They all contain many experts and—"

Alexander interrupted. "Yes, any one of those might be appropriate, and probably willing, although some might see it as irresponsible. But, for my purposes, they all undergo public scrutiny and would undoubtedly do everything possible to publicize their efforts, if for no other reason than to raise funds for future efforts. Springer's laudable rescue is a case in point. That extraordinary effort required public involvement to raise the necessary funds. I am bearing all the expenses myself, whatever the cost. In fact, while you are researching and implementing a plan, I will pay all direct and incidental expenses, including picking up half your current salary to buy you out of most, but not all, teaching obligations. Dr. Rockwell says you are a good teacher, and I don't want to see those skills diminished. But I will also pay you an equal amount directly, off the university's books."

Rudy did the math quickly, but still had to add, "It's hard to hide an orca, Mr. Alexander."

"Dr. Laguna, despite your avid interest in these animals, and your efforts to keep up with everything that has to do with them, were you aware that I had purchased and transported Makai to my facility here in Utah?"

Rudy shook his head. "Obviously not."

"Exactly. I am a very private person and want to keep this under the radar. All radar. Part of our agreement will be that this effort, up to and until a successful release has occurred, shall remain a private affair between you and me. And, even after release, I prefer to remain anonymous. All those conditions are included in the contract you will find at the back of that dossier."

"It's not my nature to be speechless, but I'm not sure what to say."

"As it should be," answered Alexander. "I've given you much food for thought. I propose you take the dossier home and read through it. Give me a call when you've reached a decision. My very private phone number is on the contract. So, unless you have any more pressing questions, I suggest Randolph and Joseph get you back to Blaine so you can meet your teaching obligations. My thanks to you for coming here and agreeing to at least consider my proposal."

Alexander pressed a button on his intercom. The door opened almost immediately, the two assistants standing just outside. Rudy thanked Alexander and followed Dum and Dee, more than a little stunned.

CHAPTER 10

Rudy started reading the dossier on the car ride back to the Salt Lake City airport, and didn't notice when they drove up to the waiting airplane.

He went aboard and continued reading.

"Jesus Christ, that poor animal," Rudy said out loud.

Makai's history was one of neglect and abuse. Separated from his family at an early but undetermined age, probably as a three- or four-year-old, he had been flown to Los Angeles and transported to Marineworld. He was placed in a small pool with some Pacific white-sided and bottlenose dolphins that apparently harassed him no end. His diet was uncontrolled and inappropriate, squid and sardines, whatever they were feeding the dolphins. Veterinary care was lax. He chewed on tank parts, wearing his teeth down. To accelerate his growth, they fed him growth hormone-laced fish supplemented with injections. This might explain his extraordinary size. Meanwhile, because of lack of exercise, he developed the deformed dorsal fin characteristic of male orcas held in captivity. The dorsal fin grows in response to water flowing over it, much as human bone and muscle development depends on adequate exercise. Makai's dorsal was bent over one hundred eighty degrees, the tip almost touching his back. Such a deformity was rare among wild animals.

Makai was an unenthusiastic participant in the circus shows at Marineworld. He refused to beach himself on the poolside and seldom leapt high for food, two of the moneymakers at marine parks because that's when audience members got to feed performing whales, for a price.

A piece of paper fell out of the folder. Picking it up, Rudy saw it was a faded black and white copy of a photo from the *L. A. Times*. Although indistinct, it showed a photo of Makai being ridden by a woman in a mermaid costume wetsuit and a large dog. The woman straddled the whale's back, just behind the dorsal fin, arms wrapped around it. The dog stood erect, just ahead of the fin. The mermaid costume had been cleverly designed so the woman could spread her legs and straddle Makai's body, but when her legs were held together it would look like a whale, or mermaid, tail.

The caption said the woman was the whale's favorite trainer, named Ariel, and the dog was called Genius. The accompanying story was short and not particularly informative, pretty much repeating the photo caption. It did mention that about the only thing Makai did with any enthusiasm was a crashing leap by the poolside that drenched the spectators.

Makai's behavior changed dramatically when a young female orca named Tama was added to the pool. She had been captured in the now greatly reviled mass roundup of orcas in Penn Cove that Alexander had recounted. After that, Makai became a star performer and seemed to teach the female many of the acts that he had refused to perform. One trainer noted in the daily log that, "Makai is an entirely different animal since Tama's arrival. It looks like he was just lonely, or maybe horny."

Part of that speculation was confirmed when it became obvious that Tama was pregnant. Marineworld had never produced an orca calf before, and the public relations staff played it to the hilt. Press clippings from the *L. A. Times* were taped onto pages in the dossier with such headlines as, "Blessed Event Expected Any Day at Marineworld." A Name-the-Baby-Orca contest was held in anticipation of the birth, encouraging school kids to submit potential names. The winning name was, suspiciously, Marina. One trainer wrote in the logbook that, "…the suits had picked that name long before and, lucky for them, a seven-year-old girl from San Fernando coincidentally submitted the same name." No one seemed to care what the sex of the baby might be.

Marina's birth was difficult. Tama was a young female, and this had to have been her first child. Marina was awkward from the start and had difficulty nursing. Marineworld staff, being unfamiliar with newborn calves, were uncertain what, if any, aid to give. Their notes sounded panicked and unsure.

Miraculously, Marina started to thrive after two weeks. Marineworld administration now had a new problem. The orca pool had been crowded with two adult whales and was clearly inadequate to house another. At the same time, they became aware of the growing popularity of orca shows in the expanding market of public-display aquaria. A deal was struck with a commercial operation in Dubai. Marina was snatched from the pool and flown off to the Middle East. No record of what happened to her/him appeared. One trainer wrote, "The front office is calling it a win-win, solving the problem of a crowded pool and reaping a large profit in financially strapped times. We on the training staff see it as a lose-lose, especially for the whales."

The trainers couldn't have been closer to the truth. As soon as Marina was removed from the tank, "Tama leapt at the sling containing her calf as it was lifted from the pool." Tama swam around the pool frantically and could be heard vocalizing continually, making sounds they had never heard before. This went on for days. She refused to perform or eat. After two weeks, the desperate staff began force-feeding her, which only accelerated her decline. Makai similarly refused to perform and swam tirelessly at her side as they both circled the tank. After a month, Tama was clearly emaciated and declining. By five weeks, she was dead. A former female trainer who had been fired from Marineworld was quoted anonymously in the *L. A. Times* as saying, "Tama died of a broken heart."

This was the end of Makai's tenure at Marineworld. He stopped performing altogether and fed only occasionally. Staff couldn't afford another death and so force-fed him. The administration, against the recommendations of the training staff, decided Makai was just lonely and introduced another orca as a companion, probably in hopes of producing additional, lucrative baby orcas. This animal, a subadult female captured off the eastern coast of Kamchatka Island in Russia, was lowered into the pool early on a Monday morning.

One of the trainers wrote at length about the events: "The new orca was placed in Makai's pool at 8 a.m., before the park opened. Makai was at the other end of the pool. At first he did not respond to the commotion in the hoist area, not surprising given how unresponsive he has been since Tama's death. But about a minute later, he rushed to the hoist area and could be heard vocalizing. The new animal was also vocalizing. Makai swam around the new animal once, then returned to the far end of the pool. We thought he would just continue his tight circles there but, instead, he put on a tremendous burst of speed and rammed the new whale full on, right in the middle of her body. He continued attacking her for a full minute, repeatedly ramming her. Blood poured from her blowhole and vent. He finally bit down on her head, and she sank to the bottom, upside down, clearly dead. Makai circled her once more and then returned to the far end of the pool and remained almost motionless. He rose to breathe sporadically."

The dead female was removed from the pool and disposed of offshore. Administration now had a large financial burden. They had spent an enormous amount on the new female and still had the upkeep on a large male who would not perform in the daily shows. The trainers were hesitant to get in the water because Makai became increasingly hostile. Anyone who entered the pool, even if only knee deep, was blasted with a painfully loud pulse of sound. Some reported that their legs felt uncomfortably hot. The decision to unload Makai took no time. What did take time was finding a buyer for what training staff said the front office called, "a liability whale."

Finally, a marine park in Mexico purchased the whale. He was shipped off, and the entries in the dossier became increasingly sketchy after that. He traveled from park to park, from continent to continent, each time receiving poor care, while being kept in totally inappropriate conditions of water temperature, pool size, food types. The only positive note was that he apparently bankrupted several corporations that had no business housing large marine mammals. The final entry in the folder mentioned a marine park in Corpus Christi that bought Makai, who was now called Tex. Soon after, the owners were prosecuted for trafficking in endangered species, mostly Australian parrots and South American anteaters. Makai/Tex became a ward of the state in the bankruptcy proceedings. Euthanasia was on the table.

Which is where the trail of papers ended. Details of his purchase by Alexander and his move to Utah were not included. The final page of the dossier was a one-page contract proposal between J. B. Alexander and Rudy.

Rudy's plane touched down at Bellingham as he was looking over the contract. Joseph and Randolph drove him directly to his house in Blaine. He thanked them for their hospitality as Cheez bounded up the driveway to greet him.

Rudy needed more background. A computer search for information on Alexander took little time because there was little information. Alexander's full name was Jacob Brigham Alexander, and he was listed in the Fortune 500 as the 186th richest person in America, between Steven Spielberg and Oprah Winfrey, net worth somewhere around four or five billion. No photo was shown on the Fortune 500 site. His money had, in fact, come from the paper industry, largely production of pulp used in household paper products. Several acquisitions and mergers were reported, only because the Securities and Exchange Commission had approved them. Little else was revealed. No mention of family (wife, children?). Alexander had managed to buy his way into anonymity. A hard thing to do in these times.

Returning to the contract, Rudy found it straightforward, as Alexander had suggested. Rudy was to be retained as an employee of J. B. Alexander Industries, LLC, with half his teaching time bought off, paid directly to Northwest, and the other half to him. His duties were stated simply as: "Oversee the rehabilitation and introduction to the wild of a male orca known as Makai, all expenses to be borne by the LLC. The source of the funds shall remain anonymous. Upon successful introduction and repatriation of the orca, Dr. Laguna will make periodic reports on the whale's behavior, time compensated at a rate of one hundred dollars per hour plus any incurred expenses."

The bottom contained places for Rudy's and Alexander's signatures. Alexander had already signed.

Rudy was comfortable with everything in the contract; he found its simplicity encouraging. He went to bed around two a.m. and finally fell asleep an hour later.

Awake at seven thirty and foregoing coffee, Rudy calculated that it was already eight thirty in Salt Lake City, not too early to call. He dialed the number that Alexander had given him.

"Good morning, Rudy. How was the flight home?"

"Fine, sir. Thank you."

Rudy decided to get to the point.

"The contract is pretty much what you told me," he said. "It's a very generous and unquestionably exciting proposition. I don't have any lawyers to check things from my end, but I can't hide my interest in attempting what you've proposed. I already have some ideas on how to go about this. The whole venture is fraught with peril and pitfalls, but I'd like to think it's more than worth trying."

"Great then," Alexander said. "Fax that thing over to me and let's get to work. We'll plan another trip out here that won't be so rushed. Let's do it soon. Welcome aboard, Rudy."

CHAPTER 11

Joseph and Randolph picked Rudy up Saturday morning, Rudy having spent most of the week neglecting his classes and going over scenarios for repatriating Makai, rejecting ideas almost as soon as they surfaced. So many complications, so many uncertainties, so many possibilities to consider. The whole project could crash and burn. Maybe it was good Alexander wanted to keep things hush hush. Would this even be possible?

Rudy walked unescorted to Alexander's office, carrying the dossier and a notebook filled with scribbling. Foregoing small talk, he got right to the subject.

"J. B., the gaps in this whale's biography are large enough for him to swim through. I know you know more than I was allowed to see. If we're going to do this, I have to have all the information. Then maybe we can avoid stupid mistakes."

Alexander nodded. "You're right, Rudy. You have all the information up until I began negotiating to obtain Makai. That process had its moments. But none of that will be kept from you."

Alexander swiveled around in his chair and picked up a cardboard box full of manila folders and eight-inch by ten-inch bound journals.

"Here are the complete records beginning with day one, when I made my first inquiries about the whale's whereabouts and availability. Enjoy."

Rudy put the box at his feet. "Thanks. This is great."

"Then on to other matters," Alexander said.

"Right. I think I have the outline of a plan," Rudy said. "But, first, I've got a couple—okay, several—questions."

"Shoot."

"The way I envision things," Rudy began, "we have to do everything we can to prepare Makai for a return to the wild as a self-sufficient, socially functioning, adult male orca. So, what has he been fed?"

"Salmon," Alexander replied.

"How much? A full-grown male orca in the wild eats four hundred pounds of salmon a day. That adds up to between twenty-five and fifty fish, depending on size."

"We're hitting the lower end of that range, but Makai probably isn't quite as active as an animal traveling fifty to a hundred miles a day chasing fish."

"Okay. What kind of salmon?"

"Pretty much whatever we've been able to get reliably."

"Dead or alive?

"Whole fish, fresh, flown in from Alaska. Never frozen."

"But dead."

"Yes. Is that a problem?"

"Not if he's going to live in a kiddie pool," Rudy said. "But he has to know how to catch live salmon if he's going to survive in the ocean."

"Okay. I can see that," Alexander said after a moment. "But where do we get live salmon? My sources haven't even mentioned that."

"From salmon fishermen. And hatcheries. I know salmon fishermen who will be more than happy to supply us with live fish if we're willing to pay enough. As far as hatcheries are concerned, I'll have to put out some feelers to state, federal, and tribal sources that run hatcheries that catch fish on their spawning runs. Our timing isn't great but, again, if we're willing to pay enough, we could get lucky. And, because of our ultimate goal, we're going to have to give him Chinook salmon."

"I don't see that as a problem. Money can perform miracles."

"Okay. I'll work on it and let you know."

Rudy had befriended the crew of the *Clarabelle*, a salmon fishing boat in Blaine Harbor. He could just imagine how happy Captain Lewmar and the *Clarabelle's* crew would be. They'd be paid top dollar to catch live fish to feed an orca, with no middlemen draining the profits.

Rudy was pacing now, back and forth in front of Alexander's desk.

"Second, we have to do something about his dorsal fin. His acceptance into orca society may hinge on fixing his deformity. Wild adult male orcas don't have a hideously bent dorsal fin. I'm afraid he might be viewed as damaged goods the way he looks now."

"And your solution to this problem?"

"Prosthesis. Done by a knowledgeable expert."

"You mean something like that dolphin in Florida that they gave a new tail fin and then made a tear-at-your-heartstrings movie about?"

"Precisely," Rudy replied. "Only I think this will be a little easier since the dorsal fin doesn't move up and down like tail flukes do. But, then again, it's never been done before."

"I'm assuming you've given this some thought," Alexander said with a smile.

"Quite a bit, actually. And some research, at least on the internet. I'm still working on the details. No matter how we do it, it's going to cost. Lots."

"Once again, money can move mountains, and I'm not going to do this on the cheap."

"Good. We'll come back to that."

He stopped and looked at Alexander, who was scribbling notes on the ever-present legal pad on his expansive desk.

"Third, we may have to do some dental work because, as is typical of captive whales, his teeth are pretty worn down, probably from chewing on concrete and metal in his pool."

"It doesn't seem to affect his ability to chow down salmon," Alexander said. "But we'll pay attention to that, just in case."

"Fourth," Rudy continued, "is the critical issue of where and when he will be released, something that will require a series of carefully planned and executed steps. We have to prepare him for living in the wild, which involves critical social aspects of his future life. Orcas live in complex social groupings with long, unique histories, customs and practices. For Makai to have a chance at surviving, he must somehow be integrated into one of those societies."

Rudy paused, because the next part was huge.

"So, the even bigger question is where to attempt this. It isn't so much a geographical question as it is a social question. Repatriation to the North Atlantic isn't even an option, because we don't know where he came from. And it's too far from here to be practical in terms of managing his introduction once he is set free. Not to mention the possibility that he might have to be recaptured if things don't go well."

"And you've got an idea about this?" Alexander asked.

"Yes. There is one social group that he may, and I emphasize *may*, have a chance of joining. This is dangerously speculative, which, if I were a more careful scientist, I'd avoid. But there is one possibility."

"J Pod," Alexander said matter-of-factly.

"Wow. You're way ahead of me. Tell me your reasons and I'll tell you mine."

Alexander smiled again. "From what we know, the only orca he's spent any time with was a female taken from J Pod. That was Tama, the female captured at Coupeville, bought by Marineworld, with whom he mated. They lived together, apparently happily, for a couple of years. During that time, his behavior changed enormously, suggesting that she had a strong influence on him. In fact, she changed him. Maybe he was a project whale for her."

"I guess the right woman can do that," Rudy said.

"Definitely," Alexander said. "If he is familiar with any cultural customs and language dialects, J Pod is the most likely candidate. And, fortunately, they are not far from where you conduct your research. In fact, I think you're quite familiar with those animals."

Rudy couldn't help but chuckle. *You sly dog, J. B.* Clearly, Alexander was with him, or even a couple of steps ahead, and had been from the start.

"Okay," Rudy said. "Have I told you anything you don't know or haven't thought of yet?"

"I'll admit I hadn't considered the dorsal fin problem. Thank you for that insight. It's pretty clear I picked the right guy for the job."

It was Rudy's turn to smile.

"Thanks, J. B. For starters, we need to play recordings of the Salish Sea acoustic environment to Makai. Then we play J Pod vocalizations to remind him of his roots. Or at least its newest branches. He needs to be familiar with the different voices in that group. Maybe it will even serve as a refresher course in J Pod dialect. It's been years since he's spoken any language, let alone to another whale."

"I like that," Alexander said. "Can you work on getting the recordings and the technology for broadcasting them into the lake?"

"I don't think either will be difficult," Rudy said. "Costs might be an issue though."

"No, they won't," Alexander assured him.

"Great. A couple more things. When we do the surgery, I'd like to avoid anesthetics if at all possible. As you know, all dolphins are voluntary breathers, and anesthetics have caused several drownings when the animal was too narked to remember to breathe. I think we need to do all the broadcasting from the dock to get him happy to be there. If we're going to have to do stuff to this whale, including ultimately giving him a new dorsal fin, we want him comfortable around us. I think we can acclimate him to a sling and hoist if the rewards are sufficient. But we may have to overcome some bad memories."

"You're right about that," Alexander replied. "When we brought him here, he couldn't get out of the sling and into the lake fast enough. We haven't tried to capture him since."

Rudy agreed. "I'm hoping what we do to him won't feel like being recaptured, just some minor and short-lived restraint. If we associate that with the J Pod recordings, he might be more willing. I think he's hungry for social contact and interaction, and that's what the recordings may provide. Also, feeding him, or at least releasing live fish, at the dock should also create positive associations. Importantly, he has to trust us, especially me."

"We've got a head start on that. We've fed him at the dock from the beginning, more for our convenience than anything else."

"When's the next feeding?" Rudy asked.

Alexander glanced at his watch. "Not for another hour. But I think we can break the schedule. My boys really enjoy watching him gobble up fish. They can't get enough of it. I think they'd do it for free."

Alexander was dialing his phone, giving instructions, and grabbing his cowboy hat from the rack all in one movement. The dog scrambled out from under the desk and stood by the door. Soon all three were in the ATV, heading down the dock, following a Charlie's Seafood refrigerator truck. Four men were crammed in the cab, which clearly was meant to seat only two.

Alexander and Rudy watched as the workers pulled big blue plastic bins out of the truck's storage compartment, large tail fins protruding. They dragged the bins to the edge of the dock, joking with one another.

Alexander smiled and nodded at the workmen. One of them pulled out a large silvery salmon and threw it exuberantly into the water. This turned into a contest among the other three, and pretty soon salmon were flying off the end.

"Hey J. B. You think I can get a job at Pike Place Market after doing this?" a burly worker shouted.

Alexander shouted back, "I don't know, Stephen. You might have to work a little more on your technique. Your fish keep doing back flips."

Everybody stopped when they saw the dome of advancing water as Makai raced across the lake, straight for the dock. His dorsal fin erupted from the surface, and Rudy could hear the explosive rush of air as the orca took a breath. Then the salmon, which were floating at the surface and a few feet down, began disappearing. Rudy was again struck by how large the whale was, a giant among orcas.

He wondered if Makai's exceptional size would make his acceptance into J Pod easier or more difficult. So little to go on, so much in the balance.

CHAPTER 12

Everything about this place was different. Better. Sam knew he wasn't in the ocean, although his memories that far back were weak. The ocean was open and endless. He remembered having to swim hard to stay next to his mother, although she never let him drift far behind. But they would swim for days and never be in the same place. This pool, he guessed it was a pool, was large enough to let him swim for several minutes without turning. Plus, he could dive deeper than he had in years.

The water was cool, a comfortable temperature, which was also a pleasurable and different sensation. The logriders were all male. One was clearly older than the others and was treated with respect. Sam thought of him as an elder, maybe a Grandpa. From all his years in captivity, Sam had learned to read their body language, their posture, their vocalizations. He couldn't begin to understand what they said, but he could sense intent. These logriders were clearly interested in him, but never required him to do tricks. He was fed regularly and well, given several types of salmon, all tasted fresh. He even got an occasional small Chinook. He recognized the different types because Nan, his mate at Marineworld during that brief happier time, taught him how to recognize them. Nan had also given him the name Sam. He had no recollection of what his name had been before that.

After several lunar cycles, a new logrider appeared, often in company with Grandpa. He was only a little older than the others, but was also treated with some deference, including by Grandpa, who was clearly his senior. Sam decided he must be an elder, although not very old. He started thinking of him as an uncle, maybe a younger sib of Grandpa. Okay, then, he was Uncle.... Who else did Nan talk about from before she was captured? An Uncle Morris? Good enough. Sometimes the two elders would sit on the wooden structure and just watch. Sometimes the new logrider would sit for hours alone. His posture and behavior were much more intent, focused. Sam would spyhop and stare at him and sensed a positive response in the male's posture. But, still, they never asked Sam to do tricks to be fed.

One day, the new male, Uncle Morris, entered the water, half submerged, his split tail fins encased in a soft, thick skin Sam remembered from the logriders at Marineworld. Uncle Morris was upright, standing on his tail fins, atop a flat log attached to the wooden structure. Sam scanned him and confirmed that he was indeed a male, that much of him was under water. Sam was tempted to blast him, but his treatment to date had been so benign that he didn't think it necessary. Other logriders passed fish to him that he then threw out in the water. At first Sam was suspicious of this new way of being fed and didn't eat the fish, which sank to the bottom or were picked at by the pesky seagulls that hung around, screaming for scraps.

Finally, when Sam felt more confident that nothing bad would happen, he ate the fish with minimal caution. Over several days, the new male threw the fish closer and closer to the wooden structure. Finally, the logrider just stood there, dangling a very large Chinook, the biggest fish Sam had seen. Sam made several passes, scanning the logrider and the fish. This wasn't greatly different from what had happened long ago, as one of the tricks he was supposed to perform. But Sam's confidence in the intentions of this male had grown. Slowly, he swam up to Uncle Morris, who held the fish out. Sam took it gently and swam off. It was incredibly delicious, like nothing he remembered tasting before.

This became the new game, Uncle Morris being the only one who fed him from the water, and only a few days of the week. The rest of the time the others tossed the fish out in the water.

Then, one day, things changed dramatically. Sam saw a group standing around on the dock, Grandpa and Uncle Morris included. They guided a long, large tube into the water that was attached to one of the moving land logs. Sam swam over out of curiosity. He heard unfamiliar noises and then, to his surprise, a dozen salmon shot past him. Live salmon! He caught enough of a glimpse to know they were chum salmon, not one of his favorites. But they were alive.

Sam took off after them and just followed as they zigged and zagged across the pool. He had never caught live fish before and was fascinated by the way the sun flashed off their sides as they turned and fled, while drinking in the sound of their swimming undulations through the water.

He must have followed them for a long time before he realized how hungry he was. Why not? He put on a burst of speed and snapped his jaws shut and came up with a mouth full of water. Live fish were going to be a challenge. After several more unsuccessful attempts at catching a fish, during which Sam grew hungrier, he blasted one with a shout. The fish immediately stiffened, then swam erratically, and finally grew still. Sam swallowed it and went after more.

The last of the fish, the largest and fastest, proved hardest to catch. But it soon succumbed to Sam's sonic blasts. Sam remembered that few of Nan's relatives could catch fish that way. Chasing and grabbing were more usual, although they often did it as a team. He resolved to learn how to do that, too, even though he would have to do it alone. This assumed the logriders didn't run out of live fish, or he didn't starve in the process.

Shortly after the live fish arrived, events took another dramatic turn. Sam heard sounds coming from the direction of the logriders' structure. He swam over to investigate and found a small round object in the water, hanging from a strand. The sounds came out of it. They stirred long forgotten memories, and Sam realized it was the sound of the ocean. Crashing, popping, gurgling, buzzing, sometimes near, sometimes distant. Many of the sounds were real and varied, others were constant, deep or high-pitched buzzes or throbs. Logrider noises no doubt. During some of his earlier captive periods, other logriders—the ones that wanted him to do tricks—had placed similar objects in the water that produced melodic sounds. But they were not the ocean sounds that Sam remembered from his childhood. They must be some sort of language the logriders used, limited in range, with repeating phrases. Pleasant enough, but otherwise uninteresting. These new sounds were entirely different and very real. The voices of the ocean.

And then, one day, while at the far side of the pool, he heard Nan's family, mixed with the ocean's voices. He rushed across the water, expectantly. Had they somehow found him? To his disappointment, the voices were coming from the logriders' device in the water. What a cruel hoax. He was about to tear it apart when he heard someone speak Grandma's name, a voice so similar to Nan's that he caught his breath. The voice asked Grandma where they were going to hunt that day and if she could remain behind and help care for a newborn. Then he heard the reply, the deep, soft, older voice that must have been Grandma's. Grandma called the other by the name Rose. Didn't Nan have a younger sister named Rose? Sam stopped in front of the device and just listened, rapt, fascinated.

It dawned on him in an instant. These logriders had showed him nothing but kindness and patience. Clearly, they had a plan for him. Why else would they find Nan's family and somehow capture their voices for him to hear? He leapt out of the water in sheer joy at the thought, his re-entry wave splashing the group on the dock. He heard them all laugh, a sound he also remembered from a few of his earlier, and kinder, captors. If these logriders wanted him to do something, anything, he would cooperate fully.

The logriders' concern for Sam's well-being was reinforced shortly thereafter. He remembered it as the night of the intruder. When his logriders—he now thought of them that way, not as his captors—moved around in the pool in their logs, they always did so slowly and quietly. Usually, they propelled themselves with long sticks that pushed through the water. At other times, they moved a little faster, pushed by a quietly buzzing, rotating fin on the back of the log. They never chased him and, in fact, seemed to go out of their way to avoid disturbing him.

Sam, on his part, occasionally swam over to where they were stopped and watched as they spent time around the structures that shot water into the air. At other times, they manipulated the long tubes that led from the land, from which water that tasted hardly of salt flowed, sometimes hot and sometimes cold. When he made such a visit, they often stopped what they were doing and looked at him and vocalized to one another. Everything about their body language made them appear pleased.

On the night of the intrusion, a very different log appeared out of nowhere in the pool. The moon was full, and Sam could see it well, in addition to hearing it. This new log was incredibly loud, both in the water and out. And incredibly fast. On it was an unfamiliar logrider encased in a soft outer skin. Sam approached, and the log turned straight towards him. In an instant, Sam realized he was being chased.

He took off away from the log, but it gained on him with frightening rapidity. Sam thought for sure he was going to be overrun when he heard and felt a tremendous *thump-thump-thump*. As he drew a quick breath, he looked up to see a giant black bird-like object descend toward the water, directly above the intruder. Bright lights shone down, illuminating the intruder, while powerful wind gusts buffeted Sam and the intruder. Sam could just make out two familiar logriders inside the object. They overtook the intruder, dropped some kind of mesh object on him, and then landed in the water. They grabbed him off his log and took him into the bird and left.

Shortly after, two more logriders came in one of the small logs with the quiet buzzing fins and towed the loud log away. His logriders were watching out for him.

Rudy's cell phone woke him up. His humpback whale song ringtone—a rising pitch whoop—made such intrusions a little less annoying. Even at this hour.

Picking up the phone and glancing at the face, he saw it was two in the morning and the number was Alexander's. Fearing the worst, he answered.

"Hello, J. B. What's happening? Tell me it's not bad news."

"No, not really. Things are under control and nobody, or at least no whales, have been harmed. But we had a little incident that I thought you would want to know about."

Rudy was wide awake now. Alexander was generally calm, but Rudy could detect anxiety in his voice.

"Okay, give me the details."

"Well," Alexander drawled, lapsing into his usual, more folksy tone. "It seems we had a little visitor tonight whose bucket list included riding his jet ski on every sizable water body in Utah."

"Oh shit!" Rudy exclaimed, not hiding his shock.

"Yes, I'm afraid so," Alexander continued. "The guy towed his ski behind a Hummer to the far side of my property, cut the fence with bolt cutters, backed the ski down into our lake, and took off after Makai. I guess he couldn't read the No Trespassing signs, even in the full moonlight. Not that cutting the fence isn't enough of a crime."

"Oh shit," Rudy said again, this time a little quieter. "Is Makai alright?"

"Yes, we're pretty certain. The guy didn't get very far. In his haste, he ignored the alarm system built into all the fencing and the infrared video cameras we've got set up around the perimeter. We knew what he was up to before he got to the lake. We have a float-enabled chopper stowed away in one of the outbuildings that we can scramble on short notice. Randolph and Joseph were airborne about the time the ski hit the water. They intercepted him a minute later. They got to use the cannon net system we keep for capturing and tagging pronghorn, something we do for the state game people.

"I bet Joseph and Randall enjoyed that," Rudy said.

"Most definitely. And they kind of neglected to be as gentle as they are with the antelopes. So now the guy's in custody at the sheriff's office in Salt Lake City, and his ski, trailer, and Hummer have been impounded. He's being held on a variety of local, state, and federal charges. He was a little combative when the sheriff picked him up, which isn't going to help his case. I'm afraid checking off his bucket list is going to be postponed for a couple of years. Sheriff Caleb Young and Judge Gideon Smith and I go way back. And I think the good sheriff has his eyes on that Hummer. For the department, of course."

"Of course," Rudy said. "Do you think I should come out and make sure?"

"No, I don't think so. We gave Makai a special helping of big Chinook a little while later. We weren't going to feed him until this morning, but decided he needed pacifying. He ate with his usual relish, so if he's upset, his appetite isn't showing it."

"Attaboy, Makai," Rudy answered. "Thanks for letting me know, J. B. And thanks for taking care of our whale."

Rudy shut his phone off and lay back in bed. It took him a while to fall back asleep. He dreamed about humpback whales.

CHAPTER 13

J oseph and Randolph arrived early Saturday, precisely at eight. Cheez had endeared himself to the retired couple next door. The dog was well cared-for during Rudy's frequent absences. Maybe too well: Cheez was definitely putting on weight.

On the flight to Salt Lake City, Rudy mentally went over his progress and plans. Makai had been under his care now for a very busy month. With Alexander's funds, Northwest hired a young woman zoologist to cover Rudy's Intro Bio teaching responsibilities. Rudy now taught only orcology, which met once a week. This freed him up to work almost full time on Makai's rehabilitation.

Captain Lewmar was fishing full time for Makai. The freezer storage space on the *Clarabelle* was converted into a live well, with circulating seawater. Lewmar somehow got a permit from the Fish and Wildlife Service to increase his allowable take of hatchery Chinook, well ahead of the regular summertime fishing season. Rudy had thought such an extension unlikely, but obviously Alexander's influence carried well beyond his circle of former and current corporate executives. It was amazing what money could do. Or maybe it wasn't.

Alexander was waiting in his office. He greeted Rudy and they talked briefly about the jet ski incident, then turned to the next steps.

"I've given some thought to where we might try to actually release Makai," Rudy said. "There are a number of possibilities, all with pluses and minuses. But I think I've finally decided."

"Penn Cove," Alexander said, matter-of-factly.

"Damn," Rudy exclaimed. "Ah, sorry, J. B. You take all the fun out of this."

"Good to hear, Rudy. But I can't think of a better place. It just makes the most sense."

"I agree, for logistical, as well as historical, reasons. And maybe even ironical. But now that we've got that settled, have you worked out the details?"

"No. That's your department, Rudy. I'm just here to make sure things happen as you plan."

"Okay." Rudy said. "Penn Cove makes sense because it's well within the feeding range of J Pod, although they don't seem to go into the cove itself. The Skagit River salmon run is just north and is one of the larger runs in the area. We know whales, including J Pod, hunt there. The cove itself is nearly ideal for holding an orca, both in terms of breadth and depth. It can be cordoned off without much difficulty, as was proven back in 1970. So, logistically, geographically, and sociologically, it's good, better than many other locales."

Rudy paused, as if collecting his thoughts.

"On the downside, however," he continued, "is politics, both whale and human. We have to make sure J Pod finds him there, given what appears to be their reluctance to visit the cove. And we have to minimize the disturbance and hubbub that's likely to occur when we put a very large male orca in a public space, not far from the town of Coupeville. He's likely to draw a crowd."

"And you've thought of a way to minimize that, I assume," asked Alexander.

"No guarantees, but I think the good people of Coupeville are probably the best folks to assure that Makai receives minimal disturbance. That community still suffers, deservedly so, from strong collective guilt. They all know that they were the site of one of the most notorious incidents in the history of human-orca interactions. You just have to go visit the little center, or chapel if you want, that they've put on the dock in Coupeville. It depicts what happened that day in 1970, with the forceful message of 'Never again!' I think if we approach the city leaders and tell them what we're trying to do, why we're trying to do it, and with whom, not only will they consent, but I think they'll volunteer to help. They would be our boots on the ground."

"Sounds intriguing. How do you think my financial resources can expedite things?" Alexander asked.

"Pretty straightforward. Coupeville holds an annual remembrance each August. That costs money, funded by donations. They do it up big time every decade. I can tell them I have located an anonymous benefactor who is willing to foot the bill for the next, say, five years."

"Make it ten," Alexander said, without hesitation.

"You drive a hard bargain, sir," Rudy said.

"I didn't get where I am by playing softball, Rudy. I trust you will do the negotiations. Just keep me up to date."

Alexander scribbled something on the yellow pad on his desk. Rudy waited until he was finished writing.

"Now to what I hope is the last big issue, which is—"

"A new dorsal fin," Alexander interjected, with a smile. Without letting Rudy toss out a compliment, Alexander continued. "What have you found?"

"My research suggests we've got two decisions, assuming we can restrain Makai long enough to cut off the top of his existing fin and replace it with a new one. I'm hoping we've gained his confidence enough that we can do that with minimal stress. The fin is living tissue, but is relatively immobile. I hope that cauterizing the stump will keep the lower part healthy. If I have this right, the new fin shouldn't need maintenance."

Alexander stood up and faced the window overlooking the lake, his back to Rudy.

"And the two decisions are..."

Rudy joined Alexander at the window. "First, choosing the material that will make up the new top and, second, figuring out how to attach the new top to the existing, amputated dorsal. One of the most commonly used prosthetic materials, for humans, and also for that bottlenose dolphin in Florida, is a silicone plastic. It's relatively inert, completely waterproof, and can be soft and pliable, or rigid, but slightly pliable."

Rudy was now pacing back and forth behind Alexander, his voice excited.

"I contacted a top plastic surgeon at the San Francisco VA hospital and a lady veterinarian who specializes in prosthetics for pets. They both agree that silicone is the way to go, but neither one knows how to fabricate a fin like that."

Rudy paused. Alexander turned around and looked at him, waiting for Rudy to continue.

"I've located a Seattle company that's developing industrial-size, state-of-the-art, 3D printers. They're excited about producing something so big and complex. A medical research program in New Zealand has developed a pliable polymer that can be combined with silicone. They're willing to collaborate."

"I've heard a little about those printers," Alexander said, "but I thought they could only produce small stuff—fingers and toes and toy dinosaurs."

Rudy grinned. "The technology is improving at warp speed. I've already contacted the company—they were more than happy to keep it confidential. Apparently, the 3D printer field is cutthroat. Their main hesitation is that the final product will monopolize their machine for a week, at considerable cost."

Rudy stopped and hesitated, making sure he had Alexander's attention. "They were doubtful we'd spring for an expense that big."

"And you told them what?"

"I told them my partner had very deep pockets and a big heart."

Alexander beamed. "Good. And what about attaching the fin?"

"I've got some biomechanics researchers at the University of Washington's Friday Harbor Marine Labs interested in handling that. I asked them about natural adhesives, and they said the strongest, most waterproof, natural bonding agent they could think of was barnacle cement."

"Say what?"

"Really. Barnacle cement. The stuff that barnacles use to glue themselves to rocks and turtles and whales. It's incredible stuff with a long history of study. Even Charles Darwin wrote about it, in his famous tome about barnacles, before he published *The Origin of Species and the Descent of Man.*"

"Hmm. Haven't read that one," Alexander said.

"Anyway," Rudy continued, "barnacle cement will stick to any surface, under any condition. Needless to say, it's waterproof. It activates quickly, so there's virtually no drying time. And it appears to be non-reactive with living tissue, so there's little chance of irritation and rejection where the new fin meets the cauterized surgical wound.

"But, just as important for our purposes, it has a bonding strength hundreds of times stronger than any human-made adhesive. A male orca can swim thirty miles per hour, creating significant drag forces across his fin, especially when making turns. Also, a male orca leaping clear of the water and landing on his side means six tons of animal impacting our fin. Think how embarrassed we, and Makai, would be if the top of his fin fell off during such a display."

"I guess that wouldn't impress the lady folk," Alexander offered.

"Exactly. The biomechanics people have been experimenting with synthetic barnacle cement to see if they can get something that works like the real thing. They're funded by the Defense Department, which might cause some problems."

"No, it won't," said Alexander. "I can make some phone calls. You'd be astonished how important quality toilet paper is to our fighting forces. Especially at a hundred fifty dollars a roll."

Rudy was tempted to comment on military extravagances but thought better.

"Barnacle cement, they've nicknamed it Barnie Goo, like most biological adhesives, is protein based. It turns out to be a phosphoprotein complex of proteins, carbohydrates, lipids, and—"

"Hold it," Alexander said. He turned back to Rudy and sat down. Rudy could hear the dog under the desk reposition itself.

"I love the details, Rudy, but I'm not a chemist. Your Friday Harbor folks think they can make enough of this stuff to glue the top and bottom of Makai's fin together so it stays, right?"

"Right. Or at least they're willing to try. I have to supply them with some test material, probably bottlenose dolphin flippers that I can get on loan from the collection at the University of Washington. My 3D printer people will give them samples of what their machine will produce. If the initial experiments of bonding one to the other work, they'll make us enough glue to do the job. The VA guy and the veterinarian are both okay with the glue approach. Things are falling into line, if you're okay with all this."

Alexander grew serious. "All I want is a healthy, happy, socially well-adjusted, free-swimming whale as soon as possible. And anonymity. That will be in all the contracts, stated in indecipherable legalese, of course."

"Great, J. B. Same here," Rudy said. "Which brings us, finally, I hope, to the question of when we operate and when and how we move Makai to Penn Cove."

"And your thinking is?"

"His behavior has changed dramatically since we started broadcasting J Pod vocalizations. I could be fooling myself, but I think he knows what we're doing, that we're putting things together. I think we just had to overcome his initial concerns about being a captive in yet another human-controlled environment. Everything we've done to and for him has been non-intrusive and non-invasive, which has to be opposite of all his previous experiences. So, he knows that we have a reason for what we're doing, and the J Pod recordings may have been the final clue he needed to figure it out. I think we can count on his cooperation. At least I hope so, because that's going to make things a whole lot easier."

"I take it you think we should operate soon," Alexander said.

"Almost. I want him to be willing to swim into a sling at the dock's edge and remain still while we lift him just enough to have the top half of his dorsal out of the water. If we do that a couple of times without complication, we can amputate and glue. Hopefully, all we'll need is a local anesthetic injected in the right places in his dorsal fin."

"How soon after the surgery might we be able to release him?" Alexander asked.

"I guess we'll make sure the healing process is complete, without infection. Then it's just a matter of making sure J Pod is in the area. And then being patient. So, we're talking maybe in a month, like sometime mid-June, if the whales show up when they usually do. And that will give me time to line up the people in Coupeville. Meanwhile, I'll put a rush on the folks at the 3D printing company and the Friday Harbor lab Barnie Goo group. Actually, I've already put a rush on them."

"Getting a little fast and loose with my money, aren't you, Rudy?"

"I've just been adhering to your mantra that money can move mountains. And, frankly, I'm afraid we've got the Cascades to push aside before we can pull this off."

"Have faith, Rudy. It *can* move mountains. Matthew 17:20."

I knew I shouldn't have brought up Darwin.

CHAPTER 14

"Yes, Mrs. Cartright?"

"A Dr. Rudolph Laguna is here to meet with you, sir."

Commander Hutto glanced at his watch. It was 1059; Laguna was scheduled for 1100.

"No need to keep him waiting, Mrs. Cartright. Please send him in."

Rudy walked into an inner office where a trim, middle-aged man in a khaki uniform, sporting a buzz cut hairdo, greeted him. Family portrait on the desk. A large American flag stood against a wall adorned with photos of the same man shaking hands with a variety of uniformed and civilian-dressed dignitaries.

"Dr. Laguna, a pleasure to meet you. I'm Eric Hutto."

"It's mutual, Commander Hutto. I appreciate you taking the time."

"Not at all, Dr. Laguna. When J. B. Alexander calls and says he has a proposition that I'll find beneficial, I'm all ears. He told me just enough to get me intrigued. Something about transporting a killer whale from his spread in Utah to a location nearby in Coupeville."

"I understand you and your Coupeville neighbors don't always get along," Rudy said. "I think what we're proposing might help."

"To say the least," Hutto said. "The civilian population here is often unhappy with our training missions. The sounds of our jets, what they call 'jet noise,' affects the growth of their flowers, or maybe their pot plants. They just can't accept it as the sound of freedom."

Rudy restrained himself. Any personal misgivings he had about the astronomic waste that the military represented, and the impact their pointless training activities had on whales, would have to remain personal.

"Well, I think J. B. and I have a proposal that might improve your image," Rudy offered.

Rudy detailed the plans to transfer Makai via military air transport from Hill Air Force Base outside Ogden to Whidbey Naval Air Station, followed by trucking the whale to nearby Penn Cove.

"Easily justified as a training exercise," Hutto said, "done jointly with the Air Force in Utah, who is happy to cooperate. As are we. The army may move on its stomach, but it can't go far without toilet paper."

"That's good to hear, sir. If our plans work out, I see beneficial public relations value in this. We will make sure the local presses—Coupeville, the San Juan Islands—receive carefully worded press releases that will first be vetted by your office. We're thinking of a headline like, 'Whidbey NAS Instrumental in Orca Reintroduction.'"

Hutto held up his hand. "That sounds very good, Dr. Laguna. One small change. We are officially NAS Whidbey."

"My apologies, sir. Of course," Rudy said. "Importantly, everything is contingent on things remaining confidential until the whale is established in the local orca community. The entire operation has to be done in secrecy, which we know is a tall order. But we think that's what you would call a mission-critical component."

Hutto had been standing until now. He walked to his chair, sat down, and leaned back, a smile on his face.

"Dr. Laguna," he said. "If there's one thing we're good at, besides flying airplanes, it's keeping secrets. Clarity of mission, unity of command. Anyone who violates my hush order can expect reassignment to Kansas. Our flyboys really like it here. Great fishing and hunting and biking. Unlike Kansas."

"Good to hear, sir. Thank you for your time. J.B. and I will be in touch. Should we contact you directly or work through a more junior officer?"

"Not for a minute, Dr. Laguna. A diversion from routine every now and then is welcome. Call me as needed. Mrs. Cartright will give you my direct phone number. Good luck."

"Thank you, sir."

And, with that, Rudy left Hutto's office, amazed once more at Alexander's ability to get things done. Check one more box.

On his next visit to Utah, Rudy recounted his activities to Alexander.

"Commander Hutto was more than happy to offer his services, including something called a C-130J Super Hercules, available on short notice. Hutto said a surprise request added value to a training exercise."

"No surprise there. How about the people in Coupeville?" Alexander asked.

"Enthusiastically committed," Rudy answered. "They're already contacting volunteers, who will keep people away from the cove. They'll patrol round-the-clock. We'll put an extra buoy line across the outer portion of the cove, a hundred yards outside the netting where Makai will live. The Coupeville folks see ample public relations benefits in their participation. I only hope their enthusiasm lasts if things drag out."

"Good," Alexander said. "So, looking ahead, we're hoping Makai will stay put until members of J Pod find him. Some pretty big what-ifs, don't you think?"

"Agreed. The netting is a minor barrier. In fact, I fully intend to make his 'escape' as easy as possible. I'm hoping he, too, will be patient. He hasn't been in the wild since he was very young. If I were in his situation, I wouldn't leave an open pen with ample food until I had a place to go and someone to go with. Admittedly, this is all something of a crapshoot."

"That's a little scary, isn't it?" asked Alexander.

"Yes, but I've tried to load the dice. It's critical that we get J Pod to come to him, so I've copied the J Pod vocalizations we've been playing to Makai, and we'll broadcast them outside the cove twenty-four/seven. Makai will know what's happening. Maybe he'll figure out we're trying to lure whales to the area, very specific whales. Then they discover Makai. That gives our whale additional motivation to remain where he is. Granted, it's a long shot, highly dependent on Makai being as smart as I think he is. But, so far, Makai has acted like he had been let in on the planning."

"I concur, although that's a best-case scenario. Aside from total failure, what's the worst case?"

Rudy hesitated. "Well, it could all blow up if some rival orca group, maybe some transients, came along and destroyed our setup. But that is clearly beyond our control."

Alexander picked up on the first ring. "Hi Rudy. I take it you got my email."

"Yes, and it was pretty vague: 'Makai accustomed to sling hoist. Details follow when we talk.' That's not very informative."

"Sorry," Alexander said. "Things were happening fast, and I figured you needed an update. We kept the tapered sling that we used to bring him here. It was designed to make entry easy, wide at the tail end and narrow at the head. We were concerned he had bad memories and would avoid it. We couldn't have been more wrong. I'm beginning to agree with you that Makai knows what we're up to."

"It's like he's signed an informed consent agreement and is waiting for us. Maybe we ought to just ask *him* what we should be doing," Rudy offered.

"That would certainly simplify things, wouldn't it? Anyway, we put the sling in the water, just off the dock, to see how he would react. We decided we might be able to entice him with food. We hung a big Chinook just inside the head end. Makai swam up and sucked in the fish while he was still outside. Oops. But then he swam around and into the sling and waited. After a while I guess he got bored and left. But he's been swimming around it now all week. He's obviously waiting."

"Well, I'll be damned," Rudy said.

"Or words to that effect. So, when do you think we should operate?"

"If Makai is as ready as he appears" Rudy answered, "why put things off?. How soon can we do this?"

"Everyone is ready to move at the drop of a hat, or fin," Alexander said.

"Great," Rudy said. "I just have to make one visit today, sort of a social call, but it may be important. Can your boys pick me up early tomorrow?"

"Be ready at, say 8:07," Alexander replied.

CHAPTER 15

Rudy stood outside the office door, his hand poised to knock. The plaque on the door read "Dr. D. L. White-salmon, Anthropology." Was he opening a can of worms or, worse, Pandora's box? Did Pandora's box contain worms? But Christianson had said she was trustworthy.

Despite all the planning, Rudy sensed something intangible was missing, something outside his personal realm of scientific objectivity. He'd consulted with everyone necessary and everything was falling into place. But he had neglected to confer with any of the dozen Native American tribes in the area, people who had a proprietary interest in orcas. They had no jurisdiction over what he was doing, but he also knew that their influence in anything dealing with ocean resources was strong. Their opposition to his plans could cause problems. Doris Whitesalmon was the only tribal member he knew. Maybe this could be treated as just a courtesy call.

He knocked.

A soft female voice said, "Come in."

Whitesalmon's office had the same gunmetal gray desk, chair, filing cabinets, fluorescent lighting that his did. The walls were pretty bare, except for a beautiful wooden canoe paddle on one wall, the blade intricately carved and painted to depict an orca chasing salmon. The carvings were traditional Pacific Northwest Native American style, with intricate repeated curves, concentric ovals, and pointed triangles. The colors were bold red, black, and white. The other wall had a blanket or mat of some sort, muted brown.

"Yes, Dr. Laguna?" she asked.

"Um, I apologize for bothering you, Dr. Whitesalmon," Rudy said. Why did he feel so uncomfortable, even intimidated? Something about her coolness was unnerving.

"Is there something I can do for you?" she asked.

"Yes. I'm here to get your opinion on a matter of importance to me. I'm not asking for your approval, nor am I expecting you to speak for your tribe, but—"

"Nation," she interrupted.

"Excuse me?" Rudy was taken aback.

"Nation. We are a sovereign, self-governing nation within the United States and prefer to be recognized as such."

How had things gotten off on the wrong foot so quickly?

"My apologies. I obviously have a lot to learn about local politics. As I meant to say, I would like your opinion and don't expect you to speak on behalf of your Nation."

"Understood. You say you want my opinion. About what?"

"I'm working on a rather complicated project that might be of interest or concern to…um…Native Americans in the area." Rudy tried to choose his words as carefully as he could.

"You mean what you're doing with the whale named Makai," Whitesalmon said matter-of-factly.

Oh boy. Here we go again. So much for the total secrecy that was supposed to surround this project.

"Yes," Rudy said, trying to regain his composure. "Can I ask how you know about this?"

"Yes, you may. But first can I ask you a question?" Whitesalmon was looking directly at him.

"Of course," Rudy replied, preparing himself.

"Are your parents alive?"

This was not what he was expecting.

"Uh, yes."

"And where do they live?" Whitesalmon continued.

"They've moved to southern California, outside San Diego." Rudy was grateful the question was simple.

"And your grandparents?" Whitesalmon asked.

"Unfortunately, they've all passed away."

"I'm sorry to hear that. Where are they buried?"

"Excuse me. What did you ask?" Rudy was now totally confused.

"I asked where were your grandparents buried. You know this, of course."

"Well, in truth, I don't. My father's parents emigrated from eastern Europe and never left the east coast of the U.S. My mother's parents stayed in the old country and we lost contact."

"I'm sorry to hear that also. I guess that means you don't know where your great grandparents are buried either."

"I guess that follows."

"I don't mean this as an intrusive exercise, Dr. Laguna. I just need you to understand how Native Americans, and First Nations peoples in Canada, relate to their ancestors. I know the resting places of all my ancestors going back over ten generations. Except for a great uncle who died in a fishing accident off Haida Gwaii in 1879 and was never found. A memorial pole was raised in his honor, shortly before his village was abandoned due to a deadly smallpox epidemic that wiped out ninety percent of our people."

"I'm sorry to hear that," Rudy said, not sure where Haida Gwaii was. "But I'm a little confused as to how this knowledge relates to your knowing about my work with Makai."

"Our 'belief system,' as you might call it, ties us closely to orcas. We refer to them by a name that, loosely translated, means 'our relatives under the water.' In our way of thinking, as has been related to us in our oldest stories, orcas carry the souls of our ancestors. When we die, we become them. Because of this, we feel it necessary to know where all captive orcas are."

"But many of the captive animals are from Iceland, and Russia, and other distant countries," Rudy couldn't help saying. "And many were born in captivity."

Whitesalmon looked at him sympathetically. Rudy felt like a slow pupil trying the patience of an aged instructor.

"First," she said, "our concern with the captive animals arises from our tribal histories, the parallels in the decline of orcas and our people since we were invaded by European colonists and, most importantly, parallels with the condition of the captive whales. We were poisoned by alcohol and, more recently, by opioid drugs brought by Europeans, and the orcas are now poisoned by the industrial products of western society. The orcas' primary and traditional food, and the food that made our cultures flourish, was salmon. We treated every salmon as a revered gift from the Creator. Europeans slaughtered them thoughtlessly by the millions, until the runs could no longer support their greed. What few remain, those that aren't toxic from industrial products, can sustain neither the whales nor our cultures. Western practices have destroyed the salmon, decimating the orcas and threatening the survival of our people."

Rudy was digesting this flood of information. He obviously had not given much consideration to the linkages between what he saw mainly as orca food and the histories of the native peoples of the Pacific Northwest. He waited while Whitesalmon seemed lost in thought. Then she spoke again.

"Like the orcas, we, too, were held captive for decades. Our children were taken from us, placed far away in residential and boarding schools and in so-called foster homes, stripped of their culture and forced to learn a foreign language, forced to assimilate. They had to perform or be denied food, and worse. So it is with the captive orcas.

"As for orcas from different lands," she continued, "while our bodies are constrained by geography, our souls are not. All sixty captive orcas that live in eight different countries remain our concern. This includes twenty-seven that were caught in the wild, like Makai, and thirty-three born in captivity, like Makai's daughter."

Rudy had been thinking to ask what happened to an orca's soul when it died, but thought better. And mention of Makai's daughter caught him by surprise, because he had never read anything referring to the gender of that baby. *Don't get distracted.*

"Is it fair to ask how much you know about my work with Makai?"

"Yes, it is, but you won't find the answer interesting. I won't tell you how I know, but I will tell you I know very little. Just that Makai was purchased from a marine park in Texas by an unknown buyer and flown to a very secretive location in Utah, where he lives in a man-made lake. And that you have made periodic visits to that lake."

Rudy felt somewhat relieved. Alexander's name had not come up. Either Whitesalmon didn't know his identity or was being discrete. Again, he remembered that Christianson said she was trustworthy.

"That much is correct. And, if I can request that what I tell you remains confidential, I will fill in the details."

"You have my word," Whitesalmon said. "Until you give me permission to share information, it will remain between us. As long as someone in my family knows where Makai is, and that he is being treated well, we all are satisfied."

Rudy decided to take a giant leap. He told Whitesalmon the entire story, everything he knew about Makai's history, leaving out only the details of Alexander's name. He then explained the process by which Makai would, hopefully, be united with J Pod and why they had chosen that group and the location of the release.

Whitesalmon said nothing the whole time. She just sat there, listening, with eyes half closed, her fingers steepled on the desk in front of her.

"…And we're hoping that the long time he spent living with the female called Tama at Marineworld will make him acceptable to the J Pod subgroup, especially since he seems to recognize their dialect when we play recordings of their vocalizations."

Rudy stopped, finished with his narrative, and waited for some reaction. He realized he had been standing the entire time.

Whitesalmon remained still for a minute, then another. Finally, without saying anything, she stood and walked to the wall with the piece of brownish cloth. Rudy realized it was a mat made of a tightly woven fiber. It was about three foot by four foot, probably made of cedar bark, a traditional material. Very labor-intensive and expensive, if one of this size could be bought.

Whitesalmon removed the mat from the wall and rolled it into a loose bundle. Rudy was surprised how supple it was, despite being woven basically from wooden strips. From her desk, Whitesalmon produced a brightly colored belt that Rudy recognized as a strip cut from a Hudson's Bay blanket. She tied it around the cedar mat bundle.

Handing the wrapped bundle to Rudy, she spoke quietly. "When you finish the operation on his dorsal fin, bring me the deformed top portion, the part you will cut off, in this cedar mat. I will see that it gets buried properly."

Rudy stood there, holding the bundle, not knowing what, if anything, to say. He hoped this was some sort of tacit blessing of his plans, or at least not complete disapproval. He muttered a thank you and realized he was expected to leave.

CHAPTER 16

S am grew increasingly restless, waiting for something to happen. The sling had been in place for days.
He recognized it from before, but decided to forget
the past. He swam to the dock each morning, whenever
anyone showed up, trying to convince the logriders that he
was ready for whatever they had planned. If they wanted
him in the sling, so be it, although he hated the thought
of being lifted out of the water, feeling the weight of his
body pressing down.

Finally, it was obvious that something was going to
happen. Only four logriders appeared at the dock, the elder
and Uncle Morris and two others. Those last two had only
appeared recently, but everyone asked them questions. All
four came down to the structure just above the water's
surface. Sam swam into the sling. And waited.

Tasks were assigned according to expertise. The veterinarian would perform the actual cutting, the plastic surgeon would apply the synthetic barnacle glue—a whole
quart of the stuff, produced at phenomenal cost. He would
also direct lifting the amputated fin top and lowering the
replacement silicone prosthetic. Rudy's responsibility was
to stay near Makai's head and talk to the animal. Everyone
agreed that the whale was most comfortable when Rudy

was nearby. Alexander gave hand signals to Joseph and Randall, who operated two small cherry picker cranes from up on the dock.

Sam felt the sling lift him slightly, partly in the water and partly out, with little weight bearing down on him. Only the top of his head and his back fin were above the surface. He felt some pricks along his back fin. Finally, things were happening. He took a deep breath and exhaled and tried to let his mind wander. Over the years, he'd had plenty of practice at forgetting where he was.

He heard a faint, high-pitched noise from behind but felt no pain, just a momentary reduction in the weight bearing down on him as he settled slightly higher in the water. He recognized a curved piece of orca back fin rising up and away, at the same time a straighter section of back fin was lowered down. All of this was mysterious, but he was determined to cooperate regardless. And then he settled back down in the water to just about the same depth as before.

The anesthetic injections, cutting, rapid cauterization to reduce blood flow, application of the barnacle cement, and placement of the new fin took less than five minutes. All had been practiced repeatedly. Everyone held their breath. Then they stood back and waited.

Rudy whispered to Alexander, "This is the critical point. He has to remain still for another five minutes while the Barnie Goo hardens."

If they don't want me to move, that's okay with me, Sam thought. *They've obviously been working up to something. I suspect they'll let me know when they're done. Nothing to do but wait.*

Alexander concentrated on his watch. He nodded to Joseph, who carefully lowered the sling until Makai was fully under water. As it opened up, Makai swam forward, out of the sling. He moved off, first carefully, then a little faster. He seemed a little unsteady, as if he were working to keep his balance. Then he accelerated and leapt high in the air, landing with a tremendous splash. Everyone on shore held their breath, again. When he resurfaced, the fin was intact. It was impossible to tell if Makai was aware of the change, but there was little doubt he was enjoying the speed, porpoising to the other end of the lake.

High fives were exchanged all around. Mission accomplished. Now to wait for Makai to adapt to his new, improved swimming style. After that came the next, equally critical, stage…the actual transfer to Penn Cove. All parties involved, from the military in Utah to the citizenry in Coupeville, were advised of the imminent date. But first, Rudy had to wrap Makai's deformed fin top in the cedar mat and deliver it to Dr. Whitesalmon.

PART THREE

CHAPTER 17

S o I said, "What are the attributes of an ideal quarry?"
And the answer was, of course, "It must have cour-
age, cunning, and, above all, it must be able to reason."
"But no animal can reason," objected Rainsford.
"My dear fellow," said the general, "there is one that can."
"But you can't mean..." gasped Rainsford.
Richard Connell, *The Most Dangerous Game*

"Grandma. Can we *please* go look for fish," Eddie pleaded.
"It's like silly for us to just follow everybody when we could
form our own scouting party. And like we could cover a
lot more territory that way, you know."

Grandma generally didn't encourage teenagers like
Eddie and Mitchie to go off on their own. These two, whom
everyone referred to as the twins, were rambunctious
beyond measure. But they were also a distraction, rushing
to the front of the family whenever anyone reported school-
ing salmon. Their actions were as likely to scare fish off as
find them, something they couldn't afford given how rare
salmon had been so far this summer.

"Oh alright. But first, I want you back before sunset.
Second, I want you to work the area north and east of us,
while we move west. Needless to say, do not go where you
are not supposed to. Third, do not eat anything. You could

scare fish off. Report back as soon as you think you have found something worthwhile. Then you can take one of your uncles to confirm and talk strategy."

The twins rankled at this final requirement. So what if they had spooked a large school of Chinook last week. It was an honest mistake, and the fish weren't that big anyway. And the time when they got everybody to chase a school of chum salmon, not Chinook. Again, an honest mistake.

"Agreed," said Mitchie, who tended to be more conciliatory, or at least tactful when dealing with the elders. "We promise."

The twins headed east until they neared the shore of Whidbey Island. Eddie turned south.

"Hey," said Mitchie. "Didn't we tell Grandma we'd go north?"

"Yeh, but like she didn't tell us not to go south, you know. We can come back here and go north later in case she asks. We almost never search like past the Double Mouth River."

"We don't go beyond that river for good reasons other than no fish. It's absolutely forbidden, and you know why."

"Oh, come on. That happened, like, decades ago. Only a couple of the elders claim to have been around. But they were, like, so little they hardly remember. I bet it's one of their silly legends about spirits of the dead, like there isn't any real danger, you know. Logriders haven't been trying to catch us since then."

"I don't know," Mitchie said. "We could get in an awful lot of trouble if anyone found out. Uncle Frank, in particular. He's such a hard-ass about observing rules."

"Come on," Eddie replied. "Like how's anybody gonna know? I think you're just scared. Uncle Frank has you spooked. Admit it, chicken."

"I'm no more scared than you are," Mitchie replied. And he took off south, fast.

The twins raced south, breathing heavily and seldom scanning for fish. An hour later they hesitated, both unsure of their surroundings. And caught their breath.

"I've sure never been here before," Eddie said. "Do you know where that horror story was supposed to have happened? Like how far south from here?"

"Why would you want to go there?" Mitchie asked nervously.

Eddie didn't answer, just continued south, but slower. Mitchie followed, and they picked their way along the coast for another hour, chattering to overcome an inescapable feeling of trepidation.

That's when they first heard J Pod whales conversing in the distance. They couldn't make out who was talking or what they were saying, but it stopped them cold.

Eddie turned to Mitchie. "I thought I heard my mother talking, up ahead of us. Like we shouldn't be able to hear them, right?"

"I wouldn't think so. They're too far away and, like, Long Island should block their voices. But I also heard someone talking."

"Do you think they followed us, like, because they didn't trust us?" asked Eddie.

"I guess so," Mitchie answered. "But that seems like a waste of their time. And how would they know where we were headed? Because that's where the voices are coming from."

Moving farther and even slower, the voices grew louder.

"Wow, that's weird," Eddie said. "Like, I just heard Grandma say something about getting ready for a clan gathering, but it's been canceled. And Uncle Frank was complaining about yesterday's hunting, but yesterday we caught a *bunch* of fish. And, like, their voices don't sound real, kind of high-pitched. This is really freaky."

"Well," Mitchie said after a moment. "If we can hear them, they can hear us. So we probably ought to stop trying to hide."

The twins swam toward the cove and discovered the underwater speaker that was playing the J Pod voices. They swam around it several times, inspecting it carefully.

Finally, Eddie said, "This has to be some sort of logrider's trick, maybe to lure us here where everybody was captured. I think we should get out of here, now."

"For real," Mitchie replied. "Everything about this—"

"Hello," shouted a deep, booming, much louder voice.

"Who's there?" Mitchie said, to himself and Eddie. "Did you hear someone?"

"Yes, I mean I think so. It came from a different direction, not from this logrider's thing. I'm confused, and scared."

"Hello, my friends. How fat are the salmon?" the deep voice repeated, this time giving the traditional greeting of the Southern Resident orcas, but with an accent the twins did not recognize.

"Maybe we should get out of here," Mitchie said. "Maybe this place *is* haunted."

Eddie's resolve was also weakening. He said, half-heartedly, "It's a legend, Mitch. Ghosts aren't real. It's just stuff the elders try to scare us with, like to make us behave. I think."

"Brothers," the voice said. "I can hear you, but you seem far off. Please come closer so we can at least talk. Isn't that what Grandma taught you?"

Invoking Grandma's name gave the twins pause. It would be rude to ignore the invitation, something that would surely get back to the family if this *was* a relative calling them, one they just hadn't met before.

Moving cautiously, they approached the cove, encountering the logriders' floating kelp lines strung across the mouth. Scanning ahead, they could sense a wall of webbing. And, beyond the webbing, an orca. An orca larger than they had ever seen before, someone who must be an elder. Their duty to honor tradition, and the need to be respectful, overcame their fear...mostly.

Mitchie stammered, "How fat are the salmon?"

The orca replied, again in an accented voice, "The fat runs through their blood."

"Who are you?" Eddie almost shouted. Then he remembered his manners. This elder had given the proper response, one only family would use.

"I am Eddie, and this is my cousin Mitchie. We are the grandchildren of Grandma and her sister Molly. Why are you here, behind the logrider's mesh? Have they captured you too, and in this...place?"

"Hello, boys. I'm very happy to meet you. My name is Sam, and we have not met before. I have heard so much about Grandma and her sisters. And I know the stories about this place all too well, the horrors that happened here. I understand your reluctance, but I promise you there's no reason to be afraid. I have thought long and hard about the chance of meeting my kin. I ask a favor of you. Please go to Grandma and tell her you have found me. Tell her my name is Sam, and I have news about her daughter, my late wife, Nan. That should assure her of my place in the family."

Both boys had heard of Nan, a great aunt who had been taken by the logriders during the tragedy, and who was never heard from again. But this stranger's request created a dilemma. To repeat his words to Grandma would mean revealing that they had not only disobeyed her specific instructions, but had also traveled to a place that was absolutely forbidden to any family member. But to not carry this amazing news, including information about a lost relative, one of Grandma's daughters no less, would be an unforgiveable violation of everything they had been taught.

Mitchie finally answered, deciding that acting respectful might soften any punishment they would receive.

"Sam, we are honored to meet you, and we will tell Grandma what you've said. We don't know what her answer will be, and it might take some time, because our family is many miles away. We had better leave now and bring your news to her."

"Thank you," Sam said. "I've waited a long time for this to happen and can wait a little longer. I have faith Grandma will know what to do."

The twins retraced their way back. Neither said much until they heard the family in the distance. It was well past sunset, adding to their unease. They stopped.

"What are we going to tell her?" Eddie asked.

"What do you mean 'we?' It was your idea to go there. I was just stupid enough to follow you."

"And you're the one who, like, told that elder we would talk with Grandma. So, don't back out now. We better come up with something fast," Eddie said.

"I guess we could just tell her what really happened," Mitchie suggested.

"Right, genius," Eddie said sarcastically. "Let's see. Like, we never went north, we went to a place that we've been told to stay away from since we were old enough to eat fish, and we're back way later than we promised. So now we're going to try to cover our asses with a story about a giant elder trapped in that place, someone who speaks our language with a funny accent and, like, knows something about Grandma's missing daughter. You're nuts."

"At least it's the truth," Mitchie offered. "She always seems to know when we make stuff up."

Without coming to any agreement, the twins reluctantly joined the trailing edge of the slowly moving group, trying to go unnoticed. That didn't work.

"Mitchell! Where have you been? I've been worried sick. Grandma said you promised to be back hours ago. We were about to send out searchers."

It was Molly, Mitchie's mom. The exasperation in her voice was pretty evident.

"Sorry, Ma. Really. Stuff happened. We're okay. But we have to talk to Grandma first."

"I'll say you do, and then we're going to have a little chat. And it won't be any nicer than what Grandma is going to say to you."

Eddie and Mitchie scanned the group and saw Grandma at the other end. They slowly made their way past a number of clearly angry family members. As they passed Uncle Frank, he gave Eddie a thump with his tail.

"Ouch!" Eddie shouted.

Frank acted as if nothing had happened.

"Grandma," Mitchie started. "I know we're in trouble, and you have every reason to be mad, but, like, there's something we have to tell you first. And we think we should keep this between the three of us."

Grandma was clearly displeased.

"I do not want to hear another one of your wild tales. You are both lousy liars and you are in enough trouble right now without compounding it with some lame excuse."

Eddie turned to Mitchie. "See, like, I told you she wouldn't believe us."

"What is it I will not believe?" Grandma asked. "Let us hear it and decide."

"Okay, here goes," Mitchie said. "I know this sounds pretty weird, but it's the truth. We didn't go north like you told us. We went through Raging Pass, beyond the Double Mouth River, south along the Long Island shoreline."

Details weren't necessary. Grandma immediately knew where they had gone.

"You did what?" The anger in her voice was clear. "We never go in those waters. Have you paid no attention to what we have taught you? What excuse can you possibly have?"

"We're not making any excuses. It's what we found there that we think will make things okay. We hope."

"I do not care if you found a hundred-pound salmon. That region is, and has been for decades, absolutely forbidden."

"We didn't find salmon," Eddie joined in. "What we found is a relative, like, someone we've never met before, and he knows what happened to Aunt Nan."

Grandma was dumbstruck. She forgot all her anger. She scanned around quickly to see if anybody else could hear them.

"What did you just say?" she asked.

"Yes, Grandma," Mitchie continued. "We found an elder, I mean, he is huge. He's even bigger than Uncle Frank. And he's in a deep bay just past Double Mouth River."

Grandma couldn't hide her shock.

"That is the Cove of Sorrows, where Nan was taken by the logriders, and where five others were captured and Sandy and Ben died. If you are making this up, you are in much more trouble than you can imagine. This is just plain cruel."

"No, Grandma, we're not making it up," Eddie said. "But he's, like, behind a logrider's web. He called to us, greeted us like a family member, but he had a strange accent. Like we could understand him, but it was hard. He talked kind of stiff-like, like he was trying to remember words. And he has a really weird back fin, like the top half is made of wood. Hey, Mitch, did you notice that?"

"Wow. Now that you mention it, there was something weird about his back fin."

"Please," Grandma entreated. "What did he say about Nan?"

"Right, sorry," Eddie replied. "He said his name was Sam and, like, we should tell you that he knew about your daughter, Nan."

"Wasn't there something about Nan being his wife, that she was late for something?" Mitchie added.

"I think he called Nan his 'late wife,' whatever that means," Eddie said. "And he said you would know what to do if we told you."

Grandma wasn't surprised to hear that Nan was dead; she had sensed it for years, but the realization hit hard. She would allow herself time to mourn, after she told the others. Right now, she realized she had to deal with this turn of events. It could be very important for the family, far beyond her own sorrow. She took a deep, calming breath.

"Your story is too fantastic to be made up. You have told me things that you could not know. We have never talked about your great uncle Sam. He died years ago. His heart was broken by the tragedy in the Cove of Sorrows, especially the loss of his niece Nan. He never recovered from that day. That this relation you have found has inherited his name, and that he claims to have been Nan's mate, and this has all happened in the Cove of Sorrows, is barely believable, but too complicated for you two to have come up with on your own. I need to think. I want you two to stay where I can find you. We will talk again in the morning. Is that understood?"

"Yes, ma'am," they replied in unison. And slipped away before she could say anything else.

CHAPTER 18

Are we human enough to extend the rights of humanity to another sentient species?

ALEXANDRA MORTON, *Listening to Whales: What the Orcas Have Taught Us*

Grandma spent a sleepless night. Memories, many very painful, flooded her thoughts. An elder named Sam existed, but she had never heard of him. That was so unlikely. He obviously had knowledge of her lost daughter. How? Now he, too, was a captive of the logriders and in that horrible place. But the logriders hadn't tried to capture anyone for years, not since that terrible day, as if they realized how unforgiveable their behavior had been. The twins didn't seem to think he was troubled by his situation, which was also strange. And this stranger seemed to think she would know what to do. So much hinged on how she handled this situation, but her information was incomplete. She had no choice. She must meet this stranger and find out what he wanted, or expected, her to do.

In the morning, Grandma confided in the aunts. She told them everything she knew and what she had decided. Although not necessarily asking for their approval, she wanted to make sure no one objected.

All were concerned, some were clearly afraid, but they

all agreed it was a situation that could only be ignored at the cost of family well-being.

Locating the thoroughly chastened twins, she addressed them formally.

"Edwin, Mitchell, you are not forgiven for your misbehavior. But I must put that aside for now because of whom you have discovered. I want you to accompany me to that horrible place so I can meet this stranger and decide what we should do about him."

It wasn't clear that the twins heard all of her lecture, except the part about taking Grandma to meet the stranger. Mitchie suppressed the urge to leap; Eddie was less successful. Then he apologized.

"When do you want to go?" Mitchie asked.

"As soon as the family decides where they will hunt, the three of us will leave. I have informed my sisters that we could be gone overnight, as this is a long journey, and I am not as young as I used to be. We will go at my pace, and you will stay near me at all times. If we encounter salmon, feel free to eat. But remember that we are traveling as straight a path as possible. To that terrible place."

Sam also spent a sleepless night. An entire moon cycle had passed since the move from the big pond to this new place, a move that had been much less traumatic than all the other moves he had endured. Again, it seemed his logriders were doing everything they could to minimize his discomfort. But still, why here, the place that Nan had so vividly described, the place where she had been captured?

Despite the association, he liked his new surroundings. It was the first time since childhood he had actually been in the ocean. The sounds, sights, and textures were wonderful. Many sounds were new and required mental cataloging. Clearly some were things logriders might produce. But, on the other hand, many had to be from fish or crabs or…who knew?

Even whales. Occasionally, far off in the distance, he heard faint conversations and foraging bursts. Again, his distant memories from childhood did not serve him well. He had been so young when he was taken that he hadn't really paid attention to what different sounds signified. Nan had taught him much and would speak to him constantly about her family and how they chatted among themselves, sometimes imitating the voices of family members. He loved to just listen to her talk.

Memories had rushed back when his logriders somehow provided the voices of Nan's family, back in the lake. At first, he was annoyed and thought of attacking the object producing the sounds, but it was so good to just hear the voices of Nan's family. He strained to hear *her* voice, but it was not, and could not, be there. He had watched her die and be taken away. He didn't think anyone came back from the dead, although how could he know one way or the other?

He heard the same conversations in this new ocean place. He could just make out the round sphere at the head of the cove, the same sphere that had carried the words and conversations of Nan's family at the lake. No reason to get excited; it was again the workings of his logriders. But why?

And then the unbelievable happened. Yesterday. He heard two young whales talking nervously. Their voices became louder and clearer. There was no mistaking. He wanted badly to call to them for fear they would just pass by. But their hesitation was obvious, and he didn't want to frighten them away. Finally, he couldn't stand it anymore and tried to sound as friendly as possible.

They were as surprised to find him as he was to find them. The conversation had, at first, been awkward. He could sense their unease. Giving them the traditional greeting had helped somewhat, but they still kept their distance. And he could feel their sonar pulses moving across his body, assessing him, stopping at his back, then turning away in apparent embarrassment. And returning. It must have something to do with his new back fin. No surprise. He, too, found it a mystery.

Asking about Nan, and especially Grandma, seemed to turn the tide. These teenagers—were their names Eddie and Mitchie?—hadn't known Nan, but there was no question that the mere mention of Grandma had a sobering effect on even them. Sam was relieved to know that she, at least, was still alive. It was also clear that they had come to a place where they shouldn't be. No wonder they were apprehensive.

That's when he realized that the only course was to request that they bring Grandma to him. Placing things in her hands relieved them of responsibility. Would they admit they had wandered into forbidden waters? He guessed that punishment would be delayed, that Grandma, in her wisdom, would minimize any consequences until the mystery of a new whale was solved. He hoped they made up a believable story.

And now he could hear three of them approaching. Faster this time. And then they were silent.

Grandma stopped as the three neared the outer float line at the mouth of the Cove of Sorrows. The twins briefly surged ahead, but quickly returned to where she was floating, motionless and silent.

"Are you okay, Grandma?" Mitchie asked.

She didn't answer immediately. When she spoke, it was almost in a whisper. "I swore I would never return to this place, that none of us would ever come here again. So much horror happened here, memories that haunt me daily. Perhaps it has taken this much time to rethink the past, maybe I have become too set in my ways. As hard as it is for me to admit, you two did right to break the rules. There are no ghosts here, only memories. Yes, I am fine. We should go."

"Hello," they heard Sam say in his deep voice. "How fat are the salmon?"

"The fat runs through their blood," Grandma replied, and she slipped under the buoyed line and up to the net, where Sam waited on the other side. His voice was incredibly low, fitting his extraordinary size, as the twins had related.

"The twins tell me your name is Sam. I am Lena, but everyone calls me Grandma. Please tell me how you came to be called by that name."

She was anxious to ask him directly about Nan, but thought that letting him bring the topic up would be more appropriate.

"Grandma, it is truly an honor to meet you."

Grandma noted that this whale spoke clearly but in a clipped, accented manner, an accent she had never heard before. So many mysteries.

"Nan spoke of you so often," Sam continued, "and in such loving, respectful terms. I feel like I have known you for years, without having actually met."

"Please tell me about my daughter, Nan," Grandma finally said, almost reluctant to know the truth. "The twins say you referred to her as your mate, your late wife. I will assume that my greatest fears are realized and that she is…dead."

"I am so sorry to be the one to tell you this, Grandma. Your grief must be great, but I assure you mine is equally so, for different reasons. We were both captives of what she taught me you called the logriders. Although short, our time together was, by far, the happiest of my life, and I live to this day with her memory. And with hatred for what the logriders did to her."

"Thank you, Sam," Grandma replied. "I sense your pain and share it. But it is better knowing than not. I am anxious to hear as much about my lost daughter as you are willing to share. But perhaps now is not the time. It would be too rushed. We will do that later. First, I must know how you came to be a captive here, and why you do not just escape? You could easily jump over this webbing the logriders have built. Why not?"

"I had no immediate reason to leave," Sam said. "I have spent my life trapped by the logriders. Sometimes they have treated me harshly and demanded I do things I resented. Sometimes, and most recently, they have treated me well. At the moment, they are providing me with good fish to eat, and this is one of the largest places I have been permitted to live in. And it's in the ocean, where I have not lived since I was very young. It seemed best to stay here until I had to decide otherwise. I resolved to not let them catch me one more time, no matter what. I have now tasted what life in the ocean can feel like, even in this small space. I will not go back to one of their unnatural places. I will stop breathing first."

This mention of suicide shocked Grandma, but she tried to hide her reaction. She knew it was something one could do to end suffering, but only once in her long life had she known a family member to take his own life. And that had been this whale's namesake, Sam.

Grandma's thoughts were interrupted by the images of several large Chinook salmon swimming on Sam's side of the webbing, in a tight and hurried school. She remembered that she had not eaten since yesterday, her mind so preoccupied with recent events.

"Do I sense salmon around you?" she asked.

"Yes, Grandma. As I said, the logriders bring them here almost daily. I have more than my fill to eat."

"Would it be a great bother for you to catch one for me?" Grandma asked.

"I'd be honored."

And Sam took off with a flick of his tail. It was then that Grandma got a good look at how large Sam was, and at his back fin, how strange it seemed. It was as the twins had described, the bottom half normal, but the top half made of something very unnatural, not muscle or tendon or bone, but something clearly a product of the logriders' craft. She hoped Sam had not sensed her intrusive scan.

The next moment, Grandma sensed a loud shout. Shortly after, Sam returned to the other side of the net with a large Chinook in his mouth. He tossed it over the netting to Grandma.

"That is a very impressive trick. I have never had anybody throw me a fish before. Usually, it is just brought to me and released for me to pick up."

"Oh, I'm truly sorry, Grandma. I meant no disrespect. It's something Nan and I would do to entertain ourselves. We were never given live fish. Often, we were never given fish at all. We were fed squid."

.Grandma shuddered. *This is something Sam should keep to himself,* she thought.

"And usually only if we agreed to do some of the stupid things the split-tails, excuse me, *logriders* wanted us to do," Sam continued. "Fish tossing was something we came up with on our own, pretending they were live."

"And that shout I heard?" asked Grandma. "It was phenomenally loud, even painful, out here."

"Again, something Nan and I practiced when we weren't being required to perform by the logriders. Nan was never quite able to do it, at least not as loud as I could. She said it was because I am so large. The fish tossing was just for fun and we both did it."

"I have seen transient foreigners toss seals in the air like that, but they use their tails, not their mouths," Grandma said. "Their treatment of seals seems rather barbaric."

"Yes. Transients. Nan spoke of them often. She didn't like them, for many reasons I never fully understood. They eat strange things, don't they?"

If that were all, it wouldn't be so bad, Grandma thought.

"Yes, they hunt and kill seals and sea lions and just about anything they can. They talk little, and we understand little of what they say. I have to admit they do us a favor by eating animals with which we compete for food, but we generally try to avoid them. A subject for another day."

This mention of food attracted the attention of the twins, who had been swimming back and forth at a respectful distance behind Grandma, trying to overhear without being too obvious.

Grandma turned to them and said, "If you boys want to go hunting, feel free. But please stay where you can hear me. I think we will all be leaving soon."

"Sam," she said, "since yesterday, when the twins told me they had found you here, that you knew Nan, and they could understand you and you them, I have had to consider what your presence means. I spoke with my sisters this morning, and we all agreed that, if I felt comfortable, you should be invited to come meet the family. I can make no promises, but it is clear you should not stay here any longer. The logriders cannot be trusted, and I feel responsible for your well-being, as if you were family. That you were Nan's mate eliminates any doubt as to the appropriateness of my decision. Family always comes first."

Sam tried to hide his delight, although he was unsure how he would react to so many strangers. He had lived alone for so long.

"I am most grateful to you, Grandma. I will try to make things as easy as possible. But I ask you to please tell me if I do or say anything wrong. Nan taught me so much about her family and its...*your*...traditions, but many of these memories have faded."

That said, he slid over the floats that held the webbing in place and followed Grandma out of the Cove of Sorrows.

CHAPTER 19

*Just because we don't think of them as humans
doesn't mean they aren't beings.*

ROBIN WALL KIMMERER,

*Braiding Sweetgrass: Indigenous Wisdom,
Scientific Knowledge, and the Teachings of Plants*

G randma told the twins to swim ahead and inform the elders they were coming, but that it would be several hours before they arrived. She and Sam followed at a more reasonable pace.

"I want you to tell me about my daughter, Sam," she began. "But, first, you should know how it was I lost her. We were celebrating our annual communal gathering, when many distant relations, our entire tribe, came together. We had encountered a large school of Chinook salmon near Double Mouth River and feasted on them for three days. Our presence was too conspicuous, maybe seventy or eighty of us altogether." *Seventy-eight. How could she forget.*

"The logriders must have been planning a capture, because they, too, came in large numbers. I should have realized on the third day that something was wrong, that there were too many of them, in their fast buzzing logs, paying too much attention to us, much more than normal for those times. I still hold myself responsible.

"Their attack seemed carefully planned, not unlike how we corral a large school of fish into a place where we can feed on them with ease. They forced us into the cove with their logs and with painfully loud noises. They even had noisy things in the sky that created strong winds, confusing us even more. We could not hear one another. They then started moving between the young ones and their parents, forcing us apart. They pushed us away from our babies with long branches. Then they pulled a mesh between us, much like the one that held you in the cove. They surrounded the youngsters in a circle of mesh from which they could not escape. There was so much noise and panic. Nan and the other children cried out to us, but we could not get to them. They just huddled together and cried for help as the logriders made the circle smaller and smaller."

Grandma's voice was breaking. She paused for a few seconds. Sam waited for her to continue.

"It was obvious they only wanted the youngest. They tied lines around their tails and heads. Nan was older than most, but I guess still young enough for their plans. Two of our family—Sandy and Ben—got caught in the mesh and could not come up to breathe. They drowned right there, in front of us, along with a member of another family. They took six children away, Nan included. There was nothing we could do."

"That sounds absolutely terrible," Sam said quietly.

"The horror and cruelty had not ended," Grandma continued. "We stayed in the cove after they took the children away. We meant to take our dead relatives and treat them with the respect they deserved, move them to the place of repose. But the logriders pulled the bodies onto land, and tied square rocks to their tails and dragged them offshore.

We followed them and swam with the bodies as they sank to the bottom, in water too deep for us. That burial place and this cove are two places we never go. Until now."

Grandma was obviously exhausted, physically and emotionally, from telling her story. Sam waited, then spoke.

"Nan came to me not long after they captured her. It was clear she was traumatized. Although I meant her no harm, she was frightened by me and, needless to say, I couldn't understand her. It took time for her to grow used to living in the tiny pool where we were kept. It took even longer for her to trust me. My large size didn't help, or so she eventually told me."

"Yes," Grandma said. "She was shy around her uncles, except for one."

"Adding to her problems," Sam went on, "The logriders made her work for food. She nearly starved before she was willing to eat what they fed us. But, slowly, as I learned her language, things improved. And that's when she started calling me Sam. She said I reminded her of an uncle whom she loved."

"Yes, her Uncle Sam. He loved her greatly. He was there when she was taken and never really recovered from losing her," Grandma said.

"I'm glad she didn't know about the ones who died and what happened after," Sam said.

"Yes, I am glad she was at least spared that. But tell me about the place where they kept you," Grandma urged. "I know so little about the logriders, apart from the way they follow us wherever we go. I feel it is my duty to understand them better."

"If you insist. The place was all smooth rock, all white, like a small cove or a large pool. It was shallow—I could

almost touch the bottom with my tail during normal surface swimming. I could get from one end to the other in
two easy strides, Nan in three."

Grandma gasped. "No! And this is where you lived, all
the time?"

"There was a side area where we would be pushed if we
did not cooperate. It was much smaller."

"And the two of you lived there alone?" Grandma said.

"Not exactly. We shared it with a pain-in-the-ass longnose
dolphin and two white-stripes. The white-stripes were okay,
maybe a little hyper. But before Nan came, the dolphin would
swim under me and poke me with his penis. I tolerated it for
a while, but I just got sick of it and finally hit him with a full
power shout. He almost leapt out of the pool. His head probably rang for days, and he never bothered me again."

"Good for you. We do not see many longnose, but I have
heard stories, and I am not surprised."

"He never tried anything with Nan. I made it pretty
clear she was to be left alone, even before we could talk
with one another."

"So, Nan taught you our language. What did you speak
before that?"

"I, too, was captured when I was young, younger than
Nan. I really didn't know my own language very well, and
I guess that made it easier to learn from Nan. And I was
motivated. I wanted company, and I wanted to talk and,
after a while, so did Nan."

"Do you remember much of your own language?"
Grandma asked.

"Not really," Sam said. "It's faded over the years."

Sam paused, lost in thought. Grandma waited for him
to continue.

"Life was better after we could talk to one another. We played games, invented tricks without being taught, and even played tricks on the dolphins. Nan was wonderful. She taught me so much, about her family and your ways. I learned the names of all her family members, of the larger clan, and the entire tribe. It made living in that pool bearable, for both of us.

"Things went well for a couple of years. And then she began to behave differently, more insistent, more intimate, less playful. Although we always swam side by side, we seldom touched. But she started rubbing against me. I didn't understand why."

Sam became hesitant, looking for words.

"Remember, I was very young when they took me and knew nothing about adult behavior. Finally, one day, without knowing what I was doing, we, uh…" Sam hesitated, embarrassed.

Grandma chided him, "Sam, I am old and experienced. I have given birth to five children and aided the arrival of many more. I know what mating is all about."

"Yes, of course. Sorry. One thing led to another and we mated. And then, after maybe two or three moon cycles, she asked me to look inside her. Even though I was taken from my family when I was little, I had learned you just didn't do that. It wasn't nice to stare. But she insisted. And I saw. To say I was shocked is an understatement. I asked her, 'Is that what I think it is?' And she said proudly, 'Yes, it is. And it's ours.'"

"Nan was very wise in the ways of the world, even at her age," Grandma said. "When other youngsters were busy doing the things that youngsters normally do, she would spend time with her aunts, asking questions. And she was present at several births, helping. So, she was no stranger to how things happened."

"Which may have helped in the end," Sam said. "Because I was pretty much worthless. Over the next year, she'd ask me to scan and tell her what our baby looked like. The logriders must have known also, especially some of the females, and they made fewer demands on her. Finally, our baby was born. It wasn't easy, and Nan said she needed help from her aunts, but what could I do?"

"Yes," Grandma said. "She knew she was supposed to have help. She had every reason to be frightened. What happened?"

"Our baby had trouble coming out, and then she was very weak, I guess from the birth. At first, she swam around with the, uh…umbilical cord and placenta attached, which made her swimming even more difficult. Until one of the female logriders came and cut it and took it away."

Grandma appeared to suppress a shudder, then tried to explain.

"Sam, you must realize that Nan was still too young to have a child. Although she was capable, if she had been with the family, she would have waited several more years, would have been larger and more knowledgeable. A birth would have been easier. But for her to become pregnant at her age? That just would not have been permitted. But neither of you could have known that. And to do all that, with no help from her sisters and aunts, is almost beyond belief."

Sam said, "No wonder everything was so hard. And then our baby wouldn't nurse and grew weaker, and Nan became very worried.

"Again, the aunts would have helped your baby learn how to nurse," Grandma said.

Sam paused, lost in thought, then continued. "Fortunately, things improved, or at least Nan got her to nurse, and our baby grew stronger. Nan named her Rosie, after one of her younger sisters. Nan said that you weren't supposed to give a baby a name until its first birthday, but that was a family rule and her family wasn't there."

"Nan was correct," Grandma said. "We do wait a year before giving a baby a name. It is an old rule that is seldom broken, for good reasons. And Nan's sister Rose is...*was* five years younger than Nan. She worshipped Nan and missed her greatly."

"The three of us—Nan, Rosie and I—played and played. Nan would sing to her beautifully, in a language I didn't understand. But it calmed Rosie, helped her go to sleep."

"Nan learned those songs when she was very young. They go back many, many generations, and the words are meaningless even to the oldest of us."

Sam paused thoughtfully, as if remembering the songs. Then he said sadly, "We even taught her some things that we did together, things that the logriders liked, or so we thought. And then, when she was only six moon cycles old..."

This time it was Sam who shuddered and whose voice broke. Grandma didn't interrupt.

"We had no reason to suspect anything, although, in the last week or so, strange logriders came and stood on the edge of our pool and watched us. Then, early one day, several logriders moved a mesh between Nan and Rosie. Rosie cried out, and Nan rushed to be with her. But the logriders pushed her away with sharp sticks. They lifted Rosie out of the pool. We both stood out of the water as far as we could to see what they were doing. We could hear her cries. Nan leapt up at our poor baby as they took her away. She shouted Rosie's name and Rosie cried out, 'Mama! Mama!'

"And then she was gone.

"I tried to console Nan. I told her maybe they just wanted to poke her and make sure she's healthy. Nan said there was nothing wrong with her. There was no reason to take her. 'My poor baby!' was all she kept saying.

"Nan kept by the side of the pool where Rosie had been taken. She spent hours lifting her head up, looking around, shouting for her. Her shouts turned into screams, and then wails of grief. She ignored me, told me to go away, said she hated me, that it was my fault, that I should have done something, anything. Nothing I said mattered."

"There is nothing worse than losing a child, no matter how," Grandma said sympathetically.

"I kept my distance, because everything I did or said just seemed to make matters worse. I then realized that having Rosie was what made life as a captive bearable for Nan. I was a companion, but her baby meant so much more.

"The next few weeks were torture. Nan cried and cried. At other times, she threw herself against the side of the pool. She never slept and refused to eat, let alone do the logriders' tricks. She was force-fed, but vomited the food up. Then she stopped swimming and would just hang in the water, and the logriders stopped trying to force-feed her. Maybe they thought she would get over it. She didn't. Losing Rosie took away Nan's reason to live. One night, without as much as a goodbye, she sank slowly to the bottom of our pool and didn't come back up to breathe."

After a minute, Sam continued. "My sadness at losing Rosie was great, but losing Nan was so unnecessary. We were fine, were happy. We did everything they wanted of us and more. They had no reason to take our baby. I considered dying myself because I was so angry. But I didn't. Maybe it was cowardice, but I guess I had been a captive for so much of my life that I had grown accustomed to it, hoping things would go back to the way they were before Nan came. And I tried to think of some way to get even. I stopped doing their stupid tricks and, if one of the logriders got in the water, I would rush and shout, and they would immediately jump out of the water. And then the ultimate insult happened."

"What more could they possibly do to you?" Grandma asked in surprise.

"Logriders don't understand us. They treat us as toys, as simple-minded things that are happy to perform for food. Maybe that works for the longnoses, but I suspect even they don't like their treatment. One day, a new female was lowered into my pool. She was young, younger than Nan had been when she arrived. The stranger was frightened to death and cried out in a language I didn't understand. It didn't take long to figure things out. The logriders must have thought I was just lonely and giving me a new mate would make everything fine. They were going to turn us into baby producers. We would go through this all over again, have a baby that they would then take away. I grew furious. Out of control. In a rage, I…" Sam stopped again, choked up.

Grandma said, "Sam, whatever you did would be justified given what you had been through. Please tell me."

"I'm so ashamed. I didn't know what I was doing until it was over. I rushed at her and slammed into her, again and again, until she stopped breathing. I…I…I…killed her."

Sam hesitated, waiting for Grandma to react. When she didn't, he continued. "After that, everything was different. The logriders pushed me into the small side pool. If they bothered to give me food, they just threw it into the water. Sometimes I ate; more often I didn't. Weeks went by and then they captured me, moved me far away, to a new, worse place. Years have gone by since then, and I have been moved several times, usually to horrible conditions. Perhaps I deserved no better because of what I did, but I don't give the logriders credit for such reasoning. I think they just didn't want me and didn't know what to do with me. Finally, maybe six or seven moon cycles ago, I was taken to a new, better, and larger place, where I have been treated relatively well, until I was brought to what you call the Cove of Sorrows."

Sam was done talking, and he and Grandma continued for a while in unbroken silence. Grandma was shocked at Sam's telling, but tried to not let it show. Were Sam's actions something to be considered in bringing him into the family? Had his years in captivity affected his judgment? She was hoping that Sam's experience living with the logriders might help her understand them better. But at what cost? At least he hadn't broken the strongest taboo of all. Or was there more? She decided to change the subject.

"Sam, it is clear the logriders have done things to you, things that are difficult to forget. And please forgive me if this is too personal, but there's something very different about your back fin. It is very handsome and tall, but the upper part seems to be made of something I have never seen before, like the soft bone of a shark, but not even quite like that. Is this something the logriders did?"

Sam didn't hesitate. "Yes, I know it's somehow different, but I'm not sure how. One day, not long ago, my new captors held me in the capture sling and stuck my back with the sleeping stick, and I felt very little sensation there. When I regained feeling and swam away, I lost my balance and my back fin hurt. At first, I thought I was wobbly from their sleeping stick, but I had the sensation of moving through the water differently, straighter if anything. It took a couple of days for the pain to go away and for me to adjust, but it seems to have worked itself out. I didn't know my fin was tall. It never was before. Nan used to tease me about having a droopy back fin, one that wobbled when I swam. Nan said she wouldn't want to be seen in public with me like that. It was kind of our little private joke."

"She would not be ashamed now, I assure you," Grandma said.

As they continued, Sam began to take more notice of his surroundings. He had been so preoccupied with recalling memories that he had forgotten to pay attention to where he was. He realized the water was deeper and colder than anything he had ever experienced, that they were swimming with a strong current, that new sounds were all around him. Just audible above the background noises around them, he heard a deep, long whistle and squeal. He scanned far ahead and saw something truly large swimming away, something he had never seen or heard before.

"What was that?" he asked Grandma.

"Oh, sorry," she said. "I was not paying much attention. What did you see?"

"Well, first I heard a lovely whistle, rising in pitch. And then I scanned and saw something huge."

"Hmm. Could have been a whale. Can you be more specific?"

"It looked like this," he said and then he turned to Grandma and, without thinking, projected a sound image at her.

Grandma was stunned. She stopped dead in the water. "Sam, what did you just do?" she asked.

"I tried to show you what I saw. Did I do something wrong again?"

"No. No. Absolutely not. Not since Nan's uncle Sam has anyone been able to project sound images of what they saw. Nan was just learning, or trying, to do it. She would spend hours with her uncle, practicing, but I did not think she knew how. It is a special gift that family history says only a few have possessed. We thought the gift died with Nan, if not with Sam. Is this something your family did?"

Sam replied quickly. "I don't think so. Or at least not that I remember, and I had never tried to do it before Nan came to me. But we had so many hours with nothing to do, and the sides of our pool were very smooth and hard, and we could bounce sounds off them and play with the sounds. So, we practiced and tested each other. Nan was much better than I was, but she was very proud of being able to teach me, and also proud that I tried so hard to learn. It lessened her loneliness. She would make sound images of her family members, of you and her uncles, Sam and Morris, and several aunts. She taught me how to identify things, especially creatures I should know about. Like white sharks, which seemed to be the only thing she really was afraid of, for what they could do to a baby."

"That is right. Fortunately, we do not encounter them often, and it would be a foolish white shark to attack one of our youngsters when we are together as a group. But you never know with sharks. They can behave unpredictably. They are more common to the south, where we sometimes travel in winter. It is definitely worth knowing," Grandma added.

Sam continued proudly, "Nan also taught me what Chinook salmon looked like and how they were different from other kinds of salmon. At first, the differences seemed subtle, but, after a while, I could identify all of them. It seemed important to her, even though we seldom got to eat them. Before I was moved to the Cove of Sorrows, when I was in the biggest pool, the logriders there fed me all the different kinds of salmon, and I knew what they were. I ate all of them regardless because, although I know Chinook taste best, any salmon is better than dead squid and herring."

Grandma had recovered from her surprise and decided this was yet another aspect of Sam's potential membership in the family that could be used to advantage; hers, his, and the group's.

"Sam," she said. "Making sound images is truly a wonderful gift, one that should be shared. But, for the time being, we should keep it a secret between the two of us. There will be a right time and place for you to show this special skill. We will know when."

"Okay, Grandma. It doesn't seem like such a big thing, but I'm happy to do whatever you feel best."

"Good. By the way, that was a long-finned whale you showed me. They are not common here, but seem to be growing in numbers. Their songs are wonderful to listen to."

Not much later, Sam heard excited voices off in the distance, voices saying things he recognized. Grandma seemed a little exasperated.

"It looks like the twins have told more than my sisters that I am bringing you. Fishing for the day is clearly over. I think you should just follow me and let me make introductions. We will go to my sisters first. After that, the uncles. Then who knows."

Sam tried to remember his manners. He made very quick scans and thought he recognized a few family members, or at least they resembled the sound images Nan had shown him, but everyone had been much younger. There was no question which one was Rose; she could have been Nan's twin. As Grandma had said, she was truly beautiful. He looked away quickly but knew she had sensed his glance.

Sam greeted everyone formally and respectfully, and each returned the greeting similarly. Except for one of the elder males, who remained apart from the gathering.

"Frank, aren't you going to come over and say hello?" someone named Michael asked.

"There's plenty of time, and lots of names and faces to memorize," Frank replied, although his tone was less gracious than his words.

Frank's reaction reminded Sam that Nan hadn't been particularly fond of "grumpy Uncle Frank." Things apparently hadn't changed, even after all these years. Sam guessed he was picking up where Nan had left off.

Sam also sensed quick, almost furtive, sonic pulses directed his way, especially from youngsters who did a poorer job of hiding their curiosity. He picked up a few exchanges: "He's so huge!" "But look at his back fin. What's wrong with it?" "Do you recognize him at all?" "How can that be? Don't we know everyone in the family?" "I guess not." "Do you think Grandma knows what she's doing, bringing him here?" "I guess we'll find out."

Grandma had moved to one edge of the group and swam up alongside her sister, Molly.

"Well, what do you think?" she asked.

"You've caused quite a stir, Lena. He certainly is big, really big. I wonder if that holds for all his parts."

"Oh, Molly. Be serious for a change. No wonder your son is so irreverent."

"Okay, I'm impressed," Molly said. "He's polite and seems gentle, especially given his size. And his back fin is just huge. Tall and handsome, but weird. Any idea what that's all about?"

Grandma decided it was best to withhold some information while the family adjusted to Sam's presence, and vice versa.

"I guess we will all learn about him in due time," she finally said. But she couldn't help wondering, *what have I set in motion?*

CHAPTER 20

*We are the only animals that tell stories
to understand the world we live in.*

SALMAN RUSHDIE, *Luka and the Fire of Life*

A few weeks later, the family had stopped for their usual midday rest. Sam was off to one side, toward the rear of the group. Grandma swam silently up alongside and said nothing for several minutes. Then she spoke.

"Sam, I know the memories are painful and what is past is past, but I still have some questions. Do you mind?"

"No, Grandma," Sam said. "I owe you that much at the least."

"Thank you. I remember you said you deeply hated logriders and that you sought revenge for what they did to you, and especially to Nan and your baby. Were you ever able to satisfy that desire?"

"Not really, I guess. The closest I got was shouting at any who got into the water, as loud as I could. I know that was painful and they got the message. But, beyond that, despite my hatred, I found it difficult. I remembered being taught, even when I was very, very young, that we were never allowed to harm split-tails, or logriders. I guess that lesson restrained me despite my feelings."

"Very interesting," Grandma said. "We have the same rule. It goes back eons, so many generations that its origins are lost. There is much legend, and no small amount of mystery, as to where it started and why. One belief passed down from our ancestors, one that we teach our youngsters, is that, when we die, we come back as logriders. Harming them would violate the respect we must show to those who died."

"But if we come back as logriders, how do you explain their cruelty towards us?" Sam asked.

"I guess it is because they have no memory of who they were. And you have to also remember that they are not *all* bad. Most, in fact, seem to treat us with a degree of curiosity and even wonder. It is only a few that cause us so much pain. Maybe those were transients in their former lives."

"That's all very interesting," Sam said a little hesitantly.

Grandma sensed his skepticism. "I learned a more pragmatic explanation from my grandmother, who led our family for many years, and was so much wiser than I can ever hope to be. She said that, early in our history, we learned that the logriders, despite their often pointless behavior, are very powerful. Perhaps it was a painful lesson based on experience. To harm them is to unleash that power. They can hurt us more than we can ever hope to hurt them. What happened in the Cove of Sorrows is an example. By honoring and enforcing the rule, by making it strict and inviolate, we protect ourselves."

Grandma hesitated, then she spoke again, almost wistfully. "There was a time when things were different," she said. "When I was very young, my grandmother told me that we once lived harmoniously with the logriders. In those times, the logriders actually moved across the water in logs, dipping long wooden fins in unison, singing as they went. We often swam alongside and even hunted cooperatively, each taking only what they needed. There were enough fish then for everyone, even though our families were much larger."

"What changed?" Sam asked. "Did we do something to anger them?"

"I do not think so, Sam," Grandmas said. "My grandmother said that the logriders changed. More of them came, ones who covered themselves in different skins and moved in much larger logs, noisy logs, many not made of wood. They caught entire schools of salmon using large webs, like the one they used to capture Nan. And they chased us away, sometimes violently. That is also when the salmon began to grow scarce."

Sam was quiet for a while. He finally said, "Whatever the reason for the rule, the lesson stuck with me, despite my hatred."

"I will admit I am relieved to hear that, Sam. For you to have done otherwise would be dangerous for all concerned, whether the logriders are our departed kin, or are petty and mean and vengeful, or even both. I would worry if you had acted otherwise."

CHAPTER 21

After Makai's apparently successful introduction into J Pod, Rudy began receiving invitations to speak in public about his studies. Most occurred at branch libraries in small towns or on islands, not surprising given how the public couldn't get enough of orca lore. But, occasionally, and even though it was midsummer, he got the call from an institution of higher learning.

Which is how Rudy found himself sitting on the stage of a lecture hall at Western Washington University in Bellingham. He had been invited to speak to the WWU environmental studies program about his killer whale research. His host, a department chair, was reading verbatim from a prepared introduction. For Rudy, WWU was a fairly elevated invitation. Small schools and community colleges were his usual academic venues, places where, if faculty conducted research at all, it was part-time and secondary to their teaching responsibilities. Places much like Northwest Washington State, his reluctantly adopted home institution.

Rudy's standing within the whale research community was complex. Before Makai, he was just another player who had only recently joined the orca research world. He lacked the essential pedigree, not having proven his qualifications while rising through the whale research ranks. He was a loner, used unorthodox methods, taught at a second- (or lower-) tier institution, and openly speculated in print about capabilities of orcas. Responsible scientists avoided such speculation, at least in print. Although, to a person, his whale colleagues loved the animals and did everything in their power to help protect them, objectivity remained paramount. Rudy had to work on that.

Even after Makai's release, he remained something of an outsider. Perhaps it was envy that he was chosen over others to lead the reintroduction. A subset of orca conservationists openly questioned the wisdom of inserting a truly foreign whale into the vulnerable and declining Southern Residents. WWU probably invited him because he was cheap and nearby, just up I-5. Minimal travel costs and no need to house him at a nice hotel.

While his host continued to read through Rudy's bio, he scanned the audience. In the front row, slightly off to his left, sat a slender young woman with long red hair, wearing blue jeans and a Western sweatshirt. Late twenties maybe. Interesting.

His host droned on. "Dr. Laguna attended Cal Berkeley, the University of Hawaii, and has a doctorate from Cornell University. His early research focused on the reproductive behavior of stream fishes, before he turned to whales. He taught briefly at Hamilton College in upstate New York before joining the faculty at our neighboring institution of Northwest Washington State."

After being summarily fired at Hamilton, Rudy would have added.

"In whale research circles…"
…which he'd love to join…
"…he is best known…"
…begrudgingly…

"…for his successful efforts guiding the team that reintroduced into the wild a male orca named Makai that had been held captive for years. So, it is with great pleasure I give you Dr. Rudolph Laguna, who will speak to us about 'Reintroduction to the Wild of a Captive Orca.' Dr. Laguna."

Rudy gave his usual forty-five minute historical account of the capture of a young whale somewhere in the North Atlantic, captivity and mistreatment at Marineworld, reputation for violent and unpredictable behavior, multiple location changes, brush with euthanasia, eventual sale to a private and unnamed benefactor, recuperation in an undisclosed inland location, surgical transplant of a prosthetic dorsal fin, transfer to Penn Cove on Whidbey Island, escape, and apparent acceptance into J Pod of the Southern Resident killer whales. Sprinkled with dramatic photos of exhaling, jumping, splashing whales and self-deprecating humor, Rudy knew most of the audience was there for the eye candy. Rotary club or stodgy academics, people loved orcas and couldn't get enough of them. If you couldn't make an orca lecture interesting, you were in the wrong business.

Rudy finished with a plea to support orca conservation efforts, several relevant organizations listed across a photo of an orca leaping out of the water against a brilliant red-orange sunset. He then shuffled the notes that he had never looked at while the audience applauded. His host thanked him and opened the floor for questions. This was met with the usual deafening silence. How could academics who loved to hear themselves talk and had just sat through three quarters of an hour of fascinating whale facts, not have a single question to ask? *Were they brain dead?*

Finally, a hand shot up in the back. Rudy groaned internally. A woman wearing a PETA t-shirt and too much jewelry launched into a diatribe about keeping orcas, or any whales or dolphins or seals or sea lions, in captivity.

"It's cruel and unusual incarceration," she finally shouted, then sat down.

Rudy had encountered this type of person and harangue before. No point in rising to the bait, at least not immediately.

He readily agreed, noting that captive marine mammals—what Paul Watson of Sea Shepherd referred to as the orca slave trade—were, in fact, falling out of favor; that fewer public aquaria displayed the animals, especially given the enactment of laws curtailing the practice; and that public sentiment had shifted against making whales perform in captivity. Rudy was gratified that he had been able to demonstrate that these animals could, in fact, be successfully returned to a free and wild existence, if the proper conditions were met. These were, of course, points he had made clearly in his talk, but it was obvious that the questioner had an ax to grind, regardless of what he had said.

"But," he added because he couldn't let the PETA lady off the hook entirely, "as is so well documented in a book by Jason Colby and elsewhere, our love of these animals is in no small part a result of the small, initial group of animals that were captured in nearby waters and held for the public to see. Until then, we knew nothing of their social behavior, intelligence, and basically gentle nature, at least toward humans. Before, they were just thought of as killers and pests, to be eliminated by any means possible."

The PETA lady's question broke the ice and several more followed. Rudy had heard most of them before and gave his prepared answers, lacing them with natural history tidbits and factoids that he had saved, deliberately leaving them out of his formal presentation.

Fortunately, no one asked about mental telepathy between orcas and humans. That question usually popped up in more public settings, like garden clubs and libraries. Rudy fought off the urge to be dismissive and usually responded with something neutral.

Finally, the redhead in the front row raised her hand, and Rudy quickly pointed at her.

"Dr. Laguna. Your study subject was captured from a very different genetic lineage than our local, resident orcas. As our knowledge of these animals grows, aren't we finding that the genetic differences among orca groups are so great as to suggest that different geographic lineages might even be different species, each group finely attuned and adapted to local conditions beyond the cultural peculiarities they display? Aren't you taking a risk that your animal would breed with one of its newfound group members, producing offspring poorly adapted to local conditions, while forfeiting a breeding opportunity with a native animal that might produce better adapted offspring in a family grouping that is, in fact, suffering from reproductive failure?"

Ouch! There it was, the zinger question, all in one breath! Who was this lady? This was a topic he had deliberately dodged in his talk, the issue the orca establishment challenged him on.

"I'd like to pretend I'm happy you asked that question," he said to a few chuckles, hoping humor would buy him a little space. "We thought long and hard about these complications as we were planning the reintroduction. Because we didn't know exactly where Makai's original pod lived, we didn't have the luxury of returning him to his home. He couldn't be repatriated.

"The choice of one of the Southern Resident pods was made for just the reason you mention. Reproductive failure among Southern Residents is, indeed, high, in part because lactating females unload their body burden of lipid-soluble pollutants to their nursing young. Mortality among adult males is disproportionately high because they can't offload pollutants the way reproductive females do. Ideally, we would have found and released an adult female, but none was available. So, we took a different approach, speculating—and I freely admit it was speculation—that outbreeding might rejuvenate the stock, that a healthy male might prove a genetic asset. Yes, this carried more than a small amount of risk. We're still waiting to see if we were right."

Rudy wasn't sure if his questioner was satisfied with that answer, but his host had the good sense to cut questions off after that. He thanked Rudy once more and invited audience members to join them for a reception at his home. All were invited. Rudy hoped the redhead would appear. He was intrigued.

CHAPTER 22

The department chair's home was located in an upscale section of Bellingham, a neighborhood of stately homes and well-kept yards, having all the earmarks of a faculty ghetto. Wine, cheese, crackers, smoked-salmon dip (locally caught, never farm-raised Atlantic salmon), and a small keg of beer for the grad students. Maybe a dozen to twenty people all told.

Rudy scanned the room. Bingo. The redhead was standing near the food table in a knot of students engaged in animated conversation. Undoubtedly, it was grad students commiserating over research failures and unappreciated teaching duties.

Talk among the attending faculty was similarly predictable. Throwing caution to the wind, he asked one older gentleman what his research interests were. Rudy was immediately treated to a discourse on the population dynamics of some marine snail. Population declines were a critical indicator of deteriorating ocean conditions, probably global warming and ocean acidification. Rudy felt like he was listening to thinly disguised justifications in a grant proposal.

The evening progressed. He waited for the cluster of grad students at the food table to disperse. The redhead was finally standing alone by the beer keg. She was still wearing the same jeans and sweatshirt, clad in running shoes. No makeup or jewelry, except for a troublesome gold band on her left hand. Rudy looked around and didn't see anyone that could possibly be her husband. What the hell.

"You pretty much nailed me with that outbreeding question," he said as he sidled up alongside.

The redhead gave him a slight smile.

"The Western audience is much too polite. Someone needed to hold your fanny to the fire. Your answer was predictable, if only weakly defensible. Tell me, had you really considered the genetic implications of the release?"

"Yes, and no," Rudy said. "But, mainly, I had a benefactor with deep pockets and a guilty conscience, someone with a desire to make amends for a lifetime of environmental despoliation. We had a whale, gender be damned. If it had been a transsexual from Transylvania, we were still going to try to set it free and hope for the best. That seemed better than swimming around in circles in a kiddie pool for the rest of its shortened life. And I'd been self-funding my whale research when I got an offer too good to refuse."

"I appreciate your honesty and question your integrity a little less. I'm Cassandra Flanagan, Dr. Laguna."

"Rudy, please, Ms. Flanagan. No one calls me Dr. Laguna except undergrads I'm trying to avoid. And I haven't been Rudolph since my Aunt Sarah died."

"Okay, then I'm Cassie. For much the same reasons. Except it was an Aunt Fiona."

"Okay, Cassie. You're old enough to be a faculty member, but you're flocking with the grad students. So, at the risk of insulting you, I'll ask what your thesis is about." *Always a safe topic.*

Cassie gave a bigger smile. "Thanks for the compliment. And, yes, I'm a grad student. I'm studying reproductive tactics in a local fish called the grunt sculpin."

Rudy liked how the conversation had already turned to sex, even if it was fish sex. He admitted he had heard of the fish but knew little about it.

"Grunties aren't exactly headline news," Cassie said. "I won't bore you with the research particulars, at least not now. I know just how captivating the details of someone else's drudgery can be. Needless to say, it involves many hours of watching fish do nothing. But I'll admit to having looked at some of your earlier papers on fish interactions and could use your insight on fish behavior to get through some dead ends. Do you still think about fish, or are you all whales all the time now?"

Rudy thought he'd think about marine snails if it prolonged the conversation. He liked the way this was going. He liked everything about this woman: smart, self-confident, gorgeous, and not necessarily in that order.

"No, I still try to keep up with the fish literature. I'll admit I don't claim much expertise in sculpin sex, but I'm more than happy to see if I can be of help."

"Great. Let's talk sculpin sex over dinner tomorrow. How about Pete's Pizza in downtown Bellingham, say six o'clock? Would that work for you?"

"Um, let me think. Why not? I teach until five, have a faculty meeting I'd love to have an excuse to miss, not to mention a faculty senate meeting at the same time. I was going to claim a conflict of disinterest, but now I can say I've got an advisory conference with a student. So, I'll drive down and see you then."

This had worked out very differently than he'd anticipated. Hoping for some small entry, this bombshell had busted the door down. There was still the issue of the gold band. She's probably just a married grad student looking for input into her research. But what the hell? Faint heart never won fair maiden. Are married women still considered maidens?

CHAPTER 23

Rudy was preoccupied the next day. He sleepwalked though his introductory biology lecture and held distracted office hours, half listening to undergrads trying to get him to reveal what questions he might ask on the upcoming exam. Time dragged, then slowed even more.

Finally, at five, he headed home, fed Cheez, took a quick shower, and headed south. The drive down I-5 to Bellingham took five minutes more than the usual half hour because of what passed for the Bellinghamsters' rush hour. Arriving at Pete's a few minutes before six, he didn't want to appear anxious, so he sat anxiously in the Volvo for a few more minutes.

Cassie was already inside, sitting alone at a table against the far wall. She looked ravishing, wearing the same jeans and sweatshirt as the previous afternoon and evening. Just ravishing. Rudy felt like a nerdy high school freshman on his first date with the hottest girl in school.

"Am I late?" he asked.

"No, I had some naughty boys in the lab who seemed more interested in one another than in the girls. So, I gave up. I'll go back later and see if they've settled down and come to their senses."

"Right, given the most carefully planned observations, under the most carefully controlled conditions, the animals will do whatever they damned please."

She nodded, "I have that taped above my desk."

Rudy said, "Have you ordered?"

"Just this beer," she said, pointing to the glass of dark liquid on the table. "And a slice of pizza. It's Thursday night, and the special is Pete's pizza. I don't think it's any better or cheaper on any other night, they just make more of it."

"Sounds fine."

Rudy flagged down a passing waitress, ordered a beer ("same as hers") and a slice of pizza. He turned back to Cassie.

"You undoubtedly heard about as much about me last night as you can stomach," he said. "What about you? Back story? You're obviously older than most of your fellow grad students, so something must have happened before you wound up at Western."

Cassie hesitated just a moment.

"Not too interesting. I grew up in an Irish Catholic neighborhood in Milwaukee. I was always interested in animals. Went through the usual infatuation with ponies, so I mindlessly took pre-veterinary classes at UW Steven's Point. That's the other UW. My parents were delighted, although they would have preferred I become a real doctor. But I found out that poking poodles fell short of the excitement I guess I sought.

"After graduation, I escaped from Wisconsin and headed for the west coast. Held a variety of jobs working with animals in various ways. Technician, field assistant, lab slave, that kind of stuff. Got tired of taking orders from folks dumber than me and looked for a route that might give me independence. One of my early jobs involved caring for fish in a public aquarium. I liked that and decided to go to grad school and study fish. And here I am, documenting sculpin sex."

Rudy asked, "Are you working on a master's or PhD?"

"Doctorate."

"Hmm. That's a little strange on two counts. First, I don't remember there being any fish behaviorists at Western. Second, Western doesn't grant doctorates, just master's degrees. Want to fill me in?"

Cassie smiled. "You're right on both counts. I'm actually getting my PhD from the University of Washington. I was enrolled in the lab of a prof at UW, who shall remain unnamed. He had trouble taking me seriously and, instead, decided I was more interesting physically than professionally. Not my first experience with a sexual predator, but I hoped academia might be different. Anyway, he hit on me pretty hard, making it clear that continued funding of my research would be contingent on acquiescing to his demands."

"Ouch," said Rudy, waiting for the other shoe to drop.

"I called his bluff. When my fellowship wasn't renewed— despite stellar grades and reasonable research success—I blew the whistle on him and went to the dean. She was sympathetic. I think there was some history to support my complaint. My major prof was a tenured senior faculty member, and he hadn't done anything legally wrong, just morally despicable. No smoking gun, just shell casings scattered around. The university mediated a consent decree. I could maintain my standing as a UW grad student, but I would be housed and supervised here at Western. I'm still funded by my ex major prof, which has to grate on him. He has no control over my activities, academic or otherwise. I report directly to the dean. And the prof has been barred from taking on female grad students in a field that is increasingly populated with women."

"Kind of seems like a slap on the wrist," said Rudy.

"More like a slap on the pecker. And it got the message out to everybody that traditional practices were no longer acceptable. I agreed to the decree because I knew I had made life better for my fellow students."

Ouch, thought Rudy. *A cautionary tale? A warning shot across the bow, or more accurately between the legs? Time to change the subject.*

"But Bellingham? And Western over the vaunted University of Washington?"

"UDub is full of great scientists," she answered quickly, "but they're all salmon-centric, and I was working on little tidepool fish. Plus, I hated Seattle. Terrible traffic, zero parking, unaffordable housing, lousy bicycling with all the hills, crowds of people walking around employing the practiced 'Seattle Freeze' city stare, eyes focused on a non-object seventy-five feet ahead while surrounded by scores of rich, passive-aggressive techies and just plain aggressive homeless people. And I'm not a coffee drinker. Bellingham is much more my speed. It has everything I need, including a Trader Joe's."

"Well that certainly clears things up. Where do you think I might fit in this picture?"

"In truth," said Cassie, "I am pretty much on my own here at Western. The faculty is good, as are the students. But my committee consists of blue water oceanographers. They look at plankton nets and spectrophotometers. Nobody else is doing anything remotely close to my stuff. I need a sounding board, someone who doesn't think fish behavior is so esoteric as to be pointless. Someone who speaks my language."

"Last time I looked, Western doesn't allow outside committee members."

"My committee is just window dressing, something to meet university requirements. I'd appreciate it if you would let me bounce ideas off you. Nothing official or formal, just essential. Would that work?"

Rudy thought for a moment. He didn't want to seem too willing, but he also didn't want to give her a chance to back out. Here he had one of the most beautiful and intriguing women he'd met in a long time asking, almost pleading with, him to be involved with her. And, in truth, he was also lacking someone to talk animal behavior with. His colleagues at Northwest were self-absorbed in topics far removed from anything he remotely cared about. Nor would he describe any of them as beautiful and intriguing.

"Okay. Let's see if we can work out something that would be mutually beneficial. I'll be happy to play backboard to your fish work if you'll agree to do some part-time work as my field assistant in my whale studies. My funding doesn't allow me to hire field help, so I have to rely on volunteers. Chasing whales in a rubber boat sounds real romantic at first, but it can be cold, wet, rough, scary, and mostly boring. The average person only lasts through the first trip, if that. How does that sound?"

Cassie smiled. "Fucking fantastic!"

He couldn't have put it better. There was still the matter of the gold band. *Another time. Don't spoil the moment.*

The rest of the hour at Pete's was spent in idle chatter, until Cassie looked at her watch and excused herself.

"My grunties call. I'll get back to you soon. I promise. Thank you, Rudy."

"Thank you, Cassie."

CHAPTER 24

"Laguna here."

"Now there's a welcoming voice. I'd hate to call you on a bad day."

Rudy snapped to attention, held the phone closer.

"Hello, Cassie. Sorry. I was off somewhere else. What can I do for you?"

"I was thinking of something more mutual," she said. "Since you're my ex-officio committee member and I'm your ex-officio field assistant, I figured we should get to work."

"Great," he said. "What did you have in mind? Do you want me to come work some voodoo on your fish, scare them with the depth of my knowledge as to how their tiny brains operate?"

"Not really. In truth, I want to help you more than vice versa. How is your Saturday shaping up, tomorrow morning? I could show you my lab setup, and then we could go out and look for whales. Does that sound attractive?"

He had plans for Saturday that were seeming less pressing all of a sudden. Despite her warnings, he still found her both attractive and intriguing.

"Hmm. I guess so. Why not?"

"Great. My fish room is at Western's Shannon Point Lab in Anacortes, near the ferries. Do you know the place?"

"Definitely. But isn't that kind of a long haul from Bellingham? It must be inconvenient for you to have to keep your fish that far away. But I guess we all make do. Grad students and beggars can't be choosers, right?"

"I make do," she said. "Where do you want to launch the boat?"

"How about the boat ramp at nearby Washington Park? We can launch the Zodiac and head south. Some whales were seen in that area earlier this week, so maybe they're still around. We could get lucky."

"Cool. I'll meet you in the Shannon Point parking lot. How does eight in the morning sound?"

Godawful. Especially if he had to get up early enough to hook up the trailer and drive an hour and a half from Blaine.

"No problem. See you then."

Saturday morning dawned cold and gray, not a rarity, even in July. But at least the weather forecast promised light wind and only a slight chance of rain. The roads were pretty much deserted, and he made good time. Cassie was standing in the laboratory's lot next to a yellow VW Beetle.

"Sorry I'm late. Traffic was a bitch."

Cassie led him into the building, down some drab concrete stairs, and along a hallway that looked and smelled damp. They stopped outside a door with Cassie's name and contact information on it.

"This is yours?" Rudy asked. "You have an entire lab to yourself?"

Cassie smiled and led him into the room.

Rudy couldn't believe his eyes. He was in an aquarium room that was easily fifty feet long and equally wide. Stainless steel shelves held dozens of glass tanks. Compressed air could be heard bubbling everywhere, pumps buzzed, relays shut on and off. Cabling and electronic gear in abundance.

"Wow! I've never seen such a fancy setup for looking at fish. And you say this is your lab?"

"All paid for by my former exploitative major professor. Part of the consent agreement. Ironic really since it came out of my unwillingness to consent. It's paid for off his grants, which must require some creative bookkeeping. I love how it must stick in his craw."

"And you can handle all this stuff just fine. It looks more than a little complicated."

"Not a big deal. I worked in a public aquarium in another life and got familiar with this kind of gear."

She explained that everything was automated, and every fish tank was video monitored, which allowed her to make observations from her office back on the Western campus.

"I only come here about once a week to check on things and move fish around. Otherwise, it's all watching video tape."

Each numbered tank housed a fish, grunt sculpins, he guessed. They looked like something put together by committee: long snout, fat body, and seemingly missing their back half. Each sat in a plastic barnacle.

"Aren't they beautiful!" Cassie gushed.

Rudy had done a little homework on grunt sculpins, wanting to show Cassie he was deeply interested. The Wikipedia entry mentioned that a female chased a male into a crevice and kept him there until she was ready to lay eggs. *Was this somehow insight into Cassie's personality?*

"Grunties try to look like barnacles, or at least the animal inside a barnacle. Unfortunately, watching their behavior can be kind of boring. I sometimes think barnacle behavior would be more interesting."

"What's with the plastic barnacles?" Rudy asked.

"Grunties fight over empty barnacle shells. I make my own barnacles with my 3D printer. I'm thinking the girls choose their mates based on barnacle quality as much as male characters."

"Gold digging female fish, eh?"

"Look. It's the fish equivalent of a dating website. You can lie about your physical features, but you can't fake how good your home is. Give the girls some credit."

Rudy just shook his head. This woman was not to be underestimated. The male grunties and her former major prof both were manipulated because they thought with their dicks.

Cassie introduced a couple of her favorite fish and showed Rudy a nicely edited videotape that depicted male-male and male-female interactions.

"All very straightforward except for the males who act like females to gain access to mates," she added. "Keeps me and the girls on our toes."

As they left the building, Rudy said, "I'll meet you at the Washington Park boat ramp in maybe five minutes. You know the way?"

"All too well. That's where we leave from when we go hunting grunties."

At the park, Rudy had to wait to back the trailer down the ramp. Another couple was launching a powerboat that dwarfed the SUV to which it was attached, the boat bristling with fishing poles. The husband was shouting directions to his wife as she zigzagged down the ramp. The shouting didn't seem to help matters much.

"He doesn't seem too sympathetic about her difficulties, does he?" Cassie said, materializing alongside him.

"Yeah. I love boat ramps. You get to watch unparalleled acts of stupidity, bullheadedness, unfounded bravado, transmission destruction, and marriage dissolution, often all at the same time."

The couple finally got the boat in the water and liberated from the trailer. Returning from the parking lot, the wife got into the boat at the floating dock without saying a word. The husband drove off, much too fast.

"Our turn," said Rudy. "Don't give me any crap."

"Hey. No reason. We've hardly met."

Rudy let Cheez out of the passenger's door and started to return to the driver's side.

The dog trotted towards the boat as usual but noticed Cassie standing at the top of the ramp. He bounded over to her and went into full puppy mode, bumping against her, his entire back end wagging. She reached down and scratched him behind the ears, talking softly. Cheez spun around in a happy circle.

"Don't blow my cover, big fella," she whispered, whacking him firmly on his backside. He turned another happy circle.

"Wow!" Rudy said, as he walked up to them. "Cheez doesn't often respond to strangers quite that strongly. He's usually a pretty good judge of character, so I guess you passed."

"Cheese?" asked Cassie, still scratching the dog.

"Short for Cheez Whiz. It's a long story, for later. We'd better get going."

Rudy backed his trailer without much incident. He took his place in the stern next to the outboard, Cassie sat on the wooden midships seat, with Cheez in his self-assigned position, paws on the bow, facing forward.

They headed out into the channel for a few minutes, and then Rudy cut the engine.

"We've got a pretty strong outgoing tide. Let's just drift and keep our eyes open for whales."

He pulled a small handheld radio out of the rusty ammo box.

"I'll keep the VHF tuned to the channel the whale-watching companies use so we'll know if anybody is seeing anything."

Turning up the volume, all they heard was static.

They drifted south for about a half hour without talking. Finally, Cassie looked at Rudy.

"I have to apologize, Rudy," she said. "I actually called you on false pretenses. I'd love to find whales, but first I just wanted to have a heart-to-heart talk with you so we don't have any misunderstandings about our relationship."

Here it comes, thought Rudy. *Fun while it lasted, although it hadn't lasted long and it hadn't really been fun.*

"Okay then," Cassie said. "We need to flesh out the details of our agreement. I'm a happily married woman. My husband, Heath, is a great guy. He's kind, considerate, good looking, built like a Greek statue, and very understanding. He drives a beer delivery truck, which keeps him in great shape. We have a wonderful relationship. He meets all my physical and emotional needs. What he can't meet are my intellectual needs."

"Uh-huh," Rudy couldn't think of anything else to say. If he considered himself at all like a Greek statue, it was more Dionysian than Herculean.

"That's where you come in," Cassie continued. "I know full well why you've agreed to help me. You're about as hard to read as a flashing neon beer sign, and thanks to Heath, I'm familiar with those. I can live with that, for the time being."

Rudy still didn't say anything. He wondered where this was going.

"We have an agreement," she said. "An understanding of mutual assistance. I will stick to my end of the bargain helping you watch whales, and you will be available to advise me about my often-uncooperative sculpins. But that's where it ends as far as I'm concerned. I don't want you to expect anything more from me. I've been over this ground before and know what men like you can expect, or hope for. Deal?"

Rudy was speechless. Refuse the deal and that would end things. Accept the deal and he would likely suffer debilitating frustration. But, he had to admit, she had him dead to rights. He thought for another millisecond.

"I guess so. I mean sure. Why not? I do need field help, not to belittle Cheez's contributions."

"Great," Cassie said. "I'm glad we've cleared that away. You've heard enough about me, but I really don't know much about you beyond the tidbits offered at your lecture. It looks like we have some time to talk. Starting with the basics. You're not married I take it."

"Correct. I was, but it didn't work out."

"Are you willing to talk about it?"

"Why not? Not especially interesting. I married a woman shortly after I finished my PhD. She was already on the faculty at Hamilton. It was ill-fated from the start. She was in the business school and I was in biology. She was pretty high powered. She specialized in corporate takeovers and downsizing strategies, made lots of money running her own consulting firm, taught one class in her specialty."

"No kids, I take it."

"Out of the question, and fortunate, given the eventual outcome. By mutual consent, we decided early on to prevent even the possibility. Children would have been career-threatening to both of us. We only stayed married for a couple of years. She was religious, politically reactionary, materialistic, didn't believe in evolution and denied climate change. I was a left-wing radical tree-hugger, biology was my god, and I taught evolution. And I drove the same old Volvo I'd had in grad school. In reality, we only had one thing in common. We were good in bed."

"That should have solved a lot of problems," Cassie offered.

"Yes, it should have. But it didn't. She quickly made it clear that she saw my interest in fish behavior as silly at best. She accused me of conducting 'so-what' science, as in 'so what does it really matter?' What difference does it make if minnows screw in the weeds or over a rock pile?

"I countered by quoting Stephen Jay Gould, that knowledge need never be justified by utility."

"'Try telling that to a funding agency,' she countered, and then wondered who would ever read my papers and care about them?

"'I can think of at least a half dozen people,' I said.

"'Proving my point,' she replied.

"I had trouble with her venality. I criticized her and her business school colleagues for their superficiality, what with their focus on stylish clothes and new and expensive cars. 'The only BMWs in the parking lots belong to business school faculty.'

"'Econ profs also own them,' she countered.

"'Proving my point,' I replied."

"It doesn't sound like either of you had much invested in making the marriage work," Cassie said.

"Correct. Two bullheaded people waving red flags at one another. Neither of us was very good at keeping our opinions to ourselves, so the house got increasingly quiet when we weren't shouting at one another. On the upside, the arguments only served to make our bedroom activities that much more intense. But our differences were pretty much irreconcilable."

"What caused the eventual breakup? Infidelity?"

"Uh-uh. Our marriage was pretty open. Our philandering was competitive, if anything. The failure, the final straw, was the one thing we had in common and my inability to keep up my end of the bargain."

"Oooh. This is getting juicy. Did you forget to take your little blue pills?"

"Oh no. I didn't need performance-enhancing drugs," Rudy said. "It was more a matter of shared responsibilities."

"And?"

"I was kind of distracted by my research and sort of got into the habit of forgetting my responsibility of keeping the vibrator charged. That was the last straw."

"Clearly, absolutely inexcusable," Cassie said. "And the divorce. Was it ugly?"

"Less so than our marriage," Rudy said. "She had drawn up a detailed prenup agreement that I had signed without reading. Basically, it said what was mine was mine and what was hers was hers. Since just about everything of any value was hers, she got the house and its contents, including the vibrator. I got the Volvo and a fifty-gallon aquarium filled with minnows."

"I guess I'll just file all that knowledge away in case I ever have need for it," Cassie said. "But I have another question, since we're digging into your sordid past and misspent youth."

Rudy looked up. They had drifted with the current almost to the shoreline, a stone's throw from a lighthouse.

"Let's putt-putt back over to the other side. Minke whales often hang out off Lopez Island, feeding on herring and sand lance schools, what we now refer to as forage fish aggregations. Although all the fishermen still call them bait balls."

Rudy started the outboard and headed west, then cut the engine.

"Where were we?" he asked.

"You're how old?"

Rudy hesitated a moment. "Forty-one...and a half."

"Hmm. Most people graduate from college around twenty-one. Take five to seven years for grad school. I detect a gap somewhere," Cassie said. "Care to fill it in?"

"Looks like we're destined to sit and wait some more, so I guess I'll subject you to another episode in the saga of Rudy"

CHAPTER 25

"After undergrad," he said, "I was a little aimless. I joined the Peace Corps and spent several years in the tropical island paradise of Palau."

"Wow. I've heard of that place. The diving is supposed to be spectacular."

"Right. I'll admit that idealistic, unselfish service to humanity wasn't my primary motivation. I'd heard the reefs were first rate. And they were. I did some fisheries work, but quickly realized I had little I could teach Palauans about their fish. They had a thousand-year head start; I had a zoology degree from Cal. It felt like cultural imperialism. I helped out at the fishermen's co-op, offloading local fishing boats. I was cheap labor.

"But mostly I dove and speared fish and caught fish any way I could. Lots of photos of a happy fisherman holding unhappy fish. One of my fellow volunteers once told me, 'Laguna, you'd rather fish than fuck. If you ever found a mermaid, you wouldn't know what to do with her.'"

"An interesting dilemma," Cassie said.

"After the Peace Corps, I hung around Palau. Got a contract job with the US government teaching high school biology. I bought a small powerboat and fished afternoons and weekends. Then, one day, an American tuna fishing boat showed up, doing exploratory fishing for the American government that controlled Palau. I hit it off with the younger crew on the tuna boat. They made oodles of dough catching tuna half the year then went on unemployment the other half and spent their fishing earnings. Everybody seemed to have crashed at least one Corvette. I signed on."

Cassie interrupted. "Weren't those the boats that used to kill a lot of dolphins?"

"Exactly. The tuna would swim under the dolphins, and we would chase the dolphins in fast speedboats until they tired. We then corralled them at the surface, the tuna all bunched up just below. Then we'd surround everything with the net and bring the net on board, fish and dolphins together. At first, I found it fascinating, catching fish by the thousands while I had always done it one at a time.

"But I started paying attention to the dolphins. Some had drowned in the net and came up dead. Others would be caught in the net and get hoisted up to the top of the boom, squirm free, and fall fifty feet to the deck. We called it 'raining dolphins' and had to duck out of the way. The ones that didn't die from the impact thrashed around and made the most horrible, pathetic squealing noises. Dead or alive they were slid overboard through a gap we called the shark chute. Sharks attracted by the commotion made quick work of things."

Rudy had been staring off at the shore but turned and glanced at Cassie. She looked horrified.

"It started to get to me. We could kill a hundred dolphins while catching a couple hundred pounds of fish, all to make tunafish sandwiches. It seemed like a horrible waste. I kept my feelings to myself 'cause clearly I was the only one with reservations. In Panama, I bought a little film camera and started filming the process. I made light of it with the crew, who would ham it up for the camera.

"I then got an underwater camera housing and slipped over the side once, before the sharks showed up. I filmed dolphins drowning in the net and other dolphins swimming just outside, vocalizing. It was pretty obvious that the ones on the outside were just as stressed as the ones on the inside. I didn't show that footage to the crew, claiming my camera had jammed."

"I think I remember seeing footage of dolphins struggling inside a net, other dolphins on the outside swimming around in a panic," Cassie said.

"Yes, that was probably my film. I sent a copy to Greenpeace. They took it public. It was the start of the dolphin-safe fishing movement. It was also the start of my interest in marine mammal conservation and, I guess, eco-terrorism. It was also the end of my commercial fishing career."

"I'd guess you wouldn't have been Mr. Popular among your crewmates."

"Or the rest of the tuna fleet for that matter," Rudy said. "I figured it wisest to hide my involvement, but everybody knew I was to blame. They didn't exactly scatter rose petals in my path. I had to get the hell out of Dodge. I headed as far away as I could, to the east coast. And eventually managed to get accepted to grad school at Cornell, as a fish behaviorist.

"Deep down, I wanted to do dolphin work, but all that was happening on the west coast. I couldn't compete with an army of applicants who had volunteered to study dolphins instead of killing them. At Cornell, I just had to complete my dissertation research and dive into the job market. Hamilton hired me after several other unsuccessful job interviews."

Rudy noticed they had drifted offshore again.

"It looks like the whales are a no-show today, Cassie," he said. "I warned you that finding them could be a crapshoot. It's what makes it hard for me to find help, good or otherwise."

"Hey, no biggie," Cassie said. "This beats watching video tapes. The weather's been good and you've kept me entertained. I have no regrets."

"You're a good sport, Cassie. Unless you think better, we'll plan another trip and hope for more cooperative whales."

At the boat ramp, they waited while someone struggled getting a boat onto a trailer. Rudy mentally played through the steps of backing the car and trailer without making a fool of himself.

"Hey Rudy. Give me the keys and I'll bring the trailer down," Cassie said.

Rudy hesitated. "Really? I mean it can be tricky and all. Manual transmission, you can't see the trailer as it heads down the ramp."

"First, I drive a beetle. Your transmission can't be any worse than mine. And I've actually done this before. Believe it or not, women can back a trailer too."

Rudy handed her the keys, figuring he could always park the boat against the dock if Cassie had trouble. Motoring slowly to the ramp, he was surprised to see the Volvo and trailer backing smoothly in a straight line down the ramp. It stopped just as the trailer tires were half under water. Cassie got out of the car and walked to the front end of the trailer, wading in the cold, ankle-deep water. She pulled out the winch rope and hooked the connector to the eye on the front of the Zodiac, grinning the entire time.

"You're hired," he said. "I don't remember putting that in your job description. But I'm impressed. 'Til next time, then."

He was impressed.

CHAPTER 26

The next time came two weeks later. Cassie called Rudy and asked him to take her out to try to see the whales again. She needed a break from bingeing on videotapes of fish doing nothing. Rudy hadn't really planned a research trip for midweek, but he had to admit that he enjoyed Cassie's company, so it wasn't difficult justifying the excursion.

They agreed to meet at the Blaine boat ramp this time, closer to Rudy's home. Cheez went into full puppy mode again when she parked her VW and walked down the dock.

"I don't know what that dog sees in you," said Rudy. "I know what I see in you, but he must have other priorities."

"Superior intelligence, I guess," Cassie said.

Walked into that one, Laguna.

Less than five minutes outside the harbor, Cheez gave a quick bark and looked toward the horizon. Sure enough, several whale spouts were visible.

"Hot damn," said Rudy. "It looks like much of J Pod is there. You're in for a treat."

Rudy gunned the motor and raced toward the spouts. As he approached the whales, he cut the engine and just drifted.

"It looks like they're in morning nap mode, breathing only occasionally while they laze along the surface. The technical term for this is logging. Did you know half of their brain is awake when they're resting, because they have to remember to breathe?"

182   GENE HELFMAN

Cassie was staring intently at the whales, transfixed, clearly fascinated.

Whales do that to people, Rudy thought.

"Hey, there's Makai," whispered Rudy. "He's swimming near J-28 Polaris, a female. I think he's sweet on her. It's pretty unusual for males and females in the same pod to associate like that, but Makai is a newcomer, so maybe they're bending the rules a little."

"That would be nice, given what he's been through," Cassie said.

"Hey," Rudy exclaimed. "That large female at the head of the group is J-2 Granny. She's usually with several of her offspring or grandkids. Yes! The two young males behind her are her grandsons, the twins, J-38 Cookie and J-39 Mako. I don't know if they're really twins but they were born the same year and are inseparable. Their mother may be J-22 Oreo. She also had another son, J-34 DoubleStuf, but he died. And over there is J-16 Slick, another older female. Her son is J-26 Mike. He's an enigma, always hangs out with the females. And that other big male is J-27 Blackberry. He and Makai are always on opposite sides of any group. I don't think they get along."

"Wow. That's pretty impressive. Like how long did it take you to learn them all?" Cassie asked.

"It's not that hard. The orca research community named them and prints out photos and biographies. Those galleries were critical in helping me understand orca social structure when I was working on Makai's reintroduction."

"Interesting you say that," she said. "In your talk at Western, you were kind of ambivalent about the orca research community, maybe even an us-versus-them mentality. But aren't you on the same page when it comes to saving the whales?"

"Yeah, I guess I let my feelings show a little too much. To a person, they care deeply about the whales and work tirelessly to reverse the declines. They hope their studies will help improve the lot of the whales. In my defense, I donate money to at least a half dozen orca conservation programs. But I guess the established researchers are just better at putting their emotional attachment aside when gathering and interpreting data."

"I'm happy to hear you admit that. I'll give you another point."

The whales were motionless, all at the surface. Occasionally, one would breathe, a condensed mist rising up from a blowhole, creating a mini-rainbow in the bright sunlight.

Rudy and Cassie sat in the boat for maybe a half hour, just watching. Rudy opened the ever-present ammo box and took out the hydrophone. He dropped it overboard and handed the earphones to Cassie.

"Even though they're resting, they tend to vocalize quite a bit," he said. "Just listen for a while."

Cassie listened. She had a big smile on her face. "Wow!" she said. "It's like they're talking to one another."

"I don't doubt it," Rudy said. "I haven't spent enough time listening to them yet, but the real experts, like Alexandra Morton—you should read her book—can even—"

"I have,' Cassie interrupted. "All of them."

Rudy stopped. "Huh? Oh. Right. Anyway, the experts can tell individuals apart by their distinct voices."

"Do you have any idea what they're saying?" Cassie asked.

"Not a clue. When we record them, they just appear as unpronounceable squiggles on a sonogram. But I have little trouble imagining it's a conversation. For one thing, they seldom interrupt each other; it's more of a back-and-forth. For another, orcas can make twenty-four different pulsed communication calls. The Hawai'ian language by comparison has only twelve basic sounds. Nobody questions the ability of Hawai'ians to engage in complex communication. Why not orcas?"

Cassie didn't say anything for another minute. Then she repeated, "Wow!"

"Yes, wow. And what makes it better is we, us and the whales, don't have competition. No crowds of whale watchers. The whales get some actual rest. This is a rare day."

Cassie took the headphones off and handed them back. "Thank you, Rudy. Speaking of other boats," she said, "I've noticed yours is about the only one around without fishing gear. For a guy who would rather fish than fuck, you seem to be lacking some important equipment."

"Well," Rudy replied. "I guess my priorities have changed."

"Why's that?"

"It's a karmic thing," Rudy said.

"Karma, Rudy? How's that?"

"Fish have been good to me, long after I pursued them by every lethal means possible. They got me a PhD and, ultimately, a job. It seems kind of thankless, ungrateful, to turn around and kill them. That could be bad karma. I think it was Henry David Thoreau who, when asked if he fishes, said something like, I can't fish without falling a little in self-respect. With every year, I'm less a fisherman."

"Isn't that a little mystical or spiritual for a hard-nosed biologist like you?" she asked.

"I guess I have my lapses." Rudy answered. "But I've been reading the debate on whether fish feel pain. I'd say the evidence is leaning heavily in favor of the fish. They're more sentient than they've been given credit. Or maybe I'm just hedging my bets, in case I don't have all the answers."

"But now you're studying whales, not fish. Wouldn't that release you from karmic responsibility?"

"Not really," he replied. "The main thing everybody fishes for here—either recreational or commercial fishers—is salmon. And my whales depend on salmon, of which there aren't enough. So, I'd be competing with my whales, literally stealing food from their mouths. Again, bad karma."

"*Your* whales? Isn't that a bit possessive?"

"Whales have that effect on people," was all Rudy could offer in his defense.

"Okay," Cassie said. "But there's another topic you brought up last time that bears scrutiny."

"What's that?" Rudy asked.

"The mermaid thing your Peace Corps buddy asked about. Have you decided what you would do?"

"I still haven't made up my mind."

"Can I offer a suggestion?"

Rudy grew intrigued. This was getting more interesting. "Sure, I'm all ears."

"Don't you think the mermaid should have some say in the matter?"

Ouch, Rudy thought. *I walked into another one.*

"Hmm. I guess that might be reasonable."

"Definitely," Cassie said. "Times have changed since you were originally asked the question."

"Granted," Rudy was forced to admit. "But first I have to find the mermaid."

"It never hurts to be prepared, at least mentally. Just in case."

Rudy was about to say something he thought was clever when the whales began to move. First slowly, then faster as they swam away.

Rudy was about to start the engine when Cassie held up her hand.

"I know we're supposed to be making observations," she said. "But if it's so unusual for them to not be chased by boats, maybe we should let them do their thing alone. Is that unreasonable?"

Rudy thought for a moment. He had to admit that Cassie was right. This was a rare occasion, and chasing the whales might even draw attention from other whale watchers. Once in a while, the whales deserved some privacy. He liked to think of himself as their friend, even their guardian. If so, he should act like one.

"Okay," he said. "I can't argue with that. It's been a good day. Let's call it a success and head back."

"That's pretty reasonable of you. I was expecting a fight. Maybe you're a decent person after all," she said. "So, thank you."

"You're welcome, I guess. But, really, the whales should be thanking you."

"Maybe they are," she said.

The short ride back to Blaine went quickly. At the Blaine ramp, they once again had to wait while an elderly couple struggled with backing their trailer. Cheez took advantage of the lull and headed for the trees.

Cassie turned to Rudy.

"Okay, something else has been on my mind," she said, "something I've been wondering about since your talk at Western. Hamilton College is a pretty prestigious institution. Not exactly Ivy League but close. Strong liberal arts focus. Great reputation. I would think getting hired there was a big deal, but you didn't stay. And, in fact, you went from big-time Hamilton to no-time Northwest Washington State. I'll bet most people in Seattle haven't heard of Northwest Washington. Why there?"

Rudy hadn't thought about his demise for a while. It was something he tried to put out of his mind. But it was clear Cassie wasn't going to let it drop.

"Well, in a nutshell. I had a dalliance with a young woman who had just graduated from Hamilton, someone who had taken my classes. In my defense, she technically wasn't still an undergrad, and I wasn't her instructor. Unfortunately, her father turned out to be a very influential member of the Hamilton community."

"How influential?" Cassie asked.

"Chairman of the Board of Regents and chief contributor to the endowment fund. His wife was the president of the alumni foundation."

"That's pretty influential," Cassie said.

"I hadn't done anything illegal, really. We were consenting adults, but I was dealing with irate, pissed off, rich and powerful parents. Hamilton's dean called me into her office and handed me my walking papers, which included a position she had negotiated at Northwest Washington State University. It was an offer I would have been foolish to refuse."

Cassie looked at him. "Come on, Rudy. There's got to be more to the story than that."

Fortunately, the couple ahead of them managed to get their boat on its trailer and were burning rubber as they moved haltingly up the ramp in a cloud of rancid black smoke.

"Our turn," Rudy said. "Are you willing to demonstrate your trailer backing prowess once more?"

Cassie reached out for the keys.

"Next time I get the full story," she said.

Rudy figured he had managed to dodge the subject, at least for now. Cassie would eventually pry it out of him, bringing back memories he had tried unsuccessfully to suppress.

CHAPTER 27

N o fish had been encountered for several days. Late summer was shaping up poorly. Everybody was hungry and tempers were growing short. The aunts had to intervene often to keep the peace.

Fortunately, the cousins with whom they shared these waters reported a large number of Chinook salmon heading toward the west side of Gathering Salmon Island, where Sam's family regularly hunted. Everything pointed to the salmon arriving early the next morning.

Grandma swam over to Sam.

"This will be your first pre-planned group hunt, Sam," she said. "There are things you need to know, before it gets hectic."

Sam was paying attention. The level of excitement in the family had crept up as the night progressed.

"Chinook salmon like deep water, the deeper the better. But they have never been here before and do not know about the shoals they will encounter. That is why we are here, waiting to take advantage of their confusion."

"I was wondering why we had stopped here," Sam said.

"Yes, this knowledge clearly works to our advantage. Unfortunately, we are not the only ones who know this."

"But I thought we willingly shared fish with our cousins," Sam said, perplexed.

"Yes, but it is not our cousins who are the problem. It is the logriders. This is one of their favorite places to catch our salmon. We hope to eat our fill before they show up."

Sam was surprised at the contempt in Grandma's voice. She seldom showed such emotion.

"We have to catch as many fish as possible as fast as possible. And Sam, you will play a special role. It is easy for us to rush into a school and catch fish, as long as they stay in a tight group. But some fish always break away and head for deeper water and we lose them. I need you to place yourself on the deepwater side of the school where such escapes occur and hit them with your sonic blasts."

Sam liked this idea. It was putting his abilities to best use, for the good of the group.

"One more thing," Grandma said. "I am asking the twins to work with you and collect injured fish so you can concentrate on your task."

That was help Sam could do without. He guessed he would just have to work as best he could, despite the twins. He would trust Grandma's wisdom. She usually knew best.

Things went pretty much according to plan. The salmon showed up only a little later than was ideal. But the family worked as a precision team, fanning out in a semi-circle just outside the visual capabilities of the salmon. Elder aunts formed an advancing front, corralling the fish. At Molly's signal, the uncles dove below the school, forcing the panicking fish toward the surface.

The salmon, easily hundreds of them, were now milling nervously in a compact ball. Grandma gave the signal. In the agreed upon order, one whale and then the next dashed into the school and grabbed a salmon, moving back into the hemisphere of whales to swallow it.

As soon as the attack began, the fish must have smelled blood or heard the crunching of teeth on bone, and fled towards deeper water, just as Grandma had predicted. Sam blasted the first, and it flailed helplessly, its back broken by the explosion of its swim bladder. Mitchie grabbed it immediately and swallowed it. *So much for saving fish for the others*, Sam thought.

"You only get to eat the first one," Sam shouted to Mitchie.

"Right, sorry," the youngster replied.

At the height of the action, when Sam thought he must have blasted at least twenty fish, he heard the buzzing of loud, approaching logs.

As the logs neared the feeding whales, the fish began to behave erratically, confused, not knowing which threat to avoid more. The unfamiliar, louder noises from the logs was more frightening than their old enemies, the whales. They dove and scattered.

"The fish are moving away and down!" Frank shouted. "Dive and cut them off!"

"What?" Michael shouted back. "I can't hear you!"

"Dive, dammit!"

But it was too late. The noise from the buzzing logs drowned out their voices. The fish turned offshore. Sensing the retreat, the family followed. But the logriders were approaching, sending out pinging sounds at the same frequency as the whales' sonar, confusing them further. The whales had to dodge a dozen weighted lines hanging from the logs, bright flashing objects attached at various depths, causing the fish to scatter even more.

It was over before anyone realized.

"What was all that about?"

The slender, young, blond woman in the sequined t-shirt turned to her much older and heavier husband. "What were those animals? Some kind of big fish?"

"Killer whales," her husband almost spat out the words. He gunned the three large outboard engines of their forty-foot fishing boat and turned sharply left.

"Whales, huh? So, all that huffing and puffing was their breathing, right? You don't sound particularly happy about them."

"Damn straight," he answered. "Those bandits steal all our salmon. It's bad enough we have to share our fish with the Indians, but those killer whales eat a lot more big salmon than all the Indians in Washington. Those black bastards swam right through our downrigger lines and probably scared every last fish over to Canada. We'll have piss little to show for the two hundred gallons of gas we used getting out here. So much for a fish dinner."

"That's okay with me, honey," she replied. "You know I don't like fish, and I didn't really feel like cooking. Let's pull up all those fishing lines and head back. We can just go to Friday Harbor for dinner. You can have a big juicy steak, and I'll have a teeny little salad."

CHAPTER 28

*What truly distinguishes humans
is that we have sex for so many reasons
other than pleasure...That animals...are [consciously]
engaging in copulation for procreation...
is probably unique to humans.*

G. J. SCHEYD, Psychology Today, Sept. 9, 2013

The morning hadn't been a total waste. Everyone had eaten, not as much as they would have liked, but at least more than they'd had the last several days.

"We have not really talked for a while," Grandma said to Sam as the whales rested midday offshore, away from the islands. "How are you adjusting to family living?"

Fog had rolled in soon after the morning's aborted hunting episode, which meant few, if any, logriders would disturb their rest. The whales enjoyed foggy days and the relative peace and quiet they brought.

"I think things are going okay," Sam replied. "I'm learning names, although I'm kind of struggling remembering all the different grandparents who are long gone. But everybody seems to feel that's important."

"Just accept it as tradition," Grandma answered. "Otherwise, how are you feeling?"

"Wonderful. I love the hunting. And I think I'm getting better at it."

"You are being modest, Sam," Grandma admonished him. "You were absolutely essential to this morning's success, for as long as it lasted. And everyone is impressed with your ability to incapacitate solitary salmon with a single loud blast. We are all eating better now that you are part of the hunting parties, despite the scarcity of fish."

Sam let that go. He had something on his mind.

"There is something that has me puzzled," he said.

"What is that?" Grandma asked.

"Well," Sam said, hesitation in his voice. "I was wondering why there are so few youngsters around. I mean really young children. I remember Nan talking about growing up with younger cousins, even infants. Is something wrong? Is this something I shouldn't ask about?"

Grandma took a deep breath and didn't reply immediately.

"No, your observation is correct, and it is fair of you to ask. Although I will admit it is a subject I do not enjoy talking about, although it is constantly on my mind."

"Well, if it's prying into something delicate, I'd understand," Sam said.

"Not that. It is important you know. And I am the best one to explain things. Whether or not we have babies is a decision we make collectively, the aunts and I, depending on food availability. The last few years have been exceptionally lean. The salmon runs have been down, especially the larger Chinook that we prize so greatly."

"So, the decision to, uh, have babies is ultimately determined by Chinook abundance?" Sam asked.

"Yes, and no. It is a little more complicated than that. Immediate abundance is, of course, important. But we also have ways of predicting future numbers. We taste the fish we catch during our winter sojourns.

Large fat fish with developing eggs are most likely to return to their homes, and our summer residence, the next summer. Large fat fish without eggs will migrate in a future year. So, we look at both present and future abundance in making decisions about mating. This information is exchanged and shared by all members of our community."

Sam broke in. "So that's where the greeting, 'How fat are the salmon?' comes from. It's an important fact," Sam said, the realization striking him suddenly.

"Yes, it is a tradition based on millennia of experience," she replied. "And because our unborn babies take over a year to develop, we need to know not just this year's abundance, but next year's also. Generations of experience, experience that has become tradition, tells us that babies born during years of low salmon abundance often do not survive their first year. And the effort of feeding them also weakens their mothers. This means that we may put off having babies while we wait for the runs to return."

"Oh. I see. I guess that's why I haven't seen many couples swimming together. It reduces the temptation to mate?" Sam said it more as a question than a statement.

"Oh, no. That is not the way things happen. I mean, yes, that is the way things happen, but not within the family. We never father babies from within the family. Again, we are talking tradition, but the old stories warn us that such babies are very weak and unlikely to survive. Mating occurs when we get together at the large tribal gatherings, with our southern cousins. And who mates with whom is often prearranged. Something the elder females in each family decide. Another of my responsibilities."

Sam reflected on this.

"I think I understand. Is that why everyone knows who their mother and grandmother is and was, but nobody ever mentions their father's name?"

"Yes, that is right. Well, sort of. It is just that fathers have very little to do with raising their babies. Everybody helps with catching fish for nursing mothers, but the youngsters they are helping feed are not their own. Their children are with the other families being fed by males who also are not the fathers. It is all mutual cooperation in the end."

"It sounds like it's well planned. I mean when or when not to have babies," Sam said.

"That's right," Grandma replied.

⁂

But not always, Grandma remembered painfully. *Not always*.

The desire to have children was strong, a desire that grew as a childless female grew. The social controls exercised by the elders battled with that natural instinct. Tradition and social rules usually won out, but, when they didn't, painful decisions were inevitable. Not that long ago, Grandma had been forced to make such a decision.

Charlotte was at least twenty-five. She had aided in several births and was a constant babysitter for these and other babies. But fish remained scarce and small over several years. The aunts again decided that it was best to wait another year before mating would be permitted. This decision was announced before the annual tribal gathering. It was also made known to all the other families, lest anyone get their hopes up.

Tribal gatherings could be chaotic. Grandma hated the idea of spying on youngsters and enforcing the decision. She just hoped that no rules would be broken.

Several months later, Grandma noticed that Charlotte was avoiding, not only her, but also the aunts. And Charlotte was participating more actively in the hunts, spending less time as a babysitter. Her increased appetite was hard to miss. Grandma finally overcame her reluctance to do a deep scan. Her suspicions were confirmed. It was obvious that Charlotte was pregnant.

Grandma was torn. The salmon run that year improved, Chinook migrating in large numbers later than usual. Had anyone predicted this change, she and the aunts probably would have allowed mating. On the other hand, Charlotte had broken a rule agreed upon by all, or at least by the aunts. Knowing how badly Charlotte wanted to be a mother, Grandma was caught between Charlotte's needs and the importance of respecting age-old tradition.

Grandma consulted first with her sister Molly, who tended to be more lenient regarding rule breaking. As expected, Molly counseled forgiveness, reminding her that Charlotte had acted responsibly for several years, despite her known desire to be a mother.

Grandma next spoke with the other aunts, including Charlotte's mother, Esther. Esther, too, was sympathetic towards Charlotte's situation, and almost begged Grandma to treat her daughter with compassion. Grandma anticipated this. It was as it should be, a mother's concern for her daughter, and a possible grandchild.

The other aunts were evenly divided, some noting the abundance of fish and the minimal pressure another mouth would put on the family. Others insisted that several other young females had given up breeding because of the restriction. Would it be fair to them now that opportunities to find a mate would be limited? And what about the need to follow the rules, to observe tradition?

Grandma did not consult with the younger females. Any who didn't resent Charlotte's behavior would likely sympathize with someone their own age. She also didn't bother the males. Caring for youngsters seldom crossed their minds. They helped, but clearly without enthusiasm. The exceptions were Michael and Frank. Michael was as good a caregiver as any of the younger females, tended to socialize more with the females than the males, and quickly disappeared at tribal gatherings when courtship and mating were foremost. Some of the females even referred to him, quietly, as "Aunt Michael." No problem there, thought Grandma. She'd take one Michael to a half dozen of the other males.

Especially Frank. Frank was totally useless when it came to helping with the youngsters. He begrudgingly hunted for salmon for nursing mothers, his attitude only too evident. Which probably made sense given he'd never been a father. At tribal gatherings, young females looking for mates avoided him completely, his reputation as ill-tempered and generally unpleasant preceding him everywhere.

With opinions equally divided, Grandma realized the decision would be hers. She told Molly she needed to be alone for a few hours, to seek the counsel of the ancestors. Quieting her mind, she projected her thoughts into the past, and listened.

But the waves were silent. They did not answer. She realized that her attempt to communicate was foolish. There was no reason for them to reply, because she knew what their answer would be. Adherence to tradition, respect for the old ways that had governed their behavior for countless generations, was beyond dispute.

The decision made, and her heart heavy, Grandma informed the aunts. The time to act was now, before the situation got more out of hand. Waiting for a late night when the sea was stormy and the noise of wind and waves would muffle sounds of argument or distress, she summoned three others. These included Molly and Esther, who had favored leaving Charlotte alone, and Frank's mother, Celia, who had predictably voiced adamant disapproval of Charlotte's flaunting of tradition.

The four approached Charlotte and asked her to swim toward shore with them. Charlotte refused at first, but Grandma made it clear that defiance was not an option. The five swam off a few hundred yards.

"Charlotte, this is hard for me, hard for all of us," Grandma began. She had decided this was not a time for recriminations or accusations. The act itself was sufficient punishment.

"We all understand how important this baby is to you..."

"No!" Charlotte shouted. "You can't! I won't let you!" The despair in her voice was clear to all.

"We are sorry, child. But we have no choice."

"Mother!" Charlotte implored of Esther. "Are you part of this?"

"Yes, my dear. I am," Esther whispered reluctantly.

"But why?" Charlotte gasped.

"It is best for everyone, child."

"Everyone but me," was Charlotte's choking reply.

And, knowing what was coming, she went limp at the surface.

The four elders took up positions alongside Charlotte, two on her left and two on her right. As a large wave broke over the group, they pressed their mouths against Charlotte's belly and gave a loud sonic blast, as loud a shout as they could. Then they were still, the aunts from exhaustion, and Charlotte from the realization of what had happened.

Grandma scanned Charlotte quickly and could see that the baby's heart was no longer beating. Grandma returned offshore slowly, Molly and Celia joining her. Esther and the distraught Charlotte were left alone, together.

Grandma had been silent for several minutes, clearly lost in thought. Sam assumed their conversation was over and was about to leave when she spoke.

"Sam, there is another thing you should know, related to the matter of who breeds with whom and when. If you have been paying attention to the rumors, you know that we will be joining a tribal gathering in two weeks. Many, if not most, of our close and distant relatives will be there. And you will be a major subject of interest. Your presence, and the scarcity of salmon, are among the reasons we are meeting not only with our southern relations but even with our northern cousins, which happens rarely. You will not know anyone outside the family, but pretty much everyone there will know who you are."

"I could just avoid it, couldn't I?" Sam asked, sensing an uncomfortable social situation. The idea of a mob scene put him on edge.

"No, that would be seen as rude. And really not necessary. Everyone will go out of their way to be polite, a longstanding rule of tribal gatherings. It is more of a celebration, and a time for all of us to learn about births and deaths, and who is finding abundant salmon and where. But there is something I need to warn, or advise, you about. And I am afraid I am going to have to ask a favor of you, something that may be difficult."

"Of course. Whatever it is, I'd be happy to do," said Sam.

"Let me explain before you say anything else. You will draw much interest and attention, including from young females looking for someone to father a child. You might be the most eligible unmated male there, because of your hunting prowess and lack of family ties to anybody else. Not to mention the allure of your exotic nature."

"If they knew the truth about what life as a captive meant, I wouldn't seem so exotic," Sam said.

"Be that as it may, I am asking you to not accept any of these advances. That will be difficult, and it may be an unfair request, but I have my reasons. Is this something you can promise me?"

Sam knew that tribal gatherings were also a time for couples to mate, but he really hadn't given it much thought. He was absorbed in learning the family's habits, and especially in the hunting. Finally, he answered.

"Well, I may not be quite as desirable as you seem to think I am, but I'm comfortable promising I will discourage any suitors, if that's what they should be called."

"Thank you, Sam. You may find it more difficult than you imagine. But I will trust you to keep your word," Grandma said.

CHAPTER 29

*I know this has no place in science...but could our
parameters on reality be set just a little too tight?*

ALEXANDRA MORTON, *Listening to Whales:
What the Orcas Have Taught Us*

Sam began paying more attention to group conversations; just about everyone was anticipating the unusually large, upcoming tribal gathering. One afternoon,
after a particularly successful hunt, he was resting and
enjoying a full belly. Several nearby females were talking
and laughing. Sam couldn't help but overhear. The subject
was sex, something increasingly on the minds of everyone,
especially now that the elder females had decided that
mating would be allowed. However, the females weren't
discussing whale sex but human sex.

"Did you ever wonder how the logriders make babies?" he
heard Camille, one of the younger females, ask. "I mean they're
always covered in so many layers of that thin skin stuff. It's like
it doesn't look like they even have the right parts to, uh...do it."

"Oh, I know a little something about their body parts,
or at least about the male logriders," a middle-aged matron
named Lillian said.

"Really?" came the surprised reply of several. Everyone
stopped and listened, slightly incredulous given Lillian's
tendency to exaggerate. But their silence encouraged her.

"Yes, really. I'll admit, it was a dead male logrider, one that I guess had drowned. He was lying on the bottom, and that skin they wear around their tail fins was all bunched down around the bottom of whatever their tails are. So, he was bare skin from his midpoint down to the bunched up outer skin. Anyway, his penis was exposed. It was tiny, I mean like no bigger than a baby herring. And it looked really soft. If that's what they use, their females are really getting the short end," she chuckled at her own joke.

This was more information than the group had to go on before. They pondered and discussed this new knowledge, after teasing Lillian for the detailed inspection she had obviously made.

Sam seldom paid much attention to these female gatherings. Their subject matters didn't interest him. Admittedly, he enjoyed watching Rose, but he did so at a distance. He tried to make it look like little more than a group scan that could easily be interpreted as trying to keep track of who was around and where they were headed. But her resemblance to Nan, even her way of speaking, was so strong that he couldn't help but be drawn to her. Nonetheless, to be caught lingering on her, knowing a longer scan would be sensed by its resulting warmth, would have been rude, not to mention embarrassing.

Despite his usual detachment from gossiping females, he couldn't help himself. He swam over and said, matter-of-factly, "I've watched them mate."

Everyone turned towards him. No one spoke, but it was obvious they were waiting for him to continue.

"When I was captive in the place where I lived with Nan, before she arrived, I saw a male and female mating, once."

The memory was strong, one of the strongest, a break from the routine. It involved his favorite female logrider, one he considered a caretaker rather than a captor. She was different from the others in many ways. She often came at night, when no one else was around. She would take off her false outer skin and slip into the water and swim alongside him, making vocalizations that were quiet, not shouts like the others. He scanned her freely. As he did, she would turn around in the water, kicking her hind fins slowly as she hung in the water, inviting his curiosity And she clearly enjoyed riding on his back. He could feel her real skin and sense the touch of her enlarged milk glands high on her chest.

This happened infrequently, but Sam enjoyed it. Her visits were a high point in his life.

Until one night.

"One female logrider treated me better than the others. She would swim with me at night, without her false skin," Sam said to the group. "That's how I learned she was female, because her vent was located on her belly where her two long tail fins met. As I've said before, where I was born, we called the logriders 'split-tails' because of the two long tail fins that help them stand up on land. That's also where the male's penis is located."

"That's right, now that I think of it," Lillian said.

"One full moon night, the female came with a male I'd never seen before. Perhaps he was her mate. She took off her false skin and slid into the water. He stood on the edge, looking at her. She called to him, and he finally he took off his outer skin and joined her. I wasn't especially happy to have this stranger in my pool, touching me. But I trusted the female. They both rode on my back, and I swam around the pool. They made loud noises that I interpreted as enjoyment. And I noticed his penis, which was very small, like you described. "

"Told you," said Lillian.

"Yes, but I think that was because your logrider was dead. When I stopped swimming, the female swam to the edge of the pool and lay down on her back on the hard land and waved a side fin at the male. He climbed onto the land and lay down on top of her, face down. She wrapped her tail fins around his back, and he moved up and down. I watched and could see his penis, which was much longer and straighter now, moving in and out of her vent, so I'm guessing that this was their mating. She started making short, loud excited sounds, noises I'd never heard before. They did this for maybe a minute. Then, suddenly, all the bright lights around the pool came on, and another male logrider came running out, shouting. This made them stop mating. They picked up their fake skins and pressed them against their bodies and ran away. I never saw her again."

Everyone was silent for a while. It was so hard for them to even imagine what Sam's captive surroundings had been, so it took a while to process the scene.

Finally, Lillian spoke up. "Maybe the salmon, or whatever it is they eat, hadn't been abundant, and they didn't have permission to mate. The other male was maybe an elder."

"Or maybe," it was Camille again, "maybe the other male was supposed to be her mate and he was jealous."

Everyone thought about this for a moment. Finally, Rose spoke.

"Or maybe, just maybe, the logriders have their own Uncle Franks, and he was just being a spoilsport."

This comment brought another round of knowing laughter, which dissolved into everyone offering their opinions on Uncle Frank.

Sam decided this was a good time to slip away.

CHAPTER 30

Sarcasm is the only truly unique human attribute.

ALBERT EINSTEIN

―――――

T he time for the traditional late-summer tribal gathering
finally arrived. The family moved north toward the traditional meeting place. Excitement was high. Keeping
the younger family members within the group required
frequent nagging and occasional threats. But it was, again,
tradition for the family to arrive together, even if this meant
swimming at an uncomfortably slow pace.

Grandma felt she was mentally prepared for the next
few days. Tradition drove every aspect of the annual gathering. Most of this was good, comfortable. The traditional
place where they converged had been agreed upon decades
earlier, after the Cove of Sorrows region was abandoned.
This newer place was actually better, geographically, lying
between the northern and southern clans.

The council of elder females wouldn't meet the first day,
so Grandma had a day to herself to see old friends and distant
relatives. At the back of her mind, though, was the phenomenon of Sam, whom she knew would be a subject of interest,
speculation, and even some conflict. He was the first total
stranger to be welcomed into the tribe. Grandma's break with
tradition was contentious. More so given she had requested
that Sam not mate with willing and eager young ladies.

Grandma's family arrived just as the other two southern clans could be heard in the distance. Soon, a great deal of jumping and splashing and shouting filled the waters. As the day progressed, northern families, some small, some large, joined, until the greetings became an uproar of shouts and splashes. Not long after that, several couples slipped off to be alone, at least for a short time.

Sam was tempted to stay close to Grandma, but she politely informed him that he would be best to not follow her, particularly when she was with the older females.

He kind of drifted off and was soon joined by Michael.

"Feeling a little overwhelmed?" Michael asked.

"Yeah, I guess so," Sam replied. He liked Michael, who had gone out of his way to make Sam feel welcome. Michael had even defused an occasional tense moment with humor when family members expressed their ambivalence over Sam's presence.

"This is all so new, on top of everything else that is so new. I don't remember ever being in a large crowd before."

"I wouldn't worry," Michael reassured him. "Folks will ask you questions. Some youngsters may even seem a little too curious, but they're all being watched by the elders. The last thing they want is to be shunted off to the naughty children's area with the infants and nursing moms and excluded from important traditional events."

"What about you, Michael?" asked Sam. "Don't you want to be a part of all the chaos?"

"To be honest," Michael replied, "I kind of like to just watch the proceedings. Much of the merriment doesn't interest me."

Sam remembered Grandma talking about Michael being a non-participant in the tribal activities, specifically finding a possible mate. Sam decided that mating was probably a topic he shouldn't bring up. Then Michael surprised him.

"Rumor has it Grandma has asked you to lay low, fend off the ladies. Is that true?"

"Right," Sam replied, glad that he had someone with whom he could confide. "I'm trusting in Grandma's wisdom. Actually, I'm grateful. I'm not sure what her reasons are, but, in truth, I'm not sure I'm ready to be a father again, not quite yet, even if the mother is from far away and our encounter is brief. I've caused Grandma enough trouble already and, if she says hold off, I'm only too happy to hold off."

"Good idea. Me, too, but for my own reasons."

That seemed to be all Michael wanted to share and Sam let it drop.

"Tell you what," Michael said, swimming ahead. "Let me introduce you to folks you should know, and others you might want to avoid."

Sam followed as Michael first took him to where the other two southern families were gathered. He made introductions, and Sam tried to connect body and fin shapes with names he had been hearing on and off. Bob and John, Andrea and Cindy. Family resemblances were strong, as were accents, and Sam greeted each and every one with the traditional "How fat are the salmon?", followed with "A pleasure to meet you," or some variant. Everybody was polite, although openly curious. Sam suspected Grandma had prepared them in advance. He did overhear a couple of comments about his size and, of course, his back fin.

He was about to suggest to Michael that he'd had enough when his host said, "Okay. Now it gets interesting. Time to meet the northerners."

"Do you mean the transients?" Sam said, astonishment clear in his voice.

"Oh, heavens no," Michael replied quickly, amusement clearly in his voice. "Those bloodthirsty, unintelligible, fin-dragging, seal eaters wouldn't come within miles of this gathering. Our numbers alone are enough to keep them away. Our northerners, two main groups, are distant relatives, salmon eaters all. Same language but with different dialects."

The first group of northern relatives spoke with a slight accent but were easy to understand. Gregor, Liam, Chelsea, Camilla. Sam was greeted with g'days, haloos, and top of the mornings. They were extremely polite. No intrusive comments or whispered asides. They made Sam feel comfortable.

"Very nice folks," he said to Michael. "Extremely polite."

"Yes, almost annoyingly so. Gets to be tiresome after a while. But the next bunch will more than make up for it."

Sam came alert. *Now what?*

They swam to where a large group was in animated conversation. From the distance, Sam couldn't understand what was being said. As he and Michael approached, a hush fell over the group.

"Greetings, everybody. I'd like you all to meet the notorious Sam."

Everybody started talking at once, interrupting one another.

Finally, Michael shouted at them, "Let's do it one at a time, alright?"

This silenced most of them, with some grumbling. Michael began the introductions, pointing out individuals as he did.

"Okay, Sam. Here's Amélie, and François, Dominique, Estelle, over there is Elise, Sebastien, Angélique, and last, but not least, Pierre."

"Pierre has much reason to be last," the female named Elise said, laughter in her voice.

Each, in turn, greeted Sam, although with some overlap. Their accent was certainly strange, and Sam had to concentrate to understand them. They soon started talking over one another, and Sam got lost.

Just then he sensed someone very close, almost touching.

"Hello, Samuelle," the female whom he thought was Elise, said softly. "You certainly are one big, handsome guy."

Sam was more than a little unnerved, by both her nearness and the blatantly seductive tone of her voice. He wasn't sure what to say, if anything.

"Ellie," another female called over. "Can't you see you're wasting your time? He's with Michael."

"No harm in trying, eh, Amélie? Really is a pity, no?." And she swam off slowly.

"What was that all about?" Sam asked Michael. "I don't understand."

"I guess they've been informed about my role as something like a chaperone," Michael answered.

"Ouch," Sam said. "Does that mean Grandma doesn't trust me to keep my promise? I'm not about to go against her wishes."

"Oh no, not for a moment," Michael said quickly. "Grandma trusts you thoroughly and told me so. She just doesn't trust this bunch. And clearly for good reason."

This seemed to mollify Sam.

"My head is so full of names and accents I can hardly think. Can we maybe call it a day with the introductions?"

"Yes, seems like a good idea," Michael answered. "Enough for—"

Michael was interrupted by a soft, familiar voice.

"Hey guys, Grandma sent me to let you know a hunting party is being organized. So, Sam's presence is strongly requested."

It was Rose. She had come up so silently that Sam almost jumped. Her mere presence always made him a little uncomfortable, clumsy feeling, like he was too big for his skin. They occasionally exchanged formal greetings but had never spent much time together, despite her being Grandma's daughter and was always somewhere nearby. Sam basically admired her from afar. She was anything but afar right now.

"Protecting her investment," Sam heard one of the females in the northern group comment, just loud enough to be overheard. The iciness in her voice was evident.

Michael jumped in quickly.

"Great! That's something Sam is good at, certainly much better than his dip into this social whirl. I'll leave you two to head back to the family."

"Wait," Sam implored. "I mean, okay, I guess."

The idea of swimming with Rose to where the family had remained frightened him no end. But Michael immediately took off in the opposite direction, leaving Sam to his own devices. An awkward silence followed.

Finally, Rose said, "Well, Sam. What do you think of this tribal gathering? It can be a little unnerving at first."

"I…uh…um," Sam stumbled over his words. He finally replied, "Yes, I think I'm suffering from information overload. Everyone is nice enough, but I'm just not used to crowds."

"You poor thing," Rose said with clear sincerity. "Michael is everybody's friend and sometimes forgets not everybody feels as comfortable around strangers. I hope folks were courteous."

"Oh, it's not that, or not *them*," Sam replied, relaxing slightly. "I really want to please Grandma and not embarrass her by saying or doing anything rude or contrary to tradition. I'm still learning so much."

"Don't worry," Rose answered. "It was Grandma who sent me to get you. She figured you'd suffered enough for one day, especially with that last bunch Michael subjected you to."

That Grandma had sent Rose, instead of one of the other males, struck Sam as odd. But who was he to question Grandma's motives? In fact, he realized he was very happy to be talking to Rose with no one else around. She certainly didn't seem uncomfortable around him, which loosened him up a bit. *But don't get up false hopes,* he told himself.

"Where is the hunting party heading?" he finally asked Rose.

"Follow me," she answered and swam off.

Sam couldn't have been happier, following her. It slowly dawned on him that childless Rose ought to be off somewhere with a potential father. It also dawned on him that this fact was something to be glad about. *But don't get up false hopes*, he told himself once more.

CHAPTER 31

The next day involved a lot less socializing and, to Sam's delight, a lot more hunting. Clearly, the promise of salmon was a prime factor in choosing these waters for the annual gathering. Salmon were abundant and the hunting was exceptional. Sam's ability to catch fish after fish brought him status among his new acquaintances. His size advantage gave him extraordinary speed and a sonic blast immobilized many an otherwise lost fish, which was quickly snapped up by a previously unsuccessful pursuer. Sam clearly enjoyed himself but remained modest throughout. His self-effacing attitude made his help that much easier to accept.

The gathering finally ended. Farewells and promises to meet again were exchanged. A few new couples reluctantly parted ways, joining their clans and families. Grandma swam alongside her sister.

"Well," Grandma asked. "What do you think?"

"I'm assuming you're asking about Sam," Molly replied.

"What else could I be asking about?" Grandma said.

"I could give you a long list of who was last seen with whom, or what outrages the northern belles committed, but you're probably concerned with more immediate issues."

"I have given up on them, or at least on their social mores," Grandma said. "Yes, I want your opinion on Sam's behavior, and whether we, or rather I, have gauged things correctly."

"Okay. Everything I saw and heard was positive," Molly said. "Admittedly he's a phenomenon, but it doesn't look like he embarrassed himself or you. On the contrary, his behavior was, if anything, admirable. A little socially awkward, but admirable."

"Good," Grandma said. "Then I take it we can proceed as we hoped."

"Why not? And the sooner the better."

"Sam, it is time you learned of a decision the aunts and I have made, concerning you," Grandma said with much solemnity.

Uh oh, Sam thought. *What did I do?* He wracked his brain trying to imagine what he might have said or whom he might have offended.

"I, uh, I'm sorry, Grandma. I tried to do and say what was expected. I hope this doesn't mean—"

"Oh no, Sam," Grandma stopped him. "You have done nothing wrong. In fact, just the opposite. I could not be happier with the way you behaved among all those strangers. I was afraid you might find it all a little overwhelming, but I, and my sisters, are very proud of your behavior. We received nothing but compliments, including from some who strongly questioned my judgment about bringing you into the family. You dispelled any doubts, even among the most tradition-bound elders. Everyone appreciates someone who contributes to hunting success and deflects compliments in the process. The only ones who showed any disappointment were a few young ladies who imagined themselves as the mother of your son."

Sam had forgotten about the incident with Elise, having been distracted by the enjoyment of hunting among appreciative company. He started to stammer something, uncomfortable with the topic of mating, but Grandma cut him off.

"It is the restraint you showed those hussies—not that I blame them for their interest—that has led us to a decision. You were not the only one whom we asked to refrain from mating."

"Oh, so that was what Michael was up to. Now I get it. I have to admit, he had me more than a little confused."

"What?" Grandma said. "Michael? Oh no, he's..." She seemed to be choosing her words carefully. "Never mind Michael. It is Rose I am talking about."

"Rose?"

"Yes, Sam. Rose. I know you admire her. You have tried to not make that known, but you are not very good at hiding your feelings. Rose has wanted to have a child for years, and this would have been her first real opportunity in a long while."

"You mean she didn't find a...uh...I mean...a mate?" Sam asked, surprised.

"No, she did not, not that there was a lack of willing fathers. I asked her to hold off, and she agreed. We, Rose and the aunts and I, wanted to watch your behavior."

Slowly, oh so slowly, Sam started putting it together.

"Does that mean that you want me and...you think I should...that we should?"

"Yes, exactly. Rose is ready, and you are ready, and you two like one another and—"

"But I, or we're...family. I thought we weren't allowed to—"

Grandma cut him off. "Sam, yes, you are part of the family. No one questions that anymore. But, at the same time, for the purposes of bearing children, you are not family. We do not know who your parents or ancestors were, but we know that you and Rose are not related in any way. Which means all traditional restrictions on mating are lifted."

Sam processed this.

"Okay, I guess I understand. I stopped thinking about my real family so many years ago. I'm so happy to be here with everyone, I guess it never occurred to me that, in important ways, I'm not really a member. But if you say it's okay, then I can live with that. But what does Rose think of this?"

"That you would even ask that question is just another reason why I am happy with my decision. Most males, given an opportunity to mate with as beautiful a young female as Rose, would not see past their penises."

For the second time in this conversation, Sam was embarrassed by the topic. As if sensing his discomfort, Grandma continued.

"The fact is, Sam, you like Rose and she likes you. With my consent and blessing, and with the approval of the aunts, you two should go off somewhere and get down to business."

And with an uncharacteristic show of frivolity, Grandma lifted her tail and brought it down just in front of Sam, sending a wall of water at him. And swam off.

Sam realized he was now alone. Or thought he was. A minute later, Rose swam up alongside him and slid gently along his side. Her intentions were clear, and Sam felt himself immediately aroused. If he had any hesitation, she made it clear with her words and her body language that she was a willing and eager partner. She moved slowly away from the group, Sam close behind.

Rudy had followed J Pod into British Columbia. Fortunately, the whales didn't seem to be in a particular hurry, some periodically leaping out of the water and crashing down in explosions of seawater. Occasionally, one or two younger animals, often the twins Mako and Cookie, would move out ahead of the group, but would soon be herded back, usually by Blackberry, one of the older males.

To his surprise, the K and L pods joined up with J Pod, amounting to the entire Southern Resident whale group, a real superpod, something he'd never before experienced. Which meant it would also be Makai's first superpod.

And then, to add to his surprise and delight, he saw a large group of orcas coming from the north. These would have to be northern residents—the A, G, and R clans—the salmon-eating orcas that frequented the waters of British Columbia. This had all the earmarks of a *super* superpod, if there was such a thing. He'd heard stories, but had never met anyone who had made detailed observations of such a gathering. This might even be worth writing up for publication.

CHAPTER 32

Buzz, buzz, buzz.

An alarm was going off. The Zodiac was climbing a wave, an impossible mountain of water, the jagged crest at the top shooting out like Hokusai's *Great Wave*, the climax scene from *The Perfect Storm*. The alarm must have been the outboard overheating. The boat's angle steepened as the white wave top launched out and over the crippled vessel. It started to flip over backward. *Buzz, buzz, buzz.*

Rudy awoke, shaken. The buzz was his cell phone, vibrating happily across the nightstand. He'd turned off the ringtone but had forgotten to silence the vibrate function. He tried to clear the recurring nightmare from his head, a nightmare he knew he shared with many boaters.

He picked up the phone and pushed a button.

"Uh, hello?"

"Rudy, I am going crazy staring at videos of pissant little fish doing nothing. I need a break. Some action."

"Cassie?" Rudy slurred. "Uh, what's up?"

"Please!" she implored. "You have to take me away from my video dungeon. I'm being held captive by sculpins. I need to see something bigger, something that moves, that behaves. I need to look at some whales."

"Oh. Hold on." Rudy sat up in bed. Time with Cassie was always more than pleasant, even though he had no intent of going out on the water again. The weather had turned to shit, even though it was summer. Yesterday had been just plain awful. Horrid weather, lack of animals, engine problems, more horrid weather. He had gotten home very late and drank a little too much to shake off the demons. No wonder he had had a nightmare. The clock on his phone said 7:23.

"It's Saturday, Cassie. Kind of early. Where are you?"

"In my office, since six this morning. And the little bastards haven't moved. Not last night, not yesterday. Not at all. They could be plastic dummies. I'm a zombie. Save me. Please. I'll owe you."

Cassie knew how to be in control, even when she sounded pathetically helpless.

"Uh, okay," Rudy finally answered. "The Zodiac is still hooked up to the Volvo. I guess I could make it to the boat ramp in Bellingham in an hour or so."

"Tell you what, Rudy," she cooed. "No need to drive all that way. How 'bout we meet at the ramp in Blaine. That's a lot closer for you."

"Right," Rudy replied, happy not to have to incur the wrath of every motorist on I-5 because he failed to go over forty-five m.p.h.

"That does make things easier for me. I'll meet you at the Blaine marina."

"Wonderful, Rudy. You're my knight in shining armor, or the aquatic equivalent. Let's go find some whales."

"Well, more realistically, let's *hope* to find some whales."

"Of course, Rudy. Anything's better than video hell. I'll be there as fast as my little Beetle will carry me. Thank you so much."

Cassie slipped her phone into her purse.

"Was that your whale-watching boyfriend again?" Heath asked.

"Damn. Busted," she answered, smiling.

"I think you're getting sweet, or at least soft, on him," Heath said.

"I have to admit, he's growing on me. Quite a bit. Do you think he believed me?"

Cassie started gathering things together and headed for the door.

"Yeah, you were pretty convincing," Heath said. "Are you going out in his little boat wearing that?"

"At least initially. I have to keep up appearances. Although he's treating me less and less like an object, more like a friend actually."

"That's good to hear. But if you're going to maintain the narrative, you shouldn't leave home without this."

Heath picked up Cassie's wedding band from an abalone shell filled with beach glass and held it for Cassie to see.

"Oops. I forgot. Thanks, Heath. You're a sweetie."

The Zodiac was tied up to the dock, just behind the salmon-fishing boat, *Clarabelle*. Rudy sat on the *Clarabelle's* stern, listening to the crewmen complain about how little they were getting for the fish they weren't catching.

"We're barely landing enough to meet fuel costs." It was the crewmember named Curly. "It's hard to ignore that fact, sorta like a half-picked scab."

Just then Cheez gave a quick bark. Rudy heard the high-pitched whine of a VW entering the cramped parking area that accommodated too few cars on the Blaine docks. Earlier, he had barely found space for his car and trailer. It promised to be a sunny, relatively warm day, and the locals were clearly taking advantage of the break in the weather.

Cassie's VW circled the lot twice, looking in vain for a parking space. The only vacant spot was right at the head of the dock, looking down on the *Clarabelle*, and had a bright red concrete bumper with "RESERVED" printed in black twice across the top. Cassie pulled in.

"Uh oh," Curly said, getting up from his perch on the piled netting on the stern. "That's Cap'n Lewmar's space."

He tossed his half-smoked cigarette overboard and started climbing the ladder to the parking lot.

Curly got to the top just as Cassie got out of her car. He took a couple of forceful steps and started to shout.

"Hey! You can't park th—"

Curly stopped mid-sentence. Cassie had on a pair of tight blue jeans and a very thin white blouse. She had a smile on her face and a bounce to her step. A pink duffle was slung over one shoulder. Cheez gave a quick bark.

"Hi, Rudy," she shouted. "Sorry I'm late."

Curly just stood there staring. He turned around, appearing sheepish, and looked down at Rudy.

"Is *she* with you?"

Rudy hadn't mentioned he was expecting female companionship. The conversation on the fishing boat had quickly turned to fishing. He smiled up at Curly.

"Yeah, that's my first mate today. Or second I guess, if you count Cheez."

The other crew members chuckled, and one said, "I guess sometimes ol' Cap'n Lewmar gets outranked."

Curly joined his crew and all stared in rapt attention as Cassie climbed down the ladder.

"Hi, fellas," she said with a wave. "Are we ready to go, Rudy?"

"Uh, yes. The outboard's all warmed up."

Cassie and Cheez took up their positions in the Zodiac. As Rudy pulled away from the dock, Cassie reached down for her pink duffle, unzipped it, and took out a very bulky hooded sweatshirt and pulled it over her head.

"Damn," whispered Rudy.

Cassie gave him a very big, knowing grin.

"Sorry, Rudy. I don't want to distract you from finding us some whales."

Rudy slowed outside the harbor, removed his handheld radio from the old green ammo box and started listening for traffic from the whale-watching boats. Things were calm and sunny. Nothing like the previous day. The radio was quiet.

"Guess we'll have to find our own," Rudy said. "I heard a report that L Pod passed by here heading north two days ago. Maybe we'll get lucky and catch them coming back."

"Hey, Rudy," Cassie shouted over the whine of the engine. "Doesn't it seem like there's a lot of wood in the water today? Big stuff, like logs."

"Yeah," Rudy answered. "Right. We just had a really big spring tide. It washed a lot of wood and other crap off the beaches and is redistributing it now. We need to watch for wood while we're watching for whales. One log can ruin your whole day."

Cassie sat facing forward, attentive. Cheez was in his usual place, front paws on the bow tube, scanning back and forth, but mostly keeping his nose up, sniffing the breeze.

"Do you think Cheez can smell whales?" Cassie asked.

"I don't doubt it," Rudy replied. "The UDub researchers have trained dogs to smell whale poop floating at the surface. They then scoop it up to do dietary analyses. That way they can study whales without ever seeing one. Folks on the whale-watching boats take as many pictures of the poop-sniffing dogs as they do of the whales."

"Have you trained Cheez to do that?" Cassie asked. "I think he's as smart as any poop-sniffing pup."

"In reality, I haven't trained Cheez to do anything. He figures things out for himself. Once he realized we were looking for whales, he came up with a half dozen ways of finding them. Smell, sight, sound, telepathy, your guess is as good as mine. All I know is he sees them long before I do. And he also figured out that Makai was special, so he gives two barks when he sees him."

Cassie gave the pup a scratch behind the ears. Cheez wagged his tail a couple times, then reassumed his alert, forward-facing position.

After a couple of false alarms by Cassie that turned out to be jumping salmon, Rudy turned back around and went north, in hopes of a chance encounter.

Ten minutes later, Cheez gave a sharp bark. He was looking straight ahead.

"I don't see anything," Cassie said.

"There must be something there," Rudy answered. "Cheez seldom gets fooled by jumping fish, or anything else for that matter."

Rudy accelerated in the direction that Cheez was facing. Cheez then gave two quick barks and started wagging his tail vigorously.

"Awright!" Rudy shouted. "He thinks he sees Makai."

"Really?" Cassie said excitedly. "Where?"

"Yes! There he is, straight ahead. Tallest dorsal fin in the Salish Sea," Rudy said with undisguised pride.

He picked up speed. Cheez barked twice again.

They approached the whale, slowed, and turned on a parallel course about a hundred feet away.

"Does he think we're chasing him?" Cassie asked.

"No, he'd move off or dive if he were avoiding us. And I'm pretty sure he recognizes this boat, and probably me and Cheez. If we were bothering him, he'd spyhop or breach or lobtail and do all the things that annoyed whales do when they're being hounded by boats. Makai doesn't do those things around us, even if other members of his group do. I know this whale and he knows me."

Sam heard the log approaching from behind. His first reaction was to avoid it, but he wanted to check out the area around the mouth of the Fat Salmon River on the chance of intercepting a school of spawning Chinook. And the log sounded familiar, its buzz irregular. He just kept moving.

The log pulled up alongside him, to his right. He rolled to his left to get a look at the logriders. Yes, it was Uncle Morris and the four-legged seal-like animal that he knew well. There was a female with him also; something about her was familiar. Probably not. His family encountered so many logriders and so many looked alike. But he could keep hunting because these logriders could be trusted.

He continued to scan for fish systematically, ahead, left, right, below. Ahead, left. Wait. Something way up ahead caught his attention, at the surface. Just at the range of detectability, between four and five hundred feet ahead. Too big to be a fish but worth investigating.

GENE HELFMAN

Rudy, Cassie, and Cheez watched the big whale moving smoothly alongside them not fifty feet away, breathing occasionally, unhurried. All three were spellbound.

Suddenly, the orca accelerated, then stopped perhaps a hundred yards ahead. Rudy gunned the engine to catch up.

The whale spyhopped, slapped his tail down and then breached, landing back in the water with a tremendous splash. Then he swam off to the left.

Cassie turned around to face Rudy.

"I know this whale and he knows me, eh?" she shouted above the engine noise.

"First time he's done that around us," Rudy answered, shaking his head. *Just plain weird.*

Rudy was looking at the whale and didn't see the log directly in their path. The speeding rubber boat collided with the massive piece of wood, or rather the outboard collided with it. The boat stopped instantly, killing the engine.

Rudy was holding on to the throttle arm and so was able to just keep his balance. Cassie and Cheez weren't holding on to anything and were launched high into the air. They both landed about fifteen feet in front of the boat in a tangle of arms, legs, fur, and a tail.

"Are you okay?" Rudy shouted when he saw them surface.

Cassie was spluttering, Cheez was dog-paddling in circles around her.

"I'm fine," Cassie shouted back, laughing. "I bet that leap was your whale trying to warn you about the log. Sorry I didn't see it."

Rudy processed the idea. Maybe she was right. Then another thought occurred to him. He wasn't worried about Cassie in the water. She could swim, once she shed her bulky sweatshirt. Orcas, especially resident orcas, didn't eat people. But what about dogs? Cheez paddling around at the surface could be considered an easy meal. Makai might live with resident animals, but his dietary history was much more complex. Rudy felt a chill run through him.

To worry him even more, the whale turned toward the two in the water, spyhopped momentarily, then dove. Nothing happened for about ten seconds. Then Makai burst out of the water.

Rudy looked to see if Cheez was in his mouth. The whale's mouth was empty.

Rudy looked again and gasped.

Cheez and Cassie sat atop the whale. Not just *on* it, but *riding* it. Cassie straddled the whale's back, just behind the dorsal fin, arms wrapped around it. Cheez was planted with all four paws just in front of the fin, wagging his tail and barking constantly.

Makai swam away for a few seconds, then turned and headed back toward the boat and stopped just alongside. Rudy could hear him vocalizing excitedly. Giving the fin a final hug, Cassie reluctantly stepped off the whale's back and into the boat. Cheez followed and shook the water off.

Rudy was speechless. He stared at Cassie, at Cheez, at Makai, then back at Cassie.

Cassie was grinning, then laughing.

"Ariel, the Marineworld mermaid," Rudy said, the truth dawning on him. It was more of a statement than a question.

Cassie smiled.

"And you"—he pointed at the dog—"must be Genius."

Cheez gave another shake, spraying water all around.

Rudy stammered, "I think I'm owed an explanation from you two, or three. Let's start with you, Cassie."

"It's a long story, Rudy. I guess I haven't told you everything about my previous life, before I decided to watch grunties for a living."

"Damn straight you haven't, Cassandra Flanagan. Assuming that is your real name."

He looked at Cheez. "And we'll get to you in a minute." Cheez was still wagging his tail. If he felt guilty about anything, it wasn't obvious.

Rudy noticed that Makai was swimming around the boat. Cassie finally put her fingers in her mouth, gave a shrill whistle, and waved her right hand in a goodbye gesture. Makai leapt out of the water once more, drenching them all. He then turned and headed north.

"Okay, let's hear it," Rudy said firmly.

"Don't you think you should do something about the outboard first?" Cassie said. "We're a long way from shore, and I'm getting kind of cold."

"I guess you're right. You're not getting off the hook though."

Rudy reached down for the large dry-bag he always carried. He took out a towel, a long-sleeved woolen sweater, and a pair of sweatpants and handed them to Cassie.

"Turn around, Dr. Laguna. A woman deserves privacy."

"Forget it, Ms. Flanagan. It's my boat."

"As you wish, Captain. But what about the engine?"

"Oh, right. Sorry."

Rudy turned around and tilted the engine up. One of the three blades of the prop was missing, sheared off at its base.

"I'm afraid it's going to be a slow and ragged ride home. Assuming the engine starts."

It did, on the third try. Rudy put it in gear, and the boat moved haltingly through the water, vibrating hard.

"Looks like we have lots of time for explanations," Rudy said, as he steered around the log. "Let's start now."

CHAPTER 33

"When I was a whale trainer at Marineworld, I had a boyfriend. Adam. He was always saying he wanted to see where I worked. I decided that could be fun. I'd introduce him to Makai, the other man in my life. And do it at night when we could be alone. Just the three of us."

"A multi-species *ménage* à *trois*," Rudy offered.

"Yes," Cassie replied. "Probably a little more than it should have been. I was in the habit of making nighttime visits to Makai and swimming with him, in the nude, alone. So, I kind of tricked Adam into joining us. Turns out Adam was a bit of a wuss and took more than a little coaxing, seemed fixated on how big Makai's teeth were, what was left of them."

"Not unreasonable," Rudy said.

"Well," Cassie continued. "One thing led to another, and we eventually wound up riding on Makai's back, both naked, me hugging Makai's dorsal fin, Adam behind me, arms wrapped around me, holding on to…" She hesitated.

"I think I get the picture," Rudy said.

"Exactly. Well, between Adam squeezing me and Makai moving up and down between my legs, I kind of lost it. I left the pool and Adam didn't need an invitation. I remember glancing over at Makai, who was spyhopping and watching us, and I was thinking, 'If I can't have you, Makai, this is the next best thing.'

And then all hell broke loose."

"It was that good, eh," Rudy said.

"Oh no. Quite the opposite. At that moment, all the lights in the arena came on, and this beefy white guy in a rent-a-cop uniform came running out, shouting. Adam jumped up just as he was coming. I got up and grabbed my clothes to cover myself.

"'It's okay,' I shouted. 'I work here.'

"I'd never seen the guy before," she said. "It turned out the regular night watchman had called in sick, and they brought in a substitute. I tried to calm him down and told him he didn't have to call anyone. He said he had already called the cops and the assistant director, which meant he had been watching us for a while, the pervert. We got dressed, and he hustled us into a storage area and we waited.

"When the police arrived, I explained there had been a misunderstanding, and I was authorized to be at the facility after hours. The rent-a-cop was pretty explicit about what we were doing, more explicit than necessary. The police were mostly amused and kept eyeing me pretty lasciviously. I finally convinced them that everything was my fault, that Adam had come with me because I told him I could bring guests. They figured no laws had been broken and said they'd leave it up to the Marineworld officials if any charges were to be pressed. They emphasized the 'pressed' part a little too enthusiastically. I was in no position to complain."

"So, you got off, er, I mean things were okay?" Rudy asked.

"Hardly. I hadn't been getting along with the admin people for weeks. I was constantly complaining about the conditions the animals, especially Makai, were being kept in. They saw this as an opportunity to get rid of me and fired me on the spot. They said there were dozens of qualified people who wanted my job, people who would be less trouble. *Adios.*"

"Wow! So that was it, just like that?" Rudy asked.

"Well, not exactly. Even though we had all signed something like a non-disclosure agreement, I was more than a little pissed. I waited a while and then contacted a reporter from the *L.A. Times*, a guy who had written a puff piece about the show but whom I knew was disturbed about keeping wild animals in captivity to entertain the public."

Rudy said, "When I was researching Makai's history, I remember coming across an old *L.A. Times* article. It had a picture of a young woman in a tight-fitting wetsuit—quite attractive even in black and white—and a dog riding on top of Makai as part of the show. The article said something about Makai favoring a particular female trainer named Ariel."

"Right. We all had stage names. I was Ariel, very Disney-like. Cheez here was just a pup called Genius, only pronounced with a long "E", like Geeeneus. The fake name thing was another reason the trainers and the Marineworld officials didn't get along. We felt it demeaned us and the animals. You don't happen to still have the article by any chance?"

"Yes, I kept it, along with several other less happy stories about Makai's checkered past."

"Oh!" Cassie brightened. "I'd love to see it. I remember when that story came out, but I stupidly didn't keep a copy. I threw it out along with all the other Marineworld stuff I had when I got fired. I wasn't particularly proud of my role in Makai being forced to perform for food. I loved him and interacted with him whenever I could, including off hours."

"Sounds like you had more than a crush on our big slippery friend."

"I wasn't the only one. Most of the trainers, the ones who stuck around despite the battles with the administration, became very attached to the animals. How could you not?"

"I've read that was common," Rudy said. "That even the people who were capturing orcas for the aquarium trade would connect with them, bond with them, very quickly. Some even released animals that they had been paid to catch and deliver, rather than turn them into performing captives. Especially after it became known that whales were dying quickly in captivity."

"The worst part of being fired from Marineworld," Cassie said, "was being separated from Makai. I *had* to see him, so I'd go to shows in disguise. I'd sit at the top of the bleachers, wearing these big sunglasses so people couldn't see me crying. I'm sure Makai knew I was there. He'd stay close to the side of the pool where I was, ignoring the trainers. That was part of what they called his 'misbehavior.'"

"And the *L. A. Times* reporter wrote a much less flattering article, which I also read," Rudy said. "It mentioned a disgruntled employee as the source. It was pretty damning."

"That could have been any number of trainers, so they couldn't prove it was me. I think the second *Times* article was the beginning of the end for Makai's incarceration at Marineworld. I hoped things would improve when they brought in a female companion for him, which happened after I got fired. They had a baby, but the suits sold it off, his mate died, and Makai reverted to his old ways and worse. So, they decided to get rid of him, too, another troublesome employee. When they sold him to that horrible marine park in Mexico, I was so heartbroken I moved away. And decided to study animal behavior. I couldn't break into the marine mammal group. I guess I was blackballed because of my dismissal from Marineworld. Fish were at least marine, if not quite as lovable and smart as whales."

Rudy interrupted her. "Hold on just a minute. If I'm hearing all this correctly, your willingness to meet with me after my talk at Western, and your bringing me on as an 'advisor' for your research, wasn't pure happenstance. It was a ploy to get back to your whale. You had this planned all along, didn't you?"

"Well, you didn't exactly make it difficult, Rudy."

Rudy acted indignant but admitted to himself he was really grateful for Cassie's subterfuge. If anything, he admired her even more for her planning and how things had worked out—were working out—between them. But did Cassie feel the same, or was it really only about the whale?

The ride back to the harbor was slow and quiet, Rudy not wanting to stress the outboard. Another thought sprang into his mind. He put the engine in neutral.

"Please don't tell me you planted Cheez, I mean Geeeneus, as an advance man in your scheme."

"Oh no," Cassie said. "My old contacts at Marineworld told me he just disappeared one day, after I was fired, when someone left a gate open. I was as surprised to find him with you as he was to find me. But it seemed karmic, like things were falling into place. Heaven knows where he's been and with whom between then and now. And how many names he's been given."

Mollified, Rudy recounted to Cassie how he met Cheez, who was then Jesus. They both had a good laugh. The dog had resumed his position up front, looking for whales.

They finally arrived back at Blaine Harbor, the dinghy limping toward the dock. Rudy noticed several of the *Clarabelle's* crew looking their way and smiling. They couldn't help but see that Cassie was wearing a different sweater and pants than the ones she'd left in. One of them glanced at his watch and shook his head side-to-side, giving Rudy a naughty boy nod. *If they only knew.*

CHAPTER 34

The next time, Rudy invited Cassie to go look for whales. In the weeks since Cassie's past was revealed, they had spoken on the phone several times. Rudy sensed a sea change in their relationship. He realized he actually thought about it as their *relationship*. Some barrier had vanished. Their conversations were more honest, comfortable, the topics expanded beyond whales and grunt sculpins. Rudy just wanted to see her again. To his relief, she said yes.

They motored out of the harbor and headed south, the outboard, with its new propeller, working smoothly. The day was as perfect as could be expected. Sunny, maybe in the sixties, almost warm, a very light breeze. The water glassy.

"Some whales were seen yesterday a couple miles south of here," Rudy said, "so maybe they're hanging around. Or at least we can hope." They continued slowly south, seeing nothing. Then Cheez, forelegs on the bow tube, gave his signal short bark. He was looking off to the right. At first, Rudy didn't see anything, but then a distinctive splash caught his eye.

It clearly wasn't a whale. It splashed again. Something was moving very fast across the surface, right to left, a couple hundred yards away. Then he saw the whales, some distance behind, blowing and swimming fast.

"Hold on!" he shouted and gunned the engine in the direction of the commotion.

"We're in luck, Cassie," he shouted over the engine noise. "I think we've got some transient orcas—Bigg's killer whales— chasing a harbor seal."

It was pretty obvious what was happening. A harbor seal was swimming for its life, four orcas in hot pursuit. About a hundred yards away, Rudy cut the engine and drifted. This was too good to be true.

Or was until the seal saw the dinghy. It made a sharp left turn and headed right for them. It didn't stop until it ran into the dinghy with a pronounced bump.

"Oh shit!" Rudy shouted. He knew what the seal would likely do next. Rudy grabbed an oar, stood up and jabbed at the seal, trying to push it away. The seal dodged the oar and tried to leap up into the dinghy. Rudy pushed it again. The seal bit the oar, pulling it out of Rudy's hands and tossing it aside.

With minimal effort, the seal leapt into the dinghy next to Rudy and snapped at him. Rudy scrambled towards the bow. Cassie didn't need to be told to move.

Cheez barked once when the seal snapped at Rudy, then seemed to think better of it.

And there they sat. Rudy, Cassie, and Cheez crowded together in the bow, as far as possible from the seal in the stern, nine feet away, next to the sputtering outboard motor.

"What's next, Rudy?" Cassie said. "Do you think they'll go away?" Her voice showed interest, not concern.

"Maybe. Probably not. But I'm pretty sure we're okay. The whales are interested in the seal, not us. Or at least that's what all the books say. Your life vest's nice and tight, right? Just in case."

Rudy was contemplating the possibility of the whales, all twice the size of the dinghy, upending them to dislodge the seal, like it was on an ice floe.

But nothing happened. Instead, the whales moved slowly back and forth, about fifty feet behind the boat.

The seal watched them.

Then the whales started circling the boat. Four large transients, led by a male with a very tall dorsal fin.

"What do you think they're doing?" Cassie asked.

"My guess, and it's only a guess, is they're assessing the situation and deciding on a course of action."

"And that might be?" she asked.

"Well," Rudy hesitated. "They clearly know the seal is in the boat, and they clearly want to eat it. I guess the main question is how to get it out of the boat and into the water."

"Hopefully just the seal," Cassie offered.

Rudy wasn't really worried about being eaten along with the seal. Orcas, residents or transients, just didn't attack people, ignoring a non-fatal incident involving a surfer off Big Sur. It was one of the ongoing mysteries about these animals. Still, the prospect of being dumped in the cold water was less than enticing, and once again he wasn't sure how the whales would react to Cheez. *Did dogs have the same immunity as people?*

Cassie must have read his mind. "I don't think we're in danger. But what about Cheez?"

All four occupants of the boat swiveled around as the whales continued to circle, getting progressively closer to the boat, one following another, the big male still in the lead. Soon they were bumping up against the idling motor as they passed behind, the seal clearly tracking their movement.

As the third orca bumped the motor, the seal leaned out and bit it on the dorsal fin.

The orcas dove.

"Oh shit," Rudy whispered. *That's going to piss them off for real. Now what? Would that act of stupidity convince the whales to overturn them?*

Rudy was fascinated, his scientific curiosity overcoming any fear. He had never really spent much time watching transient orcas, having focused on their salmon-eating resident relatives. This was a whole new data entry, maybe even a publishable note.

The whales remained out of sight.

"Have they gone away?" Cassie asked. She almost sounded disappointed.

"I don't know," Rudy answered.

But the whales hadn't gone away. About thirty seconds later, they appeared again, circling from a distance, blowing calmly. All four, one after another in a line, except now the big male was at the end instead of leading.

Again, the whales tightened the circle, getting closer to the boat with each circuit. And, again, they began bumping up against the motor, just like before.

And just like before, the seal leaned over to bite the third whale in the line. But as it did, the fourth whale, the male, leapt up and grabbed the seal's head and yanked it into the water.

What followed was as much a celebration as an attack, as the whales shredded the seal with shakes and tail splashes. At one point, the seal was catapulted high into the air, its limp body turning somersaults before landing. Soon the water around the dinghy was stained red with seal blood.

The last thing Rudy and Cassie saw was the large male orca with the seal in its mouth, swimming off, the other three whales swimming alongside, occasionally leaping from the water and landing sideways, creating huge fountains of spray.

"I'll be damned," Rudy said aloud. "That was fucking fantastic!"

He turned to Cassie. She had a huge grin on her face.

She put her arms around him and whispered in his ear.

"Yes, fucking fantastic," she repeated. "Thank you, Rudy."

PART FOUR

CHAPTER 35

The possibilities multiply exponentially when you consider projection of three-dimensional images between whales.

ALEXANDRA MORTON,

Listening to Whales: What the Orcas Have Taught Us

The year since Grandma announced Rose's pregnancy dragged for Sam. His delight at the prospect of being a father, as part of the family, was a wonderful feeling. But having experienced Nan's difficulty in childbirth, and then to have their child taken away and Nan's resulting death, all left an indelible scar. He was solicitous of Rose to the point of annoyance, constantly asking how she felt, asking Grandma about the baby's growth (he was forbidden from scanning her himself), spending time just swimming with Rose when he was supposed to be off hunting. This all added up to a growing problem within the family because they were offshore in the open Pacific and salmon were more spread out, harder to locate than during the summer. Greater effort was required to find enough food to feed the family.

Finally, one day in late autumn, with the baby due soon, Grandma took him aside.

"Sam. It is wonderful that you are excited about being a father. And it is wonderful that you enjoy being with Rose, as counter to tradition as that may be. But you are taking it too far. Both Rose and your child are fine. Everything is perfectly normal. When the time comes for the child to arrive, we will make sure you know. It may still be three months away, and your time would be better spent leading hunting parties and using your fish-catching skills to everyone's advantage. Not just Rose's."

Sam could tell by the tone of her voice that, in her own gentle way, she was laying down the law.

"I have been hearing a lot of whispering, sometimes louder than whispering," said Sam. "I guess my lack of upbringing in a family shows. If you're sure that Rose is okay and our baby is okay, I guess I'll try to spend less time with them."

It was as much a question as a statement.

"Trust me, Sam. They are just fine. I will make sure you are the first to know if there is any change. You have my word."

"Enough said," Sam replied.

He would try. Really.

They were out in the open ocean, headed north toward a winter feeding area. Grandma encouraged Sam to roam ahead as far as he liked, as much to keep him occupied as to find fish, although both were useful.

Sam was absentmindedly scanning, mostly diving deep to where big salmon, and other fish, were more likely to swim. Sam never lacked for food because he was much less particular about what he ate. Not just salmon other than Chinook, but also bottom fish. Lingcod, rockfish, wolf eels—*slippery buggers*—sablefish, and an occasional squid.

Which also meant that, when he caught a big Chinook, he was only too happy to bring it back to the group. He always offered it first to Rose, but she rebuffed such special treatment. It could only lead to resentment by other, pregnant mothers. She always thanked him and said he had already given her more than enough for both her and their growing baby.

When Sam surfaced to breathe, he made a cursory scan of the open, mostly vacant, expanses. But something in the distance, a weak reflected sound, caught his attention. Something large and vaguely familiar. Big enough to be a whale, but not.

He scanned intently and was able to make out an outline and movement. Definitely not a whale, as it was swimming with a side-to-side motion, not up and down. It was very big, swimming at the surface, so part of the back and tail fin were out of the water. Then it slipped slowly below, and he got a complete view.

White shark! It had to be. He remembered how Nan had told him the only things the family feared were the transients and white sharks. Transients would attack and kill a lone family member. But white sharks were voracious predators with exceptional teeth capable of tearing flesh from bone. While the family normally avoided transients and fled rather than confront them, white sharks were to be eliminated if possible. They posed a threat, especially to youngsters, but also to pregnant mothers who swam more slowly because of their swollen bellies. Mothers like Rose.

Sam tried to recall the details of the sound image Nan had projected of a white shark. She had only seen one once, and it was smaller, maybe a third the size of the animal Sam now encountered. There was no question in his mind what it was; the outline was identical. Nan had emphasized the conical snout and especially the equal size of the top and bottom lobes of the tail. Nan was uncertain how big white sharks got, but she'd heard stories of white sharks half as long as Sam. But this animal was much larger, bigger than he was. Was Nan's information incomplete? Nan said that white sharks could be killed by ramming their midsection repeatedly, something possible because white sharks could be outmaneuvered. But was this enemy too large for Sam to deal with alone?

He decided to alert the others and get help.

Swimming as fast as he could, he found the family a few minutes later. Breathless, he located Grandma.

"White shark!" he shouted. "There's a huge white shark headed this way."

His shout immediately drew a crowd.

Grandma asked, "Sam, are you sure? We are far north of where white sharks forage, especially this time of the year. Salmon sharks occur here and look a lot like white sharks. But they are small and eat the same things we do, mostly salmon."

"Oh no," Sam said. "This was much bigger. As big as I am!"

"Nonsense." It was Frank. "What does someone who spent his life in a small pool know about large sharks that roam the open ocean?"

Without thinking, Sam said, "It looked like this."

And he projected a sound scan of the shark he had seen.

Everyone went silent. In keeping with Grandma's request, Sam had not demonstrated his ability to project sound images. But this was an emergency. Sam had to convince them of the danger only minutes away. He wasn't sure if the group's silence was because of their astonishment at the size of the white shark, or their amazement at Sam's sound image, an ability they only knew about through legend.

Finally, Mitchie spoke up.

"Hey, Uncle Sam. Would you do that again, please? I only got a brief glimpse and—"

"Mitchell! Don't you dare!"

It was Molly, Mitchie's mother. Something in her voice made Sam hesitate, but only for a moment. He figured that he had to do a better job to convince them. He wracked his brain for the details of what he had detected briefly. He projected the image again, only this time in more detail and at larger size.

At first, he heard some chuckling. But then it got louder, and it was clearly laughter. Soon it swept through the group.

It was Frank, of course, who made things clear.

"Giant white shark indeed. I guess we should all turn tail and run from a plankton-eating basking shark. Maybe it's after our poop." At which point Frank left the group as noisily as was possible.

"A basking shark?" asked Sam. "What's a basking shark?"

"It is okay, Sam," Grandma said. "Your mistake is understandable. Basking sharks look very similar in outline to white sharks. But they are much bigger and, most importantly, they do not have any teeth. They just swim through the water with their mouths open and sweep up shrimp and little fish, nothing bigger than an inch or two. They're perfectly harmless."

"Perfectly harmless" Sam repeated quietly, as he sensed the group breaking up and swimming away, murmuring to one another. "Oh."

"Hey, it's okay big fella." It was Michael. "Just another lesson from the big bad world. Take me to where you found this shark, and I'll point out how they differ from white sharks. Besides their size and lack of teeth."

Sam reluctantly turned around and swam slowly back the way he had come, Michael by his side. He sensed someone else behind them. It was Eddie and Mitchie, chatting excitedly.

"Michael, Sam! Can we come too? We've never seen a real basking shark, only heard about them."

Sam didn't answer. He was sufficiently humiliated, and now he had an audience.

The basking shark hadn't gone very far. It was swimming slowly at the surface, its mouth wide open, its giant tail sweeping slowly back and forth. The four whales approached from the side.

"Okay, Sam. See the snout?" Michael said, bouncing a scan off the shark. "It's got a big bump at the end, over the mouth. The mouth is open like a big circle, and there aren't any teeth. White sharks don't usually swim with their mouths open, except when they're biting something. And you can't mistake the teeth. Your sound image—hey, that was amazing—was clear enough that we could all see your shark didn't have teeth."

"Right. No teeth," said Sam, sheepishly.

"Also, look at the five big slices on its side, between the head and the side fins. Water and critters go in that huge mouth and water comes out those side slices. White sharks and other sharks have those side slices but they're much, much smaller."

"Got it," said Sam, trying to be appreciative. "Big side slices. Right."

The shark seemed to be paying them no attention whatsoever. It just kept moving slowly through the water with its mouth agape, oblivious to the four whales that were jockeying for position around it.

"Grandma says these guys used to be really common when she was little," Michael added, now in full lecture mode. "But it's pretty unusual to see one. She blames it on the logriders but admits she doesn't have proof. This is only the second one I've seen. A real treat."

Eddie and Mitchie quickly grew bored with the lumbering beast and Michael's discourse. They started jumping over the shark, getting closer and closer. Then Mitchie misjudged his leap and slid over its back.

"Ouch!" he cried.

Sam gave a quick scan and could see a series of oozing tears along Mitchie's side.

"Oh, yes. One other thing about basking sharks," Michael added, clearly amused. "They're kinda prickly. Their skin is full of sharp spines, like a log covered in barnacles. Not a good idea to brush up against one."

Mitchie took off for the family, complaining loudly, blood streaming from his wounds.

"Good thing for him there *aren't* any white sharks around," Michael said. "Nothing excites them more than the smell of our blood in the water."

CHAPTER 36

T he baby finally came in midwinter. It happened on the stormiest night Sam had ever experienced. Towering waves crashed over the whales from several directions. The wind howled, throwing stinging spray at them, so everyone minimized time at the surface, taking quick breaths before heading down out of the turbulence. Sam, unaccustomed to such a chaotic sea and anxious because of Rose's clear discomfort, choked several times as waves crashed over him when he tried to breathe.

Grandma grew impatient.

"Sam, we know what to do. There is no reason for alarm. Most babies are born in winter, offshore, away from sharks. This is nothing new, and you are only in the way. Please leave us alone."

Chastened, but reluctant to leave Rose's side, Sam moved off, but not so far as to be unable to hear and make occasional, furtive scans of the scene. Grandma and three of the aunts were on either side of Rose. They were singing something with a pulsing rhythm, more a chant than a song. The words were unfamiliar, meaningless, but ancient-sounding. He could see them push against Rose's side in time with their singing. Although they, too, were battered by the surf, they seemed in control, remarkably calm.

"Sometimes you just have to have faith, Sam," Michael shouted as he bumped against Sam in the turbulence. "Rose couldn't have better care."

Michael didn't mention the few times that a newborn had drowned in the moments after it emerged from its mother and was supposed to be pushed to the surface for its first breath. Now wasn't the time for caveats.

The four elder females gave a shout. Rose shouted even louder. Then all five were silent. Sam ignored his instructions, and watched his newborn child slide out from under Rose's belly, tail first, then twist around. As Rose gave her body a snap, the umbilical cord broke. The placenta followed, which was quickly swallowed by Grandma. The newborn began to float downward, barely moving. Grandma rushed under the infant and pushed it just ahead of Rose. Rose slid under the child and lifted it up to the surface, timing the movement to occur just after a huge wave passed overhead. Sam couldn't hear his child's intake of air because of the whitewater noise, but he did hear it cry out.

All four elders then took turns lifting the child to the surface to catch carefully timed breaths. Soon the baby was swimming alongside Rose, its balance basically established, breathing on its own when he heard Rose tell it to. She spoke in words that Sam had never heard before but could sense their meaning. How truly mysterious.

When the infant's breathing rhythm was established, Grandma swam over to Sam. She was obviously exhausted from her efforts, but her voice was joyous.

"You have a son, Sam. He is perfectly normal and strong. The aunts will stay with him and Rose through the night, until this storm passes. But you can be confident that the dangers of birth are behind him."

"I…I don't know what to say. Thank you, I guess, for starters. Can I at least go look at him?"

"It would be best if you waited a little while longer. Let him start nursing and bond with his mother. At first light, if the waves settle, it will be okay to visit for a short time."

"How do we decide what to name him?" Sam asked.

"A child's first year is fraught with peril," Grandma said, her tone now quite serious. "Please remember. Longstanding tradition forbids naming a child until he is one year old. Then we will have a naming celebration. It will be a family decision. In the meantime, it is best not to think about it."

"But Nan and I named our daughter almost immediately," Sam said defensively.

"Yes, I know. You told me that when we first met. I hid my disapproval. Had you and Nan been with the family, things would have happened differently, more slowly, according to tradition. But I guess, under the circumstances, it is understandable."

Sam was silent. "I wonder if the loss would've been easier on Nan if we hadn't named her," he finally said.

Grandma said nothing.

CHAPTER 37

"Jayden. Thoreau. Johnson."

A young man in a black graduation robe strode up the stairs and crossed the stage as a small group in the audience jumped up and clapped, whistled, shouted.

"Willow. Silvermoon. Johnson."

No response. After a few silent seconds, a few people clapped, then stopped. No one mounted the stairs. The announcer looked around, shrugged, then continued.

"Ethan. Alexander. Juddenham."

Another celebratory outburst and a robe-clad young man ran up the stairs.

At the moment her name was called, Willow Silvermoon Johnson was on the 3:40 ferry to Friday Harbor for job interviews. She was fairly certain she would graduate, having strategically passed the absolute minimum of classes. Her overall grade point was a C minus.

It would have been lower had it not been for Senior Biology. It was the only class she never missed, or at least not after the first exam. Until then, her attendance had been sporadic. But she got a D grade on her test and a note at the top, "Please see me after class."

Here we go again, Willow thought. She expected the tiresome, thinly disguised "what-might-you-be-willing-to-do-to-pass-this-class?" proposition that had led to her failing several classes over the years. Too bad. She actually liked

Mr. Beezy, a kinda cute, curly-blonde-haired, youngish guy. He wasn't a bad teacher, seemed genuinely interested in the subject matter, went out of his way to make it interesting. *Men are so fucking predictable.*

She couldn't have been more wrong.

Mr. B looked up from his desk and smiled.

"Thanks for staying after, Willow," he said. "Your exam has me puzzled. Your answers to the questions, or at least the ones you bothered to answer, were really very good. You explained well why hatchery salmon aren't a wise conservation practice and were the only one who caught my deliberate numerical error on the Mendelian genetics problem."

"I've been told I have a head for numbers," Willow offered, surprised at how this conversation was going.

"I think you have a head for a lot more than numbers," Mr. B said. "You just don't seem to think it's worth using. Your grades going back years are Fs, Ds and an occasional C. If you get a D in this class, you won't graduate."

"Yeah. I guess so. Does it really matter?" Willow asked.

"Only if you want out. If you don't graduate, you'll have to repeat your senior year."

Willow really hadn't thought that one through. She hadn't kept track of her grade point. She probably would have known if she'd shown up for guidance counseling sessions.

"Um. Shit. Oh, sorry."

"That's okay. I suspected you didn't know. But I have an offer for you," Mr. B said.

Here it comes.

"I'm willing to forget this first exam, wipe it off the books, if you use what I think is your strong native intelligence for the rest of the term. An A in this class would pull your overall GPA up to a C minus, good enough to graduate."

Willow was stunned. Did she hear him right? And had he really emphasized the word "native?" Aside from a few taunts by some asshole classmates, her being part Native American just never came up. At home or in school.

"You mean," she began, "like if I ace this course I'll graduate? That's all?"

"Yes," he said. "That's all. It will take effort on your part. I don't award a lot of As. You'll definitely have to earn it. Deal?"

Willow thought for maybe five more seconds. The last thing she wanted was to spend one extra minute in this stupid school. And she really did like this class. What the hell?

"Sure. Deal."

And Willow put in the effort, never missed class. She didn't take notes; she never had. She just paid attention. Which wasn't hard. Mr. B really liked natural history, which was Willow's favorite part. He ignored the ancient, dog-eared biology textbook, with its emphasis on how groundhogs hibernated in winter and horseshoe crabs spawned in Chesapeake Bay. Instead, he talked about local animals, bald eagles and migrating Pacific salmon and orca whales and giant Pacific octopus ("largest in the world"). And he was really pissed about invasive, non-native things like European rabbits and European starlings. Willow glanced around at all her white, blonde, Anglo-Saxon classmates and realized she was the only native (or at least part native) in the class. The others were invasives.

She aced the exams and got the only A of her life.

But she had absolutely zero interest in going to graduation with all those dorks.

The ferry arrived in Friday Harbor forty-five minutes before her first interview. Walking up First Street, she stopped at the Whale Museum. A poster outside read, "Congratulations High School Grads! Free Admission all weekend!"

Why not?

The exhibits were really cool, photos of whales and whale bones and information videos, especially about the local orcas and their problems, largely brought about by invasive European colonists. There were even exhibits about the relationship between orcas and Indigenous Peoples (*super cool; she liked that term*). Sitting on a bench, she watched and listened. Leaping whales, mothers with calves, aerial footage of orcas chasing and catching salmon, a strong conservation message. Willow was absolutely fascinated. So fascinated that she didn't pay attention to the time until the video ended and the museum was closing, at 5:00.

Shit! She was going to be late for her interview. She wanted a waitressing gig with decent pay and tips. Her coffee shop earnings just didn't do it, and she had to escape Orcatraz.

At the restaurant's office, the woman manager glanced at her watch as a breathless Willow knocked on the door. Willow filled out a questionnaire (address, age, work experience). The manager was polite and quick, "Honestly, Miss Johnson, showing up late for an interview doesn't make a good impression. And your driver's license says you're twenty-three, which is a stretch. I'm afraid we're not a good fit."

She was on time for the next one. Again, the woman manager looked at her driver's license, looked at Willow, looked back at the driver's license, and said thanks, but no thanks.

Restaurant number three was on a side street, less family-oriented, more of a construction worker's hangout. The manager was a middle-aged, balding man. Willow shed her heavy plaid jacket. *Might as well use all my qualifications.*

The guy looked over her questionnaire, driver's license, and made eye contact with her breasts as much as her face.

"Right now," he finally said. "We've got an opening Friday and Saturday nights 'til closing. Do okay and we might add weekdays."

"Great," Willow said. "When do I start?"

"Next week," he answered. "Try to dress to appeal to the clients. It will improve your tips."

The upcoming summer was looking brighter.

CHAPTER 38

Fish don't lead exceptionally rich mental lives. They pass up opportunities for reflection, no regrets. It's a rare fish that spends time in self-analysis. They live largely in the moment.

Such were the thoughts passing through the garbanzo bean-sized brain of the large female Chinook salmon as she traveled south, retracing a magnetic map she had memorized five years before, when she first ventured north. She was returning home now to spawn, swimming tirelessly for hundreds of hours and miles. She relied more on reaction than reflection, but her actions were definitely more than a stimulus-response chain. She took in her surroundings, assessed the relative risk and reward, and responded in what her five years of life told her was the wisest choice. Her mantra until now had been simple: Swim to find food. Eat. Avoid being eaten.

But, unlike a Buddhist, she followed an irresistible sensory compulsion, drawn by a new urge, one she had never felt before. She had been traveling steadily south from feeding grounds off Alaska, the urge growing stronger the farther south she traveled. In five years at sea, she had become big and fat, almost fifty pounds, full of developing eggs. She was the largest fish in a mass of Chinook salmon, a swarm that had grown in numbers daily. Her large size gave her speed, placing her at the swarm's forefront. Not a leader. At this point, each fish felt a similar urge and would keep swimming south, alone or not.

She sensed a nearby surge of water, something larger than her schoolmates. Anything unusual was to be avoided. Darting away, she was overcome with internal, uncomfortable warmth, followed by an incredibly loud blast of white noise, then a jolt. Her gas-filled swim bladder exploded, rupturing internal organs and breaking her backbone. Trying to swim despite the searing pain, she could only flail in the water. Her last vision was of large, white, jagged conical shapes closing down on her head. And then nothing.

Sam grasped the salmon in his mouth. One bite ended the fish's life. When the salmon had rushed away from him, he scanned it quickly with a sonar pulse and determined it was a female. After disabling it with a blast of sound, he bit down just hard enough to crush its brain and stop its struggling. Delicious juices flowed from wounds along the fish's body and into his mouth; they were still warm from his initial sonic scan. Ruptured, oozing eggs confirmed what his scan had told him. Great. This is what he had been sent to find, capture, and bring back. Bring back despite his hunger. Despite everyone's hunger. It took an act of willpower to not swallow the fish right then and there, but that would have violated the trust placed in him.

His status in the family was still tenuous. Growing, but he knew some family members still considered him an outsider, an unwelcome stranger brought into the family at Grandma's insistence. To be sent out now by Grandma to catch the first fish was an incredible honor. She had ignored the resentment harbored by some of the uncles, those who had been passed over for the honor. Really, several had already had a chance, without success. Chinook salmon were scarce and late this year, with little expectation of abundant food even when they did show up. Grandma gave him an opportunity to prove himself, and he wouldn't let her down. No matter how good this fish tasted.

"Nice catch," said Frank, swimming up alongside. Sam detected more than a little sarcasm in the compliment.

"I couldn't have caught her if you hadn't pushed the school toward me. I've had the fun. Why don't you carry the fish back and give it to Grandma? We'll call it a team effort. We can even give the twins some credit."

"That wouldn't fool anyone," Frank replied. "One scan of the fish would show it exploded on the inside, and everybody knows that's one of your tricks. Thanks, but no thanks."

"Suit yourself," said Sam. He had tried, but knew he should still count Frank among his detractors. Frank had remained hostile toward Sam since day one, Sam's addition to the family constituting too strong a break with tradition. Maybe Grandma had been testing Sam, allowing him to garner favor among family members who were hesitant to accept him. Maybe he should have just held back until Frank made a catch. But the fish was just too tempting, and close. Could this seeming success backfire? He knew he still had much to learn about family politics. Too many years alone had dulled his social skills.

"We should head back and give Grandma *your* fish and let her decide about the hunt," said Frank. "And you can bask in the glory."

With that, Frank turned and swam off, followed by the twins.

GENE HELFMAN

CHAPTER 39

Ceremonies transcend the boundaries of the individual and
resonate beyond the human realm.
ROBIN WALL KIMMERER, *Braiding Sweetgrass: Indigenous*
Wisdom, Scientific Knowledge and the Teachings of Plants

Sam's family had congregated in a cove, inside a protective kelp bed. They were waiting for the migrating salmon to arrive, hoping. But few fish appeared, and the family's anticipation of the Chinook salmon spawning run turned to concern. Without Chinook—the largest and fattest of the salmon that swam in North Pacific waters—the summer resident orcas would slowly starve. They were more than creatures of habit. Their habit defined them. It was a social tradition turned into a necessity.

Grandma had begun to second-guess her decision to send Sam, Frank, and the twins to scout for the first incoming wave of migrating Chinook. Some straggler fish had shown up along the usual migratory paths but were small. Despite everyone's growing hunger, the whales let these fish pass. In part, it was family tradition going back generations. In part, it was a conservation practice to assure that at least some fish went up into rivers to spawn. More than once over the millennia, spawning runs had failed, and the only Chinook the whales encountered were individuals or very small groups. As hard as it was on expectant and nursing mothers, and as hard as it was to control the behavior of hungry youngsters, no spawning Chinook could be caught in the migratory corridors before early June. Grandma's word was law, enforced by all members of the older generation, especially the aunts. Until an actual wave of ripening, large fish appeared, tradition and prudence dictated restraint.

Grandma's intuition, perhaps motivated by her own hunger, prompted her to send out Sam and Frank to scout, find, and hopefully bring back a first salmon. Her decision to send those two, despite the obvious enmity that they showed to one another, was an attempt to get them to work together. They were decent hunters, but tended to be impatient and seldom cooperated with another. If only skill were needed, sending a sister or niece would have been just fine. But, again, tradition overruled logic. The first fish was always captured by an older male. No one really knew how old Sam was. That was just another part of the enigma that surrounded this newcomer. The hunting party today could go either way, or many ways. Several could be bad. Again, intuition and hunger, and maybe age, were probably affecting her judgment.

Telling the twins to go along was mainly to get rid of them before they drove her to distraction. As hard as they were to control, she felt that their respect, or fear, of Sam and Frank would at least give them pause before they did anything stupid. Maybe dealing with them would force the two older males to cooperate, or at least commiserate.

Sam and Frank's approach was met with excitement. Racing ahead, the twins let everyone know that the two older whales were returning, and Sam was carrying a large fish. As word spread of the catch, the family formed two lines parallel to the shore, moving so slowly they seemed to be floating. The older females (Grandma, Molly, Esther, Lillian, and Annie) lined up inshore, their daughters following close behind. Sam's six-month-old son swam alongside Rose, and had trouble being still. The males formed their own line slightly offshore, facing in the opposite direction, separated from the mothers and daughters by about one hundred feet. Swimming slowly, Grandma approached the last of the males, the largest male approaching the end of the female line until the family formed a large circle, head to tail, moving counterclockwise. No one spoke.

As he approached the circle, Sam worked to quell his pride in having caught the first fish and concentrated on the ritual Rose had drilled into his head, over and over.

"Forget about your accent," she advised him. "Approach Grandma slowly and in silence. Stop directly in front of her. Wait for her greeting, 'How fat are the salmon?' You reply, 'The fat runs through their blood.'

"Then you give her the fish and shut up. Your work is done. You will have made me and our baby proud."

Things went well, sort of. Grandma swam out to receive the fish, which got caught by the gills on one of Sam's lower teeth and he had to shake his head to free it. As it slipped from his grasp and began to spiral towards the bottom, a youngster gasped, but was quickly silenced by an aunt. Grandma seemed to take no notice and picked the fish up and swam back to the line of older females. Mouthing the fish, she passed it to her sister Molly, who, in turn, transferred it to Esther. This continued until all five elder females in the line had mouthed the fish. The fish was returned to Grandma, who bit through and swallowed most of it, leaving only the head and tail. Grabbing them, Annie, as youngest of the elders, swam to the outer edge of the kelp bed and dropped the remains. They sank slowly down to the sloping seabed.

"The fat runs through their blood," Grandma exclaimed.

Everyone cheered. Winter was officially over, summer had officially begun. It was time to eat. And maybe more.

CHAPTER 40

Rudy tried to persuade Cassie that, as much as they both enjoyed following whales—and as much as he increasingly enjoyed her company—July fourth weekend was terrible timing.

She called late Saturday night. Rudy had spent four days the previous week on the water and was exhausted from hauling, launching and driving his boat. He had stowed the trailer and spent Saturday afternoon going through his notes while things were still fresh. Dinner was something thawed from Trader Joe's. Tomorrow he would sleep in, transcribe audio recordings, and summarize results. He had already fallen into a deep sleep when his cell phone gave its humpback whale whooop.

"Uh, hello," he whispered, not looking to see who it was.

"Sounds like I disturbed your slumber," Cassie said. "Is this a bad time?"

"Uh, oh no. Hi, Cassie. What's up?"

"Sculpin romance has been hot and heavy," she said. "I've been burning the midnight oil and lots of candles watching the little darlings fucking and fighting, and I'm exhausted. And I realized it's a holiday weekend so maybe I should take some time off."

Rudy wasn't sure where this was going.

"Good for you, Cass. As your thesis advisor, I agree that you need to recharge your batteries every now and then. But where do I fit in?"

"We haven't been out chasing our whales for weeks. It's time your assistant lived up to her end of the bargain."

Whale watching? Please not tomorrow.

"That's great Cassie. I'd love to have some non-canine company. How's Monday sound?"

"I was thinking about tomorrow actually. I've got to switch some of the boys around Monday to keep on schedule," she answered.

Tomorrow? Sunday? July fourth? Jesus!

"Oh. Yes. I mean, sure, but you know what tomorrow is?" Rudy asked.

"Of course. It's July fourth. The summer circus. Is that a problem?"

Rudy could hear disappointment in her voice.

"No, no. Of course not. Or maybe yes. It's just that the whales have been hanging out off the west side of San Juan Island, doing the west coast shuffle. That means hauling the dinghy on the ferry to Friday Harbor, and it might be hard to get on board, with the holiday and all. Probably have to go standby. And we certainly won't have the animals to ourselves, if we find them."

"Rudy, I realize we won't have the whales to ourselves. In fact, that's part of why I want to go out. We've been really lucky up to now, very few others to contend with. But it's time I saw what our whales put up with during the summer tourist season. Maybe it's ghoulish behavior on my part, like being drawn to a train wreck. Tell you what. I'll pay for the ferry ride, take it out of my research budget. What do you say? Please."

Rudy thought for a moment. His research costs, including ferry rides, were actually underwritten by J. B. Alexander. But he kind of liked the idea of sticking it to her former major prof. Funny how he found himself taking sides against a sexual predator. A changed perspective, thanks to Cassie. And time with her, anytime, was fun. She did have a valid point about her not knowing what the whales put up with, the major obstacles they faced on a daily basis. It would be part of her education. What the hell?

"Okay, I guess. I mean, sure."

"You're a darling, Rudy. I'll meet you at the Anacortes ferry landing. What time?"

"Given the holiday madness, it doesn't really matter," he said, "'cause we'll have to wait regardless. How about ten?"

Sunday morning, Rudy lurched into action. Cheez watched until it was clear they were headed out on the water and then trotted out to wait by the Zodiac. Rudy hooked the trailer up, loaded his usual boat gear—VHF radio, water jug, metal ammo/tool box, life jackets. It was 9:00.

Cassie stood at the end of the line of cars snaking up from the ferry toll booth. Cheez didn't even have to be told to jump into the back seat. He was as much putty in Cassie's hands as was Rudy.

Cassie hopped into the Volvo, leaned over and gave Rudy a kiss on the cheek.

"I know I'm putting you out, Rudy. It's really good of you to do this for me. Your stock has risen even more," she said.

"Really not a big deal. I hadn't planned anything else for this weekend," he lied.

When they finally got to the booth, they were informed the next two boats were already full. "Standby will be a crapshoot," the lady in the booth said. "Happy hunting." They parked in the standby line and spent a pleasant couple of hours walking on the beach with Cheez.

They finally caught the 3:30 ferry to Friday Harbor, launched the dinghy at Roche Harbor and headed south. Turning the radio on, Rudy picked up chatter from the commercial whale watchers. The orcas were, in fact, down the coast. *Thank the orca gods.*

Soon they were floating along with the crowd, outboard idling, following the J Pod orcas as they moved slowly south along San Juan Island. The mob scene, easily seventy-five boats, was approaching Lime Kiln, a.k.a. Whale Watch Park, and its iconic lighthouse. A crowd of easily a hundred people stood on the rocks, whooping and hollering as the whales approached.

Glancing around, Rudy read the none-too-clever names of the boats in the armada. It was the usual smattering of terrible marine-themed puns: *Wet Dream, Fantasea, Aquaholic, Seas the Day, Liquid Asset, Gypsea, Happy Hooker*, and so on. A few were slightly more creative, proclaiming profligate spending related to business occupations: *Billable Ours, Row v. Wade, Knot On Call, Dhow Jones*. The commercial whale-watching vessels were there too. Hard to miss was the monstrous high-speed, yellow, rigid inflatable out of Victoria (*Prince of Whales*), its paying customers all clad in matching, brightly colored, foul weather gear. The larger, slower, and older boats from Friday Harbor (*Odyssea*) and Orcas Island (*Eclypse*) idled nearby.

Folks from the Whale Museum in their little Soundwatch powerboat were cruising around like a border collie herding recalcitrant pigs. They handed out leaflets and tried to get people to maintain the mandated three-hundred-yard distance from the whales, or chased down boats that raced ahead to intercept the whales farther south, a definite no-no. The commercial people were pretty good about keeping their distance, to the disappointment of their passengers. Private, recreational boaters were less observant of the rules. Cassie's head swiveled back and forth as she took in the scene.

"Kind of a circus, I have to admit," she said. "You warned me. One thing strikes me though. The really big, shiny, expensive boats, they all seem to just have a couple on board, like an older man and a much younger, attractive woman, maybe a guy and his daughter?"

"That's the May-December fleet," Rudy said.

"Oh," Cassie answered. "Like multi-generational families, I guess."

"That's another way of putting it," Rudy replied.

Commercial boat drivers pointed out the whales and shouted on loudspeakers. "Hey folks. You're in for a treat," came an amplified female voice from *Odyssea*. "That big male over there is the celebrity orca, Makai, now known as J-60, and what we're pretty certain is his new calf, J-61, who we think is about seven months old. On the other side of J-61 is the calf's mom, J-28 Polaris. Makai's especially attentive for a male orca, clearly a proud papa. It's unusual for orca dads to hang out with their babies, but Makai is one different whale. Some folks think the little guy should be named Makita, but it's more traditional to name them after their mothers since we usually don't know who the fathers are. J-61's momma is Polaris, so some folks think maybe they should name the little one Hokupa'a, the Hawaiian name for the North Star, which would recognize both parents. We'd welcome suggestions. Just send them to our website."

This announcement was met by the complaining shout of an adolescent boy on the *Prince of Whales*.

"Why won't the whales jump? Make the whales jump!"

"They won't jump because they're asleep, you little twit," Rudy said, aloud but mostly to Cassie. "Fortunately, boat disturbance seems less when the whales are sleeping. But data from years of people watching people watching whales indicate that, when whales are foraging and boats are present, the orcas—especially the females—spend less time feeding and more time traveling. The ultrasonic fish finders on boats emit sounds at around fifty kilohertz, nicely tuned to interfere with the sonar output of the whales. That and engine noise compromises their echolocation and probably communication. The whales waste energy spyhopping, breaching, and tail and pectoral fin slapping when boats are nearby. People interpret the activity as play, like the whales have nothing better to do than entertain us. But, in reality, the whales might just be saying 'go away.'"

Cassie turned to Rudy from her position in the bow.

"Oh, Rudy, this is still absolutely wonderful. Just being around them, even when they're asleep, is a thrill. But is it always like this, with a horde of boats dogging their every tail beat? It feels like voyeurism. I mean the poor whales are just trying to get some rest, and all these boats are buzzing around, jockeying for a good view."

"That's why we're hanging back on the periphery, behind the animals, and downwind, so they won't have to breathe our exhaust fumes," Rudy replied. "There's not much to see, and I don't enjoy being in the circus. It's the busiest whale-watching day of the year. If they could, the whales would do what most of the locals do and flee to Canada."

Rudy's diatribe was cut short by Cheez, who gave two quick barks.

"Yes, Cheez, you've already told us Makai is here," Rudy said to the dog.

But Cheez wasn't facing the whales. He was looking back, behind the Zodiac. And he gave three quick, unusually loud barks.

"Hey!" shouted Cassie. "Isn't that a jet ski?"

Rudy whirled around and looked north. About a mile away, a small boat was approaching at high speed, a noticeable piss-stream of water shooting out behind.

"I don't know. I've never seen one before. But it seems unlikely. They're illegal in these waters."

"Well, I've seen plenty of them," Cassie answered. "The waters in southern California were lousy with those crotch rockets for wet rednecks. No question; that's a jet ski, legal or not!"

The ski was approaching quickly, directly at them. It was now maybe a half mile away, and Rudy could see clearly that it was a guy on a jet ski. He was clad in black, probably a wet suit. The bright afternoon sun flashed off what could only be heavy gold chains around his neck. The driver was undoubtedly delighted at having a large audience and was going to give them a thrill.

Rudy quickly realized the ski was on a collision course with the circle of whale watchers and, more importantly, the sleeping whales. Rudy knew from casual reading that the obnoxious, monotone banshee wail of jet skis was louder in air than outboard motors but quieter underwater. There was a good chance the whales—because personal watercraft were outlawed locally, and their underwater sound was muffled—might not recognize the threat.

Some of the small boats around them began taking evasive action, moving to Rudy's right or left, basically clearing a path toward the whales.

"Shit!" Rudy shouted.

"Can't you do something?" Cassie implored. "He's going to run over the whales!"

Right, thought Rudy. *I could block his path, but then he'll either crash into us, or avoid us and crash into somebody else. But if I don't block his path, he's going to hit the whales.*

With the kernel of a plan, Rudy headed slowly at the ski. The distance had now closed to less than a hundred yards. As he turned the Zodiac, he caught sight of Makai, who had also turned around and was facing the oncoming ski.

At the last instant, Rudy reached down and flipped open the latch on the old ammo box. Reaching down past rusting tools, he grabbed the orange pistol-shaped flare gun, realizing he had no idea if it worked. Just before the ski rammed them, he aimed and fired. The flare shot out, trailing bright smoke. It struck the ski driver's prominent belly. Oddly, the flare didn't explode as anticipated but plopped harmlessly into the water.

Screaming and flailing, the driver flew off the ski and landed with a sizable splash.

"Guess it was past date after all," Rudy mumbled, looking at the pistol in his hand. "At least it had the desired effect."

The ski slowed to a stop, bumping gently into Rudy's boat. From the periphery of his vision, Rudy also sensed an even larger splash behind him, where the whales were. Turning around, he saw the whales take off at tremendous speed, away from the jet ski and its spluttering pilot.

The driver in the water screamed expletives and thrashed toward the disabled ski. Hearing a siren, Rudy looked north to see a black and white marine patrol boat charging their way, blue strobe lights flashing. He was now faced with another decision. Looking at the approaching law enforcement vessel, at the guy flailing in the water, and at the flare gun in his hand, Rudy pondered the legality of shooting someone, even if only with a malfunctioning flare gun. After a moment's hesitation, he opted for discretion.

"I probably ought to buy a working gun and flares," he said and tossed the gun overboard.

The sheriff pulled up alongside the ski driver, who was now treading water, looking from the police boat to his ski and back. The sheriff and a deputy, with some difficulty and minimal gentleness, pulled the guy into the boat as if they were landing a large, uncooperative giant sea bass. Spinning the guy around, they grabbed his arms behind his back and put cuffs on him.

"Hey! What the hell are you doing? Somebody shot me! You need to arrest them."

"Shot you with what?" the sheriff asked.

"A flare gun, dammit. Somebody shot me with a goddammed flare gun. You need to arrest them," he repeated.

"Where'd they hit you?" the sheriff asked.

"Right here," the ski driver said, pointing to his stomach. "I saw the smoke trail just before it hit me."

"Really now. Flares tend to be kinda hot as I recall. I'd expect to see some burn marks. All I see is a fat dimple. No smell of burning neoprene," the sheriff retorted. "Okay, who shot you?

"I dunno. I was going too fast to...," he stopped and corrected himself. "You oughta find out who shot off a flare gun."

He pointed at the remaining boats, which were now mostly sailboats and kayaks, the powerboats having taken off after the fleeing whales.

"I think it was a guy in a little inflatable, and he had a lady and a dog with him."

While this loud and animated conversation was ongoing, Rudy slowly moved the Zodiac to the other side of the cluster of remaining boats. A woman standing on the deck of a large sailboat motioned frantically for him to come over. Rudy motored alongside.

"Toss me your bow line," a man on the stern whispered just audibly.

Cassie did so and the guy quickly tied it around a cleat.

"Get on board, fast," he said.

Cheez jumped up on the sailboat without hesitation. Rudy and Cassie followed, clambering up a ladder.

"Go below 'til things cool down," the guy told them.

The woman came down the steps, all smiles, while the man stayed up in the cockpit.

"We were monitoring channel 16," she told Rudy and Cassie. "We heard the Soundwatch people call the sheriff to report a guy on a jet ski off Lime Kiln. The sheriff was patrolling near San Juan County Park, ticketing a bunch of kayakers who weren't wearing life jackets. They abandoned the kayakers and came to the rescue. Probably made their day."

Rudy could hear the sheriff's boat just outside.

"Hey. That looks like the dog," Rudy heard the ski operator say.

"Maybe so," the sheriff replied. "But unless your little inflatable transformed into a forty-foot sailboat, you haven't got much of a case. Excuse me, sir. Do you have a flare pistol on board?"

"Yes sir, officer. Flares are all up to date. Would you like to see it? You're welcome to look around."

"That's okay. We gotta book this guy and get back to our patrol. Have a good day. Nice dog you got there."

"Hey, you didn't even look," the ski operator whined.

"That's the Coast Guard's business," the sheriff said dismissively. "Don't want to get involved in a jurisdictional dispute with the feds."

He turned the patrol boat around and, despite having the jet ski in tow, took off, causing the ski operator to tumble onto the floorboards. Shouted complaints about who he was going to sue and who would lose their job were lost in the sound of the big twin outboards.

The sailboat's captain motioned to Rudy and Cassie that the coast was clear. As they climbed up the steps from the salon and emerged into the cockpit, they saw a dozen kayaks and a couple of sailboats nearby. Squinting in the sunshine, Rudy heard clapping, which grew louder until it was clear that everyone around them was applauding.

A couple in a tandem kayak paddled over, and the woman in the front lifted up a storage cover and pulled out a large green bottle.

"It's our first anniversary and we were going to drink this later," she said, handing a bottle of champagne up to Cassie. "But you've already given us something better to celebrate and deserve it more than we do. Enjoy."

Cassie thanked the kayakers and turned to Rudy.

"Any more entertainment planned for the day, Rudy?" she asked.

"I hope not," Rudy said.

Sam knew what a jet ski was and had recognized the sound immediately. His nighttime encounter being chased in

Utah left an indelible impression. Realizing how fast it was approaching and the threat it posed, he had shouted to the others to flee. But in the confusion, his baby panicked and started swimming in the wrong direction, right at the approaching ski. Just as the ski was going to ram his son, Sam leapt forward and grabbed him in his mouth, pushing him down, out of the ski's path.

The little whale cried out, "Mommy!"

Rose's reaction was also immediate and protective. Not recognizing the sound of the ski, all she saw was Sam grabbing her crying baby in his mouth.

"Let go!" she screamed. She rushed at Sam, ramming him in the side.

"Ouch!" Sam grunted. A quick scan showed him the ski had stopped, a logrider flailing in the water beside it. Sam gently brought his son to the surface and released him. The youngster quickly swam to his mother, hyperventilating. He nuzzled up against her.

"What were you doing?" Rose yelled at Sam.

"Saving our child," was his hurt reply. "What did you think I was doing?"

"I didn't know. All I knew was you were biting him and holding him down. I thought you were...I didn't know. It was terrible to watch."

Sam was angry, but he realized what it must have looked like to Rose. This was another trial, another test. Stifling any anger, he tried to explain as calmly as he could.

"The logrider was on a very, very fast log. I was chased by one of those, before they moved me to the ocean. I remembered its sound. It was headed straight for our child. The only thing I could think to do was push him down, out of its way. Is he okay?"

"Honey, are you okay?" Rose asked in a soothing voice. The child was clearly upset and confused.

"I guess so. Daddy bit me, but it didn't hurt. But he scared me."

"Let Mommy look," Rose said to him. She scanned him closely. He had tooth impressions on his back and belly, just ahead of his dorsal fin. None had broken the skin.

"Daddy was only trying to save you from a nasty logrider. I think you're going to be fine, honey. Would you like to nurse a little 'til you feel better?"

"Yes," he said. Nursing calmed him almost immediately.

"I'm sorry Sam," Rose said. "I really am. I should have trusted you. I've never known a father as devoted as you are. Please forgive me."

"Forgiven and forgotten," Sam answered. "Let's join the others and tell them what happened, and how to recognize that kind of log."

"Wow. You two sure do provide high drama."

It was Michael, who had been nearby and hadn't left with the rest of the family.

"I saw what happened. Pretty scary. That really fast logrider was headed right at you guys. Then the logrider who often follows us, the one with the four-finned, furry, seal-like animal, pointed a stick at the fast logrider. I heard a pop and the fast logrider got hit with something bright and fell into the water just as you grabbed your kid. I thought, now we've really got trouble. But it looks like everybody's okay, right?"

"Yes, Michael," Sam answered, turning to his friend. "Everybody's fine. Just a little shaken up. Thanks for filling in the blanks. The logrider with the furry animal is the same one who has been following me for months. I've come to think of him as Uncle Morris. I think he's the reason

I was set free. I guess he's keeping an eye on me. Pretty strange, but I guess I should be grateful. I keep having to be reminded that not all logriders are to be hated."

The ride back to the boat ramp was uneventful. At the ramp, Rudy saw a sheriff's car, lights flashing, parked on the far side of the harbor, over where the monstrous pleasure yachts were berthed. Curious, but not so curious as to chance being recognized, he stopped a couple walking by.

"What's up with the police?" Rudy asked.

"It's our sheriff," the man corrected him. "Seems like some idiot launched a jet ski off one of the megayachts and got caught chasing orcas. Pretty stupid. Jet skis are outlawed in this county. First in the nation to ban them," the guy said with obvious pride. "And orcas are totally protected. The guy will lose his ski, along with doing jail time. Castration would be more appropriate."

"Wow, that's pretty harsh," Rudy said, trying to sound astonished. "Maybe the guy didn't know about the law."

"Hey. Ignorance of the law is no excuse. I hope they throw the book at the asshole," came the indignant reply.

"Right," said Rudy. "I guess that would be nice."

Rudy and Cassie had no trouble getting on a ferry back to Anacortes. The holiday crowds were staying on the island for the much-heralded Friday Harbor fireworks show.

Upstairs in the ferry, Cassie turned to Rudy.

"Well, Dr. Laguna. Whale watching. Ecovigilante heroics. The prospect of champagne. You certainly know how to show a girl a good time."

"We could celebrate and open the bottle," he replied.

"No, it's too warm now. Let's save it for a later time when we can drink it cold."

"Sounds like a plan," Rudy said.

Rudy dropped her off next to her Beetle. Cassie started to open the car door, but turned around, ran up to Rudy, and gave him a very big hug.

"Thanks, Rudy. This was a truly wonderful day."

Rudy couldn't help but agree.

CHAPTER 41

Lance Thorn was growing increasingly fond of his job as a deckhand on the San Juan ferries. Working mostly night shifts was fine since he was a night person. He had left, or been fired from, several jobs for failure to show up on time, not to mention insubordination. Eight in the morning was the middle of his normal sleep cycle.

A roommate in his crowded basement apartment in Anacortes suggested he apply with Washington State Ferries. The summer tourist season was in full swing and the ferries were understaffed, especially the late night and early morning runs. The local tourist-based economy was short on workers. Almost every business had a "Help Wanted" sign in the window, but Lance couldn't imagine smiling all day at rich Seattleites and their obnoxious, demanding brats.

The hardest part of getting the ferry gig was passing the drug test. Two weeks drug-free before peeing into a cup set his nerves on edge, but the pay was exceptional and the hours perfect. He started at the bottom of the pecking order, pulling garbage bags out of trash bins, cleaning bathrooms—people actually got sick on these boats!—mopping floors, and washing greasy finger and face smears off windows. But he rose to the task, aided by pharmaceuticals and loud heavy metal through his earbuds. He quickly moved up to the more desirable position of guiding cars on and off the boats, chocking wheels, jump-starting dead batteries.

GENE HELFMAN

Most folks who rode the boats at night were also working stiffs who took advantage of the hour-plus ride to catch up on sleep, often without leaving their cars. The nighttime ferry staff was made up largely of loners, guys with minimal family life and other daytime distractions. Lance fell right in.

Because the daytime boats were overcrowded, perpetually late, frequently broken down, and used by an impatient and often irate public, staff were stressed, and turnover was high. This created shortages and Lance was happy to fill in. The chick-checking was much better on the daytime routes. Staying up twenty-four or even forty-eight hours was nothing new, especially with the right drugs. Although regulations called for periodic drug testing, these somehow were forgotten in the hectic, schedule-driven routine of summer ferry traffic.

It was on one of these daytime trips from Anacortes to Friday Harbor that Lance noticed a sleek, black Chevy Suburban pulling a trailer with a two-seater jet ski. Folks were always struggling onto the ferries pulling boats on trailers. In fact, this was one of the most amusing parts of the job, especially when drivers had to back the trailers onto the boat. More than once, Lance came to the aid of a driver who had jammed a trailer against the side rail, angry wife and crying kids shouting encouragement. Lance would ask the driver politely to get out and let him do the backing. Few refused. Lance even got an occasional tip, despite being strictly against WSF policy.

Jet skis were, however, a rarity. Maybe it was the cold water and family-oriented clientele, but it was the first one he'd seen. Lance recognized it as a very new, very expensive, Mitsubishi WaveBlaster. The owner was inspecting the towing gear when Lance approached. Lance noticed another man sitting in the cab of the Suburban, checking his cell phone.

"Hey, isn't that an LX Cruiser? Does it have the Hyper Vortex motor?" Lance asked.

The owner looked up, a smile on his face. The guy was middle-aged, a little paunchy, dressed in expensive, quick-dry travel clothes, matching shirt and pants, muted khaki.

"Why, yes. We just bought it, my partner and I. Taking it to our place on San Juan for the first time." The guy was very, very friendly.

Lance's gaydar was beeping loudly. Okay, a couple of queers from Seattle, summer home in the San Juans. The smell of money.

"Way cool, man. I've always dreamed of having one of those, but it's way out of my price range. I bet it's a blast to drive. What's it supposed to do?"

"The salesman at Kirkland Watersports promised us it could go at least fifty miles an hour, even with pilot and rider," the owner said proudly.

Gears turned in Lance's head. He'd always wanted to drive one of these babies.

"Did they give you lessons on how to operate it?" he asked. "They're kind of tricky."

The guy paused. "No, as a matter of fact, they didn't. The salesman just said to watch the video."

"I guess that would work," Lance said. "But a real lesson would be a lot safer."

"Yes, I can see that," the guy said. "Are you able to give a lesson?"

"I've driven all sorts of jet skis," Lance lied. "I'd be happy to do it, no charge."

Lance heard the SUV's car door slam. The partner came around the side. Quick dry travel clothes.

"Jonathan! Don't you think the ferry worker has better things to do than watch you play with that thing!"

"Patrick isn't quite as infatuated with my toy as I am," the owner said to Lance. "Tell you what." He pulled out his wallet. "Here's my card with our San Juan address. We're only here for the weekend. But let's keep in touch, and I'll take you up on the lesson. That might be the safest thing to do."

"Sure thing," Lance said. "That would be great."

"Yes. Of course," the owner said.

Lance glanced at the card. The guy was a CPA with a business address in Bellevue and home addresses there and on San Juan. He would check out the guy's place on the island first chance. Maybe he could figure out a way to joy ride the ski, familiarize himself with its operation.

Lance could hear angry voices arguing inside the SUV as he walked to the back of the ferry. A woman in spike heels was watching a large white poodle with a bouffant haircut taking a dump on the car deck.

On his regular interisland run, last boat of the night, Lance noticed a very attractive, young, dark-haired girl who rode the boats regularly. She always sat by herself in a far corner, headphones on, gazing out the window. Always alone, never spoke to anyone, stone-faced. Perpetual look of boredom. Great body, top to bottom. Maybe Native American features. Lance walked past her often, but she never even glanced up.

Finally, he used the excuse of emptying a nearby recycling bin to make contact.

"Hey, you want this *Seattle Times*? It's today's paper."

Willow Silvermoon Johnson looked up. She removed her earphones. "Huh?" was all she said.

"I asked if you wanted today's paper. Somebody tossed it out. Looks like they didn't even read it. Seems a waste, you think?"

"Uh. Nope." She put her headphones back on.

"You ride the boats a lot, don't you?" Lance said, almost shouting.

The girl took her headphones off again. She seemed to be making up her mind whether to brush him off or not. Finally, she answered.

"Yeah. A lot." She let it hang there.

Lance was encouraged.

"I notice you're usually on the late boats, like between Friday Harbor and Orcas. Do you work late?"

The girl looked up, a hint of a smile on her face. It was clear she knew what Lance was up to.

"Right, I have this great daytime job feeding ice cream to fat tourist kids and a nighttime gig pouring drinks in the sleaziest bar in Friday Harbor."

Lance couldn't decide if her response was a put-down or just a complaint. He didn't care.

"I'm Lance, ferry worker drone. Fugitive from the big city of Anacortes."

"Okay, Lance. I'm Willow."

She put her headphones back on and turned to stare out the window.

Lance considered this a success and knew not to push his luck. There would be another time.

GENE HELFMAN

It came a week later. Midweek, late boat. Willow was in her regular place, one of the few passengers on the boat. He walked up to her.

"Hi, Willow," he said.

She looked up, gave him half a smile. Headphones came off.

"Hi, Lance."

"I've got an idea," he said. "Something you might like. I have a friend on San Juan who lets me use his place. Great spot. Big house on the water. Really big house. It has everything. Great sound system, huge TV. Lots of rooms. Amazing stuff. I could take you there if you'd like. Get away from Friday Harbor. And the crowds."

Lance had plans. He had ridden his bike to the accountant's house off False Bay. It was a long shot, a hopeful, preparatory visit. On a hunch, he'd scouted the bushes for a hidden key and, sure enough, found one inside a realistic fake rock next to a goldfish pond. Cleverly disguised, but not clever enough.

"Sure. I guess so. When?"

Lance expected a rebuff and was caught by surprise. He improvised.

"Let's see. It's Wednesday. I can probably get Friday night off if I work through Thursday. How about the last boat Friday night, the one that arrives at Friday Harbor a little after midnight? Would that work?"

Lance was definitely stretching things. He would have to trade shifts with someone and borrow a roommate's car since his had been repossessed months ago. Not that his driver's license was valid. Minor detail.

"Okay. I'll be in the ferry waiting room," Willow said.

The headphones went back on.

Willow wouldn't normally even have responded to such an obvious come-on. But she had just about reached her limit at home. Her stepdad was worse than ever, her mom as useless as ever. She hated both her jobs. And the tall, young, lanky ferry worker was good looking, dark hair and eyes, sharp features, walked with a cocky confidence. What the hell? She could take care of herself.

CHAPTER 42

By Friday night, Lance had arranged everything. He did two shifts for a guy in return for getting Friday night off. His roommate reluctantly gave him the keys to his old Toyota pickup in exchange for a lid of Lance's best grass. The truck was a disaster, smelled like a mixture of beer and pot. After tossing the trash behind the seat, he drove with the windows open, nearly freezing his balls off. Anything for what he hoped would be a good night.

He got a ferry worker's discount for the trip to Friday Harbor but didn't leave the truck. No reason to interact with his fellow workers. Parking on a side street, he walked to the waiting room. Willow was the only one there.

"Hi, Willow. Sorry. The boat was a little late, as usual."

"Right," she said. She put her headphones into a cloth bag at her feet. "So, where's this place we're going to?"

"It's on the west side," he said. "It overlooks False Bay, right out by the entry. At night, you see the lights of Victoria. You'll love it. The house is full of stuff."

Lance had called the CPA in Bellevue on the pretense of wondering whether the guy was going to be on San Juan that weekend and was he still interested in a jet ski lesson? No, he was tied up on business. Wouldn't be up for another week. How about then?

Lance had memorized the half-hour route to the False Bay house, hoping he could find it in the dark. A long gravel driveway ended at a high fence and gate.

"They have really nice shrubs and stuff. Guess they want to keep the deer out," Lance said. Willow hadn't said anything.

He opened the gate and closed it when they were past. The fewer mistakes the better.

The house was dark, but in the full moonlight its pretentiousness was hard to miss. Huge logs, including some that passed for columns. Moose or elk antlers over an elaborate stained-glass and wood front door with a massive iron handle.

Using his cell phone flashlight, he located the fake rock, extracted the key.

The huge door unlocked smoothly. Turning on lights, they stepped onto slate floors, with more tree post columns, a high ceiling with log cross beams. A papier mache pterodactyl hung from one of the beams, its wingspan at least twenty-five feet.

"Cool," Willow said.

"Wait 'til you see the rest of it." He went to a panel on the great room wall, pushed a button. Blinds throughout the entry and great room rose slowly.

An expansive kitchen was separated from the great room by a curving wooden bar that looked like it had been carved from a single tree trunk. The kitchen appliances were all shiny black stainless steel. Very new.

"So where do you know the owner from?" Willow finally asked.

"Some guys I met on the ferry. We hit it off pretty well. Very generous."

Several bedrooms opened off to one side of the great room, and a half-step down on the other side was a den with a TV screen that had to be ten feet across, giant speakers on either side. Another room off the great room was a showcase of art. Paintings, sculptures, all erotic. Homoerotic.

Willow stopped, looked around. She smiled at Lance.

"Friends of yours. You hit it off, eh?"

"Hey, don't get me wrong. I just met the guy on the ferry, and he said I could use the place," he lied, caught off guard. "That's all. Nothing more."

"Sure. Whatever," Willow said. "Anything to eat? I'm starved."

The fridge was full of cold cuts, cheese, crackers. Some wine. Willow gobbled up the food and sipped the wine.

"Hey, here's the best part," Lance said. He motioned for her to follow, and they went down a winding metal staircase to a lower level where the sound of lapping waves was just audible.

Lance opened another door that led to a room full of antique nautical stuff, including a hard hat diving costume, a large brass compass off an old ship, and an old ship's anchor. The lights were all from old boats. Huge paintings of sailing ships with multiple masts and sails hung on the walls, framed in gold. A giant wooden ship's wheel stood against one wall. Mounted on the wall above the wheel were harpoons from old whaling ships. They all gleamed in the soft light.

"Wow, it's like some sort of museum," Willow said.

"Yeah. I knew you'd like it. And I've got one more surprise." He motioned for her to sit down on a rattan sofa in front of a glass coffee table. Under the glass was a painting of a mermaid on a rock, waves crashing.

Lance reached into his pocket and pulled out a small Ziploc bag. It contained white powder and a small plastic straw. He took a dollar bill from his wallet and laid out a line of the white powder, held the straw to one nostril and inhaled the line. He handed the straw to Willow.

She looked at the straw as if it were a foreign object, at the powder, and then at Lance.

"Is that what I think it is?" she asked.

"The finest. Top-grade coke. Go ahead," Lance urged.

"I dunno," Willow said. "I've never done cocaine before. Like, isn't it addictive?"

"Naw. That's crack. I never do crack. That's for n…n… crack-heads. This is pure coke. I swear."

Willow hesitated. Then all the boredom and frustration and trapped feelings of the last couple of years swept over her. She took the straw to her nose and inhaled. Held her breath. And sneezed.

"Shit!" she said.

"Hey, it's okay," Lance said. "Take a little less the second time. Then just sit back and enjoy the ride." He couldn't believe things were going so well.

Willow didn't feel any different, at least not at first. Then she slowly had a sense of growing euphoria. It was the first really positive feeling she'd had in months. She picked up the straw and started to inhale another line.

"Whoa, babe. Take it easy. There's plenty more. Best to spread it out over a while."

Willow felt lightheaded and confident. She knew she had a shit-eating grin on her face but didn't care. She was having a good time, for a change.

"Okay, then," Lance said. "One more surprise. Follow me."

Lance led her through another door, a replica of a steel passageway door in a ship. He spun a black wheel that released pins top and bottom. The heavy door creaked open and they stepped over a metal threshold.

They were in a boathouse under the house. A speedboat with a huge gray outboard motor bounced gently in the water, tied to a floating dock. Behind it was a shiny jet ski. Foul weather gear, wet suits, and yellow rubber boots hung from wooden pegs along a wall. Lance walked over and took a large wet suit down from one peg and a smaller one from another. He handed the small suit to her.

"Put this on. It may be a little large, but it will keep you warm. I'm getting something from the trophy room."

Willow didn't hesitate. At this point, and feeling like she did from the cocaine, she could do any damn thing she pleased. She took off her shoes and socks, stripped off her jeans and sweatshirt, down to panties and bra. The wetsuit went on with little difficulty. It was large, but it still clung to her body. Nicely, she thought.

Lance came out of the trophy room carrying one of the spear-like things that had been hanging on the wall. It was lethal looking, with a long wooden handle. At its end was a metal shaft tipped with a flat, sharpened spade, maybe two inches long and one inch across.

"It's a lance," Lance said. "Just like me. Maybe we can go stick it in a log."

Willow giggled. The lance was kind of scary, but right now she wasn't afraid of anything. Let him have his macho fun.

Lance put on the other wetsuit and clambered onto the jet ski, still holding the lance. He motioned for Willow to climb on behind. He turned a key and the jet ski started up with a roar. He throttled back to a purr.

"Hey. I almost forgot." Lance got off the ski and threw a switch on an electrical panel. A garage-type door slid up behind them. Willow turned around and saw the ocean bathed in full moonlight. It was beautiful.

"These things don't have a reverse," Lance said. He pushed back from the floating dock with his foot and they drifted out into the calm water of False Bay, the engine idling.

They sat there for a minute, taking in the scene. Then Lance twisted the throttle and they bolted forward. The water was like glass, and Willow had the sensation of flying over the reflected moon. They shot out of False Bay and into the ocean just beyond. Lance turned left and they sped south along the west shore of San Juan Island.

CHAPTER 43

The full moon shone down on the three whales as they moved slowly down the west side of Gathering Salmon Island. Hunting had been poor again and everyone was hungry. Grandma decided to split the family into subgroups to cover more territory. Because Sam was a proficient hunter, he and Rose and their son were allowed to go off alone, a smaller than usual subgroup. If they found fish, Sam could leave Rose and the little one and use his exceptional speed to return and report.

Sam and Rose's son had grown into a rambunctious child, keeping his parents busy. Normal young orcas are seldom a tail thrust away from their mothers, usually closer. But Sam often found himself pushing the child back where he was supposed to be. Then he was off again. As the three moved along in the dark, Rose kept calling him back while Sam scanned for fish.

They passed the Drying Bay lagoon opening. Rose gave the boy a quick and stern lecture about the dangers of this particular embayment. Covered with water at high tide, the large expanse dried quickly as the tide went out, the seabed dotted with large boulders. A great, great uncle had chased fish into the bay many years earlier and became stranded on a hot summer day. He died, probably from heat exhaustion and the weight of his own unsupported body. It was a lesson passed down across generations: Drying Bay was never to be entered, under any circumstances.

The sea was unusually silent and devoid of fish. Then Sam heard the faint buzz of a logrider. This was a higher-pitched sound than the deep background throbbing of the large logs, something smaller and faster. The orcas normally had the nighttime seas to themselves. But the moon was full, and logriders did strange things when the moon was full.

The buzzing grew louder and closer. Something about it made Sam uneasy. He called to Rose to keep their child close, at least until whatever it was had passed. His uneasiness grew as he realized why he knew the sound. It was one of those small fast logs, like the one in the lake in Utah, and the one that had almost run them over just a few weeks ago. Sam told Rose to stop and remain still.

———

After maybe fifteen high-speed minutes, Willow shouted that she was getting cold, could they head back. Lance was only too happy to comply. A fast turn, a curtain of spray, and they headed north. The entry into False Bay emerged in the bright moonlight, the only gap in the coastline. The house was lit up on the cliff edge, inside the bay.

Willow saw the orcas first, two large shiny objects, motionless at the sea's surface. Her first impression was of two wet logs gleaming in the moonlight. But something told her otherwise. She tapped Lance on the shoulder and shouted, "Stop!" She pointed at the whales.

"It's two killer whales," she said. "Wait, there's a third one. It's tiny. It must be their baby. Oh my god, how beautiful."

Willow didn't know if it was the cocaine or the moonlight or some combination, but the sight of the whales stirred something very deep inside her, something she didn't remember feeling before.

Lance apparently had an entirely different reaction. "Hot damn!" he shouted. "Let's have some fun!"

He gunned the ski and headed straight for the whales.

"What the fuck are you doing?" Willow shouted into his ear, but he acted as if he didn't hear her.

Willow stared intently at the whales. Her feeling about them changed. She went from appreciating their beauty to an undefined feeling of dread, as if she could sense the whales' anxiety.

The whales heard the log approach and Sam told Rose to flee. Sam veered off, circled back, then crossed the logrider's path. There were two riders on the log, a male and a female. Both were thin and wearing false black skins. They momentarily altered direction to pursue him, but then turned back toward Rose and her more slowly moving calf. The log quickly caught up with them.

Rose remembered the sound of the jet ski as it drew near. She immediately understood the danger it posed. She told her son to swim very close, no matter what. At first, she didn't understand why Sam had left them, but saw him head back toward the ski and across its path. She realized that Sam was trying to divert it away from their child. She had a moment of relief when it veered away and after Sam. But her relief turned to panic when she heard it turn again and speed directly at them.

"Swim!" she shouted to her child. "Swim fast!"

The log pulled up alongside them. They were both breathing hard. Rose tried to put herself between the shrieking machine and her child. The log turned quickly around then slowed alongside her child.

Lance had kept his foot on the whaling lance the entire time they were riding. He liked its look and feel. The primordial weapon in the hand of the primordial hunter. He reached down and picked it up, felt its heft. He hoisted the lance.

"No!" screamed Willow.

He ignored her and thrust it down into the back of the small whale.

Sam heard his son's scream of pain and fear. He rushed to them, overwhelmed by the growling of the jet ski, the cries of his child, the shrieking disbelief of his mate. Scanning and in shock, he saw the end of the lance sticking out of his son's back, saw the blood pouring out of the wound. Looking deeper, he saw the leaf shaped blade at the end of the shaft, lodged in his son's heart. He knew instantly what had happened. Engulfed with a rage he had never known, he turned toward the ski and charged at it.

Lance saw the big orca turn and rush at them. *Shit!* Twisting the throttle full, he raced toward the opening of the bay. Looking back, it was clear the whale was pursuing them, pushing a huge bow wave. But the ski was clearly faster than the whale.

At the bay's entrance, the water grew shallow, the bottom exposed in places. The tide had gone out, something Lance hadn't counted on. Ignoring the depth, he gunned the ski over the barely covered bottom, throwing up as much sand as water in its wake.

He didn't slow until they were fifty feet from the boat-house entry, then backed off on the throttle. The ski slowed, bumping on the bottom now that it had lost its ability to plane across the water's surface. Lance looked back and saw the whale was plowing along, kicking up sand and mud, struggling in the shallow water, but still moving forward, but barely. *Ha!*

Lance gunned the engine and just managed to slide into the boathouse. He cut the engine, jumped off the ski, and pushed the down button on the sliding door. As it dropped, he could see the large whale thrashing in the shallows, still pointed at the house, but making no progress. The door closed.

Only then did Lance remember Willow. She was sitting on the ski, sobbing uncontrollably, tears streaming down her face.

"Hey, babe. You okay?"

Willow looked at him, her hatred clear.

"I heard them! I felt them, not just their screaming but their anguish! The baby was crying in pain! You beast! You brute! You, you…animal. *No.* Animals are better than you. You're a fucking pathetic loser!"

"Hey, babe, they're only a couple of dumb fish. What's the big deal?"

Willow sat there, speechless. Slowly, she got off the ski, walked over to the pegs that held her clothes. Mechanically, barely controlling her rage, she stripped off her wetsuit, bra and panties and threw them down. She pulled on her jeans, sweatshirt, shoes and socks, opened the metal ship door, and stumbled up the spiral staircase.

"Hey, babe, where you going?"

Willow didn't answer.

Lance ran up the stairs after her.

In the great room, Willow picked up her cloth bag and headed for the front door, her hair wet, tears still streaming down her face.

"Hey, wait. I'll give you a ride," he shouted, standing there in his dripping wet suit.

Lance watched her walk up the driveway, open the gate, and keep walking, not closing it behind.

"Dumb cunt," Lance muttered. "Let her freeze for all I care."

He looked around at the mess they had made and decided he better clean up. Cover any evidence of ever having been there.

CHAPTER 44

Rudy woke with a start. He sat bolt upright in bed, confused. He had the sense of having had a nightmare, but he couldn't remember any dreams. A wave of unease passed across him, through him. His phone said two a.m. *Damn.*

Rudy was a light sleeper but couldn't imagine what he might have heard that would have awakened him so quickly. Anything unusual would have woken Cheez first. Stumbling into the kitchen, he found Cheez sleeping in his usual place, just inside the kitchen door. The dog got up, stretched, and walked over to Rudy, apparently sensing that something was wrong. The dog leaned against him and wagged his tail.

"Good boy, Cheez. Sorry to disturb you. I don't know what got into me."

Rudy went back to his bedroom. Cheez followed him and lay down alongside the bed. Laying on top of the covers and staring at the ceiling, Rudy tried to shake the sensation of foreboding that had jarred him awake. After at least an hour, sleep finally overtook him.

The whoop of his phone sounded far off until he realized what the noise was. Picking up the phone, he noticed that it was well past dawn. Groggily and without looking at the caller's number, he answered.

"Uh, hello?"

"Rudy, it's J. B. Alexander."

"Uh, what? J. B.? Oh right. I had a bad night and I'm a little groggy. What's up?"

"It looks like you weren't the only one. We have a problem with our boy Makai," J. B. said.

"Really? I saw him just a couple of days ago, swimming with his girlfriend and their little one. He seemed fine. What's the problem?"

Rudy held his breath. This couldn't be good.

"It seems Makai has stranded himself off the west side of San Juan Island, in a place called False Bay. I got a call from the sheriff there. Makai's pretty far up in shallow water, off to the south side in a pocket bay. He's starting to draw a crowd, mostly of people who want to help. But I'm afraid of what they might do in the process."

"Damn, J. B. I'm in Blaine, hours away. I'd have to drive down to Anacortes, take the first ferry I can get on, and drive out to False Bay. I feel useless."

"No, son. You need to drive to the Bellingham Airport where you will find Joseph and Randolph waiting in our plane. They'll fly you to Friday Harbor, where the sheriff has agreed to take you to False Bay to supervise Makai's rescue. The arrangements have all been made. Good luck. Please let me know how things go."

"Wow! I mean of course. I'm out of here. Thanks, J. B."

"No, Rudy. Thank *you*."

Rudy drove as fast as he could to Bellingham International. How had Alexander found out so quickly about Makai's stranding? The old guy was always full of surprises, with connections everywhere. And was Rudy's nightmare, or whatever it was that woke him last night, somehow related to Makai's stranding? That was just too far-fetched. More immediately and relevant, what could have motivated

Makai to strand himself in False Bay? Orcas never went in there, as if they knew it dried completely at even normal low tides. And why would he have left his mate and child? Nothing added up.

When he finally arrived at a big house overlooking the scene, he saw a couple dozen people surrounding the whale. They had thrown towels and blankets over his back and had formed a bucket brigade, drenching him with seawater as fast as they could move the buckets along. Makai was in a small bay, facing the shore and the house, one of those Montana log mansions constructed from old-growth trees, entirely out of place in the San Juans. It didn't look occupied, given all the drawn curtains. But people were streaming down from the house to join the effort. To add to the chaos, a news helicopter was hovering over the scene, a videographer hanging out the door filming.

On the ride from the airport, Rudy and the local sheriff agreed that Rudy would direct the rescue effort. Rudy asked to see some tide tables, which would determine how to proceed. The first thing was to get the damn helicopter out of there because it could only upset the whale more.

Rudy waded into the knee-deep water and walked up to Makai. The whale was breathing, rapidly and heavily, clearly stressed. His body seemed to be supported by the water, at least deep enough to keep from crushing himself. The wet towels and blankets would help prevent sunburn, and, if nothing else, make people feel like they were doing something.

"Hey big fella," Rudy said, standing next to Makai's left eye so he could be seen. "What the hell got into you? You're too smart to do something so dumb as to strand yourself here. I can't believe you were chasing fish. No fish is worth this."

Rudy didn't expect an answer, but he did hear, or rather feel through the water, the whale vocalizing. He also noticed that Makai's breathing slowed slightly. Maybe he was doing some good after all.

"Okay then, big boy. It's a full moon, so we have a spring tide. You must have come in here in the night when there was more water, but the tide would have been falling. In about three hours, we'll have a good five feet of water under you so you can just turn yourself around and get the hell out of here. And go back to your wife and family where you belong. Meanwhile I'll stay right here."

The sheriff arranged for a small inflatable dingy. Two burly deputies carried it down the beach and pushed it to Rudy, who rowed it back to the whale. All everyone could do, including Makai, was wait for the rising tide.

Rudy had read about whale stranding, mainly by pilot whales and other dolphin species. Orcas almost never stranded, at least not healthy ones. The pilot whale mass strandings were a mystery, but usually involved one whale getting stuck and others following. None of J Pod was anywhere to be seen, which also struck Rudy as odd. With Makai in trouble, he half expected to see the rest of J Pod moving back and forth outside the bay. Just when he thought he understood these animals, he was thrown another curve ball.

With a slight rise in the tide, Makai floated a little higher. Rudy was surprised to see him pushing farther into the bay, not turning around, trying to free himself. He rowed directly in front of the whale and bumped up against his snout.

"Whoa there, Makai. You are not following the script. Deeper water is the other way. There's nothing up here but rocks, sand, and an ugly McMansion. Fish and family are thataway."

Rudy pointed out to sea with an oar. Strange he didn't feel silly trying to reason with a whale. But, then again, they were usually reasonable animals.

His bump into the whale had turned the little boat one-eighty and he was now facing the shore. He noticed that the big log home actually had what looked like a boathouse underneath. Another pretension, he guessed. He also noticed someone on the shore, a hundred yards away, waving her arms, trying to get his attention. Something about her looked familiar.

It was Cassie. He shouldn't have been surprised. This was the first good thing that had happened today.

Cassie waded out to him, oblivious to the cold water.

"Oh, Rudy! This is awful. I was at the Shannon Point lab and heard on NPR that a big male orca was on the beach at False Bay. They didn't identify him, but somehow I knew it was Makai. I just caught the ferry and followed the traffic here."

She said all this as she was climbing into the inflatable.

"Can I talk to him?" she asked.

"I don't see what harm that can do," Rudy replied. "You're someone else he knows and seems to trust."

They rowed back to the whale. Cassie started crying.

Rudy positioned the boat so Cassie could reach down and put her arms around his snout and kiss him. Through the hull of the boat, Rudy could hear the whale vocalizing.

"My poor baby," Cassie said. "You've had a hard life, but things had turned for the better. Why did you do this?"

As if blocking the whale's path with the small rubber boat presented an obstacle—or was it Cassie's presence?—Makai stopped pushing forward and rested, breathing more slowly.

Rudy and Cassie sat in the boat, rowing softly back and forth, keeping in front of the whale, talking to him. Most of the people had long ago retreated to the shore because the water was getting too deep, not to mention too cold, for anyone to stand for long.

Finally, after another hour and another foot of water, the whale started making small movements with his tail. This turned him around until he faced seaward. Then, with stronger tailbeats, and leaving a trail of roiled water, sand, and kelp, he pushed out of the pocket bay and finally out to the ocean. A cheer went up from the crowd of now more than a hundred people on the shore. Rudy and Cassie didn't move until they could no longer see the whale.

Only then did Rudy pull out his phone. Hoping for coverage, he called J. B. Alexander.

The whale-watch boat *Odyssea* had just received a message from one of the spotter planes. They had seen a group of whales on the west side of San Juan Island, north of Lime Kiln. Telling his passengers to hang on, the captain raced down the San Juan coast. The whales, easily a dozen or more, were quite visible, blowing frequently. The captain went on the PA system.

"Okay, folks. Seems like we've got a large pod. From the numbers, they have to be our salmon-eating resident whales. J and K pods have been using this area the last few days, so it's probably one of them."

Pausing, the captain looked through a pair of binoculars.

"Yes, it's definitely J Pod. They're moving very slowly, almost in a line. That's strange behavior, especially for this time of day when they are usually chasing fish, not resting.

But when they're resting, they don't move so…so much like in a procession.

"Okay. I can make out J-2, the oldest female in the group and probably the leader and…Hey, we're in luck. It's J-28 Polaris. She's the mate of the rescued orca Makai. They now call him J-60. And, if we're lucky, we'll see their young calf, J-61. Folks haven't decided on a name yet—"

The boat captain was interrupted by one of his crew. They exchanged excited words. The skipper turned back, binoculars up.

"Hey," some kid on the boat shouted. "Doesn't that little whale have something sticking out of his back, like a pole?"

The captain could now clearly see that J-61 wasn't swimming alongside his mother but was being carried at an odd angle across her head. His body was lifeless. A rod was, in fact, sticking out of him.

"Oh shit," he said into the mike, audible to everyone. He turned it off, shut down the engines and drifted. The procession of whales passed the boat, slowly, solemnly. J-2 led, followed by Polaris bearing her calf, then the rest of the group. Cameras clicked, people held up cell phones, took videos, made calls.

The captain grabbed his radio mike and practically shouted, "Securité, securité," using the international distress phrase. "US Coast Guard or Victoria Coast Guard. This is the whale-watch boat *Odyssea*. We have a serious problem off Lime Kiln with the J Pod whales. It appears one of the whales has been harpooned. I repeat, we need to contact the Whale Museum or the university or a vet or…Hell, I don't know."

"Whale-watch vessel *Odyssea*. This is the US Coast Guard. You are on an open transmission line. Please observe transmission protocols, over."

"You come out here and take a look at this clusterfuck and see how observant you can be."

He shut off his mike.

Sam had eventually realized the futility of his chase. The logriders that had killed his child would not be there, at least not now. He had gotten a good look at them, especially the male, and wouldn't forget. The two logriders that had been kind to him, Uncle Morris and the familiar female from his captivity days, had appeared somehow and were clearly concerned about his condition in the shallows. He guessed they had no way of knowing why he was there, but they seemed anxious for him to leave. Maybe that was the best course of action, at least for now. He should go find the family and seek Grandma's advice. He shuddered at remembering how Nan had fallen apart when their baby was taken away, so long ago. He needed to try to comfort Rose, if that was possible. He would be back.

Grandma had never dealt with this kind of tragedy. Newborns died, sometimes soon after birth, sometimes later. It was always sad, but all mothers had been taught how precarious the first year of life can be. The consoling presence of the elder females helped ease the pain.

But never in her lifetime had a baby been killed so brutally and deliberately by a logrider. Many, many years ago, according to family memory, conflicts had occurred and logriders had, in fact, killed some ancestors, usually adult males. This saddened and angered the survivors, and some were vengeful. But vengeance was against all tradition.

Retribution by the logriders could be dire. But, still, to kill a baby? In these times of relative peace between whales and logriders? It made no sense.

Grandma knew that Rose would not part with her dead child willingly nor quickly. A time of mourning would be observed, Rose would be consoled, and eventually she would resign herself to the loss. Allowances would be made. Rose was a strong traditionalist, always had been. Grandma had faith that Rose would recover somewhat, if not entirely. Life would go on. The family came first.

But what about Sam? He was not bound by traditions that were new to him, and his hatred of almost all logriders was evident daily. She worried how he might react. She worried about the consequences. And she knew that everyone would turn to her if the situation deteriorated.

Sam did not join the family until late that day. Grandma saw him swim up to Rose, who barely acknowledged his presence. He spoke to no one. Grandma's concern over his possible reaction deepened.

CHAPTER 45

We don't know much about animals' capacity for hope.
We do know that they grieve...

MIDGE RAYMOND, *My Last Continent*

The news of the dead baby orca, and that it had been harpooned, quickly made local news, then rippled out. As days passed and J-28 continued to carry her dead calf, sometimes with the help of other whales, media attention increased. The whales were followed by helicopters filming the scene until the FAA restricted the airspace over them. Then the drones appeared, and their operators had to be reminded that airspace was airspace and they, too, were excluded. Still, daily broadcasts included footage, sometimes close up, of the baby orca with the harpoon sticking out of its back, held up by its mother.

As the infant began to decompose, close-ups became rarer, but speculation only increased. People for the Ethical Treatment of Animals, PETA, offered a one-hundred-thousand-dollar reward for information leading to apprehension of the person or persons responsible. Self-appointed experts speculated that the authorities might be able to lift fingerprints from the wooden handle of the harpoon. Forensic experts countered that such latent prints would have long ago washed off, not to mention the trauma that would be inflicted on the grieving mother—

and everyone agreed that she was grieving—by having somebody interfere with her.

―――――――

Willow was largely unaware of the aftermath of her jet ski ride. She had walked almost unconsciously a few miles in the moonlight, cold and miserable. She came upon a small shoreline home, its windows all shuttered, no lights on. Clearly a summertime residence. No security lights. These small homes were sometimes unlocked. Little worth stealing. Willow found a low window that hadn't been latched and climbed inside. She walked to the corner of a bedroom, sat down on the floor, pulled her knees up, put her arms around them, and fell into troubled sleep.

The next morning, shortly after dawn, Willow found the road leading into Friday Harbor. She put out her thumb, thinking she might catch a ride with someone going to open up their business. Sure enough, a woman who worked at the bakery stopped and picked her up. They exchanged a few words, and the woman respected Willow's need for silence. The woman even dropped her off at the ferry terminal, which was out of her way.

A scan of the incoming ferry showed no sign of Lance. Departing at Orcas, she hitched another ride home. No one was there. Not really having a plan, she packed some clothes in a backpack, grabbed an apple and a can of pop from the fridge, and left. All she could think of was to get the hell away from here, from the events of last night, from this life. She would head north. Go to Canada.

She had about fifty dollars from her earnings and a passport. Several years earlier, she and her parents went to Vancouver on vacation. It was, not surprisingly, a pretty miserable trip, and she remembered little, aside from crossing bridges over big rivers, a park with huge trees, her stepfather drinking too much, her parents fighting. But it did require they get her a passport.

In Anacortes, she walked on the Sidney, BC-bound *Chelan*. At customs, she showed her passport to the nice Canadian customs lady and finally boarded a bus to Nanaimo up the east coast. After that, she wasn't certain what she'd do. That's where her plan ended. All she knew was that she had the sniffles but had escaped. And used up most of her funds.

Lance, on the other hand, couldn't avoid the news. It was everywhere. On front pages, on the crawler at the bottom of the TV screen on the ferries, even on the morning talk show on the classic rock station from Bellingham, the one with the two caffeine-addled DJs. Even these guys were pretty worked up, bemoaning the lack of good old vigilante justice when the culprit was found. The authorities couldn't be harsh enough on the guy. *Why did they think it was a guy?* Lance considered high-tailing it, but he had no place to go, and if he didn't show up for work, people might start looking for him. Best to act as if nothing had happened, like he knew no more than anyone else, like he was as outraged as everyone. Just because of a dead dumb fish. It would blow over, right?

Rudy got caught up in the media frenzy, despite efforts not to. His phone rang constantly. He tried to remain objective, scientific. No, he had nothing to add. Yes, the mother was still carrying the dead calf. No, this wasn't unusual behavior for orcas, other whales, or even monkeys and elephants. Was it thoughtless maternal instinct or true grief? Did they know the baby was dead? It wasn't for him, as a scientist, to speculate. Yes, he was keeping an eye on Makai. Eventually, the reporters got bored with Rudy's answers and left him alone. There were many others, knowledgeable or not, who were more than happy to voice opinions.

And Sam spent his time in family activities amid Grandma's attempts at getting things back to normal. But he also made sure that his hunting took him past the opening to Drying Bay, just in case.

* * *

Jonathan and Patrick were surprised at all of the attention focused on their get-away home on San Juan. The big whale had stranded just out from their place. The video footage on the Saturday evening news showed a huge crowd on their shoreline. Patrick worried about all those people trampling the plantings. Had they shut the gate? Would deer get in and eat everything? Weren't the authorities doing anything to protect their property? Jonathan thought there was something familiar about the shape of the harpoon handle sticking out of the dead baby whale. The close-ups weren't sharp enough, but still. He didn't mention it to Patrick. The guy was a worrywart.

They decided they better protect their investment. Catching the last boat Friday evening, Jonathan saw the young ferry worker whom he had met before. But the guy seemed really busy and basically ignored him. No big deal.

When they got to their vacation home, the gate was, thankfully, closed. It was obvious all the foot traffic had been from the gate down to the shoreline. Nothing up by the house seemed disturbed. Nothing inside seemed amiss. On the pretext of cleaning downstairs, Jonathan went to what he called his "cabinet of curiosities," the nautical room.

At first things looked fine, but then he looked above the big ship's wheel. Damn. One of the harpoons was missing. No question. Thoughts raced through his mind. Should he tell Patrick? Should he notify the authorities? The answer was clearly no. Best to stay out of it. There was no way that harpoon could be traced back to them, even if it could somehow be recovered. It would all go away.

He rearranged the display so the empty space where the harpoon had been was less obvious. He told Patrick everything was fine.

The next morning was warm, sunny, windless. A midsummer day. Hot actually.

"Hey, Patrick," Jonathan said after lunch. "How 'bout we take that jet ski out for a spin? It's silly to just let it sit there, and the weather's perfect. The tide is high, and the sea is calm, and we can maybe venture outside a little. What do you think?"

Patrick was at his computer, catching up on work.

"Look," he said. "We never finished the Microsoft quarterly account summary, and it's due the end of this week. We really shouldn't be up here, fooling around. If you want to go out, fine. I'm going to do this. Somebody has to pay the bills."

"Fine," Jonathan answered. "Suit yourself. All work and no play, you know."

Jonathan found the instruction manual for the ski and the CD the broker had given them. It was pretty thorough, didn't really seem that complicated after all. It contained lots of footage of a young man driving the ski, with a scantily clad young woman sitting behind, arms around his waist, both laughing happily, hair flying, exhaust jet shooting up behind the ski.

Guess we're not their target market yet. They'll come around. Socioeconomics are always a little behind cultural change. It's being able to spot the trends that leads to profits.

He took the key and headed downstairs to the boat room. Everything seemed in order. Why shouldn't it? He squeezed into his wetsuit (*I really need to shed some of these pounds*), added a life jacket just to be safe, and started the ski. The gas tank registered a little over half full. That was strange, but Patrick had supposedly filled it. He probably got impatient, his enthusiasm for the ski being minimal from the start. *Oh well, still plenty for a quick spin. Can it really do fifty?*

The sliding door went up smoothly as he pushed the purring ski out backward. Once turned around, he tentatively twisted the throttle and almost fell off backward as it jumped ahead. Maybe a little too much throttle. Twisting more cautiously, the ski picked up speed. Soon it was on a plane, skimming across the water. *Wow! Patrick was missing something great.*

⁂

Grandma grew concerned about Sam's willingness to go off hunting alone. She had half expected him to stay near Rose, to give her moral support. Yes, fish were needed despite the trying emotional times, and Sam was one of the best providers. Still, he seemed a little too willing.

She decided today it would be better if the twins went with him.

"Please take them with you," she told Sam, above his objections that they'd probably interfere more than help. "Maybe they can learn some new hunting skills."

Sam left in something of a huff, not waiting for the twins. Eddie and Mitchie quickly caught up, talking all the way.

"Can you at least be quiet so we don't scare away every salmon in the ocean?" he said, his irritation evident.

The boys shut up, mostly.

They worked south along the Gathering Salmon Island shoreline. Sam only slowed momentarily outside Drying Bay and listened. He couldn't go inside the bay, even though the tide was high, given his escorts and their certain knowledge of restrictions about entering. Not hearing anything, he continued on.

The threesome swam for several more minutes, to the southern tip of Gathering Salmon Island. Fish were scarce, something that had become distressingly usual. Sam then turned around and headed back north.

"Hey, Sam," Mitchie said. "Aren't we at least going to go across the channel and, like, check things out on the other side?

"When was the last time you caught a fish over there?" Sam replied. "That would be a waste of my time. And even yours, not that it's worth much."

"Okay, whatever," Mitchie said, hurt showing in his voice.

Sam slowed again off Drying Bay, listened, heard nothing, and continued on. But a minute later he heard the faint but distinct buzz of one of the small logs. Could it be? He slowed, then stopped and listened.

"Hey, what's up Sam?" Mitchie asked. "I don't see any fish."

"Hush," Sam said sharply. "Listen."

The boys stopped and listened.

"Wow, is that one of those buzz logs, like the one we almost got run over by a couple weeks ago? Hey, didn't someone say that the logrider who killed your boy was riding one of those? Man, those things are loud..."

"Shut up!" Sam shouted at him.

Sam turned back toward Drying Bay and the twins followed.

Jonathan liked the feeling of speed and power that the ski produced. He started a turn back into False Bay to tell Patrick all about it, maybe convince him to come out, just for a little while. He'd see what fun it really was.

He noticed whales up ahead on the left, their spouts clearly visible! He slowed to get a better look. Yes, there were three of them. Two were smaller, but the third was obviously a big male with a very tall dorsal. Jonathan and Patrick frequently saw orcas going by their vacation home, watched them through the sixty-power Swarovski spotting scope they kept in the great room. But they had never been close to them. This was cool.

Jonathan knew the whale-watching guidelines. Stay a couple hundred yards away, don't race ahead to intercept them, don't chase after them. But the guidelines said nothing about the whales approaching you, as these certainly were. He cut the ski to an idle and sat there, transfixed. Their exhaled breaths erupted in the air; he could actually hear their explosive breathing. The three animals moved directly at him, accelerating, the big male in the lead.

Jonathan started to grow a little uneasy.

Sam spyhopped about a hundred feet from the log. Yes, it was the same one, same sound, just one rider, a male. His view wasn't complete given the distance, but he'd seen enough and had been focused on this possibility every moment for the last week. The rage he felt the night of the attack rushed back.

He charged the log at full speed and leapt into the air, his body completely leaving the water, arcing directly at the log, intent on crushing it and its occupant. At the last moment, as he twisted to watch the face of his nemesis, he realized his mistake. The rider wasn't a thin, tall male, but much shorter and fatter. Too late, he tried to twist away, but his momentum took over, and he crashed down on log and rider with all of his mass.

Eddie and Mitchie watched in stunned disbelief. Sam had actually attacked a logrider. There could be no doubt. From day one, they and everyone had been taught: no matter what, no matter how justified it may seem, never, ever harm a logrider. Sam had done the unthinkable. They left immediately.

The collision with the hard log knocked the wind out of Sam, tore up his left pectoral fin, and probably broke something deep on his left side. But the pain was nothing compared to the realization of what he had done, and what he hadn't accomplished. He would have hell to pay. Or worse.

He turned and swam away. He wasn't surprised that the twins had already left. They'd want no part of this. They had headed back to report to Grandma.

Patrick grew restless, glued to his computer on such a beautiful summer day. Maybe he should have agreed to go ride the ski with Jonathan. They could work on the quarterly report later in the day, after sunset. He walked to the window of the great room, next to the spotting scope. Taking the caps off, he scanned the bay. No sign of the jet ski. He swung the scope seaward and saw the ski flying along, south of the bay's entrance. Then he saw it stop, pointed north. Swinging the scope in that direction, he saw the whales. Three of them. Damn. Lucky Jonathan. He was going to have an encounter of the whale kind.

Patrick watched the whales approach Jonathan and stop. One of them, the one with the very tall dorsal fin, stuck his head out of the water near Jonathan. Was that what the whale people called a spyhop? Cool. Then he saw the big whale accelerate directly at Jonathan and, to Patrick's horror, leap into the air and…No. That couldn't be. It looked like the whale landed right on top of the ski. On top of Jonathan. No way. The perspective must have him fooled. But, seconds later, there was no question. Jonathan was off the ski, floating in the water next to it. And the whales were leaving.

"Jesus Christ!" Patrick shouted. He stood there. What could he do? Call the Coast Guard, the sheriff? Call 911? Did they even have 911 on this rock? It didn't matter. He had to do something.

Grabbing his cell phone and the speedboat key off the key hook, he ran down the spiral staircase. He started the outboard, put it in reverse. It wouldn't move. Of course. He hadn't untied it. Fumbling with the dock lines, he threw them off and backed the boat out. He seldom drove the boat; that was Jonathan's favorite thing to do. Buying a jet ski had also been Jonathan's idea. Now look what happened. *Jesus Christ.*

Patrick raced out of the cove and toward the mouth of False Bay. Had things happened there or to the south or north? He didn't remember! He slowed the boat and stood up and looked around. He spotted the jet ski, just to his right, maybe a hundred yards away. He approached slowly. He could hear the ski idling, purring in the gentle swell. Its plastic windshield was shattered, pieces hanging down. It was listing to the left, out of balance. Where the hell was Jonathan?

Patrick circled the ski, and then he saw him. Jonathan was face down in the water, lifeless. Patrick screamed.

Alright. Get him to a doctor. No. Call 911 and get a doctor here. That was the thing to do. First get him on board.

Jonathan's limp body was literally dead weight. With great effort, and taking as much care as he could, Patrick hoisted Jonathan up over the side of the boat, almost falling into the water himself while realizing he hadn't put on a lifejacket. He didn't know how he had the strength to do it, but somehow he got Jonathan into the boat. He lay his unconscious partner across the bench seat behind the driver's console, face up. Jonathan's eyes were open, staring at the sky. *Oh, please God, don't let him die, not out here, not like this.*

Patrick took a deep breath. Panic wasn't helping the situation. He grabbed his cell phone and punched in 911. Someone answered on the second ring. Help was coming.

CHAPTER 46

It had been a week since the killing of the baby orca. The story of the harpooned whale had slid off the front page, meriting briefer mention on the evening news. The incident still remained somewhat newsworthy, not only because of the scale of the atrocity, but because the biologists were fairly certain the baby had been fathered by the rescued male orca Makai. That added to the human interest. The Whale Museum in Friday Harbor received thousands of condolence cards and emails, addressed to "Baby Orca" and "Makai's Baby." Someone started up a Facebook page for Makai. Thousands friended him. But the buzz was diminishing.

And then the news cycle changed, and the topic moved back up to the top. Makai went from victim to perpetrator. Jonathan Winkler, a respected public accountant in Seattle corporate circles, had been deliberately crushed by a twenty-ton male orca while boating off San Juan Island. *Exaggerated size, of course*, thought Rudy. *Makai isn't a pound over fifteen tons. And hmm, no mention that it is illegal to operate a jet ski in San Juan waters.* The incident, as detailed by Jonathan's business partner Patrick Martindale, was clear. It had been a deliberate attack, no question. It wasn't a playful whale accidentally landing on someone. Experts concurred that, when orcas jump, they know where they are landing. The approach of this whale, the spyhop, and the final assault added up, plain and simple, to a deliberate act. An attack by a whale who, after years in captivity in confined quarters, had snapped, was a psychopath. Like that male whale in San Diego who killed a trainer. *Orlando, for Christ's sake.* Who had released the animal into the wild where it couldn't be contained? Why wasn't it just kept in captivity, put into a breeding program? People wanted answers. Rudy turned his phone off.

And people became fearful of orcas. No, they became fearful of what the media now referred to by the name they had used decades before. Killer whales.

Grandma was shocked and saddened at what the twins told her. Shocked, saddened, but not completely surprised. She had hoped it wouldn't come to this, but had known it was a possibility. Sam was not constrained by tradition. He had been too silent the past week, which had made her more than suspicious. It was wise to have sent the twins with him, or she wouldn't have known what happened, and wouldn't be prepared to act, to minimize the repercussions that would surely come.

First, she would have to tell the elders, knowing those who had questioned her accepting Sam into the family would feel vindicated and wouldn't hide their feelings. Her leadership would be questioned. Maybe it should be. Maybe she should question it too. Maybe she was just too old, too sentimental, to make the day-to-day and longer-reaching decisions on which her family depended. Maybe it was time to shrug off the mantle of leadership, pass it along, relieve herself of the burden of constant worry, of weighing alternatives, of deciding the best course for the greatest number. She was plagued with self-doubt.

She had no doubt about what to do with Sam. He would be banished from the family. Immediately. No one would question that. They would only question why she hadn't anticipated today's events and sent him away before something so predictable occurred. But she had felt sorry for Rose, for her loss. To ostracize Sam on top of the tragedy might be too much for Rose. Again, had she been too sentimental?

Sam did not appear until well after dark. He joined the edge of the group, swimming slowly, obviously in pain. Grandma said nothing but scanned him thoroughly, without hesitation. His condition confirmed what the twins had reported. He had three broken ribs on his left side and was bleeding internally. His left pectoral fin was lacerated. Normally, this would have been cause for quick action by the elders, for soothing words and comforting presence. That was unthinkable under the circumstances.

She approached Sam. He floated still, barely facing her.

All he said was, "I'm sorry, Grandma. So sorry."

Grandma choked up. So much was contained in his contrition. She hesitated a moment, then thought better.

"Not as sorry as I am, Sam. You know what must happen, don't you?"

"Yes, and I won't make you say it. I'm leaving. Thank you. Thank you for placing trust in me. I regret most violating that trust. Tell Rose I love her dearly and always will."

And he was gone.

CHAPTER 47

Within a day of the attack on the jet skier, Makai had disappeared. The press, while reviling the big male, was still focused, laser-like, on the plight of the mother. Images of Polaris pushing her moribund calf, the spear sticking from its side, continued to appear in blogs, newspapers, and on evening broadcasts.

This sad spectacle went on for fully two weeks. Polaris usually swam alongside family members and, at other times, was alone, keeping her calf afloat. Sometimes others, usually females, helped keep the calf afloat. The images were heartbreaking but spellbinding. Global media covered what became known as her "grief tour."

Rudy was torn. It was the height of his field season. The media circus made it easy to keep track of the whales. He was getting a wealth of data, admittedly compromised.

On the other hand, Makai was *his* whale. His emotional attachment had grown to the point of obsession. He tried to remain objective, but it became increasingly difficult. He suspected that Makai's attack on the jet ski was somehow connected to the baby whale's murder, that Rudy alone understood what had motivated—and justified—the attack. To not follow Makai now would be to abandon him.

But how? Rudy was clueless. The whale could have gone anywhere. It was a very big ocean.

He accepted that his knowledge of the whale's behavior was insufficient to handle the turn of events. He tried to think of someone who might have greater, or at least different, insight.

It was a long shot, to say the least. But what was the possible harm?

He knocked on the now familiar door. He hadn't been here since delivering Makai's fin top in the cedar mat.

The same soft female voice invited him in. Doris Whitesalmon sat at her desk. Rudy stopped just inside the door. Looking around, he noticed the place on the wall that had held the cedar mat was still empty.

Whitesalmon looked up and, in what seemed to be her practice, said nothing for a full minute.

Finally, she spoke.

"He has gone north."

Rudy wasn't surprised. Why else would he have come?

"How do you know?" he asked. There was no doubt in his voice, only puzzlement.

"The tribal fisheries, both here and in Canada, are very active right now. We have many boats and eyes on the water. Our men are watching for him. We feel great sorrow and sympathy."

"Where is he going?" Rudy asked. Then it occurred to him to ask the real question that was troubling him. "And why?"

"Your questions are intertwined," she said. "He is searching for answers, and he will go where he finds them."

Rudy would have appreciated a more direct, or at least informative, response. He knew pushing Whitesalmon for more would be pointless. She told him what she wanted to, or what she felt he deserved to know, and no more. Still.

In frustration, Rudy blurted out, "What am I supposed to do?" He immediately felt embarrassed, but then realized it was the question he'd been struggling with.

"Follow him. What else can you do? And maybe you will find some answers also."

Rudy stood there. Of course. He didn't really need to be told. He was about to leave when he noticed that Whitesalmon was writing something down. She stood and reached over her desk and handed him a piece of paper.

Rudy looked at it. She had scribbled what appeared to be hieroglyphics, script with apostrophes and superscripted question marks.

"Siʔaʔm'ac'aʔ," it said.

Rudy recognized it as a Coast Salish word, otherwise undecipherable. He attempted a pronunciation.

"Sigh-amaka?" he said.

"No, See-am-ma-tsa," she corrected.

"Okay, See-am-ma-tsa. What does it mean?" he asked.

"It is not a what. It is someone you might want to talk to," she answered. "And when you find her, show her this."

Whitesalmon opened a woven cedar purse that was lying on her desk, removed a purple cloth. She handed it to Rudy. Unwrapping the cloth, Rudy found an intricately carved statuette of an orca, glossy black, about an inch high, with inset abalone eyes. It was surprisingly heavy.

"That is argillite," she said, "a type of soft stone."

It was obvious that Whitesalmon was finished.

"Um, thank you," was all he could think of saying.

Rudy considered the logistics. Following a whale that could easily move seventy-five miles a day meant covering ground and water quickly. Pursuing by rubber dinghy was pointless. Clearly Cheez would come along. They'd just live out of the Volvo.

Whom should he tell? He could only think of two people who would care and would want to know. Cassie and Alexander.

Cassie understood immediately. She told him to keep in touch. She would keep him informed about how the media was dealing with the situation. With Makai gone, or at least out of the local jurisdiction, calls for vengeance seemed to be diminishing. The news cycle had spun off to handle recent mass shootings.

Alexander also concurred. "Don't worry about expenses, Rudy," he said. "Go keep an eye on our whale and keep him out of harm's way. Let me know how I might be of help."

Rudy packed some camping gear and dog food, invited Cheez into the car, and left for Canada. It was time to think like a whale. Resident orcas favored the east side of Vancouver Island, known as the Inside Passage. That increased Rudy's chances of encountering Makai, or at least encountering people who might have seen him.

CHAPTER 48

Heading north, far from familiar waters, Sam found himself moving through narrow passages, fighting strong currents, some that created whirlpools that he sensed initially by their sound but was uncertain what the sound meant.

He found out soon enough. Caught by surprise in a twisting torrent, he was spun around violently and found himself moving sideways, then backward and upside down, pulled toward the bottom. With tremendous effort, he righted himself, pushing hard against the flow. In a few seconds, he was free, although dizzy from the tumbling. He was still fighting a strong current, but at least it was flowing steadily against him.

Taking a huge breath, he calmed down and scanned around. A school of very large Chinook was stacked up just outside the whirlpool, facing into the flow, picking off disoriented herring that were discharged from the whirlpool. He had never seen so many big fish in one place before. He blasted one and swallowed it in a gulp as the rest of the school fled. It was the first he'd eaten in days.

Hunger satisfied and wanting to avoid more whirlpools, Sam moved closer to shore and into a rock-strewn bay. Small shapes approached and dashed by him. To his surprise, he was surrounded by a dozen young, energetic sea lions. They appeared out of the gloom, turning aside

GENE HELFMAN

at the last moment, then rocketed past. He was surprised at their boldness, by their ability to recognize he posed no threat. Here was another creature he had only heard about.

One youngster swam up and circled him slowly. Sam remained motionless, afraid he might do something to scare it off. He realized how lonely he had been and welcomed the company. A few other sea lions joined up and, the next thing he knew, he was the center of their excited attention. They basically used him as a playscape, going under, sliding over, and swirling around him. Their movements were quick and supple. The first youngster nestled against his side, barking softly under water. *That's just fine.*

Sam then heard a different sound, a shout, more like an alarm, coming from the shore. Scanning, he sensed the sea lions dashing to the nearby rocks. His companion apparently didn't hear the alarm and remained at his side.

A quick scan revealed the reason for the retreat. Transient orcas, maybe a half dozen, were approaching from outside the bay.

The transients drew nearer, then stopped. They made no sound. His new friend must have realized something was wrong and started to move toward the rocks. A transient rushed the sea lion. His friend turned quickly back toward Sam and dove under him. Another transient charged from Sam's other side, turning at the last moment. The sea lion was breathing rapidly now, frightened and confused. All six transients began circling Sam and the sea lion. Sam could hear the sea lion's breathing and even his rapid, frightened heartbeat. The transients moved closer, tightening the circle.

Deciding quickly, Sam moved toward the rocks where the other sea lions had hauled out, all looking in his, and the transients', direction. To his surprise, the frightened sea lion climbed onto his back, his side fin claws digging into Sam in an attempt to hold on. Sam could have easily shaken him off but felt this would violate the friendliness the sea lion had shown him. Instead, he swam into the shallows next to the rocks, his belly scraping the rough, barnacle-covered bottom. The sea lions on the rocks barked louder.

With the rocks so close, the transients could no longer circle but, instead, began passing rapidly back and forth, out in deeper water. Sam's new friend slid off his back and made a mad, successful dash for the safety of the rocks.

The transients retreated slightly, far enough that Sam could no longer see their outlines in the murk, but his scans revealed their body language. They were clearly enraged at this interference. They resumed swimming back and forth, getting closer. Despite swiveling as much as he could, Sam could only sense them clearly when they were ahead of him, within the beam of his sonic scans.

One broke off from the group and rushed at Sam from the side, his left side, still sore from the log impact. The transient must have sensed his vulnerability.

Sam felt the wave of water ahead of the transient. He twisted painfully and leveled a loud sonic blast at his attacker. The transient screamed in pain and turned aside, followed by his fellows.

The transients regrouped at a distance. Sam heard them talking, but they were unintelligible. They began another slow approach, separating into two groups, and staying away from the region ahead of Sam, neutralizing his sonic defense. Whenever he turned, they moved aside. He could feel their exploratory sonic scans along his sides. They became still and silent, perhaps fifty feet away. They then exchanged brief, excited vocalizations that Sam guessed were preparations for an attack.

He felt the rush of water ahead of the charging transients, then felt bodies crashing into him, teeth clamping onto his sides and fins. He was rammed and bitten repeatedly, pain shooting through his body. Each time he twisted one way, he was attacked from the other side. *So, this is how it ends.*

Just then, Sam heard a clear, loud shout of, "Now!"

Multiple black and white bodies shot past him, colliding with the transients. Bodies crashed into bodies, each with a loud thud. Sam found himself in the middle of a melee, accented voices he understood shouting tactics, others he didn't understand screaming in pain and rage. Amidst much thrashing, he felt the powerful tail beats from the retreating transients.

As his attackers fled, Sam scanned and recognized a dozen members of the northern families, crossing back and forth ahead of him.

"Iz everybody okay?" someone asked.

"My nose, it hurts," one replied.

"Your nose, it always hurts," said another. "You run into too many logs at night."

Sam heard laughter.

One of the northern whales swam up to him.

"Hello, big fellow. We heard our friends the sea lions barking alarm, no? It seems you have interrupted the transients' repast. I do not think you made those wandering bandits too happy, eh?"

"I guess I was careless. I let my guard down. Thank you! I'm certain you saved my life."

"It was nothing, my friend. I am Pierre," he said. "We met before at the tribal gathering. We are very glad we came when we did and hope those brutes learned to stay away from our home."

Sam reintroduced himself to each of the northerners. They knew of his exile and expressed condolences for the loss of his child.

"We welcome you to stay but, please, only for a little while. Although we sympathize, we too must obey the traditional rules and insist you remain an outcast. At least for now, no?"

Sam was disappointed, but he was in no position to argue, given the kindness he'd just been shown.

"Thank you once again for saving me," Sam replied formally. "I will not do anything to cause you more trouble than I already have. I will continue my journey, although I'm uncertain where it will lead."

"Life can be like that, no?"

Sam was about to swim off when he felt a bump along his side. Turning, he saw a large sea lion, one he recognized as a female. In her mouth, she was holding a Chinook salmon, still quivering. She pushed it towards Sam and swam away quickly.

"I think that was the young sea lion's mother, thanking you for saving her child," Pierre said.

"Wow," was Sam's shocked reply. Tasting the juices of the salmon, Sam realized he was still quite hungry, but not starving given his previous meal.

"It is you she should be thanking," he said. "Those transients will think twice about chasing sea lions here. Please take this."

And he ceremoniously placed the salmon in front of Pierre. His host bit the salmon in two, swallowed half, and passed the fish to an elder aunt.

"That was a nice gesture by the sea lion's mama, no? And by you, although, to be honest, we have many, many fish now, eh. It has been a good year for us. Not so good for your family, we hear. In fact, we hear things are very bad down there. It seems not fair, no? We have so many fish and you so few. We have more than we can eat, enough to share, no?"

"That is very generous of you, Pierre. Very generous. You are an excellent host."

"We would be very happy to be more than a host. More of us would make the intrusions by those seal-eating bandits even less likely. Not just you but your southern relatives too. Yes, I like that idea. But, goodbye my big friend. Until next time. We wish you much luck. To you and your kin."

The northerners moved off, talking rapidly among themselves.

Sam hesitated a moment, then resumed his journey, with much to think about.

CHAPTER 49

R udy had heard through the whale-watch grapevine that Makai was traveling north, beyond Vancouver.

He hitched a ride on a whale-watching boat out of Campbell River, a good way up the east coast of Vancouver Island. Rudy knew Gregor, the owner, through the whale-watching circuit. Business was slow, especially for midsummer. Only six clients on a boat that held thirty, so there was room. Rudy's status as the man who had "saved" Makai made him something of a curiosity, even more so now that the whale was considered something of a renegade. Cheez was allowed to come along as a novelty.

The day had been largely disappointing. Then Cheez gave his trademark bark from his position on the bow.

Gregor turned to Rudy. "What's that all about?" he asked. "Your dog just stands on the tube staring forward. Does he know we're looking for whales?"

"Definitely," answered Rudy. "And I'm pretty sure he's seen some. I'd train your glasses on the distance at one o'clock."

Cheez then barked twice.

"Good boy, Cheez. Gregor, we've lucked into the world-famous killer killer whale, Makai."

"No shit," Gregor said. "Where?"

"Right where he's telling us. One o'clock."

Shouting at the passengers to hold on, Gregor gunned the twin two-hundred-fifty-horsepower outboards. Thirty seconds later, he brought it to an abrupt halt. Makai's dorsal fin was obvious, maybe two hundred yards ahead.

"Looks like we brought the right people, and dog, with us today, folks," Gregor announced into everyone's headset. "That very tall dorsal fin belongs to no one else but Makai, the former captive, now runaway, orca. He appears to be alone, and I think I see several Steller sea lions frolicking in the water around him."

"Is he going to eat one? He's not going to eat one, is he?" It was a small girl, maybe ten years old.

"Oh no, miss. Makai is part of the Southern Resident community. Or at least he was until recently. Anyway, they're fish eaters. Never eat seals and sea lions. Those sea lions wouldn't be swimming anywhere near him if he were a threat. They know he's harmless, unless you're a salmon."

Rudy had never seen orcas and sea lions interacting before. He took out his phone and started to film. Just then Cheez gave another bark, followed by a growl. He was looking off to port. No one else paid attention because they were concentrating on the sea lions swimming and porpoising around Makai. Rudy turned off his phone and looked left.

"Uh oh. Hey, Gregor. Looks like we've got company. Bad company. Pointed dorsals."

Gregor followed Rudy's gaze.

"It looks like the game has changed, folks," Gregor announced. "We've got a pod of transient orcas headed our way, kinda fast. We almost never see resident and transient whales near one another, especially not here where the residents live."

The approaching transients caused a panicked retreat by the sea lions as they dashed toward some nearby rocks.

"The sea lions look scared," the same little girl said. "Why?"

Gregor tried to sound reassuring. "Well, these new whales are different from Makai. Unlike Makai, they *do* eat seals. But it looks like our sea lions have found a safe place on those rocks."

"But there's still a little one next to the big whale. Oh no! Those new whales are chasing it!" she shouted.

Rudy started filming again. Things happened fast, very fast. The transients made passes at the young sea lion as it dashed back and forth around Makai.

"Look!" the little girl shouted. "It's climbing on the big whale's back!"

"I'll be damned," Gregor said.

Everyone stared as Makai moved slowly toward the rocks, the sea lion clinging, head swiveling between the predators and the safety of the rocks. Makai seemed to beach himself. The water was so shallow that the transients couldn't swim between Makai and the rocks. The sea lion slid off his back and dashed to safety.

The transients moved off.

"Show's over, folks. That's one lucky sea lion, and one very smart orca. I've never seen anything like that before." He turned to Rudy. "Did you manage to get that?" he asked.

"I think so," Rudy answered. "I wasn't too steady, and I don't do a lot of video stuff, but I'll send it to—"

"Hey, those other whales are coming back!" It was one of the other people in the boat, a man this time.

Everyone watched as the transients began crisscrossing in front of Makai. Then one rushed him head on, but turned violently at the last moment. Rudy could have sworn he heard a cry. Then another transient rammed Makai on the side. Rudy grabbed his phone hurriedly and fumbled with the record button. He could see Makai twisting to fend off attacks, but he was outnumbered and outmaneuvered. Spray was flying everywhere, some of it reddened. Everyone watched in shocked silence. Only Rudy was filming, despite his concern.

"Looks pretty bad for your whale, Rudy."

Rudy was thinking the same thing and feeling helpless. He didn't say anything.

And then things got even crazier. Where there had been seven whales, there now were at least twice that number. And the new whales were clearly attacking the transients.

"Hey, that's G1 pod, our guys," Gregor exclaimed. "There's G-14 and G-19 and…and—"

"They're chasing the bad whales away!" the little girl shouted. "Hooray!"

Rudy had stopped filming, his phone battery having died. He watched as the transients disappeared to the north. Then Makai and the new whales, the northern residents, slowly swam off, side by side.

"Well, folks," Gregor said into his mouthpiece. "I guess you got your money's worth after all. This is one for the books. Dr. Laguna, can you explain what happened?"

"Not really," Rudy said into Gregor's mike. "It's just another example of how little we know about these animals, how smart they are, how they cooperate. But I don't think anyone has even suggested that Northern and Southern Residents come to each other's aid. Like Gregor said, one for the books."

As soon as Rudy got off the boat, he borrowed Gregor's phone and called Cassie. She picked up on about the fifth ring and answered hesitantly.

"Uh, hello?"

"Cassie, it's Rudy. I'm on a borrowed phone, mine is dead. I've got something that's going to blow your mind."

Rudy described the entire incident, as best as he could remember. "And I got it all on my phone. Except I can't review it until I get it charged back up. But that's just the beginning. I think we can use this is in our rehabilitation campaign for Makai. But I need your help."

"You know I'd do anything for Makai, and even you for that matter. But how can I possibly help?"

"After our little splash down and whale ride between you and Cheez and Makai, I did some background checking."

"You mean you didn't believe me, Rudy?" Cassie said, the hurt in her voice evident.

"No, not for a moment. Of course, I believed you. There was no way you could have fabricated that story. Not after what the three of you did in the water. But I wanted to check the old newspaper clippings because they had a ring of familiarity. In particular, I wanted to run down the reporter, the one you said did a follow-up exposé on Marineworld. Something about him seemed familiar."

"Oh, yeah," Cassie said. "I think his name was Sanderling, like the shorebird. I kinda remember him getting axed by the *L. A. Times* not long after that. But I don't know why or what happened to him. Too bad. He was really thorough."

"You're right about his leaving the *Times*," Rudy said. "His name is Phil Sanderlin. Like you said, he disappeared for several years and then resurfaced in Blaine as an environmental reporter for the *Northern Beacon*, the Blaine weekly birdcage liner."

"Oh, how the mighty have fallen," Cassie said.

"Seems so. Sanderlin's called me several times about Makai, and I'll admit I've kind of avoided him. His last call sounded rather prickly, like he was tired of getting blown off. Maybe I should have been more available."

"How does he fit in? And where do I fit in?" Cassie asked.

"Despite my rudeness, he still wants orca news. So, I think he's our man to start our PR campaign to resurrect Makai's reputation. I think you should call him and remind him of your Marineworld connection back when he was with the *Times*. Then tell him we're willing to give him an exclusive on an orca story, a *very exciting* orca story. Don't say any more. Between the two of us, he'll come around. Especially after I send him my video, assuming it shows what I think it shows."

"I'm on it," Cassie said.

They ended the call. After he handed the phone back to Gregor, he realized he really had enjoyed hearing Cassie's voice. It seemed like forever since they'd talked.

On the ferry ride back to Anacortes, Rudy got to thinking about his relationship with Cassie, how helpful she had been, no matter the time nor inconvenience to her. In fact, Rudy had to admit that he was very fond of Cassie, far beyond his initial attraction. Cassie would come over in the evening, and the two of them would sit in the kitchen and argue science for hours. Cassie had real insight into the workings of the biological world, especially orcas. He couldn't remember such enjoyable conversations with his ex-wife. If anything, he and Cassie covered more meaningful verbal ground in one evening—about whales and life—than Rudy had with his ex in the entire two years of their rock-strewn marriage. And Cassie seemed to have an almost spiritual connection with the whales, but it never interfered with her hard-nosed, objective interpretation of things. She was, if anything, more objective than he was.

And her work ethic was 24/7/365. And a quarter.

He really should thank the whales for bringing them together. Unfortunately, there was always Heath and that damned gold band on her ring finger.

CHAPTER 50

"Sanderlin here," said the voice on the phone.

"Hi, Phil. This is Rudy Laguna. I'm—"

"Laguna! Hey, I've been trying to reach you for months. Never even got a response. Now I'm Mr. Popular. What's the deal?"

"Sorry about that, Phil. I was under a sort of a gag order. But I've been authorized to speak to you exclusively."

It was as close to the truth as Rudy felt necessary.

"About?" Sanderlin sounded skeptical.

"I'm about to send you a text with an unedited, low resolution, jumpy video attached. It's about five minutes long, actually four minutes and forty-seven seconds. After you see it, you can call me back and we'll talk more."

Rudy hung up and sent the text.

Cassie arrived while Rudy was on the phone. She wanted to know if her earlier call to Sanderlin had worked.

"How'd it go? Do you think he'll bite?" she asked.

"I'd put money on it," Rudy said with a smile.

After five minutes, his phone whooped.

"Holy shit, Laguna! What the hell was that all about?"

Rudy explained as much as he could. He heard Sanderlin's keyboard clicking in the background. Finally, the reporter broke in.

"Tell me if I've got this right. First, you're offering me an exclusive to this story. You haven't contacted anyone else, like the big boys in Seattle or Vancouver, right?"

"Right. And none of the other people who were on the boat had the presence of mind to shoot video. They were all too awestruck. The video you watched is the only record."

"And you want me to write this up for the *Northern Beacon,* right? We're not exactly the center of the journalistic universe."

"I figure the wire services will pick it up, over your byline," Rudy offered.

"Damn straight they will. And what do you want in return? Compensation, attribution?"

"No compensation. I guess I'd like credit for the video. Plus, I have names and emails of the other folks present, including the boat operator. So, you can have a second source."

"That all seems reasonable. Almost too reasonable. Nothing else?"

"Well, yes, there is. A couple of things."

"Aha! Figured as much," Sanderlin said.

"Hear me out," Rudy replied. "First, I'll give you the complete story, but I want to meet face-to-face rather than doing this over the phone."

"I don't see a problem there. Your place or mine?" Sanderlin asked.

"I'm happy to come to your office, this afternoon."

"Great," Sanderlin said. "How about three o'clock?"

"That'll work," Rudy said.

"Okay. Drop the other shoe."

"Number two. I want to see any story you're going to print before it goes out."

"You know that goes against all journalistic policy, even at this paper. It's something I'd have to run by my editor first."

"Fine. Just show him the video," Rudy said. "My guess is he'll get religion real fast." He hung up.

Cassie had been listening to Rudy's end of the conversation. "Well, what did he say?"

"He said he'd do whatever we asked of him, or that's my paraphrase. He was practically hyperventilating."

The Northern Beacon office occupied a nondescript one-story building with a dark tar paper roof, near the Blaine waterfront. Rudy walked into an open room with a couple of desks. No receptionist, no one shouting, "Stop the presses!"

A short, stocky man with a full beard, glasses, and graying, curly hair, got up and walked toward Rudy. He was wearing jeans and a red plaid shirt.

"Laguna? Hi, I'm Phil," he said, extending a hand.

"Hey, Phil. I take it your editor gave you the green light."

Sanderlin pointed to a desk in the back of the room where a slender man with even grayer hair was talking on the phone and gesticulating with his free hand. The guy looked up momentarily, but then went back to his phone call.

"Yeah," Sanderlin said. "That's my editor, Calvin. He didn't hesitate. He told me to do whatever was needed to placate you. His exact words were, 'We don't get this kind of scoop often, if ever.'"

Sanderlin placed a folding metal chair on the opposite side of his desk. Rudy sat down as Sanderlin opened his laptop.

"That phone call from Cassie what's-her-name was a real blast from the past. Some of which I'd rather forget. Still, the coincidences are piling up."

"Yes, Ariel the Mermaid tracked you down, right to the ends of the earth. I'll admit I'm more than a little curious how one's career path goes from investigative reporting for the *L. A. Times* to writing for the Blaine *Northern Beacon*. Doesn't seem like a natural progression."

"Fair enough," Sanderlin replied. "Basically, I raked the wrong muck in LA, stepped on the toes of some influential people who used their influence to get me shit-canned."

"Sounds like how I wound up in these parts, a victim of influential people," Rudy said.

"I thought I was the cat among the pigeons," Sanderlin replied. "But it turns out the pigeons were armed and dangerous. The *Times* poisoned the waters for a job at a real newspaper. No one would even talk to me. I left a trail of unanswered phone calls up the west coast. I was headed for Canada but stopped in Blaine to pee…too much coffee. Almost drove right past the office but stopped in on a lark. I caught Calvin over there short a reporter who was also willing to sell advertising. I don't know if he even made phone calls. So here I am."

Rudy smiled. "It sounds like the fates have brought us together," he said.

Sanderlin cut him off. "Tell me about the video and what went on up there."

Rudy retold his tale while Sanderlin hunted and pecked on his computer. He stopped Rudy occasionally to get a detail but otherwise concentrated on his notes.

After about half an hour, Rudy said, "There's not much to add, at least not right now. I think you should have enough for a piece, right?"

"Damn straight," Sanderlin said. "I've got work to do."

He didn't look up as Rudy left the office.

A week later, the front page of the *Northern Beacon* carried the full story, under the bold headline, "Orcas Join Forces to Save a Sea Lion." *Nice alliteration*, thought Rudy. The story was pretty much as Rudy had recounted and even had a frame capture from Rudy's video, a less-than-perfect photo of the little sea lion clinging to Makai's back. Rudy's observations were backed up with quotes from the boat captain and two of the passengers, including an eleven-year-old girl. *Kids in a story always add a human interest angle.* At Rudy's suggestion, Sanderlin quoted one passenger as saying, "Gee, maybe that big whale isn't such a bad guy after all. I mean like maybe somebody on a jet ski harpooned his baby. Maybe he was attacking the jet ski and not the rider. I sure hate jet skis."

Sanderlin, to his credit, was thorough. The story ended with comments by a self-appointed authority on killer whale biology, who dismissed Rudy's interpretation of events as uninformed, emotional, anthropomorphic speculation.

"Wow," Cassie said, after she read the article. They were sitting in the kitchen of Rudy's rental. "This is good stuff, except for the last part. Talk about character assassination, of both you and the whales. Hey. Can Makai sue for libel?" she asked.

"It's the court of public opinion that concerns us most," said Rudy. "And I don't think an alternative, less emotional explanation will gain much traction. The public is much more interested in compassionate whales than swimming black and white automatons. Sanderlin said his mail is running ten to one in favor of Makai as a hero. Lots of touchy-feely letters to the editor. My guess is, if Makai ever comes home, he won't face a lynch mob."

"Do you think J Pod will accept him back?" Cassie asked. "I can't believe he left completely on his own. Maybe he was no longer welcome."

"That's a hard one to know without speculating wildly and emotionally. And I don't see where we can have any influence on the matter, aside from our efforts to improve his image among our species. We're not his people."

CHAPTER 51

*I have little patience with scientists who take a
board of wood, look for its thinnest part, and drill a
great number of holes where drilling is easy.*

ALBERT EINSTEIN, 1949

R udy decided to go back up Vancouver Island, hoping
to make occasional contact with Makai. It gave him
the feeling of doing something. Another series of long
ferry and car rides. His mind wandered.

Rudy wasn't prone to self-reflection or analysis. That
just hadn't been part of his personality. But thinking about
Makai and Cassie got him assessing his current condition
and how he got here. Maybe he should send a thank you
card to Hamilton's dean for banishing him to the academic
hinterlands of the Pacific Northwest. Otherwise, he'd still
be at Hamilton, destined to becoming the world's authority
on the behavior of New York minnows, referring to himself
as the "Minnow King." He would churn out paper after
paper, reach fifty in years and publications, and look back
and probably say, "so what?"

Instead, he was now committed to something bigger.
The value was clear, to him and to Alexander and to Cassie.
Especially Cassie, which he had to admit took on special
significance. And, also, to people like Doris Whitesalmon,
or why else would she have asked for Makai's fin and

entrusted him with the orca carving? These were all people who had become important to him. He couldn't remember many such people in his previous life. His work and goals had always been self-centered. Important people were those who could advance his career.

But now his motivation was different, focused outward not inward, and he had to admit he liked it. He was convinced he was trying to undo some of the harm humanity had wreaked upon the ocean and its inhabitants. Maybe he could help make the world a better place for a magnificent and imperiled species. Helping place Makai into J Pod had seemed the right thing, or had until his baby was murdered. Making the world a better place wasn't so easy after all. If only he knew where and how it would all end.

Rather than undertake what might be a fruitless search for Makai, he decided to return home and launch Plan B, the resurrection of Makai's public image, while hoping the whale would also come home. Plan B was at least positive action.

He decided to start with jet skis. That seemed promising. Or at least it seemed like where Makai had started. Something caused the whale to attack a ski, or its driver. Makai had, more than once, demonstrated that he did things with forethought. It was a long shot, but Rudy had little else to go on.

The ski had been driven by the CPA from Seattle, who owned the large house where Makai got stranded. The newspaper accounts identified him as Jonathan Winkler. His business partner, Patrick Martindale, had been interviewed extensively after the attack. Rudy reached Patrick by phone after finding their business website.

"Hello, this is Dr. Rudolph Laguna," Rudy began. "I'm a killer whale researcher."

"I've made all my statements to the police and the press," was Patrick's terse reply. "I really don't have any more to say."

"Understandable," Rudy replied. "Do you mind if I ask if Jonathan is okay?"

"I guess not. Most of the reporters want to know more about the whale," Patrick said. "They didn't show much concern for Jonathan beyond describing his injuries and wanting to know how much our San Juan house was worth. Jonathan seems to be recuperating, thank you. He may be released next week."

"I'm glad to hear that," Rudy said. "I guess it could have been much worse."

"I think we're counting our blessings right now. Is there anything else?"

"Yes, there is. I feel kind of responsible for what happened. I'm the researcher who led the team that set the whale free. We had no idea that he was aggressive. Nothing in his past suggested he would attack someone." *Well, almost nothing.* "We want to learn from this tragic incident, learn what we might do to prevent future incidents. Would you mind terribly if I came out to talk with you and go over details of the attack? I'm not sure I trust the accuracy of the newspaper accounts." *Like their failing to mention that jet skis were illegal in the county.*

"I guess not," Patrick said. "I can't see the harm. I like whales, always have, and we both get a thrill whenever we see one from our home on San Juan. It was one of the selling points of the house, seeing them going by. Kind of ironic, I guess."

"Yes, it is," Rudy said. "I make many of my observations right along your coast. I'd be happy to meet you there, at your convenience."

"Sure, why not? I'm coming up this weekend, tidying up for Jonathan's return. How would Saturday afternoon work?"

"That would be great, really," Rudy said. "Saturday afternoon. I'll try not to take too much of your time."

Patrick gave Rudy the address, which was unnecessary since Rudy had been there already during Makai's stranding. No reason to complicate the matter.

Rudy caught a midmorning ferry to San Juan Island, killed time taking in the exhibits at the Whale Museum in Friday Harbor, and knocked on the huge door of Patrick and Jonathan's home promptly at one o'clock. He hadn't really paid that much attention to the house when he and Cassie were coaxing Makai out of the small cove. One look made him also wonder just how much it might have cost.

Patrick invited Rudy in, and they sat in the great room. Rudy paid his host several compliments about the design and décor, then got down to business. After small talk about orcas, Rudy's research, and Makai's repatriation effort, Rudy pulled out a press clipping of the attack and read it.

"So, is anything missing?" he asked.

"No, not really," Patrick answered, too quickly, his eyes looking anywhere but at Rudy. Rudy sensed Patrick's unease and decided to wait for more. When Patrick said nothing else, Rudy decided to change the subject. He was certain Patrick was hiding something.

"Hey, I've got an idea. Would you mind terribly if I took a look at the jet ski? The press report made it sound like a real wreck."

"I guess not. Sure. Follow me," Patrick said.

He led Rudy down a spiral staircase and into a room full of nautical stuff, expensive, old stuff. Large paintings of old sail boats, an old ship's wheel. Lots of brass and polished

348   GENE HELFMAN

wood. He would have looked longer, but Patrick practically pushed him through the room to another door that had to come out of a submarine, with a big metal wheel you had to turn to open. It led to floating docks under the house.

The jet ski was tied up behind a small powerboat. The ski was smashed, the windscreen lay flat and shattered, the steering handles mangled and drooping, splintered fiberglass and loose wires everywhere. Two things immediately caught Rudy's attention. First, the ski was a two-seater, a detail not mentioned in the news accounts. And second, everything was crushed as if the blow had been off to the left, as if Makai had tried to land to one side, not directly down. That seemed odd if the whale's intent had been to kill.

"Wow! It's amazing Jonathan wasn't hurt even more. This ski is a mess."

"Yes," Patrick said. "I guess we feel lucky."

Rudy looked at the ski more carefully. He tried to imagine what had happened, picturing the incident from above, as if filmed from a drone. Mentally reenacting Patrick's newspaper account, he imagined Jonathan driving the ski, stopping, idling, and then Makai leaping into the air to land. But the image in Rudy's mind began to take a different shape, different images. Were there two people on the ski now? And Makai wasn't leaping, he was swimming away. And the ski was chasing Makai's mate and the baby whale.

"Hey, are you okay?" Patrick was asking.

"Oh, yeah. Sorry. My imagination ran away with me. I really can't help but think Jonathan's lucky to be alive."

"Yes, thank heavens. He had a concussion and some serious bruises, a dislocated shoulder, but amazingly, no broken bones."

Again, Rudy thought, *that seemed odd if the whale's intent had been to kill. As if Makai somehow minimized the impact.*

They went back inside the room with the nautical antiques. Rudy looked around.

"This is really impressive. Much of this stuff looks like museum quality," Rudy said.

Patrick hesitated before answering. "This is Jonathan's favorite room. He collected all this over several years. It's his pride and joy."

Rudy scanned the room, then his gaze stopped. "It's all so perfectly arranged," he said. "Except that one wall." He pointed to a space on the wall above a ship's wheel, the paint slightly lighter than the surrounding area. "It looks like something's missing there," he said.

Patrick hesitated again.

Rudy could tell he was wavering.

Patrick took a deep breath. "Well, actually, yes," he said. "There is something really strange about all this. I don't know if I should be telling you. Can I trust you to keep this in confidence, not run to the papers with stuff?"

"You have my promise," Rudy said. "I'm a researcher, not a reporter. I want to prevent future problems, not exploit past ones."

"Okay, I'm going to trust you," Patrick said. "Jonathan bought an old whaling harpoon at an auction in New Bedford. It had a wooden handle and a long metal shaft, ending in a flat tear-dropped blade. I think it was technically called a lance, for finishing whales off. It used to be on that wall, right there."

Rudy held up his hands. "Whoa. Are you thinking what I'm thinking?"

"Yes," Patrick said. "The baby whale was harpooned with something just like that. And now it's missing."

Harpooned whale, smashed jet ski...no, smashed Jonathan's jet ski and Jonathan's harpoon was missing.

Rudy tried hard not to overreact. "Does Jonathan know the harpoon is gone?"

"I don't think so. I tried to ask him about it, at the hospital. But he was still heavily sedated. He mumbled something about other whales and a guy on a ferry. It didn't make much sense. Do you think I should tell the authorities? Are we complicit in the death of that baby whale? I mean do we have legal liability here?"

Rudy recognized the moral quandary, and realized that Makai's attack on Jonathan might, in fact, make sense.

"I don't see how anyone can connect you and Jonathan to events, unless the harpoon is recovered from the baby whale and somehow traced to you, both of which seem unlikely."

"Yes, unlikely," Patrick repeated. "I feel really guilty, but maybe it's just a coincidence. I guess staying quiet is the right thing to do, at least for now."

Rudy wanted to run out of the house with this new information. These complications needed to be thought through. At least he should get Cassie's opinion.

"I agree. Your chief obligation is taking care of Jonathan. I appreciate your telling me all this."

"You will keep this quiet, right? We have an agreement," Patrick said.

"Yes, we have an agreement."

CHAPTER 52

"Sanderlin here."

"Hey, Phil, it's Rudy Laguna. If you're busy, I can call back. This could take a while."

"Hell no, Laguna. You're my fairy godmother. Calvin's taken me off advertising and wants me full time on what he sees as 'science reporting.' Right now it's sea star wasting disease and sewage leaking from Victoria. What have you got?"

"Lots," Rudy said, feeling emboldened. "I think I have a follow-up to the Makai saga."

"Great!" Sanderlin said. "Hit me."

"Okay. That quote you got from the whale-watching passenger, not the little girl, but the other guy. The one who suggested Makai maybe wasn't such a bad guy. That comment got me thinking," Rudy lied. "It reminded me of something, and I put two and two together."

"Equaling?"

"Four or five, or maybe more."

"Hold it," Sanderlin said.

Rudy could hear him banging on his keyboard.

"Okay, I'm taking notes."

"Good," Rudy said. "Some of this is publicly available, other parts are stuff that you'll just have to take my word for."

"Let's start with the public stuff, which I can check," Sanderlin answered.

"Last year, July fourth to be specific, a jet skier almost plowed into J Pod right off Lime Kiln Park on San Juan Island. The guy was arrested by the county sheriff. It made the papers there, and the arrest record should be in the sheriff's files."

"Okay, that's certainly verifiable. What's the connection?" Sanderlin asked.

"I happened to be out in my inflatable when it happened, and what didn't get reported was that Makai's youngster came close to being run over by the ski."

"So, you're telling me that Makai may have recognized the jet ski was dangerous? Okay. That's part of a story. Fill it in," Sanderlin said.

"Alright. Here are the parts you'll have to take on faith. Makai had an earlier encounter with a jet ski when we were rehabilitating him at a location I can't disclose. He got chased by one, probably frightened. The important thing is that, unlike the rest of J Pod, Makai knew what jet skis were and that they could constitute a threat."

"That's a little far out for responsible journalism, Rudy, and you know that."

"Here's the clincher. The guy who got crunched by Makai, the one who was riding the jet ski—"

"The CPA from Seattle, John Something."

"Right. Jonathan Winkler. Jonathan collected marine antiques, kept them in a special little museum downstairs in his McMansion on San Juan Island, and—"

"Is that the same place where our whale friend managed to beach himself?" Sanderlin asked.

"Exactly," said Rudy. "The same place where the jet ski that Makai crushed was originally housed."

"Hmmm. I detect a thickening plot," Sanderlin said.

"But wait, there's more. Among Jonathan's maritime antiques was, and the operable word here is *was*, a whaling lance—"

"Like the one stuck in the back of the baby whale."

"Exactly," Rudy said. "You're connecting the dots very well."

"Wait a minute, Laguna. How do you know this? I don't remember anything in the news releases or interviews."

"I did my own dot connecting. I met with Jonathan's partner Patrick at their home, on the pretext of having an interest in the orca I had released. What we could learn from this tragedy."

"And Patrick agreed to talk with you?"

"Yes, after a while. It was obvious he had a guilty conscience. He basically wanted to confess something, but only after I agreed to keep what he told me in strictest confidence."

"Which you're violating right now," Sanderlin said.

"Only because I'm trusting you and your journalistic integrity and creativity to somehow use this information without revealing the source."

"Lay it on thick, Laguna. But go on."

Rudy recounted the details of his visit with Patrick.

"And why are you telling me all this?" Sanderlin asked when Rudy finished. "You know I can't use it without confirmation. And I can't go to this Patrick guy because that would violate your agreement."

"I'll be honest with you, Phil. My concern is with my whale. He's being vilified. He attacked a jet ski that I'm convinced was involved in the murder of his calf. I don't want him hunted down as a dangerous animal, like some rogue grizzly bear or white shark. I'm trusting you to work bits and pieces into an interesting story, a more sympathetic view. Make it speculative, piece the puzzle together, lay the blame for the speculation on me. The public loves orca stories, and you can keep them happy."

"Thanks a heap, Laguna. Maybe I should have stayed with dying starfish and poop out of Victoria."

"Any time, Phil."

Then Rudy called Cassie and brought her up to date.

Rudy was impressed. Sanderlin wrote an op-ed piece under the headline, "Rogue Whale – Perpetrator or Victim?" The article was accompanied by the now-famous photo of J-28 Polaris, carrying her dead baby, the harpoon clearly visible in its back. Rudy's accounts were attributed to him, especially about the Lime Kiln incident, setting the stage for connecting a jet ski with the harpooning. And Rudy was quoted as saying, "Maybe, just maybe, whoever harpooned that baby had been riding on a jet ski."

In the interests of responsible journalism, Sanderlin once again interviewed the guy who had dismissed Rudy's earlier account of the sea lion rescue. This time he characterized Rudy's story as "supposition, speculation, and fantasy, entirely lacking empirical support. Laguna has turned coincidence into evidence and seen correlation as causation."

It didn't matter. The article had just the result Rudy had hoped for. The public heard what it wanted to hear; sympathetic letters poured in to the editor of the *Northern Beacon*. They exonerated Makai, pleaded for understanding, and even called him a misunderstood and bereaved parent, justified in his reaction to the hated jet skis. Advertising was also up considerably.

Guess I took one for the team, Rudy thought. *I can live with that.*

CHAPTER 53

S am kept heading north and west, to open water. The waves grew rough, steeper, breaking, the wind a howling gale. Each time he rose to take a hurried breath, the wind snatched away his exhalation, swallowed it in a thick, billowing fog. Despite wind and seas, he found plenty of salmon. *So different from home. Few logriders, lots of fish.*

Home. It pulled at him. Rose, his dead child, Grandma, Molly, Michael, the twins, even Frank. They were his family and he missed them. He had known loneliness for much of his life. But the present loneliness was so much stronger, contrasting starkly to the joy of togetherness he had come to experience with his family.

Sam realized that being alone was not his natural state, was not the way things were meant to be. He even flashed back briefly to his childhood, dim and fleeting memories of being with other whales, something he hadn't thought about for years. As the realization that he was an exile grew, so did the pull of returning. And as that pull grew, so did an idea. The idea became a plan, the plan a solution, a solution to not just his problem but many of the problems facing his family.

He soon found himself amongst a new series of offshore islands, far removed from larger land masses. Fish abounded, logriders were scarce, some actually moving in quiet logs propelled by wooden fins dipped rhythmically into the water. The logriders here never approached him but, instead, stopped while he passed. He sensed they somehow respected him.

He came to a decision: *return with the plan, no matter the cost.*

He headed south, moving faster, with purpose, traveling day and night. It took only a day to arrive near where he had saved the young sea lion and, in turn, been saved by his northern cousins. Soon he could hear them talking in the distance. He called out and, immediately, their conversation stopped. A familiar voice shouted his name. He swam in that direction.

"Our big friend, we have found you." It was Pierre.

"I, uh, didn't know you were looking for me," Sam said. "I didn't intend to be hard to find."

"Finding you is not difficult. You are hard to miss. But we have important news for you."

Sam's mind raced. He wanted news, but feared that it might be bad.

"Please tell me," he said.

Pierre paused, then spoke quietly. "It concerns you and the elder we know as Lena, she is called Grandma in your family, no?"

"Yes," said Sam, "Grandma. Is she alright?" Sam feared the worst.

"We have few details, but she is ailing and asked we find you. She requested you return home."

Sam wasn't certain he had heard correctly. This was good news *and* bad.

"You are certain I am supposed to return?"

"Yes, most definitely. And quickly if you can."

"Thank you so much, again."

"Good bye again, my big friend. And good luck. But, please think about our offer. Come back, with your kin."

CHAPTER 54

Rudy felt better after telling Sanderlin about the jet ski connection, or at least felt he had done something positive. But he was still left with an empty feeling, looking for a solution to a poorly defined problem.

It was a rare rainy night for late summer, not that rain was anything rare in Blaine. But Rudy also heard distant rumbling thunder; electrical storms were a definite rarity. Sure enough, less than ten minutes later, lightning flashed, followed quickly by booming thunder. Then the power went out.

Rudy rummaged around in various drawers and cabinets and finally found what he vaguely remembered he had stored away. Candles. Old candles, left over from his days teaching at Hamilton. So much water under that bridge.

He lit the candle and placed it on the kitchen table. It cast a warm, albeit faint, glow.

Sitting at the table in what would otherwise be romantic candlelight, Rudy took stock of his situation. He could not shake the sense of responsibility he felt for Makai. He had almost single-handedly created the situation in which the poor whale now found himself, worse off than before, alone, an outcast, probably brokenhearted. What, if anything, should Rudy do? What, if anything, *could* he do? Rudy felt he had no control over the situation, if he ever had.

He was jarred out of this reverie by his phone.

"Rudy, it's Cassie."

"Hey, Cass. Do you have power?" he asked.

"No, it went out a half hour ago. I'm at the Shannon Point lab. They have backup generators that keep the seawater pumps going, but not much more. So, I can't get any work done. But that might be a good thing."

"How's that?" Rudy asked.

"Well, I can't keep my mind on sculpins, I'm so worried about Makai."

"Seems to be a trend," Rudy offered.

"Yeah. I'm not surprised. In fact, I'd be more surprised if you were thinking otherwise. But, more importantly, there's an old guy here, a night watchman and custodian named Henry—I don't know his last name—been here forever. He and I often talk because we're the only ones around late at night. He's a local, part Native American. Actually, more Native than part. Very spiritual, although he usually doesn't get too heavy with me 'cause I think he senses I'm not particularly inclined."

"Hey," Rudy said. "You're safe with me. I've been accused of having the spiritual depth of a bedpan."

Cassie hesitated, obviously lost in thought. Rudy waited. Cassie usually didn't waste his time, especially when it came to their whale.

"Well, tonight was different, really different," she said. "We got on the subject of orcas. He started talking about how his family was orca clan, all the ancestor connections and stuff. I encouraged it. It's really fascinating. I told him about Makai. As much as I should, maybe a little more. Sorry about that."

"No, I understand perfectly," Rudy said.

"Good. I thought so. Anyway, we got into the problem with Makai, losing his calf, having to leave his family because of attacking the jet ski, and going north, and how we, you and I, were worried about him and what might happen now that he was no longer with his adopted family."

"And?" Rudy asked.

"Henry got really quiet. He closed his eyes and didn't say anything for a long time. It looked like he was praying or meditating. He's prone to periods of silence, like you wonder whether he's really listening."

"I know exactly what you're talking about," Rudy said, thinking of his interactions with Dr. Whitesalmon.

"Well, but then it's always obvious he really has been listening. Because he said a name. It was an Indian...Native American, name. I'm probably blowing the pronunciation because it came from deep in his throat, but it sounded like Shee-ma-ta-sa."

"Shee-ma-ta-sa?" repeated Rudy, "or more like See-am-ma-tsa?"

"Hey, that's right, better than I did in fact," Cassie said.

"I've been practicing," Rudy said.

"How's that?" she asked.

Rudy described his latest visit to Whitesalmon.

"Wow," Cassie said. "Maybe this is making sense after all. Henry said See-am-ma-tsa is his aunt, really old. I sometimes think everyone's his aunt or uncle. I know this sounds totally nuts. But he said See-am-ma-tsa is old orca clan, knows more about orcas than anyone alive, can communicate with them. He said she knows powerful medicine. She lives up in BC, on Vancouver Island, somewhere on the road to Bamfield Inlet, west of Port Alberni. I guess that would make her a First Nation's person, not a Native American. Anyway, he said you should go find her and ask her how to help Makai. He seemed really positive, like it was his duty to help."

"I think I know what you're getting at," Rudy said.

"I know it sounds ridiculous, Rudy. It's not much to go on, like all we've got is the name of a Native woman who lives somewhere on Vancouver Island. But he seemed so positive, so determined to help. And now we've got two people telling us about her. You've got to go find her, Rudy. I'd be happy to go with you if you'd like, keep you company."

Rudy was tempted, but thought better about it.

"No, that's fine Cassie. Thanks. It's more important you monitor the situation here, so much better than I seem able to. Plus, I've got Cheez for company, and I don't have grunt sculpins to babysit. Anyway, I'm at my wit's end. This is, at least, something to do. It's probably a wild goose—or whale—chase. But what else is there? I know the road to Bamfield, been there before. Seems British Columbia calls me once more."

"Rudy, please let me know what happens and if I can help in any way. Call me."

"Will do, assuming there's cell reception. Thanks, Cass, really," Rudy answered.

Rudy pulled the piece of paper that Dr. Whitesalmon had given him out of his pocket, the one with the woman's name. Giving the matter serious consideration, it was, in fact, pretty ridiculous. A whale witch doctor on the road to Bamfield. But it was the same name that Cassie had been given. This seemed like more than a coincidence. Here he was an objective, rational, logical research scientist. Spiritual quests were way above his pay grade, not even in his job description. But objectivity was of no help now, as he tried to influence the sequence of events surrounding

Makai, a sequence that he had set in motion. Rudy felt like he was kayaking in dense fog, sailing into an ocean that wasn't on his charts,

What the hell. Why not?

"Hey, Cheez, time for another road trip."

CHAPTER 55

To get to Bamfield, Rudy had to drive across the Canadian border to the BC Ferry terminal near Vancouver. With no letup in the rain or wind, he didn't have much competition catching a ferry across the Strait of Georgia to Nanaimo on Vancouver Island. *Nice weather for slugs.* He then drove up the island's east coast and inland to Port Alberni. That's when it got interesting.

Rudy had been to Bamfield before, on a visit to the Canadian marine lab there. The lab was accessed via a spine-jarring, thirty-mile gravel road that took three hours of dodging potholes, washboard ruts, and behemoth, hell-bent logging trucks. The trucks plowed up dust in the summer and mud in the winter. It was summer now, so why was it raining?

The rain landed with an intensity unmatched by the sweep of the Volvo's eroded windshield wipers. The scenery couldn't have been less promising, had Rudy been able to see it. With each growing mile, mud accumulated on the car, as did Rudy's misgivings about the trip. His mind drifted as he weighed the potential of this venture, about Makai's plight and, in fact, the plight of the Southern Resident whales.

Maybe halfway along the road to Bamfield, between nowhere and nowhere, he was jerked back to the present by the unlikely sight of someone walking along the road. He slowed, then stopped. The person turned around just enough for Rudy to see that she was inappropriately dressed.

Totally inappropriately, like in jeans and a hoodie sweatshirt, wearing thin sneakers. Not carrying anything. No question it was a woman, or girl, because the rain-soaked sweatshirt that clung to her thin frame left no doubt. Her dark hair hung down, dripping water across a miserably unhappy face.

"Get in back, Cheez," Rudy said. The dog hesitated in protest, then jumped into the back seat. Rudy leaned across and opened the passenger door, letting in a gust of rain.

"Hey, can I give you a ride?" he asked, trying to sound as unthreatening as possible. It seemed like a no-brainer, given the weather and the deserted nature of the road. The girl looked at him with piercing dark eyes, suspicion and exhaustion both evident. She shivered and sniffled and got in, sniffled and shivered some more, and appeared to fall asleep.

"Can I ask where you're headed?" Rudy said.

No answer.

"I guess you don't know. As a matter of fact, that makes two of us."

The girl was clearly cold and undoubtedly sick, given her labored breathing. Rudy cranked the heat up and drove on, wondering what to do next. He had expected to encounter occasional turnoffs or isolated houses, but had yet to see one. All he knew was he was looking for an elder native woman who talked to orcas. And now he had a sick passenger to complicate things.

Finally, a couple miles farther, he saw lights off to the right. As he got closer, a cluster of trailers emerged from the rain. A garish orange security light illuminated machinery in various stages of repair in the yards. The roof of one trailer was covered with a blue tarp, held down by tires. He realized he was stereotyping, but the scene said First Nations. He hoped he was right.

Rudy pulled off the road. The girl didn't move, although she groaned weakly, sneezed, and mumbled incoherently. The trailer with the blue tarp had the most lights on, so Rudy figured that was as good a place as any to inquire about…a woman named See-am-ma-tsa, assuming he was pronouncing it correctly.

He got out of the car and was greeted with wind-driven rain. Back in for his raincoat. *Idiot!* Shoving his hands into the pockets, he felt a strange lump, then remembered it was the stone orca carving. Cheez jumped out and took off for parts unknown.

Hesitantly, Rudy sloshed across the yard and climbed three steps to a small wooden porch. No overhang to keep the rain off. Bluish light from a television flickered through a window. Rudy could just hear loud voices inside. He knocked tentatively.

No one answered.

He knocked again, harder this time. After a few seconds, the door opened partway and he was staring up at a very large teenage boy, with dark skin and native features. The kid wasn't smiling. He looked at Rudy and said nothing.

"Um, excuse me. My name is Rudy Laguna, and I'm looking for a woman named See-am-ma-tsa, or I think that's how it's pronounced. A woman named Doris White-salmon in Blaine and a man named Henry"—*damn, no last name*—"who lives in Anacortes, in Washington, said she might be able to help me."

The kid stared at Rudy for another ten seconds, then closed the door without saying anything. Rudy stood there, feeling foolish.

Having decided this was a mistake, Rudy turned around and was about to descend the stairs when he heard the door open behind him. This time a woman was standing there, looking at him. Silently.

"I'm really sorry to bother you folks," Rudy said as he turned toward the door, "but I was hoping someone could help me find a woman named See-am-ma-tsa, who is supposed to live somewhere around here. I need her help."

Then remembering his passenger, he added, "And I picked up a young girl on the way here, who was walking by the road. She was underdressed and soaked to the skin, and I think she's not feeling well. I guess I should take her somewhere to…"

Rudy didn't finish the sentence. The woman turned and shouted something in a language Rudy didn't understand. Immediately, the teenage boy who had first opened the door brushed past Rudy, leapt down the stairs, and ran to the car. He reached in the car and lifted the girl from the front seat. Carrying her cradled in his arms as if she weighed nothing, he quickly walked past Rudy and into the house.

The older woman was barking orders into the trailer. Rudy could now see it was full of people, young and old, from toddlers on up, a dozen or more. The kids were horsing around or staring at Rudy or the teenager carrying the girl. Adults were scurrying about as if they had just been given tasks. The older woman said something else and pointed down a hallway. The boy carried the sick girl to the end of the hallway and disappeared behind a door.

Rudy was still standing in the rain, but the door hadn't been closed on him. Raindrops were starting to drip onto his shoes. Since no one had said otherwise, he stepped inside and closed the door behind him.

All heads, all with dark eyes, turned his way, except for some women in the kitchen, who were busy cooking something on the stove. The woman who had come to the door walked up to him. She was short, stocky, wore a simple print dress and had long gray hair in braids.

"Tell me again why you are here," she said.

Rudy repeated what he had said to the boy, about Whitesalmon and Henry suggesting he find someone named See-am-ma-tsa. He was absentmindedly fingering the statuette in his pocket.

"Oh. And Doris Whitesalmon said I should show See-am-ma-tsa this," he said, holding the orca figurine for her to see.

The woman stared at the statuette, then at Rudy. For a full minute, she said nothing.

"You have to realize that you are an outsider and not exactly welcome here," she finally said in only slightly accented English. "However, because you brought that poor young native girl with you for help, we are giving you the benefit of the doubt. Otherwise, you probably would have been asked to leave the first time you knocked. Or more likely just ignored. And you have been entrusted with a very sacred object. You say you are trying to find See-am-ma-tsa. May I ask why?"

The moment of truth, Rudy guessed. Exactly why *was* he here? He wasn't sure what he should say, what this woman would think of his quest. Yes, he guessed it was a quest: Ahab, Diogenes, Don Quixote? Those comparisons all seemed kind of presumptuous. But it was important and, maybe, just maybe, there were answers in this unlikely place to questions he hadn't completely formulated. He decided a partial explanation would be less than truthful.

He told the woman everything, from the beginning. Makai's captive history, his time in Utah, Rudy's involvement in preparing him for release in the wild, the details of joining up with J Pod and its rationale, Makai's acceptance into the orca family, birth and death of his calf, the jet ski connection, and what appeared to be banishment from the Southern Resident orca community to northern waters.

The woman listened in silence, her eyes closed. *That seemed familiar.* When Rudy finished, perhaps twenty minutes later, he realized that several other people were standing and staring at him and also listening. No one had spoken, nodded, commented, or asked questions. Rudy was uncomfortable being the center of attention.

"I am See-am-ma-tsa," she said. "It is clear you have a sincere concern for the whale you call Makai. We know him by another name—that is not important. And we will talk at length about him. Meanwhile, we are grateful that you brought the sick child here, which we also take as a sign of your trustworthiness. She is one of us, but right now she is too ill for us to know who her relations are. She is running a very high fever and is delirious and needs rest and healing thoughts and some strong medicine."

Rudy was grateful that everything she said was positive, although he was a little concerned that these people were going to start some sort of medical care for the girl he had brought. What was his responsibility towards her? Was this a simple Good Samaritan incident? Did they have Good Samaritan laws in Canada? *That's a stupid question. It is Canada, for Pete's sake.*

On the other hand, he didn't know anything else to do, so he pushed his doubts aside and remembered Cheez running around outside in the rain.

"Thank you," he finally said. "I hope it's not a problem for me to stay until you decide she's okay. I need to check on my dog, and then can we talk about the whale?"

"Yes, go check on your dog while I tend to the child. Then come back and have something hot to eat and drink."

She made no mention of Makai.

Rudy stepped outside. It was still raining, but he really hadn't needed to worry about Cheez. The big dog was romping around in the front yard with a couple of mongrel puppies that were chasing and nipping at him. Cheez was acting in a most undignified manner, so Rudy decided not to interrupt and went back inside.

He sat down on an overstuffed armchair. Almost immediately, a young girl brought him a bowl of hot soup. He guessed it was some sort of vegetable concoction with large nuggets that looked like corn, dark green beans, and chunks of some sort of squash. Whatever it was, it tasted great, and he realized he hadn't eaten in hours. He looked up to thank someone, but everyone had gone back to whatever they had been doing. Being ignored was better than being an object of curiosity.

Still, he did want to ask about his whale.

See-am-ma-tsa emerged from the room down the darkened hallway where they had taken the girl. She said something in the same undecipherable language, and two other older women immediately hurried down the hall, disappearing into the room at the end.

Rudy looked at his watch. It was almost eleven. He had lost track of the time. The younger children had been slowly drifting away, and he was now among the few people remaining, all adults. See-am-ma-tsa returned from down the hall.

"You are welcome to spend the night, if you like," she said. "My sisters and I are caring for the young girl. She is still feverish, speaking incoherently. Surprisingly, the women think she is actually mumbling in something akin to our language. Given her condition, they are keeping a vigil on her, so you need not be concerned. They will decide in the morning whether she can and should stay or be taken somewhere else, probably her home. That decision will be made in the morning."

"And my need to talk about the whale?" Rudy asked, frustration showing in his voice.

"That will also be done in the morning," she said, making it clear that the matter was settled. "Come, I will show you where you can sleep."

Rudy followed her to the first door on the right of the hallway. Pushing it open, he saw several young children fast asleep on pads on the floor, some alone, some snuggled with an older child. An army-style steel frame bed with a mattress stood unoccupied in the corner, a pillow at one end and colorful blankets folded neatly. Rudy guessed that was his.

"I, uh, had better see to my dog first," he told See-am-ma-tsa.

"Of course," she answered. "Then make yourself comfortable."

Rudy went outside and whistled for Cheez, intending to let the dog sleep in the car. Cheez emerged from under the trailer, followed by two small, furry mongrels.

"I guess you've found family, too, eh, fella? Have a good night."

Cheez shook one time, turned around and walked back under the trailer, the two pups dutifully dogging his steps.

CHAPTER 56

We need another and a wiser and perhaps a
more mystical concept of animals.

HENRY BESTON, *The Outermost House*

⸻

nside the back bedroom, things were anything but peaceful. Willow Silvermoon Johnson was on the bed, sleeping fitfully. The three women were sitting in metal folding chairs to one side, watching her. See-am-ma-tsa reached up and placed a wet washcloth on her forehead, then turned to the others and whispered.

"I think her fever has broken, poor child. She is lucky that man found her when he did. This is terrible weather for someone as sick as she is to be outside."

"Are you worried, sister?" asked another woman.

"No, I think she will be okay, if her fever does not go back up. The herbal soup we gave her will help. We should just focus our thoughts and prayers on her and be watchful."

Willow moaned and turned over. She opened her eyes, tried to focus.

"Where am I?" she asked, her voice weak and troubled.

"Don't worry, child," said See-am-ma-tsa. "You are with friends and family. You just need to rest."

"I was so cold," she started. Then, "How can I be with family? My family is on Orcas Island."

"Your family is in many places, not just where your home is."

"But that's where my mother and brother are. And my... stepfather."

"Do not trouble yourself right now, child. We will help you get back to them. Right now you need to rest."

"I don't want to go back, not to that awful man. Please don't make me go back."

"No one will make you do anything, we promise."

Willow paused, then spoke again, "I had the strangest dream," her voice trailing off.

"Tell us about it, child," See-am-ma-tsa said. "Dreams can be meaningful, or meaningless. But they should be shared."

Willow hesitated. The dream had left her feeling very uneasy. It didn't make sense and, at the same time, *did* make sense. But she felt comforted by these three old women, felt she could trust them. When they called her "child," she felt it was lovingly. She thought about the dream and, as she remembered it, she began to speak, almost in a trance.

"I, uh, saw people on a beach, near a stream or small river. The people were very thin, almost ghost-like. Some were very old, others not so old, and even children, including a woman carrying a baby in a kind of backpack. They were all standing near the water's edge, looking out to sea.

"I heard one, an old woman, say, 'Help us. Our people are starving and dying. The ocean is full of fish, of salmon, but they are too fast, and we are too weak to catch them.'

"Then a giant black bird flew down and hovered over them, the wind from its wings so strong it pushed the weakened people to the ground. Everyone was clearly frightened, except the old woman who had cried out. She stood back up.

"The giant bird spoke to them, or more like *ordered* them. It told them to go into the water.

"'But we have no canoes,' the woman cried.

"'Go into the water, right now!' the bird commanded.

"The oldest woman waded slowly into the water, followed by two other old women. As soon as the water got above their ankles, their legs began to turn black. The deeper they waded into the water, the more their bodies turned black and shiny. They looked down at their bodies and turned toward the others standing on the shore, troubled.

The people on shore began to cry out in alarm.

"Then the bird said to a man standing on shore, 'What, you who claim to have been a brave warrior? You let these old women do ocean work for you? Have you no shame?'

"The old man was obviously frightened, but he waded into the water with the women. And his body turned black. When all four had darkened, they grew fins and lay down in the water, half-submerged, facing the crowd. It was obvious they had become orcas.

"The giant bird shouted, 'Now go catch salmon for your people!'

"But the water was too shallow, and they were stranded and couldn't turn around. The old woman orca cried to the people, 'Come. Push us into deeper water!'

"Then some of the people on shore rushed into the water. They didn't become orcas. At first, they couldn't turn the whales around, but, when more people joined them, they managed to turn the whales so they faced out to sea.

"'Push us out!' the whales cried.

"But the whales were too heavy. No matter how hard they tried, they couldn't move the whales.

"Then, on shore, I saw the baby in the backpack. Her mother had propped the backpack up against a beach log. The baby started to struggle and jerk back and forth, until the backpack fell over. The baby wriggled out and crawled on her hands and knees to the water. When she got to where the oldest female whale was stranded, the baby leaned against the whale and pulled herself up. She began to push with the others. That made the difference. The people pushed first one and then another of the whales far enough to where they could swim away. They immediately started chasing and catching salmon. I could see fish in their mouths."

Willow stopped and looked around. She felt uncomfortable, self-conscious, almost foolish. Her story, her dream, maybe it was silly. But the three women sat perfectly still, eyes closed, concentration on their faces. This encouraged her to continue.

"Then the whales spoke to the giant bird. 'We have eaten enough to regain our strength. But how can we feed our relatives?'

"The giant bird told the people on the beach to run to the stream. Then it said to the orcas, 'Form a line and herd the fish to the stream. Work together as your people worked to help you.'

"Which is what the whales did. They pushed the salmon into the shallow river and the people ran into the water and started picking fish up with their hands and throwing them onto shore. Soon the shore was covered in thrashing fish.

"But in their excitement, everyone had forgotten about the baby, even her mother. She turned back and saw her baby's body floating in the surf. She screamed.

"The giant bird swooped down and landed in the water next to the baby. The mother cried out, 'No! Don't take my baby.'

"But the bird didn't carry the baby away. Instead, it pecked at the feet, legs, body and head of the drowned baby and it, too, became an orca. It quickly swam to join the other four whales who had gathered together off the beach.

"'When you die, you too will become orcas,' the oldest female orca said to the people standing on the shore. 'And we will return each summer and chase the salmon up the river for you to catch. But allow the first fish to pass unharmed and then catch only what you need, to ensure salmon for future generations.'"

"And that's all I remember," Willow said. She seemed exhausted by the retelling.

She looked up. All three old women were sitting stock still, upright, eyes closed, hands folded in their laps. They had been silent for the entire recounting of the dream, other than an occasional "*mmmm*."

They smiled at one another, and See-am-ma-tsa spoke to Willow.

"Your dream is a story we all know," she said. "It is one version of what the Anglos like to call our creation myth, the story of our beginnings as Orca Clan, of which you are clearly a part. Although in our reciting of the story, there is no small child. Do you remember someone telling this story to you, perhaps your mother?"

"Uh, no. I don't think so," Willow replied, her voice showing surprise. "No, my mother almost never talked about being Native American or part Native American. She was ashamed of that and kinda always avoided the subject, 'specially around my stepfather."

"How unfortunate. But, certainly, you would have heard it from someone. How about your grandmother?"

"Oh her. Yeah. I kinda remember her. She was very old and wrinkly. Oh, sorry, that was rude."

"No problem, child. No need to apologize. We are very proud of being old and wrinkly. But tell us more about your grandmother."

"Well," Willow went on. "She died when I was really young, like maybe four or five. But I remember she used to tell me stories all the time. My mother always called them fairy tales, but Grandma would look at her and say something like, 'Have it your way, dear,' and then turn back and tell me another story. I don't remember the stories, but I do remember really liking them and her."

See-am-ma-tsa nodded to the others.

"That is most likely where you heard our creation story, child. But now there is something else. All three of us feel you are hiding something. It is a strong feeling, unmistakable. While you were sleeping, before your fever broke, you kept saying something like, 'I can feel it. It's horrible.' Something is troubling you deeply, either something in your dream you did not mention, or something related to the dream that frightens you. You should tell us this thing."

Willow couldn't believe they knew. How did they know? Should she tell them? She was so ashamed, so horrified, it haunted her continually. But she trusted these women.

"I did something terrible. I didn't mean to. And it wasn't my fault, really. At least I don't think so…" Her voice trailed off.

"Please, unburden yourself, child."

It was See-am-ma-tsa, and her voice was soft but forceful. Willow felt carried by the voice.

"I …I…I…killed a baby whale."

Willow stopped and looked at the women. She half expected, *no*, she *fully* expected to see shock on their faces, to be met with instant condemnation. The three women sat there, impassive.

See-am-ma-tsa said, "How did this happen, child?" It was a simple question, containing no judgment.

It was as if someone had reached down inside her and pulled the story out. She related everything, left no parts out, from meeting Lance on the ferry, going to the large house, his giving her the cocaine, the jet ski ride, pursuing the whales.

"I could hear their concern, as if they were talking to me as much as they were talking to each other. And when that loser speared the baby, I heard its screams, crying to its mother in pain. I could feel the baby's pain and the mother's anguish, the horror in the mother's voice. And then we ran away from them, but the bigger whale, I guess the father, chased us almost to the beach, but we drove right up over the shallow water and he couldn't go that far. And then I ran away."

"You did not kill that whale, child. The man did. No one would ever hold you responsible, in any way. Free yourself of that guilt."

It was a command. Willow felt it deeply, so deeply it was as if she had been lifted off the ground, following a monstrous weight lifted off her soul.

All three women got up as one.

See-am-ma-tsa turned to Willow. "We are happy you are better, but we should not rush things. It would be best if you tried to go back to sleep now. Powerful dreams can be exhausting to recall."

With that, the three women walked slowly out of the room, softly closing the door behind them.

Willow lay back down, her head spinning. How could she go back to sleep now?

Within two minutes, she did. A peaceful, dreamless sleep.

The next morning, Rudy got up, stepped over a few sleeping bodies, and went outside to give Cheez a bowl of dry food. The pups immediately pounced on the food. Cheez, to Rudy's surprise, let them feed right under his nose without so much as a growl.

Going back inside, someone handed Rudy a cup of coffee, already sweetened. He smiled and said thank you.

Sitting in the same overstuffed armchair, Rudy mentally recapped the incidents of the past day, trying to put pieces of an unlikely puzzle into a rational whole.

See-am-ma-tsa joined him, sitting in his armchair's mate. "The girl you brought here is named Willow," See-am-ma-tsa began. "Her home is in the San Juan islands. We, my sisters and I, are confident that she is better, regaining her strength. Thank you for helping her."

"That's good to hear," Rudy said. "Can I ask you about—

See-am-ma-tsa interrupted him. "You came to find answers to questions about the whale you know as Makai. Questions about what you might do to help him. In truth, you brought the answers with you."

Rudy listened, confused, "All I brought was my dog and that young girl and the orca carving. How—"

See-am-ma-tsa interrupted him again. "I suspect from our conversation that you probably do not consider yourself a spiritual person. But, whether you admit it or not, you are. How else could things have happened as they did?"

Before Rudy could answer, See-am-ma-tsa told him some of what they had found out about the girl named Willow. And her part in events.

"She is escaping from things that happened there involving the orcas you are concerned about, that she felt responsible for," she added.

Rudy was stunned to hear that Willow had witnessed the murder of Makai's calf.

See-am-ma-tsa paused, seeming to check herself.

He waited, then filled the growing silence. "So that's why Makai was so focused on jet skis," he said. "And it all makes sense, confirms my suspicions. The ski he attacked was the one from the big house near False Bay. The place where he stranded himself. Same ski, different rider. Probably mistaken identity. Realized his mistake too late it appears. Still, it explains much. I'm not sure what I can do with this information. Maybe Willow can help identify the guy who speared the whale."

"I would not push too hard on that, not yet," See-am-ma-tsa said. "She is traumatized by the event and recovering from her illness. Her mind is as frail as her body. We have faith that justice will be done, somehow. Please trust our wisdom."

Rudy considered telling Sanderlin and getting the word out through the press, to somehow flush the perpetrator out of hiding. But he also realized he was swimming in unfamiliar water again, dealing with these people and their way of doing things. Perhaps it was best to be patient...for now.

A little later, Willow appeared, barefoot, in baggy sweatpants and a University of Victoria sweatshirt. Despite her sleepy appearance, Rudy could tell she was really quite beautiful. But she was also quite young, a childish quality to her beauty. A vulnerable child in a woman's body. And she looked vaguely familiar. He shrugged it off.

Life in the trailer still seemed rather chaotic to Rudy, but he guessed that was the norm. Everyone now ignored him. The rain appeared to have let up, although it was still very gray outside.

While Rudy was outside checking on Cheez, See-am-ma-tsa joined him.

"The elders feel confident that your young charge can go back. She does not belong here, at least not now, not until all these events are past her. The family has packed some food, dried her clothes, and feels it is time for both of you to leave. And, Rudy, they are truly grateful you brought her here. That counts for a great deal."

Rudy thanked her, knowing nothing else to say. Willow came down the steps of the trailer less enthusiastically than he would have liked.

He imagined it would be a long, quiet ride to the ferry.

As soon as he got to Port Alberni and back into cell phone range, he pulled over and checked his messages. He had one from Cassie.

"Rudy, call me ASAP. First, Polaris is no longer carrying her dead calf. That seems to be over, thankfully. But more important, Grandma is sick. All the whale-watch boats have been reporting on her condition. She's much too thin, and she stays at the surface when the other whales dive. Everybody's worried. And Makai was spotted heading south by the folks in Campbell River. He basically blew past their whale-watch boat, against the current, right through some whirlpools at the worst possible time. He seemed unfazed. Call me, dammit…"

CHAPTER 57

S am headed south nonstop, covering ground in days that had taken him weeks before. He didn't stop to eat, but he was aware that fish became scarcer as he traveled homeward. This realization strengthened his resolve.

He didn't slow until he arrived at the northern limit of the family's usual summer hunting area. Stopping, he listened intently. But, if the family was nearby, their conversation was drowned by the multitude of sounds produced by the logriders. Again, the contrast with the quiet of northern waters struck him, something he hadn't even considered before.

Finally, after two days of fruitless searching and an increasing sense of dread, he heard familiar voices. They were subdued, almost hushed. No careless gossip, playful exchanges or conversations. He approached the group quietly, restraining his desire to shout out.

Everyone was at the surface, barely moving, all in the same direction. A scan showed several of the aunts around Grandma. Sam listened carefully and could detect Grandma's labored breathing. As he approached closer, the group parted to allow him to pass. He stopped alongside Molly. She whispered to him, somehow knowing he was nearby.

"Sam. How good of you to come. I am so happy word was passed to you. We will have to thank our relatives up north as soon as possible."

Molly's normally easygoing, even flippant demeanor had changed. She was uncharacteristically somber, serious.

"Please tell me what's happening, Molly," Sam pleaded. "All I know is that Grandma is ailing, nothing more."

"I fear it is serious, Sam. For weeks now, she has been listless, unwilling or unable to make decisions, even confused at times. Our poor hunting success is not helping, and she refuses to eat, saying fish should be saved for others. When she speaks clearly, she questions her past actions and her ability to lead. And she often asks for news about you. I think, I *hope*, your presence will calm her. Wait here."

Molly swam off toward the group around Grandma. They moved to let her through, and he heard her talking quietly with the matriarch. Then Grandma turned, gasped for breath, and swam toward him. The others moved aside.

"Sam, oh, Sam," Grandma said.

He couldn't tell if he detected relief or anxiety in her voice, maybe both.

"Sam, I truly feel we have wronged you. I have wronged you. We acted hastily in forcing you to leave. Please forgive us."

"There is nothing to forgive, Grandma," Sam replied. "I acted stupidly. I let my rage overcome my judgment. I broke rules our family has followed for generations. I left on my own. You never had to tell me what I had to do."

Grandma hesitated, then spoke between labored breaths. "No, Sam. It is I who acted hastily by not trying to discourage you from leaving. You cannot, and should not, be blamed. We...I...failed to consider the circumstances of your upbringing, your years of captivity and mistreatment by the logriders, and your lack of having been schooled in our traditions regarding not harming them. And, most importantly, the extremely cruel and unforgiveable nature of your son's murder. We have no reason to prevent you from rejoining your family. Welcome home."

In his haste to comprehend fully this turn of events, Sam realized he was exhausting the old matriarch. She was gasping for air, her speech halting. Molly came up alongside, her intent obvious.

"Thank you, Grandma," Sam said, moving aside to allow Molly to be near her sister. "What you've said is enough. I'm truly grateful for your decision. If you forgive me, then I will find it easier to forgive myself. But now I can see it is time for you to rest."

As Molly and Grandma moved off slowly, Sam knew Rose was nearby. She started to speak, but Sam hushed her.

"Rose, Rose, Rose. I've been thinking about you constantly. The hole created in my heart by our son's loss has only been made larger by being apart, at a time when I should have been here to console you, if that was possible. I—"

She cut him off. "Sam, my grief is no less, but no one holds you to blame. Nor do any question your justification for acting like you did. I certainly don't. My main regret is that it appears you weren't successful in exacting the revenge we both seek."

"Thank you for your understanding," Sam said.

"Please, let me finish," Rose said. "I have things I must say. After the initial shock of those terrible events, and after I was persuaded to stop carrying our dead child and permit a traditional parting with his spirit, Grandma and the aunts gathered. They talked and talked. The family has never before encountered such a complex, disturbing, devastating turn of events. It was Grandma who finally convinced the others that we acted in haste, that you should not have been turned out."

"How serious is her condition?" Sam finally had the courage to ask.

"As serious as it can be. Her age and the strain of leadership have put her in a state of self-doubt, which may be the hardest part for her. None of us have faced this sort of thing before, but something deep inside tells us that her decline is irreversible. How and why we know this is another mystery."

Sam was wrestling with the current situation and his plan, wondering how his ideas would be received, whether they would be viewed as a solution or a complication. Taking his idea to Grandma now appeared impractical; she seemed to have ceased to lead. From what he had seen, Molly was the individual to whom everyone turned. He thanked Rose once more for her understanding and told her he needed to talk to Molly about something important.

Sam swam up to where Molly and the other aunts had taken positions around Grandma.

"Molly, can I speak with you alone for a moment?" Sam asked.

Molly hesitated. She scanned around, first at Grandma, then at the others. She turned to Sam. "Is this really important, Sam?" Reluctance was clear in her voice.

"I think it is. Very. Please," Sam answered.

Molly moved off, Sam following. When they were out of earshot of the group, she said, "Alright, Sam. What is it? Please be quick."

Sam had always liked Molly, her irreverent take on most things, her willingness to let tradition slide when necessary, her ability to pick her battles. But her carriage, her voice, everything about her now was different. Serious. Sam addressed her more formally, and slowly. He felt uncomfortable calling her Molly but didn't know what else so he didn't use her name.

"I'm deeply saddened by Grandma's condition and know this weighs heavily on you, as does the position of responsibility into which you have been forced. What I have to say is of the utmost importance to the future of my family, *our* family." He hesitated, waiting for a reaction.

Molly said nothing. She was clearly there to listen, nothing more.

"In my travels north," Sam began, "I witnessed much that was surprising. I will save many details, but the most important fact is that food is abundant, very abundant. Enough for both our northern relatives and us. And logriders are scarce, very scarce."

"But those salmon feed our northern cousins," Molly replied, surprise in her voice. "We never intrude there. It goes beyond tradition that we forage only in our home waters when the salmon are spawning. Those traditions, both ours and the northerners', go back generations beyond memory. What makes you think that our intrusion there would be welcome?"

"I met our cousins twice," Sam offered. "And each time they made it clear that they are aware of our plight, at the danger of starvation that we face. Their leaders are young and less bound by tradition. And they emphasized that salmon were abundant, more than enough to meet all our needs. And our presence would lessen the threat they are experiencing from the seal-eating transients."

"You are certain of this?" Molly asked, skepticism obvious in her tone.

"Yes, certain," Sam tried to sound reassuring, despite lingering doubts. It was more than worth the risk. His family's current condition was past recovery. He knew it when he left. In the brief time he had been back, he could see that many of his relatives had lost weight, Rose in particular, although the stress of her tragedy could have been partially responsible. That Grandma had stopped eating could be as much from self-sacrifice as from failing health, or both. He saw no other path.

Molly had been silent. Finally, she spoke.

"This is a drastic idea. Beyond drastic, Sam. No one else would have even entertained such an idea. But I guess you are less bound by tradition, which makes such an unorthodox idea imaginable. I cannot decide this alone. I have to confer with my sisters, and with Grandma. Despite her condition, she alone still decides matters of such importance."

"Thank you for hearing me out, Molly. You are still Molly to us, aren't you?" Sam asked.

Molly smiled. "At least for the time being, or until someone comes up with a better name behind my back." And she left him.

Sam was relieved to know that she still retained some of her sense of humor.

Molly returned to the group around Grandma. She tried hard to weigh the pros and cons of Sam's bold idea. She hesitated to bring it up at that moment with the others, at least not before she talked with Grandma. Despite her condition, Grandma was still their leader and nothing so momentous could be considered without her agreement, or acquiescence. It really was an existential decision.

Later that evening, everyone broke up into small foraging groups. With fish scarce, they decided to hunt only at night when logriders did not follow them. It gave Molly a chance to talk to Grandma alone and uninterrupted. Molly hesitated to trouble her with such a serious matter, but the old whale's spirits seemed to have been lifted by Sam's return. *Now or never*, Molly thought.

"How are you feeling, Lena?" Molly began. "You seem a little better today."

"Yes, definitely. I feel less guilty now that Sam is back. Things will be better. Rose will be happier, and we so badly need Sam's hunting skills. If there are fish to be found."

Exactly, Molly thought.

"Lena, Sam has proposed something different, something extraordinary, as a solution to our problem of lack of food."

"It would take someone with Sam's different history to come up with a solution. I feel even better now about his return. But I sense hesitancy in your voice, Molly. If it is a good solution, what can be wrong with it?"

"Because it flies in the face of tradition," was her answer.

"He is not suggesting that we eat squid, is he? I don't think that would meet with much enthusiasm. I can just imagine Frank's reaction."

Molly was heartened by her sister's almost lighthearted statement.

"Even Sam knows better than that," she replied. "But his idea is an almost stronger break."

"This is hard to imagine. I am prepared. Please, tell me," Grandma turned serious once more.

"Sam said that, during his travels, he found abundant fish, great abundance, and far fewer logriders. He also met twice with our northern cousins, and those meetings were meaningful. Importantly, the northerners expressed a willingness to share that abundance. Sam feels we should move there, to the north."

"But we are southerners," the surprise in Grandma's voice was clear, her reaction immediate. "We have always been southerners. We have known no other way for countless generations."

"Yes, Lena. But we are starving southerners. Our children die before their first birthday—even those who are not killed by logriders—because their mothers cannot produce enough milk. And even those who are fed grow sickly because something is wrong with our milk. You know this, I know this, we have spoken of it many times. Our future here is uncertain. No, it is bleak. Sam has offered a solution, a difficult one, but still a solution."

Grandma spoke again, the weariness returning to her voice. "I do not know. I cannot know. This is too much to ask, to think about. I understand how desperate our situation is, that I am responsible for how things have gone. Bad decisions, wrong choices. I just do not know…" Her voice trailed off.

"Lena. No one doubts your wisdom, questions your decisions—"

"Perhaps they should have."

"No. You have led us well for so many years, through many years of plenty, and now through times of lack. You are not responsible for the lack of fish nor for what might be in them that is unhealthy. Many of us blame the logriders for both. No one blames you."

Molly moved closer to her sister, close enough that their flanks were touching.

"I know my time is past, and you know your time has come," Grandma said, barely audible. "I am sorry that this falls on you in such difficult times. I am just too tired. I cannot make a decision without consulting with our ancestors. They will give me guidance. Please, leave me alone for a while."

"As you wish, sister. Seek the guidance you need. You know we trust your wisdom."

Molly watched Grandma move from the group, expecting her to stop just far enough away that others would know not to disturb her. But Grandma continued to swim off. Molly decided to follow at a distance, without scanning and therefore remaining undetected.

After about ten minutes Grandma slowed, then stopped. She paused, then slowly sank below the surface. Molly could no longer contain her concern and briefly scanned her sister. Grandma was immobile, sinking, off balance, deeper and deeper. Molly rushed forward, scanning furiously and calling out, first to Grandma, then to the others.

"No!" she screamed as she saw Grandma collide with the bottom, headfirst. Then her lifeless body settled slowly on its side.

It took only a moment for Molly to gain the composure she needed. Grandma had truly gone to consult with the ancestors, leaving Molly to lead in her place. Molly realized that her sister could not bring herself to break so strongly with tradition, to abandon their ancestral home and go north, to become northerners. Lena's last act was to free Molly to decide what she thought was best for the family, unimpeded. But first they would have to mourn, according to tradition.

The news of Grandma's death moved quickly through the worlds of both the whales and whale watchers. K and L pods knew within a day; elder females immediately came to pay their respects. Shortly after, K and L pods sent messengers to inform the northern families. Although memorials were required and would happen, by tradition they would be delayed until the end of summer's foraging period. J Pod would grieve on their own for the time being. But everyone's heart was heavy. A legend, the oldest of the old, was gone.

Grandma's absence was only too obvious to the whale-watch community because the rest of J Pod was accounted for. Rudy got a call from the captain of one of the Friday Harbor boats. He had been mentally prepared for this, but it still hit him very hard.

He called Cassie and could hear her sobbing.

"Call me later and we'll talk," he said, sensing she needed to be alone.

After a week without reports of seeing her, the media picked up on the buzz and even published obituaries.

CHAPTER 58

Following Grandma's death, Molly was immediately recognized as leader. As the eldest female and closest relative to Grandma, her assumption of responsibilities was automatic. This was how it had always been done, through countless generations. But adherence to the old ways was weakening, undoubtedly accelerated by Molly's more liberal take on many subjects. Still, a generational divide developed. Older family argued against any break with tradition. Younger members felt differently.

Debate centered on two courses of action. First was the possibility of moving to northern waters, where food was more abundant and logriders less so. Second involved somehow exacting revenge on the killer of Rose and Sam's child. Older members objected to both, on traditional grounds. Younger members favored both.

"We are tired of starving for the sake of tradition, and we want to be allowed to have children, children who will not die because of tainted milk."

It was Charlotte, the young female who had been forced to lose her unborn child because of scarce food. Despite her young age, she had achieved a leadership role among the younger family members because many felt she had been treated unfairly.

However, all understood that the two courses were likely to intersect, with consequences. Action against logriders would likely result in dangerous reprisals, which would, in turn, make a permanent move to the north a necessity. Molly tried hard to remain neutral, knowing her final decision would be the deciding factor.

She was saved from a difficult choice. During one of the more heated exchanges, actually a shouting match, Frank's loud voice silenced everyone. He had been mute for days, mourning the loss of Grandma.

"Enough already! What fools you all are. We sit here arguing when our future is at stake. Do you think the ancestors would counsel suicide? Because of the logriders, we are starving. Our elders are emaciated. We cannot have children because there are too few fish. The logriders have taken our fish and poisoned the few that remain, and even those are sickly and crawling with parasites. By standing on tradition, we are dying. Death by tradition. We have no choice. If our northern cousins will welcome us, and I think I am not alone in questioning Sam's insistence that they will, then we should move north. We have no future here. At least up north, there is a future."

The silence that followed Frank's outburst lasted more than a minute. Long a staunch traditionalist, his reversal and senior status made the difference. Without comment, family members began to disperse. It was obvious to all that the argument was settled. At least within the immediate family.

Molly's next challenge was to somehow convince the remaining fifty southern community members that it was in everyone's best interest to move north. She wasn't surprised to find a great deal of skepticism, tempered by the same issues her family had faced, namely starvation and failed reproduction. Finally, it was agreed that the decision would ride on the willingness of their northern cousins to accept another seventy-five hungry mouths. A delegation was sent north, one from Molly's family and two equally senior aunts from the other two families.

A whale-watch boat out of Sidney, British Columbia, was surprised to see three female orcas swimming steadily north, far from the migratory paths of incoming Chinook salmon. What drew more attention was a report from the Whale Museum. A photograph showed clearly that they were from J, K, and L pods, three older Southern Resident females that were seldom seen this far north nor together.

"Just shows how little we really know about these, the best studied orcas in the world," the director of the Center for Whale Research was quoted as saying.

Meanwhile, Sam and Rose plotted revenge. It required cooperation of the entire family, so they were heartened when Molly announced a provisional plan for the family's move north, to occur when and if the elder females confirmed they would be welcomed.

Fortunately, all of J Pod had grown increasingly sympathetic toward Sam and Rose, contemplating how they would feel had one of their babies been so brutally, willfully murdered. With a decision to move more likely, Sam and Rose felt they could reveal their plan. Revenge had to be carefully choreographed, accomplished at minimal cost to the family, and to all orcas for that matter.

Despite the family's encouragement, Sam remained reluctant about one aspect of the plan, an aspect that put Rose in potentially grave danger. But she was willing to do anything to exact revenge, willing to act in ways that Sam couldn't even contemplate. Her desire for vengeance was much greater than his. Sam couldn't help but think that Rose truly was the sister of his long-dead mate Nan.

Sam started searching for the logrider who had killed his son. The image of the logrider driving the log was burned into Sam's mind. He could see him standing, harpoon in hand, as the log roared up alongside. Having spent years among the logriders during his captive periods, he became adept at recognizing individual differences.

He focused first on the small and medium-size logs that surrounded them during their daily feeding forays, but he never saw anyone even distantly resembling his quarry. Next, he followed larger logs that were continually present. Scanning their riders was challenging, but no one matched Sam's memory of the logrider, although some came close.

Then, by chance, one of the very large, green and white objects the whales called rumble-logs crossed paths with a smaller log that he was following. Sam saw, standing on the back end of the rumble-log, a male logrider that caught his attention. Tall, thin, dark head fur, hunched shoulders. *Yes!*

Sam turned and made a beeline for the rumble-log. The tall logrider looked up and saw Sam and immediately turned and ran into the dark recesses of the rumble-log. It had to be him!

Sam noted the sound of that particular rumble-log. Many looked alike both above and below the water, but each had a characteristic, individual and unmistakable sound. Sam followed the log until it stopped at the shoreline, but the logrider did not appear again. It didn't matter. Sam knew the log and just had to study its pattern of movement between the islands.

"I've found him!" Sam shouted breathlessly to Rose when he returned after his successful search.

She knew immediately whom he meant. They could now put their complicated plan into action. It had gaping holes that were evident to everyone. That didn't matter.

Sam spent the next day teaching Rose just what the hated logrider looked like by projecting a precise sound image of the man. He did it over and over until they both were satisfied that Rose would be able to recognize the logrider when she spyhopped and looked, from any angle.

Then Sam spent a week establishing which rumble-log the hated logrider rode. That was easy as he was on a rumble-log that regularly traveled through the whales' home waters.. The rumble-log emitted an unmistakable throbbing and had a unique-sounding bow wave.

Whenever Lance was working, a large male orca appeared, day or night.

"Is that damn whale always following us?" Lance complained to a fellow ferry worker on the *Elwha* about a week later.

"Naw, Lance. I guess you're just lucky to be on board when he does," was the reply.

Lance tried to hide his concern.

"Yeah, just lucky," he grumbled.

Things fell into place when the three aunts returned from their northern mission. They reported that the northerners not only welcomed them, but anxiously sought their presence. Transient whales were increasing in northern waters. Northern families speculated that a recent increase in dolphins, seals, and sea lions—transient food—fueled a transient population explosion. Although the roving bandits focused their attacks on dolphins and seals, they had also recently killed a young northern whale who had wandered away from his family. If the southerners moved north, the increased vigilance would make things safer. Food availability was not an issue. There was plenty to go around.

Now it was just a matter of Sam and Rose finding the right moment.

And wait they did. Although Sam shadowed the rumble-log over two weeks, hardly stopping to rest, he rarely sighted the logrider at a time when he could act. And he struggled to coordinate his family's movements with the rumble-log schedule. For one thing, the rumble-log seldom crossed paths with migrating salmon. And although the whole family sympathized with Sam and Rose, they were hungry and much more interested in finding food.

False alarms interfered with feeding and didn't help. The only positive note was that the twins, Eddie and Mitchie, had more than enough energy and were well-fed because they frequently went off on their own to find salmon, or something else. They happily volunteered to help out. Sam recruited them to follow the particular rumble-log when he checked other logs for the hated logrider. He also gave them a quick course in sound image projection on the off chance they might encounter their logrider quarry. The boys thought this was really cool and spent hours practicing on their own, with a modicum of success. As it turned out, their assistance proved critical.

CHAPTER 59

Rudy drove south with the young Native American woman whom he now knew as Willow. The tribal members insisted that she return to her mother, her stepfather's behavior notwithstanding. They felt she could grow into her new identity, strengthened by the knowledge that she was part of something larger. Willow saw few options and begrudgingly agreed. She, however, remained silent for the entire five-hour drive to Sidney.

Cassie, bless her heart, agreed to meet up with Rudy and Willow at the Sidney ferry terminal. She volunteered to take Willow home for a few days, if for no other reason than to let the exhausted girl sort things out in her head in the presence of compassionate female company. Rudy thought he had acted fairly compassionately but admitted his company wasn't what Willow needed.

At the Sidney Border Services kiosk, Rudy showed his passport and Cheez's vaccination record. Cassie had her documents in order. Willow was concerned that maybe her mother had reported her missing and she'd be picked up trying to cross back into the States. She assumed a fetal position in the back seat next to Cheez and feigned sleep. She had given her passport to Cassie earlier, who insisted that Willow was her niece and was getting over a bad stomach bug and they hated to wake her up.

Sneaking a peak at Willow's passport, Rudy saw the Orcas Island address. So that's where he had seen her before, the Orcas Island coffee shop. So long ago, but here she was. Another coincidence?

The customs agent, volunteering that she had a daughter about Willow's age, waved them through. Willow was actually asleep when they drove onto the *Elwha*, the old rustbucket having been put into international service because of a breakdown by the usual, and equally ancient, Sidney boat, the *Chelan*. Cassie and Rudy decided to leave Willow alone.

Up in the passenger cabin, Cassie sat down in a corner, away from the large summertime crowd. She gently slid aside a half-completed jigsaw puzzle on the table, most of its corners in place. She went back to reading the annual newsletter from the Whale Museum that she had brought with her on the trip.

Rudy, returning from the men's room, walked right past her, he was so lost in thought.

"Hey! Space cadet. Over here," Cassie called.

"Uh? Oh wow, sorry. I guess I was preoccupied."

"Care to share?" Cassie asked.

"I might as well, 'cause I'm in need of a reality check, bad."

"You're usually pretty grounded in reality," Cassie said. "This must be something out of the ordinary."

"To say the least," Rudy began hesitantly as he slid in across the table from her. "I know this is going to sound weird and squishy and woo-woo, but I feel like I've stepped into a parallel universe, where things and people somehow converge. It's like I'm being drawn into connected events that violate all my ideas of how the world is ordered, outside the realm of science. I'm being asked to suspend disbelief when, all my life, I've been a disbeliever."

"How so?" Cassie asked.

Rudy sensed no skepticism in her tone and felt encouraged to continue. "Well, let's start with the fact that I've met Willow before, a couple of years ago, I think, when I was just starting to study whales. It wasn't anything significant; she was working in a coffee shop on Orcas..." he stopped. "Wow, there's another one. She was working in a place called Orcas, even though the name has nothing to do with whales."

"Whoa. You've lost me there, Rudy. Wanna back up?"

"Sorry. I'm now looking for connections a little too hard. Forget it. Anyway, I stopped for a cup of coffee, and she served it to me. It was completely forgettable, or at least forgotten. And now I pick her up on the road to Bamfield while looking for the Native woman you and Doris White-salmon said I should find..."

"Okay, I'm seeing a pattern there," Cassie commented.

"I think so," Rudy continued. "Right now, I'm trying to connect the dots. So I'm trying to find this Native American, or First Nations, woman and, in the process, I pick up Willow and take her to a trailer in the middle of nowhere, and See-am-ma-tsa just happens to be in the trailer. I guess there weren't too many other places on the road to Bamfield to stop at, but still. And then it turns out that Willow was on the jet ski with the jerk who harpooned Makai's baby. What are the chances of that?"

"Slim and nil, but go on," Cassie said.

"Okay, let's go back. To you and Cheez. What are the chances that you two would connect with me? And with Makai?"

"I don't know about Cheez. He could have been moving from owner to owner, looking for the right companion. You said the right things and acted the right way. As I recall, you even called out his name, or something close enough, right?"

"Yes, I guess."

"And who knows how many places he'd stopped before that. Plus, you had a boat, which, as I recall, is high on his checklist of important criteria. And you took him out to look for whales. He probably thought he'd won the lottery. Dogs adopt people all the time and seem to know when Mr. or Ms. Right comes along."

"Still," Rudy hadn't quite given up.

Cassie continued. "As far as my presence and connection, I wound up in Seattle as a grad student after wandering aimlessly. I suspect the orca culture in these parts was part of the draw. I always paid a lot of attention to orcas because of my Marineworld experience, and paying attention was easy because they were always in the news in the Northwest. And when it became known that you were responsible for Makai's repatriation, I figured it was worth a try to ingratiate myself. As I said before, you didn't make it difficult."

"I guess I should feel like I was being used, huh?" Rudy said.

"Happens to women all the time, Rudy. Turnabout is fair play."

"I'll grant you that. By the way, have I ever thanked you? I mean life has taken a sharp upward tick with you and Cheez along, now that I'm in the mood to reflect and confess."

"No, you hadn't. But you're welcome," Cassie said sincerely.

"So anyway," Rudy went on, a little embarrassed, but happy with her reply. "I've got this series of linked events swirling around in my brain. They seem too coincidental to be coincidences, but I guess they can all be explained away if I try hard enough. Still." His voice trailed off.

GENE HELFMAN

"But it seems like it all ends here, right?" he picked up his thread again. "I mean not much else can intersect. Some sort of circle seems to have closed, mostly. We can hope Willow goes to the authorities and they try to find the guy who killed Makai's baby, although, if I were the bastard, I'd head for Mexico. The people in Bamfield felt Willow was too vulnerable right now, given how sick she was, not to mention traumatized by the events of the recent past. But maybe, in a little while, she'll do the right thing."

"I'm not sure even that would accomplish much," Cassie said. "I did some reading. The criminal penalty for killing an endangered species is like a year in jail and a hefty fine. Far less than killing a person. And the court case could be weakened by a smart defense attorney. The killer's word against Willow's, the other witnesses being the whales. The evidence is largely, no entirely, circumstantial, given there's no body and no murder weapon. I'm afraid legal action isn't going to provide the justice we want, and the whales deserve."

"Ouch," Rudy said. "That's depressing. I hadn't thought about that. So, I guess we'll just take Willow back to her awful existence on Orcas and go back to what we were doing before. My semester starts in a couple of weeks, and your sculpins must be missing you. We'll just hope things work out for our whales."

"We won't know until we know," Cassie said. "Or we could go back to See-am-ma-tsa and ask her what happens next."

"I doubt she would tell us," Rudy said. "We'll just have to live with the suspense."

CHAPTER 60

*We've seen animals work together toward
a common goal...Despite what many believe,
they are not so different from us.*

MIDGE RAYMOND, *My Last Continent*

The twins had been dutifully following the rumble-log they had nicknamed Thumper when they spotted their quarry. They rushed to where the family and a bleary-eyed Sam were working. The whales had found a school of Chinook and were planning their approach.

"Hey, hey, everyone!" shouted Eddie. "We got the guy, on the right log. It's not where it usually is, but it's like right up the coast from here."

"You're sure?" asked Sam. He was only marginally confident that the twins could get it right, on both the log and logrider.

"No question, man," Mitchie answered. "Same logrider, same rumble-log, just like you described them."

At which point he projected a blurred, distorted and only sort of recognizable sound image of the logrider.

Close enough, thought Sam.

"Good work, boys. This may be our chance. Is everybody ready to go?"

Family members responded, some more enthusiastic than others. Someone said, "No, not again." But they were all accustomed to working together, so as soon as a few left to follow Sam and the twins, the rest joined in.

The family swam north until they heard the rumble-log. They leapt and saw it in the distance, heading south. Sam called a halt.

"Let me go check, just so I'm not wasting everybody's time."

Eddie and Mitchie started to complain about their identification being questioned, but everyone ignored them.

Sam swam ahead, scanning and raising his head slightly to make sure it was the right log. It was, but, after circling the log, he didn't see anyone that resembled the logrider. The last thing he needed was another wild goose chase. It was obvious that the family was losing patience with the repeated false alarms. Then he sensed Rose swimming alongside him.

"Uh, hi, Rose. You kind of snuck up on me. Anyway, I don't think anything worthwhile is happening here. Another dead end."

"I had a funny feeling," she said, her voice distracted. "Something was drawing me. But I don't think it's the logrider, or not the one we seek. It's something else, stronger and more positive."

"That's great, Rose. But I'm afraid we're losing support with all the aborted efforts. We should just head back."

He turned and started swimming south.

"No! Wait! I know what it is, and *who* it is that I sense. Yes! Tell the others. We have to do it. Right now!"

The urgency in Rose's voice was so obvious, her conviction so strong, that Sam had no choice but to do as she wished. He returned to the group, ran through the drill they had practiced, and swam to intercept the boat. And he continued to worry about the danger Rose was willing, even anxious, to face.

"Attention Washington State Ferry riders. This is Captain Richmond from the bridge," came the announcement as the *Elwha* entered US waters. "Looks like you're getting a bonus on this busy, late-summer Sunday. There's a large group of orcas, killer whales, directly ahead, and they're engaging in a lot of surface activity. We're going to slow down and watch a while. Our apologies to anybody hoping to catch a flight out of SeaTac, but I-5 southbound is a parking lot, so a few more minutes here won't make much difference."

Rudy and Cassie waited for the rush of passengers to gather on the observation deck at the front of the boat. Approaching the back edge of the jostling crowd, they stood off to one side. The whales lobtailed, spyhopped, and erupted from the ocean, throwing water everywhere.

"Quite a show these guys are putting on," Rudy said to Cassie. "It looks like just about all of J Pod is here, including Makai. I guess he really *has* rejoined them. That's about the only good news we've had for a long while. Maybe the circle, or whatever, really has closed."

"Any idea what's going on?" Cassie asked. "I mean it hardly seems appropriate to be celebrating, what with the death of a baby and Grandma's passing. You'd think this kind of behavior would be out of place, and—"

Rudy cut her off. "Yeah, I agree, it's strange. What's also strange is I'm sure everyone is here except Polaris, Makai's girlfriend."

"I don't find that surprising given her baby was killed," Cassie said. "That kind of grief is impossible to overcome, regardless of what everyone else may be doing. Good on her."

"I guess so," Rudy said. "I mean, yes, I agree, but it's still a little strange. I hope she's okay. But there's something about all this frolicking that strikes me as odd, as if the whales were deliberately trying to keep our attention. I just have a weird feeling, something I can't define."

Down on the car deck, the crew members, Lance included, moved toward the bow to watch the whales. But when he saw his nemesis orca cavorting with the other whales, Lance beat a hasty retreat for the stern. He stopped near the restraining rope and lit an illicit cigarette since no one is watching.

Not only was Sam participating in the acrobatics, he was shouting orders to everyone about how to act. Just to heighten the excitement, he threw in a couple of back flips followed by an airborne somersault that ended in a tremendous, thundering splash-down, all tricks he had been forced to perform during his years of captivity. He ignored the remnants of pain from his injuries. *Anything to create a diversion. At least this part is working.*

Willow had dragged herself out of the car and gone upstairs because she had to pee. Returning from the restroom, she spotted Cassie's Whale Museum newsletter and sat down on the lumpy plastic upholstered seat. Knees drawn up to her chest, she absentmindedly added pieces to a half-finished jigsaw puzzle depicting Big Ben. She ignored the whale-oogling crowd and remained where she was. She felt uncomfortable watching orcas, still processing what she had learned in Canada and how the whales had further fucked up her already fucked up life.

"Sister Willow. Bring him to me."

Willow looked around to see who was speaking, but the cabin was empty.

"*Sister Willow. Bring him to me.*"

She knew no one was speaking; it was more a thought in her head, but a spoken thought.

"Who's there? What do you want?" she said, not knowing if she'd spoken or was just thinking the words.

"*Avenge our child. Redeem yourself. Bring him to me. I implore you.*"

Willow stood up and moved toward the bow where the crowd had gathered.

But the voice told her, "*No, not that way. The other way. Come down to the ocean.*"

Willow walked almost trance-like away from the crowd. She descended a stairwell, pushed open a heavy metal door as if it weren't there, and stepped onto the car deck. She looked toward the stern and saw Lance standing there, smoking.

"*Now is the time. Give him to me.*"

Willow walked slowly toward Lance. He saw her and started to smile.

"Hey, babe, long time no see. I hope you're not still pissed at me. We could have lots of fun if you wanted."

Lance had turned around, his back to the water, facing Willow as she approached. Willow saw a swirl of water just off the stern and thought she saw the form of an orca just below the surface. Shouts of excitement could be heard from the crowd on the other end because the boat was coasting along in neutral, the engines barely audible.

"*Now! Give him to me!*"

Willow reached out as if to embrace Lance. He smiled and was just about to give her a hug, when she pushed him with all her might. He stumbled backward, caught his balance right at the edge of the boat, and turned to look at Willow.

"Hey, babe. What's that all about?"

At that moment, a large black shape rocketed up onto the deck of the ferry. Somehow, Willow knew it was the orca who had been talking to her. The whale grabbed Lance by the leg and he fell over. The whale held the screaming, thrashing Lance in her mouth.

"*Sister Willow. Return me to the water.*"

Willow ran over to the whale. Lance reached out desperately to grab her, but Willow slipped his grasp and leapt past him to just behind the whale's head. The deck was slippery from the water that came on board with the whale, but Willow got a toehold on a hatch cover on the deck surface. She put both hands on the side of the whale and gave a shove.

"*Harder my sister! Harder!*"

Willow summoned strength she didn't know she had, coming from a place she had never experienced. Digging her toes into a groove around the hatch cover, she pushed with every muscle in her body. The whale moved slightly, then a little more, and then slid off the stern and into the water, Lance still in its mouth. They disappeared below the surface.

Willow moved to the edge and looked down. She saw nothing. She waited maybe fifteen seconds and still saw no sign of the whale nor Lance.

"Hey girl! Get away from there! You wanna fall off? Jesus!"

A male crewmember in black coveralls and a neon yellow jacket came running up and pulled her back.

"Don't you kids have any sense? You fall overboard, you freeze, or you drown, or you get chopped up in the prop like a Cuisinart."

Willow shook off his grip and backed away from the end of the boat, still looking at the water. When she ducked under the restraining rope across the deck (a thick rope she didn't remember avoiding earlier), the ferry worker, satisfied she was moving, turned back toward the cars.

———

Rose held the logrider down for maybe thirty seconds, long enough to shout to Sam that she had him. Sam signaled to the rest of the family to stop their display and to head away from the rumble-log.

———

The whale surfaced alongside the ship, about thirty feet ahead of the stern, tucked under an overhang where they couldn't be seen by anyone on the boat. Lance spluttered and coughed but was surprised that he hadn't been bitten in half. In fact, the whale was holding him tightly, but gently, face up, so he could breath. *Must be some sort of game these dumb fucking fish play.* He expected to be released and would swim to safety, hopefully very soon.

He was correct about the release part. However, the whale kept him pinned against the side of the huge ship. Lance heard the seven-thousand-horsepower engine start up and felt the throbbing of the huge propeller as the boat gained momentum. He remembered his orientation briefing and that the thirteen-foot diameter prop rotated at an amazing hundred and sixty revolutions per minute. "That's almost three times per second, folks, chopping large logs up with ease," the instructor had said.

As the boat moved forward, the whale swam along at the same speed, still pinning Lance against the metal hull.

"Hey! Lemme go, dammit!"

Which it did.

To Lance's horror, his attempt to swim away from the ship was useless given the suction of the giant screw, suction that pulled him inexorably down and back. He reached out for something to grab, but all he got was bottom paint and rust under his fingernails as they scraped along the hull.

Willow glanced behind the boat at the wake, a red stain quickly dissipating in the churning water. Looking farther back, maybe one hundred yards, she saw a female orca leap high from the water and splash down. She heard, or thought she heard, "*Thank you, sister Willow. Thank you.*"

As if on signal, the rest of J Pod joined the orca, and they swam off, two young males leaping and landing in unison.

Willow walked slowly back upstairs, wondering if she had imagined it all. But she could still feel the skin and underlying muscle of the whale. Her hands and body tingled from the effort and the intimate contact.

"Boy, did you miss a terrific orca display," Rudy said to Willow when they returned to their seats.

"Yes, honey, I don't think I've ever seen so much jumping, not in the wild," Cassie added.

"Sure," Willow mumbled without looking up, as she put the clock face piece of the Big Ben jigsaw puzzle down in no particular place.

CHAPTER 61

We ask for open eyes and open minds,
hearts open enough to embrace our more-than-human
kin, a willingness to engage intelligences not our own.
ROBIN WALL KIMMERER, *Braiding Sweetgrass: Indigenous*
Wisdom, Scientific Knowledge and the Teachings of Plants

The remainder of the ferry ride was uneventful. Willow maintained her sullen silence, although she appeared agitated, moving puzzle pieces hastily. She begrudgingly consented to going home with Cassie for the time being, where they would let her mother know she was safe. Willow didn't seem to think Rudy and Cassie should worry too much about that.

For his part, Rudy felt bone dead tired. He hadn't slept particularly well in the trailer. The day had taken its toll, with the long drive to Sidney, the hot wait for the ferry, concern over basically sneaking Willow back into the US, the ferry ride, and finally the hour and a half ride back to Blaine. He zombie-walked into his rental, fed a hungry dog, and sat down at the kitchen table with a beer, intent on going to bed when it was finished. It was already ten p.m.

Cassie cajoled Willow into calling her mom. The phone conversation started off less than enthusiastically, Willow assuring her mother she was fine. No mention of where she'd been or why. But, shortly, Willow sprung to life.

"No shit!" she exclaimed. "Hot damn. Good riddance to bad garbage, or whatever they say. Yes, I'll be home in a day or so, now that the creep is gone. And Mom."

Then Cassie heard Willow say something unintelligible, in a totally foreign language. Sort of guttural. Willow paused and listened, then smiled.

"Yes," she said. "And, Mom, I think I'd like to know more about Grandma. Bye, Mom."

She turned to Cassie.

"I got great news, the best. My asshole stepfather is in jail, where he belongs. Has been for a couple of weeks. He was pumping a septic tank in some trailer park on the mainland and flashed an eight-year-old girl. She was home alone and didn't like the jerk's behavior, so she secretly videotaped him. When her parents got home, she showed them the video. They went ballistic and called the cops. He'd left a bill, so he was easy to find.

"They raided our house. My pest of a little brother knew where the asshole had hidden a laptop. The cops took it away and found lots of kiddie porn on it. He's probably going to a special prison just for sex offenders. I hope he gets corn-holed to death." She was almost laughing.

Cassie congratulated Willow on the good news. Exhausted from the long day, she offered Willow her bedroom and then threw some blankets and a pillow on the living room sofa. Turning on the TV, she intended to fall asleep to the ten o'clock news.

And she almost did. But when the woman newscaster showed a jerky video of orcas jumping and leaping and cartwheeling, she sat up. It was shot by an unsteady tourist on the *Elwha*. But it was obviously the same display she and Rudy had watched.

"Those ferry passengers were certainly lucky," the newscaster said to the neatly dressed man next to her, also with perfect hair. "Whale-watching trips usually cost around seventy-five dollars, so they got a free show."

"In a related story," her male counterpart added, his voice more serious. "A ferry worker thought to have been on that same boat has been reported missing. Washington State Ferries are trying to locate him. They figure he just failed to sign out at the end of his shift and will turn up. If he doesn't show for his next scheduled shift, the search will become more focused. Now this from Golden Threads Assisted Living."

Cassie was awake now. A thought she had been toying with, actually living with, resurfaced. She had been thinking about orcas more and more lately, daydreaming about them while watching grunt sculpin videotapes. Today seemed to cap it all. There was no escaping what was clearly an obsession. She got up and started to pace.

After about ten minutes, she said out loud, "Yes, dammit. Why the hell not?"

She hastily scribbled a note to Willow. "Make yourself at home, there's lots to eat in the fridge. I'll be back sometime in the morning. Got something to take care of."

She packed an overnight bag and headed for the door, then stopped.

"Of course, silly," she said to herself. Returning to the kitchen, she grabbed the bottle of champagne from the jet ski/flare gun incident out of the fridge.

It was half past ten.

Driving north, all doubt was erased by a local news announcement on the Bellingham NPR station.

"We have an interesting story out of Vancouver, BC. Some more news about our endangered resident orcas that put on a show for ferry riders this afternoon. These same whales, what the researchers call J Pod, joined up with the other two groups of Southern Residents, the K and L pods. About seventy-five or eighty whales were seen swimming north across Boundary Pass, heading for Canada."

The announcer added, "Since then, the same whales were spotted shortly after sunset by passengers on a British Columbia ferry, still heading north. Even more interesting, they were now accompanied by an even larger number of orcas identified as Northern Residents from A and B pods. It was getting dark, but passengers reported a great deal of leaping and splashing."

"In other developments, the City Council, in special session today, voted thirteen to one to…"

Cassie turned the radio off. She wondered if Rudy knew about this. Well, he would soon enough.

Rudy fell asleep sitting at the table, his beer half drained. The unmistakable sound of Cassie's VW outside brought him awake, barely. Wasn't she supposed to be keeping an eye on Willow? *I guess it must be something serious or she wouldn't have come this late.*

Cassie had a big smile on her face as she opened the door to a tail-wagging Cheez. She pulled the champagne bottle out of her overnight bag and placed it on the table.

"We have lots to celebrate," she said. "Do you have champagne glasses?"

Rudy rummaged around in a cabinet and produced two plastic cups.

"Totally gauche, Rudy. This is really good champagne. But I guess they'll do."

Cassie deftly twisted the cork off, which shot across the room. She poured two full glasses and held hers up.

"Here's to the whales, and us," she declared.

"I'll drink to that," Rudy replied.

"Okay. For starters," she said. "I heard on the news that it looks like J Pod and the rest of the southern families have headed north. Like, really north, into northern resident territory. They've been seen mixing with the northerners amidst a lot of celebration."

"Huh?" Rudy said. "You mean like they're giving up on the San Juans? Are you sure?"

"That's what it sounded like, from the brief news broadcast. It was kind of sketchy, but that's what people were speculating."

"Let's make a phone call and find out," Rudy said. "I don't think it's too late."

He found his cell phone and punched in numbers, put it on speaker.

"Whales Galore, Captain Gregor here."

"Hey, Gregor. It's Rudy Laguna. We're hearing reports that our whales have escaped to Canada like a bunch of Vietnam-era draft dodgers. Any truth to the rumors?"

"Damn straight," Gregor said. "We got wind this afternoon that your whales were in our water. Which was good news, because yesterday our whales were way down south. Too far south, but, apparently, they were just an escort service for yours. I headed out just to see for myself. It's true. I spotted the largest gang of whales I've ever seen moving north. Must have been a hundred fifty animals, most of which I didn't know. Except for your boy, Makai, who's hard to miss."

"Wow! Thanks, Gregor. Do me a favor and keep me posted. It looks like your business is about to pick up."

"Fer sure," Gregor said. "And Rudy, if you ever want to see your whales, you're welcome up here any time, eh. Just bring that dog of yours. Or just send him; we don't really need you."

"You've got a deal, Gregor. Take care."

Rudy hung up and looked at Cassie, grinning.

"Of course!" he exclaimed. "Now it all makes sense. Attaboy, Makai. So that's what you were doing up there. Scouting things out. And now you've taken your family to where the fish are. Maybe it couldn't happen while Grandma was still alive. Maybe her passing was a blessing. Maybe she even knew."

"Wow!" Cassie said. "I hadn't thought of that, but I can see your logic. And his."

They touched their cups together and took a good sip.

"Good, now number two, the 'us' part. It turns out I kind of lied to you," she said as she slid into the chair across from Rudy. "Again, I guess."

"I'm detecting a pattern here," Rudy said.

"Please let me explain. Heath and I were never married. The wedding ring was sort of a flag of convenience, or a protective force field. It kept most guys from hitting on me. At least the honorable ones."

"I'm not sure which slot I fit in, at least now."

"Exactly," she said. "You started off in the bad boy category, but morphed over time. Big time. You treat me like a person, not an object, and have for months. Which takes me to number two, or is it three? It doesn't matter."

Cassie hesitated a moment, then reached across the table and took both of Rudy's hands.

"The important thing," she said, looking directly into his eyes, "is that Heath moved out to live with his boyfriend. That moves you into first place to meet more than my intellectual needs, if you're interested."

Rudy was clearly caught off guard but recovered.

"When wasn't I?" he replied, returning her gaze.

"Oh yes, I know. But you were too much of a lecher for me. Sexist pigs like that are a dime a dozen. But, as much of a jerk as you were at first, I saw promise, or at least potential. You acquiesced to my rather unreasonable initial demands. That gave me reason for hope. And I think you've come around, in many ways. Maybe the whales have made you a better person. Maybe the whales have made us both better people. You gave up a lot to save a whale, showed real devotion. Your quick thinking using a flare gun against the jerk on the jet ski was pretty selfless, and pretty brave, actually.

"Anyway, I find all, or most, of your behavior admirable," she continued. "And your willingness to help Willow was a good sign. You were genuinely concerned about her, treated her like a human being in need. I don't think the old Rudy Laguna would have been quite that compassionate in the presence of a beautiful, nubile, young damsel, in distress or otherwise."

Rudy hadn't really thought about that. Maybe his horizons had broadened. Maybe the whales had made him a better person. Or maybe Cassie had. Or both. He certainly was a lot happier since Cassie entered his life. In fact, if anything, he depended on her greatly. It was more than dependence, it was a much deeper feeling. She filled a void that he hadn't even known existed. He certainly didn't remember feeling that way toward his ex-wife. This was much more meaningful.

"Okay, I can't argue with that. I'll admit to having been less than an admirable representative of my gender, and even maybe a better person now, if you think so."

"I do," she said.

"But before I put in my application for sainthood, what about our wandering waif? Is she willing to go home, or are you going to have to adopt her now that my status as a project appears to have been upgraded?"

"See, you're showing concern about her, or maybe just changing the subject. Either way, that's another thing," Cassie said with a yawn. "I convinced or, I guess, *demanded*, that Willow call her mom. Talk about pulling teeth. But her world has brightened somewhat. Her mom told her that her stepdad—'that asshole' is how she refers to him—was arrested for child molestation. He got caught exposing himself to some little girl and then had lots of child porn on a laptop. He's in jail, awaiting trial and will undoubtedly get put away for a long time. Willow practically turned a cartwheel, figuratively speaking."

"Sounds like he had it a long time coming. So, is she willing to go home?"

"She's willing to go home and even seems like she's giving her mom a second chance. And, anyway, she can't live with me, because that's the fourth thing."

"Which is?" Rudy asked.

"I've been thinking a lot," Cassie said. "I just don't have the fire in my belly to play voyeur to a bunch of underperforming grunt sculpins. Even if they were over-performing. Rudy, I want to change my dissertation topic and study orcas. With you. It's like I've woken up from a long sleep. It's where I started, and I now know I want to go back, probably always have."

Rudy hesitated, thinking of the implications, mostly very favorable. Still.

"You'd be giving up a lot, your primo lab setup, all the time you've spent. I can't offer anything comparable to the sculpin Hilton you've grown accustomed to."

"It's a small price to pay to work with animals I love," Cassie said. She hesitated as if there were something else she wanted to say, then continued.

"So, the bottom line is, Ariel the Mermaid has made up her mind. She's moving in. All of her: physical, emotional, and intellectual. If you'll have her."

Rudy hesitated just long enough for a pout to start to spread across Cassie's face.

He said, "That would make me very happy."

"Whew," Cassie whispered. "You had me worried there. Great. There's more to talk about, but I think it can wait 'til morning. Right now, I'd like you to help me get to sleep. It's been a long and eventful day."

The next morning dawned gray. To Rudy, it was glorious. He awoke to the sight of Cassie lying next to him, her long, red hair spread out on the pillow. Her face was a study in tranquility. Rudy felt jubilant. Yes, he was thrilled that Cassie would move in, that they would spend more time together. But he also had a sense of relief, like a weight had been removed. It seemed like more than Cassie's turnabout, but he couldn't think what else. Maybe it was the culmination of so many events. Regardless, it was worth enjoying.

He slipped out of bed as quietly as possible and went to the kitchen to face the challenge of making coffee that Cassie might find acceptable.

Cassie joined him at the kitchen table a few minutes later. She took a sip of coffee and didn't grimace.

"Rudy, I was thinking. It's great that our whales have gone north to a better life. But that kind of leaves us with a problem. Like, how can we study orcas if there aren't any orcas to study?"

"Yeah, it looks like we may be out of business just when you made your big career move," Rudy said.

"Well, it's not like there's a paucity of problems still facing the whales," Cassie offered. "And there are always the transients."

"I guess so. I know the transients are orcas too, and highly intelligent and interesting but, somehow, I have trouble getting as excited about them. It's like being asked to root for a team you've always looked upon as the opposition."

"Hey, our orcas adapted to the new conditions," Cassie said. "We should be able to do as much."

EPILOGUE

Rudy was out in the driveway trying to put a patch on the Zodiac. A small, rusty blue pickup truck pulled to the curb and stopped. The driver got out with a big smile on his face. "Jesus!" he shouted.

Cheez sat up, started wagging his tail, and bounded over to the truck. The guy scratched Cheez behind the ears and smacked him a couple of times on the rump.

"Hi there," the guy said to Rudy, finally looking over at him.

Early twenties Rudy guessed, as a deep sense of foreboding came over him. Deciding to face something he had dreaded, he replied, "Looks like you know my dog."

"Jesus. Oh yeah. We were best buddies back when I was in school here. Before I graduated. I wondered what happened to him. Oh, sorry. I'm Tom McNeil."

"Rudy Deluna," Rudy replied, walking over. He offered his hand, thinking, *so this is the jerk who abandoned Cheez.*

"Yeah, Jesus and I hung out together big time. He's really an amazing dog, isn't he?" McNeil paused for a moment. "But he isn't really my dog. He's more his own dog. He just showed up one day when some friends and I were playing basketball in our driveway. One guy hit a three-pointer from about thirty feet out and I shouted, 'Jesus Christ!' and the dog trotted up to me, tail wagging. It took us a couple of minutes to figure out that was his name, or close enough to it for him to recognize. So that's what we called him.

"And he kind of adopted us. Didn't require much care really. Kind of used us as a home base. He loved to ride around in the back of my pickup. And he really likes boats, 'cause one of my buddies has a Boston Whaler knock-off and Jesus somehow knew when we were going fishing and was in the truck as soon as we started loading up fishing rods. Always rode up front in the boat.

"Then when we were packing the truck for leaving he disappeared. We guessed we had just been a stopover on his way somewhere else. Are you his owner? He's a helluva smart dog, well trained. You did really good."

Rudy relaxed. So this was the story, or at least part of it. Clearly there were blanks and many miles to be filled in between Marineworld and Blaine but finding them seemed unlikely. However, stranger things had happened.

"Jesus—we call him Cheez Whiz—and I met under sort of similar circumstances. I've uncovered a little more of his past through some strange events that would take too long to explain but otherwise he sounds like the same dog you knew. Are you, uh, reclaiming him?"

"Oh hell no. I'm just in town for the day, hanging out with my old buddies. I live in a tiny apartment in Seattle now, no pets allowed, and a lousy place for an outdoors dog like Jesus. Or Cheez Whiz. I doubt he'd stay in Seattle for a day. If he's happy here it's not my call to try to claim him. I see you've got a boat, which makes sense. Like I said, he's his own dog. This is great! Wait 'til I tell the guys. They'll be stoked. Nice to meet you, Mr. DeLuna. Take care."

McNeil got in his truck and drove off. Shortly after, Cassie came out of the house, holding Rudy's phone.

"You had a call. But first, what was that all about? I was watching through the kitchen window. That was quite a commotion. You looked really worried at first but it looks like things worked out."

"It's a little complicated. Let's go back inside and I'll explain."

Rudy recounted his conversation with McNeil. Cassie nodded.

"Genius, Jesus, Cheez Whiz. A dog of many faces. Anyway, you've got a call. Kind of mysterious, some man asked for you and I said you were outside talking with someone. He said his name was J. B. and you should call him back."

"Oh. That's something else I need to fill you in on if we're going to work together, transients or not."

Cassie handed him the phone and Rudy dialed JB's number.

"Hi J. B. What's up?"

"Rudy, my boy, how are things out there on the coast?"

"Just fine, sir. All the reports are positive from what little information we get from up north. Makai and his family seem to have adjusted well to life in Canada. It's kind of lonely here now, but I think we all have reason to feel satisfied."

"Well and good, then. But actually, that's not why I called. I have some news I think you'll find interesting."

"I'm listening," Rudy answered. He could sense that Alexander was enjoying drawing this out.

"Well Rudy, it looks like we've found her."

"And who would that be, sir?" Rudy asked, playing along.

"Marina," Alexander said matter-of-factly.

"Marina?" Rudy asked. "The name rings a bell, sort of. Can you give me a clue?"

"Ask Ms. Flanagan who Marina is." Alexander answered.

Rudy put his phone on speaker and turned to Cassie.

"Do you have any idea who Marina might be? JB Alexander says they've found her."

Cassie thought for about a half second. Then she screamed, "Oh my God, you're kidding! That's fantastic! Where, how?"

Rudy repeated his question, now to both of them, "Who is Marina?"

"Makai's daughter!" Alexander and Cassie answered in unison.

"Of course," Rudy said. "Damn. I should have known that. Where is she? What are the circumstances?"

"She's in captivity, in a whale circus in Dubai," Alexander said. "And quite unhappy from the reports I've been getting. The seller is motivated. Are you up for another round of whale redemption?"

Rudy thought for about two seconds. He looked at Cassie. "Well?" he asked.

"It looks like I've found the beginnings of my new dissertation topic," was her quick reply.

"Okay J B, you're on. But only if I can bring my new assistant on as part of the team," he said.

"I don't see a problem," Alexander said. "My boys will be there to pick you up this afternoon at, let's say 3:35. Will that work for both you and Ms. Flanagan?"

It dawned on Rudy that he'd never mentioned Cassie before. How the hell did Alexander know about her? He shouldn't have been surprised.

"We'll be waiting, J. B."

Acknowledgments

A large community read all or parts of earlier versions of this book and offered advice that was or should have been heeded. Regardless, any inaccuracies or errors, made inadvertently or for the sake of fiction, are mine. More on this in a moment.

I want to thank, in no particular order, Harold and Ruth Van Doren, Mike and Sharon Flanagan, Lisa Muehlstein, Jim Beets, Vita Rose, Luanna Helfman, Arthur Meador, Betsy Hanson, Elizabeth Menozzi, Iris Graville, Deborah Nedelman, Betty Jean Craig, Dac Crossley, Karin Fitz-Sanford, Deborah Giles, Audrey Holloway, Jason Colby, Irene Skyriver, and JoeAnn Hart. Kristi Hein and Shannon Cave provided indispensable editorial advice, although I'm still unconvinced about the inviolability of the Oxford Comma and the deadly sin of head-hopping. The folks at Luminare Press guided me unerringly through the publishing maze, especially Patricia Marshall, Kim Harper-Kennedy, and Claire Flint Last.

Although most of the important places in the novel are real, I've taken more than a few "fictional liberties." Northwest Washington State University (go wolf eels) does not exist. Blaine really is a nice seaside town with a lovely harbor and shoreline. Lopez Island has a diverse community and more Subarus than Volvos. Some readers doubted a prosthetic dorsal fin would remain in place. Barney Goo is in fact based on the incredible adhesive properties of barnacle cement and has been synthesized, albeit in small amounts. The creation story recounted by Willow to tribal elders in Chapter 56 is entirely of my making, as is the First Salmon Ceremony of the whales described in Chapter 38 (although greeting ceremonies of a similar type have been observed when different orca clans meet). Rudy's *super* super-pod involving both Southern and Northern residents (Chapter 31) is one such fictional liberty.

Facts about orca biology and behavior are presented as accurately as I can where they are known. Because orcas are my super-heroes, I've endowed them with special powers based upon speculated but as yet unproven traits. These include but are not limited to: blasting prey into submission (but read about the "terminal buzz" emitted by feeding dolphins); midwife orcas attendant at births (although nearby females are known to guide a newborn to the source of milk); and sound image projection (suggested by Alexandra Morton a couple of times).): The forced abortion scene in Chapter 28 is entirely of my doing. Transient/Bigg's killer whales are intelligent, social, complex organisms. They are vilified here solely to endow resident orcas with the universal (human) cultural trait of xenophobia (see E. O. Wilson's *On Human Nature*). Then again, transients have been known to commit infanticide, something resident whales, real or imagined, would have to consider abhorrent.

As far as orca language and the names they use among themselves are concerned, to quote Rudy, "they just appear as unpronounceable squiggles on a sonogram." I admittedly used a lot of license here. And again, any inaccuracies or errors, made inadvertently or for the sake of fiction, are mine.

Orcas in the Pacific Northwest, especially the wonderful Southern Resident individuals that I get to view from a respectful distance on happy occasions, are in fact endangered for all the reasons repeated throughout this novel. "Whale Wise" guidelines for watching them are published widely and should be observed. The various orca and whale conservation organizations listed in Chapter 9 are real and deserve financial support; any profits arising from the sale of this novel will be spread among several of them.

If you want the unvarnished facts, the scientific literature on orcas is rich and active. The conservation organizations provide bibliographies on their websites. Some useful lists with summaries are linked on the Orca Network website (www. orcanetwork.org) under "Orcas/Natural History/Resources." Books that stand out include those by Ford, Ellis, and Balcomb; Ford and Ellis; Hoyt; Colby; Morton; Baird; Shields; and Knudtson. The lists don't include the large universe of young adult and children's stories about orcas.

And finally, my wife, Dr. Judy Meyer, has lived with and improved this novel in its various incarnations over the years. What merit exists on these pages is in no small part due to her patience, efforts, and sage advice. Any inaccuracies or errors, made inadvertently or for the sake of fiction, are mine.

About the Author

GENE HELFMAN is an animal behaviorist turned conservation biologist. With a PhD in ecology from Cornell University, Gene was on the faculty of the University of Georgia for thirty years, authoring four books on fish and marine conservation and dozens of related scientific papers. He spent much of his professional career underwater demonstrating that fish are smarter than conventionally thought. In an effort to get the message to a larger audience and on the premise that more people read fiction than nonfiction, he has turned to writing screenplays and novels. Gene and his wife, Dr. Judy Meyer, an aquatic ecologist, live on Lopez Island in Washington State.

For more on orcas, etc, visit:
https://genehelfman.pubsitepro.com